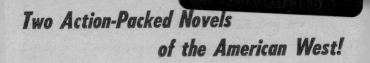

Two Action-Packed Novels
of the American West!

SIGNET BRAND
DOUBLE WESTERN

POWDERSMOKE FEUD

and

CLATTERING HOOFS

SIGNET Brand Westerns You'll Enjoy

POWDERSMOKE FEUD

(Original title: *This Nettle Danger*)

and

CLATTERING HOOFS

by

William MacLeod Raine

A SIGNET BOOK
NEW AMERICAN LIBRARY
TIMES MIRROR

Powdersmoke Feud COPYRIGHT, 1945, BY WILLIAM MACLEOD
RAINE, COPYRIGHT RENEWED © 1975 BY PATRICIA RAINE HIGSON

Clattering Hoofs COPYRIGHT, 1944 AND 1945, BY WILLIAM MAC-
LEOD RAINE

Published by arrangement with Houghton Mifflin Company. Orig-
inally appeared in paperback as separate volumes published by
The New American Library.

 SIGNET TRADEMARK REG. U.S. PAT. OFF. AND FOREIGN COUNTRIES
REGISTERED TRADEMARK—MARCA REGISTRADA
HECHO EN CHICAGO, U.S.A.

SIGNET, SIGNET CLASSICS, MENTOR, PLUME AND MERIDIAN BOOKS
are published by The New American Library, Inc.,
1633 Broadway, New York, New York 10019.

FIRST PRINTING (DOUBLE WESTERN EDITION), FEBRUARY, 1980

1 2 3 4 5 6 7 8 9

PRINTED IN THE UNITED STATES OF AMERICA

POWDERSMOKE FEUD

CONTENTS

1. The Wire Cutters

IT WAS A NIGHT of scudding clouds from back of which a pale moon emerged occasionally for a few moments. Out of the darkness the mountain range came vague and shadowy. A trail of sorts, steep and rocky, ran up the hogback, one good enough for a horse but impossible for a wagon. Looking up at it, the cap rock seemed a sheer precipice, but Bruce Sherrill knew there was a break in the wall through which the cowpony could pick a way. The animal took the last stretch with a rush, scrambling up like a cat, the hard muscles of the flanks standing out like ropes.

From the far end of the cleft Bruce looked down into a black gulf of space at the bottom of which Squaw Creek followed its winding course. A pinpoint of light stood out of the emptiness like a beacon. It was from the Gilcrest ranch. The roan picked a footing through the obscurity with the sureness of a trained Western mount.

The lower slope was dotted with small pines, but the grove ended before Bruce reached the creek, giving place to thick brush that slashed his legs and snatched at the stirrups. A trace paralleled the stream, and he took it out of the gulch into a small park where the light he had seen from the summit of the hogback reappeared. He opened a poor-man's gate and closed it behind him.

When he rode into the yard he found three other horsemen waiting there. One of them, Pete Engle, was holding Dave Gilcrest's white mule Jenny.

" 'Lo, Bruce," Pete said. "All here but Flack."

Pete was a small man, his face lined with wrinkles of anxiety. He wore dusty boots run down at the heels, soiled jeans, and a patched shirt that had once been blue before many washings had faded it. Care rode heavily on Pete's narrow shoulders. Five reasons made the struggle to earn a livelihood harassing. He had a wife and four children and it was impossible to forget that the wolf was never more than two jumps from the door of his cabin.

Gilcrest came out of the house followed by his wife, a tall gaunt woman in a loose gingham dress. She had apparently been good-looking once, but years of toil and worry had etched lines in her face and dried the sap from her body. She might be twenty-nine or thirty.

The newcomer swung from the saddle to meet her. Unlike most of these nesters, Bruce was instinctively courteous to women. This was something they could not get from their own men, and they liked it in him. But tonight Sarah Gilcrest was preoccupied with her fears. She brushed aside his greeting.

"This is a crazy business," she broke out sharply. "They'll lay for you-all. One of these nights there will be a rookus—and then what?"

Sherrill's smile was friendly and disarming. "Don't worry, Mrs. Gilcrest. We expect to use wire cutters for weapons."

"I s'pose that's why you're all packing guns," she retorted tartly. "If you want to know, I worry every minute Dave is night riding."

"There are a hundred miles of wire around the Pitchfork spread," Bruce reminded her. "What chance would they have of picking us up at any one point?"

"Now, old woman," Gilcrest interrupted mildly. "If you would just quit frettin'." He was a big hulk of a man, bowlegged and barrel-chested, with a long drooping mustache too large for the homely, puckered face.

The sound of hoofs came down the wind. Out of the darkness a big bony horse took shape. Riding it was a man with a sly hatchet face and small searching eyes set too closely. He carried a long muzzle-loading rifle.

"Just in time, Flack," Engle said.

Bruce glanced around. "If you're all ready, we'll start," he suggested. The youngest man present, he had been tacitly chosen as leader. Soft-spoken and gentle of manner, he had, however, a driving force.

With the exception of Pete Engle, who was an old-timer and knew this country from the grass roots, all the others but Bruce had within the past few years come a thousand miles in covered wagons to try a hazard of new fortune in this raw frontier land. Bruce was of another genus. He was from a good family, well-educated, and had brought with him the means to buy several hundred head of cattle to stock the ranch on Bear Creek that he had homesteaded. But this fight was his as well as theirs, for he had filed on land upon which the cows of a big outfit had run for a dozen years and had fenced a stretch of the creek to keep out Bar B B stuff.

They rode down Squaw till it emerged into the open foothills leading to the undulating plain. The stream took a sharp turn to the east, but they still pointed south to avoid climbing the spurs that, rooted in the range, ran down to the flats below. For the most part they traveled in a silence broken only by the creaking of saddle leather and the sound of moving horses. These men were going on a grim and perhaps dangerous errand. They were not gay and casual young cowboys who joked about everything.

Flack drew alongside Bruce and moved knee to knee with him. "Looks like rain," he said. "This country sure needs it. I don't ever recollect seeing Squaw so empty of water before."

8

Sherrill agreed briefly that this was true. He did not like Flack. The fellow had a mean spirit, and there was something ratlike about the quick beady eyes in the long-jawed face.

"I'm certainly a chump," Flack continued, with a furtive look at his companion. "I done forgot my clippers."

"Thought you were going to a dance, I reckon," Bruce replied, a touch of contempt in his voice.

"I sure must be wool-gathering, doggone it," Flack admitted humbly.

Bruce did not accept this explanation. His guess was that the man had left the cutter at home deliberately, to mitigate his offense if they should be caught.

"Anyhow, someone has to hold the horses while the others work," Flack mentioned more cheerfully. "I can be the wrangler."

"So you can," Bruce answered dryly. "And if Daly's riders jump us you'll be all set for a getaway."

"Now that ain't nice," reproved Flack virtuously

Bruce made no comment. A spur touched the flank of his mount lightly. The roan began to dance. "Steady, Blaze!" its rider ordered. By the time Bruce had the cowpony quieted, he was riding beside Cal Malloy, a tubby little man with a round moon face.

"Flack forgot his clippers," Bruce told the fat man.

"The damned yellow-belly is full of tricks," Malloy snapped, disgust in his voice. "He'd be a fine partner to side a fellow if he got in a jam."

Engle pulled up his mount and the others joined him. They had come to a barb-wire fence. Bruce turned his horse over to Flack, but he carried his saddle gun with him. The sound of the clippers punctuated the silence of the dark night. All three strands of wire were cut between each post for a hundred yards, after which the men remounted and rode along the fence for a quarter of a mile and repeated the demolition for another stretch. This was not the first time they had slashed the "bob-wire" of the enclosures of the big ranches, and they went at the job with ruthless efficiency.

While the others were at work Flack took charge of the mounts, but apparently there were too many of them to manage easily. They bumped into one another as they swung to and fro restlessly.

Cal Malloy called to the wrangler irritably. "Bring those horses nearer and keep them close to us. If you can't handle then I'll swap places with you."

"They're millin' around," Flack explained. "Keep your shirt on, Cal. I'm bringing them up."

The nippers were getting dull. After the third attack on the barb-wire Bruce called to Pete, who was at the head of

9

the line, "We'll call it a day." He straightened, nerves suddenly tense. On the light night breeze there had come to him the drum of hoofs. "Fork your broncs, boys," he cried. "They're on us."

The nesters raced for their mounts, grouped half a stone's-throw distant. Pete stumbled on a grass bump and went down. Saddle gun in hand, Bruce waited for him to pick himself up.

Out of the darkness a rider galloped, far ahead of his party. He dragged his horse to a halt and fired at Pete, who was just getting to his feet. The bullet plowed into the ground. His second shot was a hit. Pete ran, limping. Before the rider could pull the trigger again Bruce had his saddle gun in action. The weapon dropped from the hand of the rider. He clung to the horn in front of him for a moment then slid from his seat.

With one sweep of his eyes Bruce took in the situation. Flack had not waited for his companions but had turned loose the horses and was galloping away to save his own hide. Three of the wire cutters had reached mounts. One of them, Dave Gilcrest, was holding a pony for Pete, now only a few yards from him. Blaze was vanishing in the distance, running at the heels of Flack's big bay. The attackers were coming out of the murk not a dozen yards from him.

Bruce caught the rein of the riderless horse beside him and vaulted into the saddle. He swung the animal round, pulled it to a gallop, and sent it over grounded wire into the big pasture.

2. On the Dodge

THERE WAS A MOMENT before the clatter of the guns sounded, the time it took for the cowboys to realize that Ben Randall was lying on the ground and one of the wirecutters escaping on his horse. Bruce lay low in the saddle, driving the buckskin to its fastest speed. Bullets whipped past him. One thudded against his calf just above the boot top. In a dozen seconds he was out of range of accurate shooting.

But he held the horse to a gallop, for he knew that already the pursuers must be pounding across the pasture. First, he must see they lost him in the darkness. After that he must make plans for the future. This would be no safe country for him if he had killed Ben Randall. Old Jeff Randall would see to that. The Diamond Tail was lord of justice in this part of the territory, and the rough old-timer who ruled it would be no impartial judge.

He had been lucky in the horse he had commandeered. The buckskin had a broad deep chest and a big-barreled body.

It was not overbred. Bruce guessed that its legs would stand up for the grueling test they might both have to face. The rider swung sharply to the left, still traveling rapidly. The black night surrounded him like a wall. He had no time to let the horse pick its way. All he could do was hope that a leg would not be broken in a gopher hole.

Presently he pulled up to listen. A coyote yelped in the distance, but no rumor of horses breaking through the brush reached him. For the time he had evaded the enemy. This did not greatly elate him. He knew that before morning every mountain pass would be blocked and every ranch on the plains be on the lookout for him. He must have been recognized. Bill Cairns had been staring at him when he jerked the horse around to start his flight.

He kept going, but at a more reasonable gait. He was not quite sure why he had cut into the pasture, unless it had been to divert the hunt from his companions, particularly poor Pete. It would have been safer to make directly for the mountains and try to get over one of the passes before it was closed. The chase would concentrate on him. He was the only one of the raiders yet identified and the one who had shot young Randall.

Not counting the peril into which the shooting had brought him, Bruce was unhappy at what he had done. He was no killer any more than he was a horse thief, but now the word would go out that he was both. What else could he have done? Before Pete reached the horse Gilcrest was holding for him Randall would have finished him if he had been let alone. Bruce had been given a fraction of a second to decide. It had to be Pete or Ben. A man in a fight had to stand by his own side.

The boot of the fugitive was already soggy from the blood dripping into it. When he had time he would have to give it attention. But he could not do that now. He was cut off from his own ranch, even if he had dared go there. Before daybreak he must be out of the valley and in the hills. There were draws and pockets where he might find a temporary hiding place among the aspens or the scrub oak. Down here in the rolling plains he would not have a chance. He decided to make for the Sleepy Cat Range.

Bruce did not deceive himself about what would befall him if he was captured. He had been too long a thorn in the side of the big ranches. His cool light insolence, the lash of his quick tongue, the encouragement his aid gave the hoe men, had marked him for punishment even before the jaws of this trap had closed on him. Unless he had miraculous luck he was due to be rubbed out before the sun of the coming day set.

He pointed northeast, holding the buckskin to a road gait. It would not do to be in too much of a hurry. The strength

11

of the horse must be conserved. It would have to travel far over a wild rough country, and it must have enough stamina left for a hard race if he were seen by one of the posses combing the hills for him.

Light was already breaking in the eastern sky when he cut the wires of the Pitchfork pasture and rode out of it into a draw leading to the foothills. A small stream ran down it, and he plodded beside this for miles, working steadily deeper into the approaches to the range. He found what he wanted at last, a gulch running into the cañon, its floor sown with young pines behind which he could conceal the buckskin. Without unsaddling, he tied. There was no feed here. The animal would have to wait till he found a grassy pocket higher up.

Bruce limped back to the brook, the saddle gun in one hand. The wound in his leg was paining a good deal. That was something he had to endure. Before it was better it would be a good deal worse. Beside the stream he sat down and pulled off the boot. His blood-stained stocking clung to the calf. It took more resolution than he had to tear the cloth free. Instead, he put the leg into the running water and let the current wash the stocking loose. This hurt, but he stuck it out. His hope was that the clear, cold runoff from the snow would cleanse the wound and prevent poisonous infection. The handkerchief that had been around his neck he washed, and after it had dried in the warm sun he tied it around the wound. The sock he threw away. Slowly he inched the boot on again, setting his teeth to keep from grunting. He drank deeply, and washed his face in the cool water. After the buckskin had drunk he headed again upstream.

He had not gone a dozen yards when he heard voices. A party of his hunters were coming up the cañon. Swiftly he wheeled the horse, rode back to the gulch, and moved into the pines behind a great boulder. Bruce watched the party draw up to water. His stomach muscles tied into a cold hard knot. He could see the discarded sock lying beside a rock not a dozen yards from them.

"Might have gone up this gulch," a cowboy said.

"Not unless he could climb out by his eyebrows," another differed. "There's a twenty-foot rock fall straight up and down at the top. Could be hiding in the pines."

The man who spoke next was Bill Cairns, wagon boss of the Pitchfork. He was a wall-eyed man with a leathery brown face. Hard muscles packed the frame of his big body. "Could be, but isn't. Not that bird. He's way up in the range, ridin' like the heel flies are after him. He'd be a chump to fool around down here."

"Mebbe so." The cowboy who had spoken first pulled out

12

a revolver and sent a bullet crashing through the pines. "That's for you, Mr. Sherrill, if you're roosting there."

Cairns turned on the young fellow angrily. "What you trying to do—warn him we're around?"

"You said he wasn't there," the young rider retorted sulkily.

"He isn't. But don't pull any of that funny stuff when we get higher, Wally. Save your bullets till you see the son of a gun."

The foreman pulled his horse, splashing as it went, out of the water. He rode upstream. The others followed in single file.

Bruce reclaimed the sock and buried it in the creek beneath a rock.

A mile below this point he had passed a rocky forge down which in the rainy season a torrent poured. He rode back and turned into it. Looking up that boulder-filled steep, Bruce doubted if a horse could make it. But he had not any other choice. He could not turn back into the valley. Nor could he follow the creek, knowing that Cairn's posse was ahead of him. He set the buckskin at its job.

He had to get out of the saddle long before they reached the top. Every step on foot up the gorge tortured him, but he set his teeth and took the pain. All his thought had to be given to the task of maneuvering the reluctant horse up the narrow rock-stewn bed. They made it, after a hard pull.

Bruce found himself on a plateau, one side of which dropped down to a small mountain park and the other fell almost sheer to the foothills below. There was on it no sign of human life. He rode to the end of the prong and looked down at the sea of grass stretching to the far horizon. In the pleasant sunlight it was a fair sight to see. No doubt a gentle breeze was rippling through it, though he was too far away to verify his guess.

He made out the windmills of the Pitchfork, and nearer a sparkle of light that must have come from the sun glinting on a line fence. Bruce frowned. That fence was a symbol of war, the spoils of which were the water and the grass on that wide undulating plain.

It was unfortunate, Bruce thought wryly, that he was of a temper that saw both sides of a question. Better be a thorough partisan and know that you are a hundred percent right and your enemy entirely wrong. The tired nesters and their gaunt parched women could vision only one angle to this quarrel. They had come a long weary trek to homestead this land and these insolent cow barons flouted the law and made it impossible for them to live in their homes.

All of Sherrill's sympathies were with these poor underprivileged nesters, but there was some justice too in the claim

13

of the cattlemen. For a score of years they had been the Men on Horseback, lords of all they surveyed. They had fought the Sioux and the Cheyenne, had endured droughts and blizzards while building up their herds. Their cattle had roamed over a hundred miles of free grass. By use they had a claim to it, if not by law. Then the hoe men came in to fence the creeks and plow the meadows, cutting off the cattle of the big ranches from feed and water. In retaliation, to protect their herds, the old-time cattlemen began to fence all the land in sight.

Though the sympathies of Bruce were with the newcomers, he had an uneasy feeling that nature was on the side of the range men. This was pasture land, too dry for farming. The plow would destroy the native grasses, and the land would be lost forever.

None of which reasoning justified the big outfits in fencing thousands of acres of government land to prevent the small fry from running their poor herds on it. The arrogance of the Randalls and the Dalys and the Applegates would not in the end avail them. They could frighten away this or that homesteader. They could rub out another accused of rustling calves belonging to the Pitchfork or the Bar B B, but they could not stop the tide of hoe men looking toward the cow country any more than Canute could sweep back the sea. The empire of the cattleman was doomed.

Bruce dropped from the plateau to the mountain park that bounded it. At the far end of this was a thick clump of aspens running up into the entrance of a small gulch. He rode across the park, skirted the aspens, and descended into a pocket where the grass was good. After he had picketed the horse he pushed up into the gulch to a cluster of great boulders tossed together fifty feet from the floor of the trough. He lay down to rest and in spite of his throbbing calf fell into troubled sleep.

Hours later he was awakened by rain beating in his face. The sun had vanished, and the whole sky was a heavy gray. It had set in for a long rain.

He limped down into the pocket and saddled the buckskin. If any of his hunters came this way they would notice the circle of cropped grass where the pony had been picketed. But that was a contingency against which he could not guard. The weakness of his situation was that no planning could extricate him. It was not possible to know in what direction he might run into enemies.

3. Linda Applegate Shows Anger

WITHIN THE HOUR he caught sight of riders moving along a ridge above him, their figures vague in the misty rain. He drew back into the pines and waited until they had passed from sight. Already night was beginning to fall, earlier than usual on account of the heavy weather. He decided to stay in this timbered park until daybreak.

That he would have a bad night he knew. The cold rain had chilled him to the bone. He was very weary and in a good deal of pain. For twenty-four hours he had been without food, and he guessed he was running a fever.

After several attempts he got a fire started close to a projecting sandstone bluff. The wood was wet and several times the struggling fire threatened to give up the ghost. It ran to smoke rather than heat.

There was little hope in him. The mountain passes must both be guarded. He dared not shoot game. Twice he had crossed streams in which he had seen trout. They might as well have been in Africa for all the good they did him. Eventually he would be forced to work back to the ranch country from which he had escaped. He was cut off from his allies as completely as if a prison wall had surrounded him, and in any case they were too weak to help him.

He slept fitfully, waking now and again from the pain of his wound and from the penetrating cold. Dawn broke clear. He was saddling when he saw riders once more on the lip of the park, this time traveling in the opposite direction from those he had sighted yesterday. One of them pulled up and pointed a finger down at him. Somebody let out a yell of triumph. The hunters scurried about, trying to find the quickest way down from the rimrock.

Bruce pulled himself into the hull and made for the opposite ridge. When he reached the top he looked back to see riders strung along the flat he had just left. He had no choice now. With the hunters so close to his heels he had to let himself be driven back into the ranch country and hope for a miracle. Recklessly he raced down the steep slope, rubble slithering from the hoofs of the buckskin. He galloped down precipitous gullies and came to a long ledge overlooking the plains. Perhaps he was trapped. All he could do was to keep going, watching for any break in the rock that might lead to the foothills below.

His pursuers were out of sight for the moment, and they had not yet appeared when he found a rain gutter made by flood streams and turned the horse into it. This was a beggar's choice, but the buckskin reached safer ground below, during half of the descent sliding on its haunches.

A hill crease tempted him, and he took it instantly. Far back he heard the shout of one of the posse, but at least they had lost him for the moment. The draw led to open ground. There was a fence before him and beyond that the buildings of the Bar B B ranch house. He grinned wryly. His long flight had brought him to the very door of his chief enemy. Most of the cattle shut off from water by his homestead fences belonged to Cliff Applegate.

Linda was making a rice pudding when she heard a horse moving toward the house. She glanced through the window. The buckskin was the favorite mount of her cousin Ben Randall, but the man in the saddle was not Ben. She was startled. Ben lay at home, near to death. That villain Bruce Sherrill had jumped his horse and escaped on it. Except at a distance she had never seen the fellow, but this must be the man. Her stomach muscles tightened, not from fear. While he lowered himself from the saddle, heavily, as one does who has been hurt, her gaze did not lift from him. He came to the porch, limping.

The girl was surprised at the appearance of the man she saw in the doorway. He was haggard, his eyes sunken from pain and fatigue. One shoulder leaned against the jamb, as if for support. She guessed he was completely exhausted, though his twisted smile was one of mocking self-derision. What very much astonished her was that she found no evil in the face of this man whom she had for years heard denounced as a scoundrel.

"Couldn't make it," he said, lifting the Stetson from a head of crisp reddish hair. "Your friends were too smart for me. They cut me off from the passes."

The planes in the fresh young face set like those of a hanging judge. She was thinking of Ben Randall, the boy with whom she had gone to school and ridden the range and hunted deer. Her heart hardened, to reject any appeal this young fellow might make.

"So you come to me for help—after killing my cousin," she flung at him bitterly.

The news that Randall was dead disturbed him, but he had no time for dwelling on that now. "Thought you might like to be in at the kill," he corrected, still with the thin brittle smile. "They are beating the hills back of your place. In ten or fifteen minutes they ought to be here." His body sagged a little. He leaned more heavily against the jamb.

"If they find you here——"

"There won't be any time for last words, will there?" he cut in flippantly.

"Get on that horse and ride away," she ordered, stormy lights in her dark eyes. "I can't save you—and I wouldn't if I

16

could. You'd better hurry." Her gaze swept out of the window to the hill folds back of the house. No horsemen were yet in sight.

He came into the room and put a hand on the back of a kitchen chair to steady him, still with that fixed ironic grin turned on her. There was something a little wild in his look, as if he might be out of his head.

"Don't you hear me?" she snapped. "If they are really there, as you say, they'll take you out and hang you."

"Sounds reasonable," he agreed.

"You fool!" the girl cried. "Haven't you a lick of sense? Fork that horse and light out, if you don't want to get what you deserve."

"You're a true Applegate," he said. "No fooling you. Give the dog a bad name and hang him."

Anger boiled in her, and back of it an increasing dread. She hated this insolent scamp, but there was a growing panic rising in her. She did not want him taken to be killed—not here, before her eyes, after she had seen him in such dire need.

"What is it you want—food?" she demanded. "If it's that, I'll get you some. But I won't have you here."

"Quite right," he agreed. "Evil communications corrupt good manners. I learned that in my copybook."

Her exasperation was about to burst over him, but he did not give it time. His knees collapsed, and he pitched down at her feet in a faint.

4. A Good Samaritan

LINDA STARED DOWN in great surprise at the prone lax body of the fugitive. From it her gaze went through the window again to search the hill creases. She caught sight of a horseman for a moment and then he disappeared in a draw. Sherrill had told the truth, they were hard on his trail.

Already she had decided to save him if she could. Her thoughts came in stabbing flashes. First, she must get the horse out of sight before they emerged from the foothills. That done, she must hide the hunted man. Not upstairs in her bedroom. She could not carry him up. In the storeroom off the kitchen. Neither her father nor her brothers went in there more than once a week.

She ran out and pulled herself to the saddle on the buckskin. There was a brush-filled gully at one side of the house where old tin cans and garbage were flung. It angled in the direction of a hayfield for a hundred yards or more. Near the lower end she led the animal down the steep bank and tied it to a young willow.

As she hurried back to the house Linda saw that the hunters

17

were out of the foothills and moving toward the ranch. In another five minutes they would be tramping up the porch steps.

She caught the unconscious man under the armpits and dragged him across the kitchen floor into the storeroom. A flour barrel and one containing molasses stood at the far wall and behind these she left Sherrill. His hat and the saddle gun she brought in and concealed under some empty gunny sacks. There was no time to make sandwiches, for she could see a group of men coming through the gate, but she took in and left her unwelcome guest a jug of milk and a plate of bread and cold beef. The door of the storeroom she closed.

When a rap came on the door she was stirring the pudding, a song on her lips. She stopped singing, "Don't you remember sweet Alice, Ben Bolt," to let in Bill Cairns and four Pitchfork cowboys.

"Morning, Miss Lindy." On the ugly mouth of the foreman was an ingratiating smile. Ever since the girl had been fifteen Cairns had looked at her with a covetous eye. "Haven't seen anything of that young fellow Sherrill, I reckon?"

Linda's eyes were wide with surprise. "Is he around here, Mr. Cairns?"

"You bet he is. Not far away. We drove him down from the hills and lost him at the rimrock. But he had to come this way. If you'd been lookin' you must of seen him pass."

She stared at him. "You mean—right by the house?"

"Mighty close, headin' for the river."

"Unless he's around one of the ranch buildings," Wally Jelks amended. "Hoping after we've passed to cut back into the hills."

Cairns showed his tobacco-stained teeth in a grin. "Smart boy, Wally. Maybe you're right. Have a look-see in the stable and the bunkhouse."

"How about that coffee you promised us, Bill?" a youngster asked.

"I'll make some right away," Linda said. "Won't take me but a few minutes. If one of you will grind some in the mill."

Three boys headed for the coffee grinder, but in spite of his bulk the foreman was there first. "Take the others with you, Wally, and search the buildings. Make sure he ain't squattin' behind the roothouse or anywheres. I'll stay with Miss Lindy, seeing as she's got a license to be scared of this murderin' scoundrel."

"I'm not afraid of him," the girl said promptly, an angry flush on her face. She had noticed Wally Jelks's satiric grin as he started to follow the others from the room. His thoughts were as clear to read as the open page of a book. Cairns wanted to be alone with her. Probably the range rider had observed the sly greedy looks with which the foreman had watched her furtively at dances.

"You're a young lady and don't understand," the Pitchfork major-domo told her with smug righteousness. "Some of these fence-cuttin' hoe men are bad characters—this fellow Sherrill, f'rinstance. A girl like you, pretty as a painted wagon, ought to have a good man to protect her."

"I have three—my father and two brothers," she said stiffly. "Nobody with any sense would dare to insult me."

Her dark hard eyes drilled into his. His reputation with women was bad. If he had any ideas about her he had better forget them now.

"Right," he agreed. "Still and all, Cliff hadn't ought to have left you alone while that villain is still prowlin' around."

"Perhaps you had better tell him so," she suggested, with a thin contemptuous smile. Cliff Applegate was not one to take advice on so personal a matter, certainly not from a man with Cairns's record.

An angry red poured into the back of the foreman's leathery neck. He was thought to be a tough hard fighting man, and he was full of vanity. To have this young woman tell him off so neatly was annoying. He was a man of no subtlety and blurted out his resentment.

"You got no call to ride me because I'm trying to protect you from this skunk we're aimin' to rub out. You've always been so high and mighty. What's the matter with me, anyhow?"

"If you'll finish grinding the coffee I can start making it," she suggested.

"You've always acted like you hated me," he complained.

She corrected that impression. "You're quite wrong. I'm afraid I've never thought of you one way or another."

He strode up to her, his face purple with rage beneath the tan. His strong fingers closed on her shoulders and bit into them. "By God, you will," he swore. "No woman can talk thataway to me."

Her small fist smashed into his face.

A man had opened the door and was standing there. He said, in burlesque of the current melodrama, "Unhand that villain, maiden." Rod Randall, an older half-brother of her cousin Ben, was smiling at them in frank enjoyment. He was a lean-loined, broad-shouldered fellow, dark and good-looking, with black eyes and a strong jaw. Linda called him cousin, but he was no kin except by the courtesy of marriage. She had seen a good deal of him, but she did not understand him very well. She was a little afraid of him. He had the unconscious arrogance of one who means to take from life what he wants. It sometimes made the girl uncomfortable to suspect that one of his unnamed wants was Linda Applegate. She thought about him a good deal, as a young woman does concerning a man who may some day be important in her life. Her instinct warned her to avoid him. She suspected he was ruthless, that no woman would mean enough to him to find happiness beside him. And yet somehow he fascinated her.

It was like him not to rush forward to her assistance, to act as if this were a pleasant comedy for his entertainment.

"He's making an annoying fool of himself," Linda told the newcomer. "But I don't need any help. I know how to handle his kind."

Randall laughed. "Pick on someone of yore size, Lindy," he drawled. "Bill doesn't weigh much more than two hundred pounds." He offered mock sympathy to the Pitchfork man. "Maybe I could hold her long enough for you to make a break for yore horse and a getaway."

"I wasn't hurtin' her any," Cairns growled.

A change came over young Randall's face, amusement banished from it as the flame is from a blown candle. His eyes had grown hard and cold, the warning of half-scabbarded steel in them.

"You'd better not," he said, his voice and bearing arrogantly contemptuous. "Keep yore dirty looks on yore own kind. If you ever annoy Miss Applegate again I'll cut your hide off with a quirt."

"I was jest funnin' a little, Rod," the foreman mumbled. "No need to get so bossy about it. Why I stayed here to protect her from that fellow Sherrill."

"Her own family will do any protecting that's needed," Rod answered. "Don't forget that."

They heard the cowboys coming back. Their spurred boots dragged across the porch.

"Nothin' doing," Jelks announced. "He isn't here."

"Who isn't?" Randall asked, and the situation was explained.

"We'll take off," Cairns announced, his voice a snarl.

"Not without our coffee," a towheaded cowboy objected in surprise.

"Of course not," Linda said. "I'll hurry it up."

"Sherrill has probably ridden across the pasture to the river and will try to hide in the bushes," Jelks guessed.

"I could of told you that all the time," Cairns flung out spitefully. "He's not jugheaded chump enough to stick around here to be caught."

They drank their coffee and left. From the window Randall watched them ride down into the pasture.

"I'll drift along after them presently," Randall told his hostess as he sauntered back. "Like to be there when they get the fellow."

20

She thought he moved with the undulating grace of a panther. Sometimes it seemed to her there was menace in his motions, a suggestion of a banked power to pounce if the occasion came. He flicked at the table with the end of his quirt.

"So Mr. Cairns has ideas," he mentioned, his smiling eyes on her.

"I'd rather you didn't say anything about this," she said. "I'll handle it."

His grin remained. "You already have, I'd say. Competently."

Linda did not like that. As a younger girl she had been known to have a gusty temper not under very good control. For the past year or two she had been trying to live this down.

"What could I do when the fool laid hands on me?"

"No criticism here," he said.

"How is Ben?" she asked.

"I've been riding all night," Rod answered. "But a Diamond Tail hand reached our camp this morning with the news Doc says Ben might make it if he has luck. Why in time did he have to race in before the others and get a slug put in him?" He moved to the door. "So long, little wildcat. Be seeing you."

She watched him ride away, a flatbacked graceful figure, and as soon as he reached the pasture she opened the door of the storeroom. The wounded man was conscious.

His gaze took in the slender graciousness of her young body, the face with a beautifully modeled bone structure. There was a hint of temper, perhaps of willfulness too, in the hostile eyes. No doubt she had been spoiled. He thought her capable of violent emotions.

"You have visitors," he said.

"They have gone."

"Didn't they want to meet Mr. Sherrill?"

His insouciance set a spark to the resentment in her. "I'll make this clear," she declared coldly. "I'm not going to joke with you. There's no friendship between us. To me you are just a killer I hate. But you're here—wounded. There's nothing I can do but take care of you."

"A good Samaritan."

"As soon as my father comes you'll be his responsibility." She said it with angry bitterness. "Now I'll look at your wound."

He shook his head. "No. Why take trouble to patch me up for so short a time?"

She glared down at him. If she had been a little girl she would have stamped her foot. "Haven't you any sense?" she cried, withdrawing her threat illogically. "I want to fix you up so you can travel, so that you won't be killed here by my people."

"Fair enough," he agreed. "Inconsiderate of me to drop in

but your friends were crowding me. Any port in a storm, you know. Too bad I had to annoy you. The patient is ready, doctor."

She brought water and clean rags, knelt beside him, and dressed the wound. It was a neat job.

"Doc Bradley couldn't have done better," he said approvingly.

She noticed that he had drunk the milk and eaten some of the bread and meat. "I'll get you a snack to take with you," she said.

He got to his feet slowly, still light-headed. "Why?" he wanted to know. "I'm just a killer you hate. Your conscience is clear now. I can make it off the Bar B B without any more food. Thanks for your charming hospitality."

"I'm not thinking about you." She wanted him to be sure of that. Her voice was sharp with censure. "I want you to get far enough away so that it won't be Applegates who meet you."

He hobbled into the kitchen and his glance went out of the window. "Sorry to disappoint you. We're a bit late. Enter Cliff Applegate all loaded for bear."

Her glance shuttled to the window and back again to him. The color had drained from her cheeks. "I'll help you upstairs," she told him instantly. "Quick."

He hesitated. "What's the use? You can't keep me hidden here, even if you wanted to."

"Do as I say." She caught at his arm and drew him toward the stairway. "Hurry—hurry!"

He limped up the stairs, leaning on her, and was pushed into a bedroom. "Don't make a sound," she warned.

"Lindy!" her father's voice called.

"Be right down," she answered, and shut the door behind her.

The first glance told the uninvited guest that it was the girl's own bedroom. The furniture was plain and simple, but everything in the room had the woman's touch that made it homelike and attractive. Dotted muslin curtains hung at the window. A neat rug was on the floor. On the bed a patchwork counterpane made perhaps by Linda's mother was as fresh as if it had been finished yesterday. His eyes picked out the titles of half a dozen books on a shelf—the poems of Tennyson and Longfellow, *David Copperfield, Guy Mannering, Jane Eyre,* and a three-volume edition of Shakespeare. The exquisite neatness showed that the young mistress gave her belongings scrupulous care.

He tiptoed to the bed and sat down on it. He knew this would be only a short reprieve, but she had wanted it that way and he had not found physical strength to resist.

5. Breakfast at the Bar B B

CLIFF APPLEGATE SAID, "We're hungry as wolves."

He was a big man, with a broad reach of shoulders, a thick chest, and the heavy muscular spread that comes to an active outdoor man in the fifties. The eyes in his bony determined face had been bleached from squinting into ten thousand summer suns. They held a touch of arrogance, due to the power that success and possessions had brought him. His sons, Cliff and Brand, were tall, long-legged young fellows, strong and spare of flesh, but it was an easy guess that in time they would look very much as their father did now.

"I suppose you haven't had any breakfast," Linda said.

"We've forgotten what little we had," Brand laughed.

"Have you heard this morning how Ben is?" young Cliff asked.

"Still hanging on," his sister answered. "Doc Bradley says he has a slim chance. Rod told me. He was here for a minute."

Linda looked at the pudding in the oven, found it done, and put it on a side table. She began preparing breakfast for her men. It occurred to her that it might be wise to show an interest in the chase from which they had just returned.

"Did you get Sherrill?"

"No. He seems to have found a hole and pulled it in after him," Brand replied. "But he can't get away. The passes are plugged up. He'll be driven down into the valley."

"Bill Cairns and four Pitchfork boys dropped in and stopped for coffee. They said they jumped him up in the hills but lost him afterwards."

"Then he is still in the hills," Cliff, Senior, said.

"Not if they are right," Linda explained. "They think they drove him down to the river right close past the house here." She put roasted coffee beans into the mill and ground them.

The men went out to wash up while she made biscuits and cooked the steaks. But before she started she flew upstairs to her patient. She had intended to tell him to lie on the bed, but she found him already there, his dusty boots on a newspaper.

"You'd better have them off," she said, and caught hold of a heel and toe.

"Don't bother," he advised her, "unless you don't want me to die with my boots on."

She paid no attention to his sardonic remark. The boot on the wounded leg she eased off as gently as possible. Beads of perspiration stood out on his forehead. His teeth were clenched.

"I'll get you water soon as I have time," she promised curtly.

23

"I say thanks. You haven't told them yet."

"That's my business," Linda replied brusquely. "You stay here and keep quiet."

"Why not?" An ironic smile twitched at his mouth. "This isn't my day for whooping it up. I can get along without visitors nicely—except you."

An angry flush swept into her cheeks. "I'm not doing this for you, but to keep my folks from being the ones who kill you."

She left the room and hurried downstairs. Swiftly she put three large steaks on the stove to cook and measured coffee from the drawer under the grinder into the pot. Her motions as she mixed the biscuits, rolled them out, and put them in the pan were sure and fast. When the men came stamping into the house she was nearly ready for them.

"It's time Bud Wong came back from town," she told her father. "He's had time to gamble away all his money and get on several sprees. If I were bossing that Chinaman he wouldn't get off so easily. He's been away nearly a week."

"Do you good to cook for a spell, honey. We can take it."

"You'd better. First one complains I resign."

They ate like men who had been starving on a desert island. Linda brought plate after plate of hot biscuits to the table. She watched them vanish almost as if a magician had waved them away.

The girl gathered information while they fed themselves. "How did this man Sherrill come to shoot Ben?" she asked. "I know Ben and some of the Diamond Tail boys caught him cutting wires."

"That's the answer," Brand said. "Guns started smoking."

"Who began firing?" Linda persisted.

"I reckon Ben did, but that doesn't matter. He was on his fast buckskin ridin' hell for leather like he always does. Soon as he got close enough he cut loose. Bill Cairns says Ben hit one fellow. He could see him limpin' as he ran. Then Sherrill shot Ben outa the saddle, grabbed the buckskin, and lit outa there before they could get him."

"Ben was shot in a fight then. He wasn't ambushed."

"That's right," her father confirmed. "But there wouldn't have been any fight if these fellows hadn't been cutting Pitchfork fences." After a moment the ranchman added: "There's nobody in the world I have less use for than this man Sherrill, but I will say for him that I don't think he would kill from ambush. He's a hardy devil and doesn't fear God or man."

"How did the Pitchfork riders know they would be cutting wire at that place just then?" Linda inquired.

There was a long moment of silence, broken by her father. "Don't ask so many questions, honey," he told her.

24

His answer surprised her. She could see no reason for secrecy, unless perhaps the cattlemen had brought in a range
detective to check on the nesters, one whose identity must be
kept under cover.

Brought up in a world of men, her impudence encouraged
since she could first toddle, Linda was not easily suppressed.

"What's the matter with that question?" she demanded.

Brand grinned at her. "Little girls should be seen and not
heard."

"Maybe they oughtn't to be seen either," she said, a little
heat in her voice. "I've decided to accept Aunt Mary's invitation to visit her. I won't be gone more than two or three
months."

"Now—now, honey," her father interposed. "Don't get
sore. Brand is just foolin'."

"I'm not sore," she flung back. "I just want to go away and
play with my dolls for a while—to some place where a lot of
men won't always be dragging mud into the house for me to
clean up—and dropping their clothes any place they take them
off—and coming home at all hours for meals—and giving
me such a nice time generally. I'm damned tired of it."

The ranchman was shocked. "I haven't heard you use that
word since you were a little trick about four years old. It's not
nice for a young lady."

"Oh, I'm a young lady now, am I, too old to be spanked?"

"I paddled the boys too for letting you hear them use the
word," he reminded her. A bit fearfully he took up her complaint. "I didn't know you were so tired of us, honey."

The gentleness of his voice reproached her. She knew that
of all the world he loved her most. Her warm fond eyes smiled
at him. She did not know why she had flared up anyhow.

"Forget it, Dad. Once in a while I get tired of staying at
home and running the house, especially when you come home
with secrets I'm not to know because I'm only a girl and of
no importance."

"Who said you were of no importance?" he asked. "You
know better than that, Lindy. It's only that we're kinda
pledged not to tell anyone that particular thing."

"That's all right, then." She turned on him her mocking
impudent grin. "I won't have to accept Bill Cairns's offer to
become his missus, will I?"

Her father's hand stopped, with a buttered biscuit halfway
to his mouth. "Did that scalawag dare——?"

She interrupted his resentment. "Not quite. What he said
was that I needed a good man to protect me. I told him I had
three. I gathered that the good man he was thinking of
wouldn't leave me alone to the mercy of this desperado Sherrill the way my men do."

"Maybe he is right. I ought to have left one of the boys here."

"Do you think Sherrill would hurt me?"

"He's in a bad jam. You can't be sure what he would do."

"Don't worry about him," Cliff, Junior, said. "He's not going to be with us long."

"About Bill Cairns," Brand commented. "If he bothers you any, sis, let me know."

"Are you the head of this house, Brand?" his father inquired with displeasure. "I'll look after my daughter when it is necessary."

"It won't be necessary," Linda told them decisively. "I can take care of Mr. Cairns without any help. I've already put a flea in the ear of the big lug."

"If he crooks a finger at you I want to know it." The ranchman looked at Linda sternly. "And don't let me hear of you flirting with this scoundrel the way you do with half the boys you meet. He's no good."

"I'm certainly dumb," she told herself out loud. "I ought to know by this time you can't take a joke. I would not look at Bill Cairns if he was the only man in the world. And I don't flirt with anybody. I have to be polite don't I?"

Her father ignored the question. "We'd better make the calf cut this afternoon. Some of our boys ought to be getting back soon."

He caught up his hat and left the house.

6. Linda Changes Her Father's Mind

LINDA GAVE HER PATIENT A DRINK and washed his face with cold water. She looked down at him, frowning.

His twisted grin was apologetic. "I'm a white elephant on your hands, Miss Applegate. Sorry."

She was worried. The buckskin in the gully would be discovered soon, and then the place would be searched. She could not keep the wounded man here without somebody finding out he was in the house. Yet it was plain he was in no condition to travel. He needed a doctor, but he would have to do without one. Before nightfall he might be beyond medical aid, unless he was still concealed.

"I don't know what to do with you," she answered. "If you stay here my father will find out, and even if you could travel I couldn't get you away without being seen."

"Better tell him I'm here," he advised. "You won't be to blame for what happens to me."

"I don't see why you had to come blundering in here of all places," she broke out in exasperation. "You know how we

26

have despised and hated you for your contemptible conduct. On top of that you have to shoot my cousin and come here to hide."

"Annoying," he admitted. "There isn't any out for me, Miss Applegate. I'm throwing in my hand." He started to rise from the bed, but her strong arm pushed him back.

"I'll decide what's to be done," she told him sharply.

"I have a slight interest in this," he reminded her dryly. "Much obliged for your kindness, but I won't impose on it any longer."

"You'll stay right there till I make up my mind."

She spoke imperiously, but it was her anxiety rather than her anger that influenced him. He might as well let her have her way. It would make no difference in the end.

He gave a gesture of surrender. "All right. Whatever you say. Fix it up so you won't get into any trouble."

She left him, to go down and wash the dishes, her mind greatly disturbed. Her father was not a cruel man, not ruthless like her uncle Jeff Randall, but he could be stern and stubborn. There was no man he felt so bitterly toward as the one upstairs, and now the fellow had added surplusage by shooting down his favorite nephew. It was not likely he would show any mercy for him now. Probably he would not himself execute what he considered justice but would turn the offender over to the Randalls for punishment. At the Diamond Tail Sherrill would meet his jury, judge, and sheriff.

A jubilant shout outside startled Linda. She heard her brother Cliff's voice, excitement racing in it. "Look what I found in the gully, Father."

The girl's heart went down like a plummet. She knew what he had found. With the dish towel still in her hand she walked out to the porch. Cliff was leading the buckskin across the yard to the blacksmith shop where his father and Brand were standing with their saddled mounts.

"Ben's horse," the ranchman said, and a moment later added: "The Pitchfork boys were right. They drove him out of the hills."

"Where to?" Brand asked. "Where is he now? Did he hide the horse, figuring he had a better chance to slip down to the river on foot without being seen?"

"Or is he on this place right now?" his father asked. "We'll find out about that first." He turned to his daughter. "You didn't notice any lone rider around here, Lindy?"

She cried, to gain time, "Why, that is Ben's buckskin."

"Yes. Sherrill must have been on it. He's either here or headed for the river on foot."

She nodded quickly. "Like Brand said, getting rid of the horse so as not to be noticed."

27

"Stay here with yore sister, Brand," the cattleman ordered. "Cliff and I will search the outbuildings. If he's not there we'll go through the house. He might have slipped in while Lindy was busy."

"Just what I did," a voice said. "But it was no go. I'm bucked out."

Their eyes converged to the doorway. Bruce Sherrill was standing there, his hands in his trousers' pockets. The other men stared at him, for the moment dumb with surprise.

"That's a lie," Linda said angrily. "I hid him in my room." The guns of both her brothers covered the fugitive.

"What crazy nonsense is that, girl?" her father demanded.

"Can't you hear?" she retorted. "I hid him—from Bill Cairns and his men—because he is wounded and I didn't want him murdered here, no matter what he has done. And when you came I hadn't made up my mind what to do. So I didn't tell you. I thought he might have a chance to slip away. Then somebody else could deal with him, not on our place."

"Have you lost your mind?" the ranchman bellowed. "Trying to stand between me and this killer. My own daughter. Goddlemighty! You ought to be whipped. Butting into other folks' business."

She faced Applegate, her eyes hot with anger. "He's been wounded, I tell you. He fell fainting at my feet. I had just time to hide the horse and drag him into the storeroom before the Pitchfork men came. Would you want me to turn over to Cairns to be hanged a man who might be dying? Or to you either?"

Her father struggled to control his temper. Her defiance was outrageous. "Why can't you act like a lady—instead of a——"

Words failed him. He could not find a simile. His face had dyed to a rich purple. As yet his rage was turned against the girl. He would deal with his enemy later.

"I don't claim to be a lady, whatever that is," Linda flung back furiously. "How could I be, brought up in a house filled with savages? If you were civilized you would understand that a woman can't turn a wounded man over to be slaughtered even if she does hate him."

Applegate threw up his hand in a gesture that flung the girl aside for the moment. He glared at the man in the doorway—haggard, sunken-eyed, unshaven, but with the look of one unbroken and indomitable in the grim reckless face.

"You've gone too far at last," Applegate cried harshly. "When you shot Ben Randall you tied a noose around yore neck."

"I shot him because he was trying to kill a man he had already wounded," Sherrill answered. "A friend of mine."

28

"That doesn't go with us. Yore friend was cutting a Pitchfork fence. No doubt he is a rustler."

"No," the wounded man denied. "Just a plain homesteader fighting for his rights, a poor scrub nester no better than a worm in the eyes of you exalted bullies."

"Even if Ben lives it won't do you any good. You've come to the end of yore trail, Sherrill. You've been warned times enough, but you were hell-bent on forcing a showdown. Well, you've got it."

Bruce Sherrill flashed a quick look at Linda. She had not told him young Randall was still alive. He was glad to know it, even if it would not profit him.

"What are we going to do with him?" Cliff, Junior, asked. "Take him over to the Diamond Tail?"

"I reckon that would be best," his father said.

"Can't you see he is sick?" Linda broke out. "He can't ride."

"He's been riding for most two days," Brand said callously. "He can make out to do twenty miles more."

"What kind of men are you?" the girl cried desperately. "Apaches torture their prisoners. I thought you were decent white folks."

"Keep outa this," the cattleman ordered her. "I won't stand for any more interference from you. Go into the house."

She steadied her voice before she answered, to convince him that this was no hysterical outburst. "I want to talk with you, Father—alone," she said in a low voice.

"I've got more important business on hand," he told her roughly. "Later I'll tell you plenty."

Her eyes held fast to his. "We'll talk now—or never. I'm of age. I'd rather work in a railroad hash house than live here with men who have turned a wounded prisoner over to be murdered by his enemies. I'll leave—and never come back."

Cliff Applegate stared at his daughter in astonishment. She had been pert and impudent often enough and had let her gusty temper fling her into occasional tantrums, but she had never before set her will to stand against him on a matter of importance. There flashed to his mind a vivid picture of how bleak and desolate life would be without her. But he brushed it aside. He was not going to let a slip of a girl, his own daughter at that, give orders as to what he could and could not do.

"I'll lock you in yore room, missy. I'll show you who is boss here. You've been spoiled. That's what is the matter with you." He took a step or two toward her threateningly.

Her gaze did not falter. "I mean what I say," she answered, still very quietly. "If you take this man over to the Diamond Tail or if you send for Uncle Jeff to get him, I'll not stay here another day."

Cliff reined in his anger, checked by a warning voice inside that was close to fear. He might be on the verge of a bad mistake. Linda was both proud and obstinate. Any one of a dozen young fellows in the district would marry her if she snapped her fingers at him. If he drove her too far, she might do just that, and regret it later.

"What is it you want me to do?" he asked harshly.

"I want you to keep this man hidden here till he is able to travel, then turn him over to the law."

"The law!" snorted her father. "And have a rustlers' jury turn him loose to start his deviltry all over again."

"Of course it isn't fair," she admitted. "I know that. But there's nothing else we can do."

"When we started to comb the hills for this fellow it was to rub him out for shooting Ben—and that's what he deserves," the cattleman retorted. "This is man business. You've got no place meddling in it."

Linda ignored that. "If you'd met him in the hills and he had died fighting, that would be different," she persisted. "But he dragged himself to our house sick and wounded. Let him stay here till he is well, anyhow, and then make up your mind."

"And if our riders tell the Pitchfork and the Diamond Tail that he is here, what then?"

"They don't need to know he is on the ranch. Nobody need know except us four."

"But Wong would know, after he comes back and starts cooking," Cliff, Junior, suggested.

"Leave Bud to me," his sister replied. "He'll be close as a clam if I ask him."

"She's got an answer for everything," Brand said with a sarcastic grin. "Soon as she is boss of the Bar B B we'll have to ask her may we wipe our noses."

"You're blackmailing me," the ranchman told Linda bitterly.

"I'm keeping you from doing something you would always hate yourself for having done. We've got to be fair even to an enemy. We can't revenge ourselves on him by being a party to his murder. I don't like him any better than you do, but I'm not going to lie awake nights ten years from now because I was afraid to tell you the truth."

The ranchman turned his resentment on Sherrill. "Get back into the house," he ordered. "Before some of our riders drift back and see you. I haven't made up my mind what the hell I'm going to do, but there's no sense standing out here yapping about it." On Brand he swung round irritably. "Better put this fellow in yore bed, boy, till I decide what's best."

Linda knew she had won a victory, for the present at least. She was wise enough to make no comment and to become as unobtrusive as possible. Her father was furious at her, even

30

though his judgment was already telling him she was right. A dominant man, his pride grudged being set straight by his own daughter.

The girl went into the house and stewed a chicken for their unwelcome guest.

7. Bruce Makes Himself Popular

BEFORE BRUCE SHERRILL had imposed himself upon them the Applegate family had been a friendly and closeknit one, but now their casual carefree life had been disrupted. None of them were happy. Linda was in the doghouse. Her father spoke to her only when necessary, and her brothers blamed her for the unfortunate predicament in which they found themselves. Though secretly glad they had not turned their prisoner over to the Randalls, they felt that they had betrayed their friends.

Brand came back from a visit to the Diamond Tail in a sullen temper. The family were at dinner when he walked into the room and joined the others.

"How is Ben?" Linda asked.

"Better. Doc thinks he has a good chance to make it." Brand plumped out the grievance in his mind. "I'm not going back there again. I felt like a skunk, sitting there and keeping my trap shut then the boys got to guessing where Sherrill could be. Whose side are we on anyhow?"

"I've wondered about that myself," his father said bitterly.

"One thing is sure," Cliff, Junior, contributed. "When this gets out we won't have any friends among those we have always trailed with. They'll change the name of this ranch to the Double Cross."

"We're doing the only thing we could do," Linda submitted, rather humbly. "You good as told me so yesterday, Brand."

"You oughtn't ever to meet any of yore enemies, except with guns in yore hands," Brand flared out. "Take this guy upstairs. You look after him when he is sick and wounded, and you find out the cuss is human same as yoreself."

Unexpectedly his father came out in support of the course they had taken. "We'll live down any feeling there may be. I've been thinking that if Ben gets well even the Randalls may be glad after a while they didn't get a chance to hang Sherrill. But I'll be mighty pleased when he's well enough for me to take him to town and turn him over to the sheriff." He added quickly, "I don't like him any better than I did. He's one of these smart-aleck brash birds."

"I never did meet a nester like him before," Brand said. "Most of them are sad-looking trash, meek but obstinate as

31

a government mule. When one of them drops in at a round-up you feel like throwing a rope on him to drag the poor cuss up and fill up his belly with steak and flapjacks. But this guy is different. He turns that you-be-damned grin of his on you and wants to know when the hanging is going to be."

"Truth is, he isn't by rights a nester," Cliff, Junior, cut in. "He bought some of his land, and he is grading up his stuff same as we are. That whiteface bull of his is a jim-dandy. Trouble with him is he horned in too late and tried to grab off our range. Then when we wouldn't stand it he threw in with the covered-wagon riffraff."

"Thanks for explaining him to us," his father said sourly. "He may be Jay Gould for all I care. He's a pain just the same. A born trouble-maker. Men like Sherrill have ruined this country. It was the finest place in the world when you were children. What will it be like in ten years?"

Since the first day of Sherrill's arrival Linda had seen almost nothing of him. Bud Wong prepared his meals for him and served them in the bedroom. From her brothers she learned that the wound was healing and that in a few days he would be able to travel. It would be a relief to get him safely out of the house.

One afternoon he hobbled downstairs and came into the sitting room where she was dressmaking.

"What are you doing here?" she asked. "Don't you know that one of the ranch boys might drop in any minute?"

"They are all down in the south pasture working stock," he told her.

"A neighbor could come. They do almost every day."

"I'm betting this is an off day," he told her coolly.

"Of course it wouldn't matter to you if my father and brothers get in bad for protecting you," she said, a small whiplash in her voice.

"You don't like me, do you?"

"No, I don't."

"Yet you saved my life."

"We all make mistakes."

He smiled. "I'm not going to get any change out of you, I see."

She looked straight at him. "You don't think I interfered on your account, I hope."

"No, I'll acquit you of that. You were worried about the family conscience. But since it meant a good deal to me, you mustn't blame me for feeling grateful."

"You don't need to. It might have been anybody."

"But it happened to be Bruce Sherrill."

"Unfortunately."

He looked her over carefully, and what he saw he could

32

not help liking. She had long well-fashioned legs, a lovely body slenderly full, a face a man could remember in his dreams. She moved with the fine animal vigor of one who loved the air and the sunshine, and in spite of her willfulness there was a certain gallant and defiant courage in her to which his heart responded.

"Some day you are going to change your mind about me," he said, smiling at her.

"Am I?" Scornful words poured out to punish his audacity, but she felt a faint quickening of the blood. "I see," she replied with a curl of the lips. "You're one of these barber-shop mashers who slay girls. You ought to have a nice little silky mustache."

His smile persisted. "Wrong guess. I'm not like that at all. But I don't need to tell you that. You know it."

She felt herself flushing beneath the tan of her cheeks. He was quite right. She did know it. The look of scorn she had flung at him was not genuine. It was true that a flame of resentment against him burned in her, but it was also true that he interested her more than any other man she had met, unless perhaps it was Rod Randall. Her father and brothers were tough game Westerners, but their courage was fierce and defiant. Sherill could meet danger with a mocking smile that denied its importance. His cool politeness could cover the sting of a whip. What was he like, back of this reckless front? He had given her a chance to find out, but she closed the door on it.

"It doesn't matter," she said carelessly. "In a day or two you'll be gone. I'll probably never see you again." A heat beat into her voice. "I hope not. Ever since you came there has been nothing but trouble in this house."

He asked if he might smoke and when she gave permission rolled a cigarette. "Trouble is good for people sometimes," he suggested. "It shakes them out of their complacency and forces them to face the truth."

"What truth does it make *us* face?" she demanded, sparks of anger in her eyes.

"You're beginning to see that God didn't make this country millions of years ago just for the convenience of a few arrogant cattlemen. You'll never again hold the smug undisturbed belief that they are justified in trampling down poor settlers."

She swept aside the waist she was making and rose, a tall slim figure stiff with rage. "That's a fine thing to say, after my father and brothers hid you here and saved you, their worst enemy, protecting you from the just punishment you had earned. I knew you were a hateful person, from the first time I ever heard of you. I am surer of it than ever. Don't speak to me again, please."

33

She walked out of the room into the kitchen, where Bud Wong was making apple pies.

"You want tell me something, Missie?" he asked.

"No." The repressed violence in her exploded. "That loathsome man! Is he going to stay forever?"

Bud Wong liked their guest, who made little jokes showing friendliness. "He plitty flesh," the cook conceded.

"Fresh!" she repeated. "He's the most impudent ungrateful scoundrel I ever met, as full of conceit as an egg is of meat. I wish I had let Father take him to the Diamond Tail."

"He all light." Bud turned his slant eyes on his mistress with a smile. "He think Missie plitty nice."

"He takes a strange way of showing it. Not that I care. He's a detestable person, and I hope he keeps out of my sight till he goes."

They heard him limping across the sitting room to the stairway and slowly taking the treads. Presently Linda went back to her sewing, anger still churning within her.

She did not mention to the rest of the family the quarrel with Sherill. It was her own private affair and she did not need any help from them. But she rehearsed what had been said after she went to bed, and the resentful memory of it was with her in the morning as she passed the door of his room on the way downstairs.

Her father was standing by the table reading something written on a page torn from a cheap tablet. He handed the paper to her.

She read:

I've stolen another horse to get to town. I'll leave it with Sheriff Humphreys. Thought it better not to outstay my welcome. You do not want thanks from me for what you did, but you are getting it none the less.

Bruce Sherrill

"He's giving himself up, I reckon," Cliff said.

She tossed the paper back on the table. "We can do without his thanks. I never was so tired of a man in my life. He told me yesterday he had been doing us a favor by staying here because he had shaken our smug belief in our right to fight the nesters. His vanity is colossal. He needs a lesson."

"He'll get one," the cattleman answered grimly. "I'm glad he has gone. I've made up my mind to come clean with your uncle about this whole business. He'll raise cane, and I'll have to take whatever he says."

"Do you still blame me so much for what I did?" Linda asked gently.

"No. You were all right, honey. We couldn't turn him over to be hanged after he had come here wounded. I see that plain as you do now."

34

He put an arm around her shoulders and gave her a little hug. She felt a warm glow in her heart.

"The fellow must of got up in the night and slipped out," Cliff said. "He was keepin' us fooled about not being able to travel. Only yesterday he told Brand that in three or four days he figured he would be able to make it to Redrock."

"Yes, I expect he's chuckling now to think how he fooled us—after using us to save his life. He's one of these slick fellows smooth as butter."

She turned away, hot anger in her dark eyes, to find out from Bud Wong whether breakfast was nearly ready. She hoped she would never see him again as long as she lived.

8. Jeff Randall Uses Bitter Words

LINDA SAT BESIDE HER FATHER in the buckboard when he drove down the valley to the Diamond Tail. She went for two reasons, because she wanted to see for herself how her cousin Ben was getting along and also because she wanted to be present when Cliff told her uncle what they had done in order to take her share of the blame.

The day was young, and the sun rising above the sandstone cliffs sent a sheen across the gray-green sage to the foothills across the valley. Hill-prongs jutted out from the mesa above into the plain, some of them eroded into shapes reminiscent of the fabled castles she had read about in Scott's novels. The pungent scent of sage mixed with dust rose to her nostrils. Once she caught sight of antelope in the distance slipping single file through the brush.

She had been born and brought up in this country, and all its scents and sounds, the hundred changing atmospheric appearances of desert and mountain, had been a part of her heritage. Life in the high plains, spent largely outdoors with sun and wind beating on her, had contributed to the radiant health that gave her eyes, her face, her hair, such an exciting vitality.

Her father pointed out men in the dip to the left of them stringing wire. He said grimly, "Some the nesters cut ten nights ago in the dark of the moon."

"You don't know who they were?" she asked.

"We don't *know*. They got away without being caught that time. I reckon yore friend Sherrill was one of them."

"Is he my friend more than yours?" she inquired.

"No, he's no friend of any honest person who runs cattle here."

"Will there be any more trouble? Or have they learned their lesson?"

"There will be more trouble—plenty of it. No way of ducking it. A slather of these poor fools who want free land are coming into the country to homestead. They don't use their heads. When they look over this open country, they never figure that it is all grazing land, too dry for the crops they are used to in Iowa or Tennessee. The only way to keep them out is to fence."

"Isn't the government going to put a stop to that?"

He shook his head. "I don't know. We've got a lot of wise lawyers back in Washington making laws for this cattle country without ever having seen it. They don't understand the conditions, and they don't take the trouble to find out. Our own Congressmen and Senators are all right, but they can't make those Easterners see how things are. Fact is, the general idea at Washington is that the West doesn't amount to a hill of beans anyhow, and it sounds good for them to make a hurrah about keeping the land open for the common people. Consequence is, a lot of no-account folk who can't make a go of it anywhere move out here and starve, after they have ruined the land for those of us who can use it."

Linda had heard the cattlemen's side of this question for years, and she had always assumed it to be the right one, but now an unpleasant misgiving lurked in her mind. Maybe the homesteaders might have a just claim too. She brushed this out of her thoughts, resentfully, for she knew that Bruce Sherrill had planted it there.

The Diamond Tail ranch house was a long rangy log building, to which several additions had been made in the course of years. Looking down on it from the ridge above, one could see a huddle of other buildings—a bunkhouse, sheds, blacksmith shop, and small cabins. In contrast to the Bar B B, the place gave an impression of untidiness. In one corner of the big yard were wornout wagons, buggies, disconnected wheels, and rusty tools.

A boy of about seventeen shouted greeting to them as they drove into the yard. Linda waved a hand. "Hello, Ned! How is Ben?" Ned was a younger cousin, a long-legged gawky lad who was just now wearing a friendly grin.

"Doing fine. Eats like he had been ridin' the range all day. He'll be tickled to death to see you, Lindy."

Ben had gained ground surprisingly in the past two days. He was a dark lithe young man, very good-looking, with a gay and reckless charm that made for popularity. At sight of Linda his eyes lit.

"Time you came to see me," he approached, and drew the girl's face down to kiss her. "Didn't you hear how close I was to Jordan's bank?"

"You had us all dreadfully worried," she told him. "I never

36

saw such a boy for getting into trouble. We're so glad you're better."

"Can't keep a good man down," he answered cheerfully. "Though I will say that Bruce Sherrill made a good try at it."

"You think he meant to kill you?" she asked, to find out how he felt about it.

"You don't shoot at a man to do him any good," he replied, with a laugh. "Not that I blame him any. My gun was smokin' too."

"Do you have to get into gun fights?" she chided.

His eyes twinkled. "It's a bad habit—like flirting."

"I don't flirt," she said in swift defense. "When a man shows an interest in me I can't hurt his feelings, can I?"

"I reckon not. Anyhow, they all recover after a while. I haven't seen any die of love yet. What would you think about not hurtin' the feelings of a cousin who showed an interest in you?"

"I would talk over with him the other seventeen girls he is showing an interest in," she told him, eyes dancing. "Since I was told to stay only three or four minutes I must go now." After a moment, she added seriously: "You're going to hear something about me you won't like."

"You're not engaged?" he flung at her.

"Nothing like that. This is something altogether different. After we have gone your father will tell you, if you ask him."

She left him filled with curiosity and joined her father and uncle on the porch. The first glance told her that Cliff had blurted out his confession. Applegate was glaring at his brother-in-law, a stubborn set to his jaw. Randall's mouth was a thin tight slit, but the eyes were the principal barometer of his rage. A bleak blaze of anger shone out of their flinty depths.

He was a bullnecked man, strong-jawed, with harsh features tied together to form a gross powerful face. There was a shapeless lumpy quality about his rounded shoulders and big body that sometimes reminded Linda of a swollen toad. But in spite of his weight there was no fat on him. A steel band of muscles crossed his thick stomach, and his great thighs were hard as steel. By reason of the drive in him he had become the leading man in the district, and he held his sway sometimes by bullying, again with suavity, but always to get what he wanted.

"So you had him in your hands and turned him loose," Randall said, an ugly rasp to his voice.

"Put it that way if you like," Applegate answered. "He slipped away in the night."

"He couldn't have slipped away if you had turned him over to me."

37

"That's what Father wanted to do, Uncle Jeff," Linda cried. "At first. But I made such a fuss, on account of the man being wounded, that he gave way."

"You made a fuss—and he let you have your way." The biting scorn in Randall's voice stung like a lash. "After this fellow had killed Ben, far as you knew."

A dull flush burned into the face of the Bar B B man. "Soon as I had time to think I knew she was right," he said dourly. "I hate this scalawag as much as you do, Jeff, but I couldn't turn a wounded man over to you to be killed after he had come to the ranch for shelter."

"Very noble of you," the other man jeered. "Of course it wasn't your boy he shot down. Why should you care? What's a double-cross among friends anyhow?"

"You've no right to say that, Uncle Jeff," Linda retorted. "Father wouldn't throw down a friend any more than you would. He had to do what he thought right."

Jeff turned his washed-out blue eyes on her. "What you made a fuss to get him to do," he corrected. "Who runs the Bar B B—Cliff Applegate or a crazy girl he can't keep in her place?"

"That'll be enough, Jeff," his brother-in-law warned. "Linda is not in this. I played the hand."

"You certainly played it fine. If there is one man I thought would do to ride the river with, I would have put my money on Cliff Applegate, and he cuts loose from his crowd to back the play of a murdering scoundrel who has done nothing but make trouble ever since he came to the territory."

"We'd better go, Father," Linda said in a low voice. "There's no use talking to Uncle Jeff while he is in this mood. Pretty soon he'll say something we won't be able to forgive."

"So you're the ones that have the forgiving to do," sneered Randall. "Well, you can't get out too quick to suit me. And tell your friend Sherrill when you see him that I aim to hang his hide up on a fence to dry one of these days."

Cliff rose, reluctantly. If they left now it would mean the break of a long friendship, but to stay longer would result in the exchange of more bitter words.

Two little girls rode into the yard and slid from their saddles. They turned their horses over to Ned and started for the house, each carrying schoolbooks in a strap. At sight of their cousin they broke into a run, pigtails flying.

"Lindy—Lindy!" they cried, and flung themselves into her arms. "Mother's visitin' grandma. She'll be back in two-three days. She says she'll bring us over to see you awful soon. The pinto mare has a foal—the teeniest prettiest little thing. An' we have a holiday Friday." They poured this information at Linda, interrupting each other eagerly.

38

Their father ordered them into the house gruffly. This scene of happy reunion did not fit in with his own feeling toward the Applegates.

The children were surprised and distressed. They had heard Jeff explode in anger, but he was seldom harsh with his little girls.

"Can't Lindy go with us and see the colt?" Molly asked.

"No, she can't." He added brusquely: "She doesn't want to see it or you either. Get along in."

Lindy said, gently. "We have to go now, Molly, but I hope you and Pearl can come and visit us very soon."

Jeff set his stubborn jaw. "They can't. If you're lining up with the sodbreakers, we'll start from the chunk right damn now."

The unhappy frightened children looked from one to another of the grown-ups and moved reluctantly into the house.

9. "As the Sparks Fly Upward"

SHERIFF HUMPHREYS WAS NOT GRATEFUL to Bruce Sherrill for waking him at five-thirty in the morning to give himself up. What Humphreys wanted to ask him was why since he had got this far he did not keep going till he was out of danger. The truth was that this young man just now was dynamite to handle. From Randall the officer had received an indirect message to keep out of the hunt for Sherrill and let the cattlemen handle the matter. The sheriff had no desire to barge in, even though he was on the opposite side of the political fence from the big ranches. He had been elected by the votes of the little fellows opposed to the large outfits, by townsmen, nesters, rustlers, hoe men, and a few small stockmen. But he saw no use in raising an issue. His policy was to get along peaceably with as many citizens as he could. Now Sherrill had come along and dumped trouble in his lap.

For what stood out like a sore thumb was that he could not please both parties. The only hopeful feature of the case was the news that Ben Randall was getting better. If the boy had died old Jeff would have been quite capable of bringing armed men from the ranches some night and storming the jail to hang the enemy. Now he would not dare go quite that far. At least the sheriff hoped so.

"What you want me to do—have you tried for assault with attempt to kill?" Humphreys snapped.

"I thought maybe you would want to send posses out to arrest Bill Cairns and Ben Randall too," Bruce suggested blandly. "Three men were wounded that night. Ben shot Pete

Engle and Bill Cairns sent me a pill. I don't suppose you share old Jeff's idea that it is all right to rub out us small fry but lese majesty to hurt a Randall."

"You know doggoned well I can't do that without starting a war," the sheriff said irritably. "Why couldn't you let sleeping dogs lie? If I put you in my jail they're liable to come hell-roaring in here to get you."

Bruce laughed. "I didn't think you would kill any fatted calf when you saw me."

The officer relaxed. "Well, come in and have a bite of breakfast. You can tie your horse to that young cottonwood."

"I don't think I had better," Bruce differed. "It's not my horse, but one I stole." He tied the reins to the saddle horn and gave the cowpony a cut with a quirt. The animal started down the street at a gallop. "Hope he knows enough to go home."

"Where is home for the horse?" Humphreys asked.

The face Bruce turned to him was as blank as a wall. "Where he ranges," the young man said.

"I notice you kept the pony so the brand was on the other side from me."

"That might be because I thought you had better not know who owns it," Sherrill answered, smiling by this time.

"Suits me," grunted the sheriff. "I don't want to know. I've got troubles enough."

The mirth died out of Sherrill's eyes. He looked solemnly at his host, who was a pillar of the little church at the end of the street. ". . . Affliction cometh not forth of the dust, neither doth trouble spring out of the ground; yet man is born unto trouble, as the sparks fly upward," he quoted.

The sheriff grinned at his irrepressible guest. "No use quoting Job to me," he said. "I haven't his patience."

Bruce pointed a reproachful finger at Humphreys. "You don't know your Bible, deacon. Not Job, but Eliphaz, a gent who came to have breakfast with his friend Job and certainly rubbed his troubles in plenty."

Mrs. Humphreys came down stairs to start the day and was surprised to see Bruce on the sofa rolling a cigarette. She had known him as a small boy before either of them had come West. He jumped to his feet. "I've ridden forty miles to get my teeth into some of your beaten biscuits, Mrs. Humphreys," he told her. "Ever since you introduced me to them last time I ate here I've been dissatisfied with other food —so here I am."

She was fat and forty, a wholesome good-looking motherly woman. "My goodness," she said, "I thought——"

Her glance whipped to her husband for instructions. The

situation was not clear to her. She did not know whether this cheerful young man was a guest or a prisoner.

"You thought I had forgotten those biscuits—and the fried chicken—and the raspberry jam. No, ma'am. When I am your husband's regular boarder do I get you for a cook?"

Mrs. Humphreys laughed. She had not put on her stays yet, not knowing they had company for breakfast, and her plump flesh shook like a jelly. She liked Bruce, as most people did. It was a relief to know his dead body was not lying crumpled in some fold of the hills, as her imagination had pictured. Instead, he seemed not to have a care in the world.

"I can't give you fried chicken for breakfast, but you're welcome to the beaten biscuits and the raspberry jam." She asked her husband, from force of habit, "Did you grind the coffee last night, Tim?"

"Don't I always?" he asked.

Bruce thought them a well-mated couple. The sheriff was a fat, friendly, easygoing man, and his wife had an unbounded admiration for him tempered by a maternal feeling that at times he was only a little boy acting big.

After the edge of their appetite had been dulled Humphreys raised the question in his mind. "What in heck am I to do with you?"

Sherrill helped himself to more raspberry jam. "Is that a rhetorical question, Sheriff? Or do you want advice?"

"I ought to put you in the calaboose," Humphreys said, answering himself. "But nobody wants you there. I sure don't. Your friends don't. I don't suppose you want to be shut up. The cattlemen would rather have you at your ranch or in the hills where there is no closed season on you."

"Your reasoning points to one conclusion, doesn't it?"

Humphreys glowered at him. "I'm sheriff of this county, young man, and sworn to do my duty."

"Regardless of who it pleases." Bruce nodded approval. "But what is your duty? Let us look at the facts. The big ranches put themselves against the law by fencing government land. We cut the fences. Are we breaking the law? If so, point it out to me."

The sheriff eased himself irritably in his chair. "You know blamed well you were waving a red rag at the big outfits."

"You're ducking the point. Of course it annoyed them. It annoys a burglar to be bitten by a bulldog while he is robbing a house. I claim we were inside the law. Any remarks?"

"Go on," Mrs. Humphreys said. "Tim is listening."

"While we were peaceably cutting bob-wire——"

"With guns in your hands," Humphreys barked.

"That country is filled with rattlesnakes and they are all out at night," Bruce mentioned. "Well, while we were at work

41

along come a bunch of warriors and start shooting. Pete Engle is wounded, and young Ben Randall races after him to cut Pete down before he can reach a horse. I fire once. Far as I know that was the only shot from any one of our party. Isn't that a pretty good self-defense case? Pete and I are both hit. We are not really asking you to arrest young Ben Randall and Bill Cairns. Nobody is asking you to put me in jail."

"What are you here for, then?"

"To put myself right with the law. Arrest me, then release me on bond. Everybody satisfied, including your conscience."

"A lot you care about my conscience," the sheriff grunted.

His wife said: "Still, it's a good way out, Tim. Bruce has a right to claim self-defense, so without deciding on the merits of the case you release him on bond for the courts to settle the right of it later."

Her guest nodded approval. "A Daniel come to judgment! yea, a Daniel!"

"Hmp! Maybe Jessie is right at that. I'll see Judge Lanigan. You stay right here till I've talked with him." Humphreys rose from the table and put on his dusty old black sombrero.

After the sheriff had gone Bruce suggested that he would like to saw wood for his breakfast if there were any chores about the place to do. His hostess told him there were none.

"How about me hoeing that corn in the garden?"

"Tim said you were to stay indoors," Mrs. Humphreys told him. "You look fagged out. No wonder, after riding all night. And you said you had been wounded. Where?"

"In the pasture. The night they jumped us."

"You know that's not what I mean, Mr. Smarty. What about your wound? Is it serious? Hadn't I better have Doctor Bradley see it?"

"No need. A good fairy doctored me."

She looked at him with shrewd inquiring eyes. "You're keeping something quiet. All right. That's your business. But I'll bet a doughnut there's a woman in this somewhere."

Bruce was quite willing to follow her advice about resting. He lay down on the bed in the room to which she took him and immediately fell asleep. When he awoke the sun was just sinking in the west.

Mrs. Humphreys heard him stirring and called from the foot of the stairs that supper was just ready. Sherrill washed his face and combed his hair.

There was fried chicken for supper.

"Everything arranged," the sheriff said. "Light out when you like."

Bruce said he thought he would get into another jam so that he could come back to this cooking and stay more permanently.

"If you are starting on your travels again what do you expect to do for a horse?" the sheriff inquired. "By your way of it you have stolen two in a week. If you keep on helping yourself maybe some owner after a while will get narrow-minded and not like it."

"Thought I'd have Sheriff Humphreys go down to the Elephant Corral and hire me one," Bruce replied, a twinkle in his eye.

"Not on your life," his host refused promptly. "I'd look fine getting you a horse to skip out on."

"If you feel that way about it I'll mosey down and get one for myself." Sherrill took a large helping of whipped mashed potatoes and put it beside the chicken leg and wing on his plate. "I'm going to hate leaving you, Mrs. Humphreys. If you ever think of taking a second husband I'd like to file an application."

"I like the husband I have pretty well," she said. "But I'm some worried about you, Bruce. Where are you going from here? Are you sure you'll be safe?"

He did not tell her where he was going. The less the sheriff knew of his whereabouts the better. Whimsically he tilted an eyebrow at her. "Now who would want to hurt *me?*" he asked.

10. Bruce Takes a Train

BRUCE CROSSED THE BRIDGE and moved across a vacant lot to the corral. His eyes were vigilant and wary. Since he did not want to be recognized by anybody meeting him, his hat was pulled well down on his forehead. In a city a stranger aroused no comment, but in a small ranch town of the frontier he was observed and there was speculation as to the reason for his presence. Sherrill knew that one of the town loungers seeing him would not be quite satisfied until he was close enough for an identification. And if the man made out who he was everybody in town would know about it inside of half an hour. The cattlemen had spies in town of course. Before the sun set tomorrow Jeff Randall would get word that he had been here.

He got into the corral over the back fence and moved forward in the dark shadows of the wagon sheds. A man came out of the small office near the gate.

" 'Lo, Prop," drawled Bruce. "How you doing? Still got the idea that three kings beat a flush?"

The owner of the corral whirled on him. "What you doing here, you crazy galoot? Haven't you got any sense a-tall?"

He was a little man, excitable, with a high thin voice. His

43

nickname was Prop because in an errant moment he had commissioned a wandering sign painter to hang from the box frame over the gateway a legend which read,

MATT ZANG, PROP,
ELEPHANT CORRAL, REDROCK

Another man came out of the office and gaped at Sherrill. "Well, what d'you know?" he exclaimed. "If it ain't Bruce!" The man was Flack. He had been caught unaware. The lantern by the side of the office door lighted the sly mean face and caught the look of startled apprehension. More than once there had been an ugly thought in the back of Sherrill's mind. He had put it away, only to have it return. He could not believe that Bill Cairns and his riders had discovered them cutting wire by sheer chance. Somebody had given him a tip, and nobody knew in advance of the raid except those expecting to ride on it. Bruce remembered that Flack had come without his wire clippers, that he had volunteered to hold the horses and had kept them some distance from the men at work, and that at the first alarm he had turned the mounts loose instead of waiting for their riders. Had he expected the attack? It looked like it.

That Zang could be trusted, Bruce knew. He flung questions at Flack. How was Pete Engle? Had there been any trouble with the cattlemen since the night of the raid? Did anybody except themselves know who were the wire cutters that night?

Flack was suavely ingratiating. He was tickled to death to see Bruce. All his friends had been worried for fear he had been killed in the hills. Pete was doing all right, but somebody had burned his cabin down while he was staying at Gilcrest's recovering from his wound. Nobody had been at home when it was done. Flack was sorry to have to report that two of the haystacks in Bruce's meadow had been fired and his fences cut in forty places. There had been an attempt to destroy his house but his three cowboys had shown fight and the attackers had given up without success. The homesteaders felt pretty bitter at the high-handed outrages of the stockmen.

"Where are the Engles staying now?" Bruce asked.

"At the Gilcrest place. We're building them a new house right where the old one was. All the neighbors have turned in to help." Flack went on to explain that he had come to town to get a new wheel for his wagon on account of a bust-up from a runaway.

"And while you were here you thought you might as well get a new hat and suit," Bruce suggested.

Flack looked down at his new clothes uneasily. It was well known that he never had a dime to spend. "My father died and left me some money—not much, just a little—and I fig-

44

ured I had looked like a tramp long enough and had better fix myself up decent like white folks." His oily smile was not very sure of itself. "Well, I'll tell the boys I saw you. They sure will be pleased."

"Have you got your new wheel yet?"

"No. Yates didn't have one. He's sent an order to Cheyenne for it."

"You're starting for home tonight?"

"Thought I would. I'll break the journey down the road a ways."

"I might as well see you started," Bruce said. "You can tell me all the news as you think of it."

"That's right. And of course the boys will want to know how you made out so long in the hills without any grub and just where you holed up so you couldn't be found."

"Tell them I found manna in the wilderness," Bruce answered lightly. "With all the game and fish in the hills a man can't starve."

Sherrill stayed with Flack until he saw him disappearing down the road in the darkness. He had come to a sudden decision and he did not want the man to have an inkling of what it was.

Bruce returned to the corral.

"I want to borrow five hundred dollars, Prop," he said. "Do you know any guy can lend it to me?"

Zang rubbed his bristly chin in thought. "I could get it at the bank tomorrow," he suggested.

"I need it tonight," Bruce explained. "I'm taking a long trip on a train, but I don't want anything said about it."

The keeper of the corral was a little surprised. Somehow he had not expected Bruce Sherrill to let himself be driven away.

"I reckon that's smart of you," he replied, unable to keep a touch of disappointment out of his voice. "They'll sure get you if you stay."

"I'll be back—in about ten or twelve days, I should think. How about Kilburn? Think he could get it for me right away? I want to start for Casper soon as I can."

"I'll ask him. Wait here till I come back."

In a little more than an hour Zang returned. He handed Bruce a roll of bills, and the ranchman put them in his pocket without counting the amount. "I'm much obliged to you, Prop. Mighty few men would dig up so much for a friend without asking a single question."

"Hell," Zang said, "you're good as the wheat. None of my business where you are going—or why."

"I reckon you had quite a job getting Kilburn to open the bank and get the money."

"He kicked some, but not too much. I didn't tell him I wanted it for you."

"Good. Now I want a horse that will take me to Casper."

Zang had only two. He recommended a flea-bitten gray. "Not much for looks," he said. "But how that broomtail can travel!"

At Casper, Bruce took the train for Cheyenne. There he bought a ticket for Washington.

11. A Bullheaded and Cantankerous Man

CLIFF APPLEGATE DREW UP in front of the Humphreys house and helped his daughter out of the buggy. The sheriff and his wife were old-time friends, and when Linda came to town she always spent the night with Jessie. There was a hotel in Redrock, but it was used only by poor derelicts who had no better place to go.

Jessie Humphreys ran out to meet Linda and kissed her warmly. "Time you came to see us, after all your promises," she cried.

"Father had to come for supplies, and as I wanted to match some dress goods I made him bring me," Linda explained.

"I'll drive down to Prop's corral and leave the rig," Cliff said.

"Be back in time for supper," Jessie told him "Tim will sure be glad to see you."

Linda cleaned up, put on a fresh dress, and went downstairs to join her friend in the kitchen. They chatted while Jessie worked. In the girl's mind there was something particular she meant to find out, but she wanted to have the other woman introduce the subject.

And presently Mrs. Humphreys did. "You'd never guess who slept in your room last." Since Linda gave it up, her hostess said, "Bruce Sherrill."

"Oh, that scamp." Linda's voice and manner were hostile.

Jessie was a forthright person. What she thought, she was not afraid to say. "I'm not so sure about that. Of course all of you at the Bar B B detest him. But the fact is I like him."

"I think he is the most conceited, insufferable pup I ever met," the girl answered with sharp emphasis on the adjectives.

Jessie's bright eyes fastened on her guest. "When I was at the ranch you told me you did not know him."

"I didn't then, but I do now." Linda poured out the story.

"So you're the good fairy who doctored him."

The young woman flushed angrily. "He told you that, did

46

he? That's like him—to boast about what I was forced to do. How could I help it when he was sick and wounded? Sometimes I wish I had let Father turn him over to Uncle Jeff."

"He didn't say it was you. Only that a good fairy had looked after him." Jessie added: "It must have been hard on you all—especially on Cliff—to shelter the man he was hunting, one he hates so much."

"Hard on us!" Linda exploded. "When we told Uncle Jeff he practically flung father and me out of his house. Where do you think we stand with our friends? We're traitors—double-crossers—turncoats who have thrown in with the trash nesting in the hills. Oh, I know you feel differently about these settlers. They all voted for Tim. But when we see them plowing up good grass land——"

"It isn't because they voted for Tim that we feel sorry for them," Jessie interrupted, quietly and firmly. "You ought to try to be fair, Linda."

The girl repented swiftly. "I know it isn't, Jessie. You and Tim are the salt of the earth. Sometimes I get all mixed up about these homesteaders myself, especially lately. They are awf'ly poor, some of them, and they have families. But we were here first, and if they had a lick of sense they would see this is grazing land, except some pockets along the creeks, maybe."

"I think Bruce feels a sort of responsibility for them, even though he isn't a farmer himself," Jessie said.

"What did he come here for—to give himself up?"

"He wanted it understood he wasn't an outlaw. If the law wanted him, here he was. But Tim felt there was no sense in putting him in jail. It was easy enough to get someone to go bail for him."

"Where is he now?"

"We don't know. He didn't tell us where he was going. He rented a horse from Matt Zang and disappeared. That was three days ago."

"I suppose he has gone back to his ranch to make more trouble."

It was in Jessie's mind that some on the other side made a good deal of trouble too. News had reached town that poor Pete Engle's house had been burned down while he was still recovering from his wound. And Pete had a wife and four little children.

After supper Tim and Cliff sat on the porch and smoked. It was pleasantly cool there after a hot day, and when the dishes were done the women joined them. They were thinking about going back into the house when heavy footsteps clumped along the sidewalk and turned in at the gate. A squat ungainly figure shuffled up the path to the house.

The visitor was Jeff Randall. He peered at those sitting on

the shadowed porch and let out a grunt of surprised exasperation.

"Quite a bunch of Mr. Sherrill's friends present," he jeered.

The sheriff ignored that. He rose. "I'll bring out another chair, Mr. Randall," he said.

"Not for me." The owner of the Diamond Tail waved the offer aside contemptuously. "I don't belong here. I'm just one of those damned cowmen you were elected to fight, Humphreys. I wouldn't expect any justice from a nesters' sheriff, and I'm not one of the kind of cattlemen who sit around and chin with fellows trying to ruin the country."

The sheriff's voice was carefully amiable. "Now you have that off your chest, Mr. Randall, I'll be glad to hear what I can do for you."

"You can tell me where that skunk you turned loose is holed up."

"Meaning Sherrill, I reckon."

"Meaning Sherrill." Randall added bitterly. "The guest you had staying with you while you were fixing it with Lanigan to free him."

"He left here Friday evening. I haven't seen him since."

"When he left town he was riding Prop Zang's gray."

"Was he?"

"You know damn well he was. Where did he go?"

"I don't know." Humphreys repressed a desire to tell the arrogant ranchman that he would not give the information if he had it.

"I wouldn't be surprised if he had come back and was in this house right now."

"He isn't here, Uncle Jeff," Linda said.

Randall glared at her. "Do I have to believe you—after you hid him from me for several days?"

"You don't have to believe any of us," the sheriff said firmly. "I'm sorry you feel so hostile, but there's nothing I can do about that."

Cliff had had about enough of his brother-in-law's domineering ways. "What are you beefing about, Jeff? Tim hasn't got Sherrill tucked away in his pocket. You sent him word you could take care of the fellow without any official help."

"So I could of, if you hadn't thrown down on me and hidden the scoundrel." Randall slammed a heavy fist down on the porch railing, venom glaring out of the bleached blue eyes in the sun-and-wind-weathered face. "If he ever gets where I can throw a gun on him, I'll blast the life out of the scalawag, even if he is yore friend."

"That's wild talk," Humphreys said. "I hear Ben is getting along fine. Sherrill is under bond to appear here if the law wants him. After all, the Pitchfork boys wounded two of the other side. Doesn't that make it even steven? Once a feud gets started a dozen men might get killed."

"The damned nesters were cutting a Pitchfork fence, weren't they?" Randall snarled. "If they had all been shot into rag dolls they wouldn't have any just complaint. Don't think we're gonna lie down and let them ride over us."

"Pete Engle's house was burned the other day. Haystacks have been fired. This can't go on. There is law in this country. In the end it will win out." The sheriff spoke quietly, but with conviction in his voice. Back of his good-nature there was resolution in the man, and a stiff pride not easily aroused.

"If you're claiming I fired Engle's house you're a liar, Humphreys," the Diamond Tail man flung out harshly, "though I tell you straight that I'd back up whoever did it. Law! What kind of law do you call it that helps riffraff rob decent men of all they've been building up for twenty-five years? To hell with it."

Randall turned and lumbered down the path, slamming the gate behind him. The clumsy tread of his feet died away in the distance.

A rueful smile creased the lips of Applegate. "He always was bullheaded and cantankerous," Cliff remarked. "But I'm with him in most of what he claims."

A shiver of prescient dread ran through Linda. "It's such a lovely country," she said with a sigh. "And we are filling it with war and hate."

The others made no comment. They were of the same opinion.

12. Ramrod Meets a Killer

RAMROD SPINDLER, in charge of the Quartercircle D C during the absence of Bruce Sherrill, did not take his responsibilities lightly. He and the boys under him had repelled the attack on the ranch house made one dark night but they had not been able to prevent the firing of two haystacks and the cutting of the wire fence. Cattle had strayed, and Ramrod had not felt it safe to let Neal and Mark ride the range except together and armed with rifles. He was worried also about Bruce, but not so much so since he had received the letter from Denver telling him to have one of the boys meet him at Redrock when the stage arrived on the seventeenth.

What Bruce was doing at Denver Ramrod could not guess. The old cowhand had been afraid that his employer had been drygulched in the hills, though somehow he could not quite believe it. Sherrill was so vitally alive it was hard to think of all that energy stilled forever. Still, the coming of the letter had been a comfort. There was no other person in the world Ramrod could not spare rather than the man he served.

He decided to go to Redrock himself to meet Sherrill. Neal and Mark were top-notch boys, but the weight of years had not quelled their carelessness. The wagon boss had been brought up on the frontier. He had been all through the Indian troubles, and when there was danger around he could be wary as a coyote. It was his job, one to which he had secretly pledged himself, to keep Bruce alive if possible, and he was not going to delegate the task. Since Redrock was the nearest town, both factions traded there. He would not have his friend step down from the stage into an ambush. That was one of Sherrill's weaknesses. He was too foolhardy—walked grinning into danger as if he thought God was carrying him in His pocket.

Ramrod started before daylight and reached town in the middle of the afternoon. Redrock was a cow town. It had been laid out by a Texan who had come up the Chisholm Trail and pushed his longhorns through Colorado to Wyoming. There was an old-fashioned courthouse square with business houses on the four sides facing it. Most of these had false fronts, on which were announced ownership and occupation. In some cases the signs were superfluous. On the sidewalk before the entrances to the Legal Tender and the Palace gambling houses old cards were littered. A cowboy sleeping off a drunk lay in the street close to the sidewalk where he had been deposited by a bartender just before Jake's Place closed. Somebody had thoughtfully put a hat over his face to protect it from the sun.

The foreman of the Quartercircle D C tied at a rack in front of Doan & Devon's general store. He stepped to the sidewalk, rifle in hand. Since he had no other place to keep it, his idea was to ask permission to leave it back of the counter for an hour or two. This weapon was of no use to him in the town, where already he was facing enemies.

Bill Cairns and Wally Jelks were standing in the doorway talking with a Diamond Tail rider known as Quint Milroy. Cairns stopped, to watch Spindler as he came forward.

"I see you've turned into a two-gun man, Ramrod," he jeered. "Taking after yore boss, I reckon." His gaze shuttled from the rifle to the revolver in the Quartercircle D C man's belt and back again.

"A three-gun man," Jelks corrected. "I'll be doggoned if he hasn't got a Winchester cased beside the saddle too."

Ramrod shifted the rifle to his left hand casually, to wipe the perspiration from his face with a handkerchief. His guess was that the big bully was merely needling him.

"Hot as Billy-be-damn today," he mentioned. He was not

expecting trouble in this public spot, but it might jump up at him and it was well to have his right hand free.

"A regular walking arsenal," Cairns prodded. "A sure-enough wolf on the prowl. His night to howl, I expect, Quint."

Milroy said nothing, but his glittering eyes did not lift from Spindler. Quint was a lithe slender man, poised and wary, with a reputation as a dangerous gunfighter. He was a recent importation at the Diamond Tail. The general impression was that he had been brought in by Jeff Randall on account of his prowess as a warrior.

Spindler was no "bad man." He belonged to the class of quiet resolute pioneers who had redeemed a hundred localities from the dominance of the swaggering killer and the furtive outlaw.

"You rate me wrong, Bill," he said, with surface amiability. "When a rifle needs fixing you have to bring it to town to a gunsmith."

Cairns had a notoriously bad temper, which he let slip the leash when he did not think it too dangerous. "Did it need fixing the other night when you were plugging away at some guys from the ranch house?" he demanded.

Ramrod smiled blandly. "Oh, you've heard of that little rookus. Not much to it. Some boys had got hold of too much tanglefoot and were celebrating the Fourth of July a bit premature. You know how it is when whiskey, a gun, and a cowpuncher get stirred up together—they make considerable noise but usually don't do much harm." He added, lightly, "Be seeing you, Bill," and pushed past him into the store.

The Pitchfork foreman glared after him, his ugly mouth set to a snarl. He did not like Spindler any more than he did the man's boss. Half a mind to follow, he hung for a moment undecided.

"That will be all for now, Bill," Milroy told him in a voice low but cold as a breath of wind over a glacier.

Sulkily Cairns nodded. It had not been his intention to call for an immediate showdown. What he wanted was to devil Spindler, roil his temper, and get away with it. Unfortunately the Quartercircle D C man had not been at all disturbed. It was Cairns himself who had boiled to impotent anger.

"Let's go get a drink," he said abruptly, and clumped down the sidewalk.

Jelks followed him. Milroy stayed where he was, a thin smile on his saturnine face. He understood men like Cairns. They blew off to relieve their bilious tempers or to work up their rage to a fighting point. That was bad medicine. Much better not to insult a foe unless you were ready instantly to carry through. Even then words were generally surplusage. Quint Milroy did not waste his force in anger. He had schooled himself against emotion. Now close to forty, he had

51

killed eight times. While still a boy, he had shot a rival in a quarrel over a woman, but since that day there had been no hatred in any of his shooting affairs. The instinct for self-preservation was well developed in him. He never boasted or swaggered, never traded before the public on his reputation. He kept to himself if possible, a man gentle of voice and manner, scrupulously polite. When he killed it was strictly in the way of business.

From a clerk he bought a cigar and lit it. Leaning easily against a counter, he was a picture of one at peace with the world. But he stood, as he always did, where nobody could get at him from behind. For him vigilance was the price he paid for life.

He watched Ramrod making purchases for the ranch, the alert brain back of the quick eyes studying the foreman. Some day he might be called on to deal with Spindler. Before that hour came, if it did, he wanted to know all he could about the reactions of his victim. Milroy did not depend only upon his deadly skill with a forty-five. He knew how to set the stage to minimize the chance of an opponent. It was his pride that he had no weakness, none of the handicaps of other professional gunmen. He did not drink or quarrel or embroil himself with women, had no Achilles' heel through which he might be destroyed.

13. Back from Luncheon at the White House

THE ARRIVAL OF THE STAGE was the liveliest hour of the day at Redrock until the rattle of chips began after nightfall. For when Hank Sowers drew up in a cloud of dust opposite the courthouse, he brought with him news of the outside world. Ten minutes before the Concord showed on the hill summit at the end of the street, Ramrod tied two saddled horses at a rack in front of the hotel just below the stage office. In order not to call attention to them he withdrew to the hotel porch and joined the chair sitters there.

Most of these were antiques, retired from the activities incident to making a living. Their main interest was gossip, and they turned on Ramrod with questions about the recent trouble between the cattlemen and the sodbreakers. The Quartercircle D C foreman showed a childlike innocence. He did not know what had become of Bruce Sherrill or how Pete Engle's house happened to catch fire. In a vague way he recalled that he had heard something about fence cutting, but the particulars had not reached him. There was a rumor, he admitted, that Ben Randall had been in bed from a gunshot

52

wound. Maybe he had shot himself by accident while cleaning the pistol, if it was a pistol that had done the damage.

While Ramrod answered questions he kept an eye on the saddled horse. There was a rifle in the boot beside the saddle, and he did not want anybody to remove it while he was not looking. Spindler still was not expecting any trouble in town, but he had observed that Cairns and Jelks were crossing the courthouse grounds to the stage station.

They stopped in the road beside the hitch rack. Since they belonged to a cattle outfit they had of course read the $\overset{\frown}{DC}$ brand on the shoulders of the horses Ramrod had just tied to the pole. They stood beside the animals discussing the meaning of this. Spindler had come to town alone and had brought two saddled mounts with him. One of them was Blaze, a roan never ridden by anybody but Bruce Sherrill. Did this mean that the foreman had come to town to meet his boss?

Cairns stepped to the side of the nearest horse and put a hand on the rifle in the case. For a big man Ramrod moved swiftly. Half a dozen reaching strides took him to the sidewalk.

"I wouldn't monkey with that gun, Bill," he warned. "It might go off."

"Had it fixed, have you?" Cairns wanted to know, with a nasty laugh. "Lear must of worked fast."

Ramrod pushed between him and the roan, brushing his hand aside. "Don't you know better than to fool with another man's gun, Bill?" he snapped.

The dull red of anger flushed into the leathery face of Cairns. "Keep yore hands off me, fellow," he snarled

"Did I push against you? Sorry." Ramrod's voice did not sound like an apology. It held a sharp note of command.

"This the gun Sherrill shot Ben with?" the Pitchfork man demanded.

"I wasn't present at any such shooting," Ramrod answered stiffly.

"I was," differed Cairns. "A lot of scoundrels were cutting our fence. Too bad we didn't bump off some of them. We will one of these days."

"Y'betcha!" agreed Jelks.

"You talking about fences on government land?" Ramrod asked.

"Never mind what fences. When we put up bob-wire it's there to stay. You tell that to yore hoe-men friends."

"I'll let you tell them," Ramrod replied.

His gaze strayed to the end of the street. The stage had reached the hill summit, and the horses were pounding down the hill at a gallop. Hank dragged them to a halt in a cloud of yellow dust exactly in front of the stage office. The two

53

Pitchfork men sauntered forward to watch the passengers pile out of the Concord. From it emerged a fat drummer, a lanky cowboy in chaps and big sweat-stained hat, and a young lady who had come to teach school at Redrock. The eyes of Cairns fastened greedily on the young woman, but deserted her at the sound of a cool mocking voice. Bruce Sherrill had stepped down from the seat beside Hank.

"Nice to meet you again when you are feeling peaceable, Bill," it drawled. "Last time we met you were pouring lead at me."

The startled young woman heard the words and glanced in alarm from one to the other. The younger man was smiling derisively, but the big fellow to whom he spoke was bristling like a turkey cock. She hurried into the office. Wild stories about the West had reached her in Ohio, retailed by friends who were sure that a Wyoming cow town was no place for Mattie Adams, just graduated from Oberlin College.

"That's right," boasted Cairns. "You had just shot Ben Randall and stolen his horse. You were gettin' the hell outa there so fast I didn't get a good crack at you."

"Maybe next time he won't be so lucky, Bill," volunteered Jelks. "A guy don't always have gilt-edged luck."

"Another county heard from," Bruce told the cowboy cheerfully. "When you talk so ferocious, Wally, chills run all over me."

Ramrod moved into the picture leading the two horses. "Welcome home, Bruce," he said.

"If he had been smart he would have stayed away after he lit out," Jelks cut in sourly.

"The Pitchfork boys are a little on the prod today," Bruce told his foreman. "We'll have to try not to worry about that."

Sherrill's glance picked up Quint Milroy across the road. He was leaning indolently against the fence, a cigar in his mouth. Though he was watching the group, he gave no indication of declaring himself in on any argument that might arise. The boss of the Quartercircle D C was glad of that. When Quint moved into a controversy the shadow of red tragedy was hovering close. But the killer's actions were unpredictable. He might be making up his mind at that very moment. It was time to go.

Bruce swung to the saddle. With Ramrod beside him he rode down the street and out of the square. Cairns watched angrily the two flatbacked riders disappear. Neither of them looked back to see if their enemies were drawing a bead on them.

"That bird Sherrill is the doggonedest cool son of a gun I ever did meet up with," Jelks said with reluctant admiration.

"He'll be dead inside of two weeks," Cairns predicted. Almost in a murmur he added, "Maybe in two hours."

For a man with a time limit on his life Bruce appeared unduly lighthearted. "Good to get home again," he said, and his glance swept the brown plain beyond the small town and the blue ridge of the mountain range on the horizon. "This is where I belong."

Ramrod looked at him doubtfully. "I wonder if it is," he questioned. "There's trouble ahead, and you're in the middle of it."

"I like elbow room," Bruce continued. "We've got it here. Back in the East you can't get away from crowds."

"You been back East?"

"To Washington. I had a long talk with the Great White Father."

The foreman stared at him. "You mean the President?"

"Yes. You knew I was in his Rough-Rider regiment—got pretty well acquainted with him in Cuba. He's a man you can talk with easily. Had a ranch himself in Montana."

"Hashed over old days, did you?"

"Some. We talked about bob-wire fences too." He added, casually: "While we were eating lunch at the White House."

Ramrod guessed this for a merry flight of fancy. "Hmp!" he snorted skeptically. "Funny he didn't offer to make you ambassador to Great Britain since you are so chummy."

"You don't try to get chummy with the Colonel if you have any sense," Bruce explained, disregarding his friend's sarcasm. "He's a man you could ride the river with, but he has plenty of dignity too. Nice and friendly, but you don't cross the line."

"Did he have any ideas about bob-wire?" Ramrod asked.

"He did before I left. Of course, he didn't take my word about the situation. There's going to be an investigation."

"I've heard of 'em," Ramrod said dryly. "When the committee reports, you'll have long white whiskers."

Bruce differed. "The Colonel is a hurry-up gent."

From Doan & Devon's store a voice hailed them. Rod Randall sauntered down the steps. "Want to see you, Sherrill," he said. The words fell curt and crisp. Men on the street stopped to listen.

"It costs nothing Mex," Bruce answered coolly, and drew up.

Randall crossed the street with long light strides, gracefully as a cat, each step flinging up a spurt of dust from the road. The eyes of the men on horseback did not lift from him. They knew him to be reckless as well as arrogant and fearless.

"Thought you had lit out," he said insolently.

"Wrong report," Bruce replied. "I own a ranch on Bear Creek."

Ramrod shifted his position, so as not to be back of Bruce. "Don't crowd me, Ramrod," drawled Rod. "No showdown today."

55

"Good," the foreman said. "Gun fighting is bad medicine."

"But necessary to get rid of pests." Randall's voice was cool and scornful. "I'm serving notice on you, Sherrill. If any more Diamond Tail fences are cut I'll come at you with a smoking gun."

Bruce said quietly, "I don't want any difficulty with you."

"Then quit devilin' us, you fool, or I'll blast you sure as the sun sets tonight." Rod turned comtemptuously and walked back to the store.

The riders moved on. Ramrod said, "Mr. Big serves notice, son."

They dismounted in front of the sheriff's house. Bruce knocked on the open door. "Important guests arriving," he announced.

Mrs. Humphreys came to the door. She called over her shoulder to her husband, "Here's your horse thief, Tim."

Ramrod reproved her gravely. "Don't call him names—not this Big Mogul. He's been eatin' at the White House with his side kick T. R."

"Not really!" Jessie exclaimed.

"Honest Injun!" Bruce grinned at her. "And the Colonel's cook isn't a patch on you."

"He's fishin' for a supper bid," Ramrod mentioned.

"I know he has kissed the Blarney Stone," Jessie said. "He is not fooling me a bit. Well, come in and wash up, as you had to do at the White House—if you ever were there."

"That's a right big if," Ramrod commented.

Bruce gave his hostess a hug. She had once been his next-door neighbor and Sunday-school teacher, before either of them had seen Wyoming or Tim.

"Just like his impudence," Jessie declared, blushing, and vanished into the kitchen.

"Does a lawfully married husband have to stand for this?" Tim inquired.

Bruce clapped him on the back. "Pistols for two, Tim," he said, "but not until I've had one more of Jessie's suppers."

The eyes of the sheriff twinkled. He was not at all displeased. "Wish I had had your cheek when I was a young rooster," he said regretfully. "You sure throw a long shadow with women."

"They are sorry for me," Bruce explained.

"Hmp! There was one here the other day isn't sorry for you. She's one you can't get to first base with, young fellow me lad."

"Do I have to guess who she is?"

"Name is Linda Applegate. I don't know whose good fairy she is, but she sure makes it plain she is not yours."

"Afraid she doesn't like me. Anyhow, she did her Christian

duty. You ought to have seen her stand up to her father when Cliff wanted to turn me over to Jeff Randall for a Roman holiday. Nothing doing, she told him, and he had to take it."

"Jeff dropped in while the Applegates were here. The old wolf is plenty sore at them. Feels they are traitors for shielding you."

At supper Ramrod revived again the topic of Sherrill's visit at the White House. "Did the President feed you beefsteak like this?" he inquired.

"I'll have to ask all of you not to say a word about that," Bruce answered. "He's sending a man out here to investigate conditions and I don't want the enemy to know about it until a report has been made. Our Washington representatives would start putting a lot of pressure on T. R."

Ramrod said, "I'm gettin' so I almost believe yore fairy tale."

"I think you made a wise play, Bruce," the sheriff approved. "Nobody in Washington understands the West better than the President. 'Course we can't tell how he'll look at the thing. He used to be a cattleman himself. They say he approved of hanging rustlers when they controlled the law and couldn't be convicted. When our Senators and Congressmen get to him he'll hear the other side of the story. They will pour it on thick."

Bruce knew that was true. But the President had already declared himself on the subject of fencing government land. Moreover, he had a strong instinctive feeling for the underdog. He did not like to see little people trampled upon by the powerful.

The whiplike crack of a rifle outside startled them. They stared at each other a moment before Bruce rose from the table.

"Stay here," he ordered.

In the hall he picked up his saddle gun and cautiously opened the door part way. A bullet crashed through a panel. He closed the door. Ramrod and the sheriff were hurrying out of the parlor where they had been eating.

"Put out the lamps and get Jessie into the cellar, Tim," he said. "Someone has shot Blaze. I'm going out the back way to see if I can find out who did it."

Ramrod went with him. They made a wide circuit, to strike the road fifty yards below the house. Darkness was falling fast, and at a distance they could not be seen. The shots had probably come from a grove of cottonwoods close to the bank of the river. They moved as fast as they could without making any noise. As soon as they struck the stream they followed the bank toward the shadowy bulk made by the trees. They heard the stir of horses, the creaking of saddle leather, and then the thump of hoofs pounding down the road

57

at a gallop. Whoever had made the attack was getting away before the way of escape was closed.

There was nobody in the grove, and it was too dark to pick up any sign that might be there. The Quartercircle D C men walked back to the house. Blaze was lying in the dust before the hitch rack. The horse was dead.

"We ought never to have stopped here for supper with Bill Cairns in town," Bruce said.

"Right," agreed Ramrod. "If we had come out before it got dark, one of us would have been lying there."

The sheriff joined them. "Better stay overnight," he said.

"No," Bruce decided. "We've brought enough trouble to you. I'll get another horse and start for home."

Half an hour later the two men were riding into the darkness.

14. Ben Faces a Showdown

MARY RANDALL, third wife of Jeff, came back from visiting her people at Redrock with a queer rumor she had heard, to the effect that the Applegates had picked up Bruce Sherrill, weary and wounded, had fed and nursed him, and sent him on his way. Of course there could not be any truth in it, since the Bar B B was tied up with the Diamond Tail and the Pitch fork in the fight against the hoemen. Nonetheless it disquieted her, for she had learned the story on pretty good authority. If there was anything in it, she knew her husband would be foaming at the mouth.

She found him irritable as a bear with a wounded paw. He was nursing not only a grievance but a hurt. The marriage of his sister to Cliff Applegate had cemented their friendship. He had liked all of the children. Now he felt an obligation to hate the whole tribe, and he had to stay angry at them to do it with vigor.

After two or three unhappy days she took her problem to Ben, whom she found sitting on the porch reading a magazine. Neither Ben nor Ned were her own sons. Ben had been six and Ned only a baby when at seventeen she married Jeff Randall, already close to fifty and with grown sons in homes of their own. Mary had been a good mother to her husband's little sons, and she had continued to love them even though she now had two girls of her own.

Ben put down his magazine and rolled a cigarette. He knew Mary was troubled and he could guess why. The situation did not please him either. The young Applegates had been his most intimate companions. His status with them was more that of a brother than a cousin.

"It's your father," she said. "He is unhappy, and all he can do about it is make life a burden for the rest of us."

Ben nodded. He was very fond of this dark-eyed young woman who had given him love and care. More than once he had stood between her and his father's stiff intolerance.

"If there is anything I can do about it——" he said.

"I don't suppose there is. He sits there and broods, and if the children get in his way he barks at them."

"Father has a memory like an elephant. Mighty little chance of his forgetting or forgiving. Matter of fact, I don't blame Uncle Cliff much—or the rest of them. What could Lindy do when Sherrill showed up wounded with Bill Cairns and his wolves hard on the fellow's heels?"

"Your father won't take that into consideration. Bruce Sherrill had shot you down, so they ought to have turned him over to us."

"I don't like these homesteaders any more than he does, but you have to look at things as they are. Sherrill wasn't gunning for me. He knocked me off to save that nester Engle. In a way I'm kinda glad he did. Engle has a mess of kinds, and I'd feel like the devil if I had killed him."

"Could you tell that to Jeff? Would it do any good?"

"I can tell him. Some day I'd have to get it off my chest anyhow. I'm not going to join him in a feud against the Applegates."

"There are the children," she sighed. "They don't understand it. How could they? All their lives they have adored Lindy and liked the boys. Now they mustn't have anything to do with them or even mention their names. It's not reasonable. They'll come to hate their father."

"The thing is poisonous," Ben agreed. "Hand me my stick, Mary. I'll have it out with the old man. He'll probably skin me alive."

"I don't know what I would do without you, Ben," she told him gratefully. "You have more influence with Jeff than anybody else."

"Yeah," he scoffed. "You sure owe me a lot. I started the whole mess. Serve me right if I got flung out on my ear."

Mary gave him the walking stick and he hobbled to the small disorderly room his father used as an office. It was furnished with a plain table and two kitchen chairs. There was no carpet. A saddle with a broken stirrup and a bridle hanging from the horn had been flung into one corner. On the spare chair were a clutter of newspapers, a pair of run-down-at-the-heel boots, a dusty hat, a corncob pipe, and a sack of tobacco. Jeff Randall's huge shapeless body was huddled over the table. With a stub of a pencil he was working out the net returns from several carloads of beef he had driven to Casper and shipped from there. He squinted up at his son and said, "In a minute."

Ben put the hat, the pipe, and the tobacco on the table. The rest of the litter he swept from the chair and sat down. His father's school education had consisted of one term at a country school, and it made him sweat to get the correct answer to a simple problem in arithmetic. At every step of the process his mouth whispered figures sympathetically. Ben did not hurry him. He knew that what he was going to say would bring an explosion from the old man.

Jeff looked at the sheet of paper dubiously. "You might check this, son," he said. "Save me from doing it over. I might of made a mistake."

The young man added the columns, made the subtractions, and handed the paper back to his father. "Right," he said.

"I had eight of Cliff Applegate's stuff in one car," Jeff mentioned. "I'll have to send him a check. He and I won't be doing business together any more."

"Why not?" Ben asked.

Jeff glared at him. "You know dadgummed well why not. Because he turned out to be a traitor."

"Aren't you taking it too hard, Father?" Ben asked. "Uncle Cliff had to do what he thought was right. He held Sherrill a prisoner till he found out whether I was going to make the grade. Knew our boys were so mad they were liable to act crazy."

Jeff pounded the table so hard with a big fist that it jumped. "Now my own son is throwin' in against me," he shouted. "By God, I won't stand it."

"We want to be fair to Uncle Cliff, don't we?" Ben protested, voice and manner placatory. "He had a wounded man who had flung himself on his hands for protection. He couldn't have done less for a stray dog."

"This wasn't a stray dog," his father roared. "He was our enemy—and his. The fellow had killed you, far as Cliff knew."

"Look at it this way," argued the young man. "I rammed in with my gun smoking and likely would have killed Engle if Sherrill hadn't stopped me. If that raft of kids had been left fatherless because of me, I would have felt like a murderer."

"You talk like a fool. I won't discuss this with you. Shut up yore mouth and do as I say." Jeff was so explosively full that he reversed himself immediately. "Engle had a gun in his hand, didn't he? You're too soft for this country. I ought to have whopped hell out of you when you were growing up and made you tough."

Ben smiled, a bit grimly. He had not yet entirely forgiven

his father for the numerous thrashings he had endured for boyish offenses.

"Get this," Jeff stormed on. "We've got to fight against this riffraff—or be licked. It's war. Either they lose or we do. It's not yore fault Engle has a passel of young uns. If he wanted a safe life he shouldn't come homesteading my water and plowin' up my land."

"I understand that," Ben agreed. "What worries me is this business of Uncle Cliff. Say he did make a mistake. We can't cut loose from him."

"I have cut loose from him," Jeff corrected. "It's done."

"If we don't make up with the Applegates, Mary will be unhappy," Ben continued. "So will the children. They have been close to us long as I can remember. It's like cutting off an arm."

"Don't tell me what I'm to do," Jeff cried angrily. "I'll decide who will be our friends and who won't. That girl Lindy may boss the Bar B B, but long as I'm alive I'll run the Diamond Tail and dictate its policies. Neither Mary nor you nor the children have a thing to say about it. I've been too easy with you all, but you'll walk the straight line now. Without making a chirp. Understand?"

For the first time in his life Ben had come into direct rebellion against his father. He was an easy-going young fellow who liked his fun, and he preferred the line of least resistance. But this involved a point he could not dodge. He had to stand his ground or admit himself a weakling. His eyes met those of the older man steadily.

"I'm not trying to run the ranch or decide its policies," he said. "This is a personal matter. I'm telling you that the Applegates are our kin. We can't forget that. It's not reasonable to like them one day and hate them the next because you say we must."

"I don't give a damn whether you hate them," the old man broke out. "What I'm saying is that you are not going to have anything to do with them. Tht's an order."

"I'm sorry."

"Be sorry, but don't come sniveling to me about it. Just remember that I make the rules here."

"I mean I'm sorry that I can't obey your order."

Jeff's bulging eyes stared at his son, "What?" he demanded.

"I'm a man," Ben told him quietly. "Free and twenty-one. I'll go with you far as I can, but I won't follow you when I know you are wrong. You ask too much."

The ranchman jumped to his feet. For a moment Ben thought his father was going to attack him physically. Rage almost choked the huge cattleman.

"Then get out—and don't come back, damn you. Who the

hell do you think you are? You eat my food and spend my money—and then tell me what you will and won't do. There's only one boss here—and I'm that boss. Get out, before I break every bone in your body."

Ben walked out of the room. He realized that he had only made matters worse for Mary and the children. His father would be almost impossible now. But he did not see what else he could have done except knuckle down, and if he had done that he would have hated himself.

Jeff Randall was piling up trouble and misery for himself and for others, Ben knew, but the old man had fought his way to the top so ruthlessly that he had come to think his will was law. This corner of the world was his to rule. With the growth of power a stubbornness had developed in him that had become tyranny. Of late the challenge to his dominance of the homesteaders had filled him with anger. What the Applegates had done was a more bitter and personal affront. Now his favorite son had sided with his enemies. Ben was afraid that the savage obstinacy of the man would drive him to excesses bound to recoil upon himself.

15. Linda Looks for a Way Out

BEN RANDALL drew up at the Bar B B ranch house and shouted, "Hello the house!" He was very tired from the long ride, and his side was aching. Both hands clung to the horn of the saddle.

Linda answered the call. Her sleeves were rolled up to the elbows and there were dabs of flour on the forearms. She had been making apple pies. That was one thing she did better than Bud Wong, and her father was particularly fond of the flaky crust. The sight of her cousin surprised her.

"Aren't you out of bounds?" she asked him coldly. The girl had nothing against Ben, but she did not mean to show any warmth until he had made known his own attitude.

He turned on her his winning smile. It had got him out of a lot of scrapes in their school days. "I've come to take an interest in you, so you can't hurt my feelings," he said, using her own words.

The eyes of the girl lit. She was much pleased that he had not joined in the animosity of his father.

"Does Uncle Jeff know about this interest you are taking?" she asked.

"I mentioned it to him."

"And he said you were showing a nice neighborly spirit?"

"He told me to get the hell out of there and not come back."

Mirth fled from the girl's face. "Oh, Ben, you mustn't

quarrel with Uncle Jeff. Even though he is wrong, still he's your father."

"The quarreling has all been done, and it was one-sided. I was meek as a lamb—tried to reason with him. He wouldn't have it."

"I'm so sorry you had trouble on our account," she cried.

"I didn't. It was on my own account. If a man is pushed to the wall he has to stand on his feet and say his piece. I said mine. I wasn't going to let him bully me into siding against you-all. Mary feels as I do, but her hands are tied and she can't do anything about it."

He swung slowly and heavily from the saddle. She ran forward to help him, distressed at his condition. Of course he ought not to have ridden so far. Leaning on her, he got into the house. He lowered himself into an armchair and slumped down completely exhausted.

Her brothers were breaking horses in the corral. She ran to the door and called them. Brand was fastening a saddle cinch on a colt. He left the other men and moved to the fence.

"What do you want?" he shouted. "We're busy."

"Come now, please," she urged. "Ben is here."

Brand helped his cousin upstairs to a bedroom.

"I'd better get Doc Bradley," he told his sister a few minutes later. "Ben looks like a mighty sick man to me. He was crazy to ride so far."

It was ten days before young Randall left the bed.

"We're turning this ranch into a hospital," he said to Linda one day with a wry smile when she appeared with his dinner on a tray. "I should think you'd hate to see a guy ride up to the house for fear he would fall off his horse and say, 'Nurse me.'"

"I hope you'll be the last," she admitted.

"I reckon nobody has heard anything of Sherrill since he left Redrock on Prop's gray," he said.

"Yes, he's back at his ranch. I didn't tell you while you were so sick. He came in on the stage one night and had supper with the Humphreys. While he was there somebody shot the horse he had tied in front of the house."

Ben looked worried. "Do they say Father had it done?"

"No-o. Bill Cairns was in town. He had words with Sherrill. Folks think he did it, but there was no proof."

Ben was silent for a minute. "Funny how one step leads to another. If I hadn't happened to be at the Pitchfork when word came that the nesters were going to cut the fence that night, I wouldn't be lying here, Sherrill wouldn't have been hunted, and you wouldn't have had to look after him. Father wouldn't have got mad at you and then at me. All the trouble since then flared up from that one night."

She shook her head. "No. It was coming anyhow. I see that

now. You just set a match to an explosion ready to go off."

"Maybe." He put words to another thought troubling him. "I wish I could have got along without leaving the Diamond Tail, but I don't see how I could. You know how bullheaded Father is. In his mind he'll pile the quarrel with me on top of everything else. I'm scared to think what he will do."

"You don't mean against you or us?"

"Lord, no! He'll take it out on the homesteaders, or on one of them. On Sherrill probably. He'll blame him for everything that has gone wrong."

"What will he do?"

"I don't know."

Their eyes met. He did not want to tell Linda what he feared. He was thinking of Quint Milroy, the quiet deadly killer who had dropped in at the Diamond Tail and gone on its payroll. Ben did not believe his father had hired the man to shoot down his foes. He had employed the fellow on account of his reputation, to frighen and scare away the homesteaders who were annoying him by interfering with the grass and water he needed for his herds. But given such a handy tool, in the state of mind to which Jeff Randall had worked himself, what more likely than that the old man would use the gunman to rub out the leader of those interfering with what he considered his rights?

"Is there anything we can do about it?" Linda asked. There was a tight cold lump in her stomach. Two pictures flashed into her mind. One of Bruce Sherrill standing before her, gay and nonchalant, a whimsical smile on his face, making light of the danger crowding close to him. Another of him lying crumpled on the ground, a bullet in his heart.

"Not a thing."

"We can warn him," she protested.

"He doesn't need any warning—not after being hunted over the hills for days, not after having his horse shot down almost before his eyes. Of course the heat has cooled off a lot, since I took the right turn and made the grade. There isn't exactly an open season on him now. But he knows the old man isn't going to quit."

"So we've got to sit here and let murder be done," the girl cried unhappily.

"It may not come to that. If he is on his ranch he won't take any chances."

"How can he help it, if somebody lies in the brush waiting to get him? There must be a way to stop it. What's the law for? Why doesn't Tim Humphreys do something?"

"What can he do? The law moves only after crime has been committed, not before."

"So we had better just forget the whole thing and let your

64

father kill Bruce Sherrill," she said bitterly, in a surge of revolt.

He looked at his cousin, a new thought back of the watchful eyes. Was it possible she had any interest in Sherrill outside of that dictated by impersonal humanity? The man had been in her house a week, so close that she could not escape his presence. There were qualities in him that might touch a woman's fancy—his good looks, gay insolence, and that manner of easy contact which the outside world gives. Add to that the situation, a fugitive being hunted for his life, with her standing between him and death.

Linda must have guessed what he was thinking. A wave of color beat into her cheeks and up to the roots of her hair.

"I don't like him any better than you do," she whipped out. "I detest his impudence—and what he stands for—and everything about him. But that's no reason why I should stand aside and let him be killed by an assassin. We've got to do something, Ben."

Ben loaded his fork with mashed potatoes and gravy before he answered. "Nothing we can do," he retorted, sharp irritation in his voice. "It's got beyond us."

His resentment was not at her but at the situation that had trapped him. He understood her horror at waiting with folded hands to let tragedy develop, and to a degree he shared it. Yet what responsibility of his was it if Bruce Sherrill got himself killed because he had hell in the neck and would take no warning? Ben and the Quartercircle D C man were lined up on different sides of this feud. They had never exchanged a civil word. How could he prevent a bitter and vindictive old man from following his urge to destroy an enemy he hated?

Linda's reply touched this very point. "If we could get Uncle Jeff to see he is in the wrong, that there is a better way to settle this trouble——"

"What better way?" he demanded. "You can't compromise this fight. Either the cattlemen win or the homesteaders do."

"I know." She hesitated, and then made the plunge, color beating into her cheeks. "Could Rod do anything with your father—if I could get him to try?"

"What makes you think you could get him to try?" he asked quickly, watching her steadily.

She began to arrange the dishes on the tray, to avoid looking at him. "He's always been nice to me," she said. "I think he likes me."

Ben was sensitive to atmospheres. It had more than once occurred to him that there was some undercurrent of emotion drawing these two together, perhaps in spite of themselves.

"And you like him," he suggested.

"Well, he's my cousin, sort of, isn't he?"

65

"It couldn't be that you're in love with him," he said, with an intonation that made the statement a question.

"No, it couldn't," she flashed at him indignantly.

"Because Rod wouldn't be good for you. He's too like Father—too hard and too bossy. No woman—even if he loved her—could bend him an inch from the line he chose to follow. Rod has taken his stand on this matter. He's right in front of the fight, and he wouldn't say a word to hinder Father. Fact is, I don't know anybody more likely to shoot down Sherrill than Rod. He'd do it openly, in a fair fight. No ambush stuff for him. Rod isn't afraid of any man alive."

"Do they think they are God—Rod and your father?" she flung out in hot anger. "Who made it their privilege to take other men's lives? Doesn't it ever strike them that they can be wrong too?"

"Maybe we're making too much of this, Lindy," her cousin said. "Maybe all they will do will be to burn Sherrill's ranch house."

She changed the subject. What was the use of talk?

16. Washington Takes a Hand

THOUGH BRUCE SHERRILL never let it disturb the casual ease of his manner, he knew that he was walking through the valley of the shadow. From the earliest frontier days the cattle industry had been a violent and precarious one, its prosperity threatened by enemies that had to be overcome. Indians, rustlers, blizzards, drought, overfeeding, wild beasts, and poisonous plants had all to be whipped, depressions and bad markets to be roughed through. The ranchman had survived because he was an individual strong and rugged. Too often law on the high plains had been something written in a book, without force to give it practical application to the needs of the community. Cattlemen had fashioned their own law, and the moral value of it depended upon the character of the enforcer.

The homesteader had either to be accepted or to be fought illegally. Men like Jeff Randall and Ned Daly justified their highhanded methods on the ground that only terrorism would protect their rights. They had plenty of precedents to guide them. In Texas and Arizona, as well as in Wyoming, hired assassins known as stock detectives had shot down offenders from the brush.

Bruce had survived so far because he was not a rustler preying on the stock of the big ranches, and even though he was a far more dangerous enemy they had hesitated to sacrifice him. But he felt he had worn their patience too thin. The shooting of Ben Randall had been the last straw. By the nature of his business he was forced to live outdoors, and though he took what precautions he could he knew that he never swung to the saddle without the possibility of having a bullet whip across a hillside at him before he came home.

Ramrod worried over him as a mother does over a wayward son. "I saw you riding the south prong yesterday," he protested. "A mark asking to be picked off."

"I was looking for the heifer that got out of the big pasture," Bruce explained.

"Are you the only man in this outfit can ride?" Ramrod asked in exasperation. "What's the matter with telling Mark or Neal or go? Or me? I'm still able to fork a bronc."

They were at breakfast. Neal walked to the stove, got the coffee pot, and poured himself a cup. "Anybody else?" he inquired.

Mark gulped down a last swallow and pushed his cup forward. "Seeing you're up," he said. "And I think Ramrod is right, Mr. Sherrill. Leave us do the hill-ridin' for a spell."

"I can't wrap myself up in tissue paper and mothballs," Bruce explained. "This is my scrap, not yours. Maybe the man in the bush with the rifle might not have good eyes and couldn't tell one of you from me at a hundred and seventy-five yards. He probably would not want to come closer to make sure. I'd feel fine passing the buck if he mistook one of you for me. It's been done before, you know."

Ramrod was reaching for another slice of ham. He waited, fork poised, while he glared at the boss. "Holy smoke! The boys are he men, ain't they? You don't have to tuck 'em up in bed nights. Anyhow, old Jeff isn't trying to collect him a two-bit compuncher. He's after big game—you, Bruce Sherrill."

Neal backed the foreman's argument. He would be nineteen in a month, and he had done a man's work for three years. One thing he did not want was to be babied. "That's right. Mark and I are just two spots in this game, but don't count us out." He grinned, to make sure the others would know his next remark was a joke. "We are two of the heroes at the siege of the Quartercircle D C where there was a pint of lead spilled and nobody hurt."

"I wouldn't ask for better men," Bruce said. "But after all, as I told you before, this is not your fight. I advise you to leave. You are under no obligation to stay."

Neal flushed angrily. "How come you think we're quitters? I aim to stick around."

"Same here," Mark agreed. "In pitch a deuce is sometimes

good as an ace. When a guy shoots the moon a two-spot can knock him galley west." [1]

Bruce was touched at the loyalty of his big broad-shouldered young riders, but he did not embarrass them by mentioning it. "Fact is, we don't quite know where we are, he commented. "All the fireworks may have been to scare me and other homesteaders away. Nobody has been killed yet."

His foreman snorted derisively. "You sure take a lot of convincing. Rod told you his piece the other day, didn't he? And his father. Do you want an affidavit from old Jeff that he means business?—'To Whom It May Concern: I'm not foolin' when I shoot up Bruce Sherrill and attack his ranch and burn his haystacks and comb the hills to drygulch him and kill his horse. I mean to fill him full of slugs.' Signed J. Randall."

Mark glanced out of the window and reported a guest. "Dave Gilcrest on his white mule Jenny," he said.

Gilcrest bowlegged into the room and tossed two letters in front of Bruce. "Picked 'em up in yore mail box as I came along. How's everything on Bear Creek?"

"No complaints," Bruce answered. "Grass fine. How about Squaw?"

"About as usual. Pete Engle's house is finished and they have moved in."

"Sarah all right?"

A grin touched the big man's homely puckered face, and he tugged at his long drooping mustache. "Still worryin' some about me, but no more than usual. All I weigh is two hundred-odd pounds, and I'm strong enough to throw a yearling across the crick by its tail."

"No new trouble with the cattlemen?"

"No. Couple of Pitchfork riders drifted up the crick yesterday and stopped to watch the Engles moving in. One of 'em was that fresh guy Wally Jelks. He made a sarcastic crack about what a nice little house it was and how he hoped it wouldn't burn down accidental like the other one. But there's another thing. Two fellows rode in yesterday with a pack outfit and set up a tent. Claimed they came to fish. Might be, but I got to sorta wonderin'. Folks don't usually pack a couple hundred miles just to fish."

"Give their names?"

"Barnard and Sawyer. They drapped in to our place for milk. Asked a lot of questions about the trouble between us and the cattlemen. Course, tenderfeet always are poppin' off with fool questions. That may not mean a thing."

"But you think they may be stock detectives?"

---

[1] In pitch, a card game played much in the cattle country, when one shot the moon he engaged to take high, low, jack, and the game or else be set. If an opponent held the two-spot he lost the bid.

"Yeah, or gunmen brought in for a showdown. We don't know what the hell old Jeff and his friends will do next."

Bruce slit with a table knife the envelopes of his letters and read the enclosures. The first was not signed. Two sentences were written on a sheet of paper in a neat Spencerian style, probably by a woman. He thought he could give her name.

I am not your friend, but I don't want you murdered. For God's sake, if you have a lick of sense, get out in time.

The other letter bore a Washington postmark.

"Don't worry about the fishermen," Bruce told Gilcrest. "I'll ride over today and have a talk with them. I've a notion I know this Barnard. If he is the man I'm thinking of, he is all right."

Bruce rode back with Gilcrest over the hogback to Squaw Creek. He found the fishermen's camp a mile above the Gilcrest place. The men were just tramping back in when he arrived. They carried rods and creels.

"Any luck?" he asked.

They showed him four fish, a very small take for a morning on a first-rate trout stream. A fair guess was that they had been fishing only as a blind.

"They weren't biting," the older man explained. He was red-faced, bald, already beginning to carry surplus fat about his waist. But his eyes were keen and quick.

"Mr. Barnard, I reckon," Bruce said, and gave his own name.

"We were going to look you up," Barnard said. "But you have beaten us to it. News must travel fast here. Mr. Sherrill, this is Mr. Sawyer, a Denver representative of our office."

"A letter reached me from Washington today," Bruce told them. "But not before a rancher was in my house with word that strangers were on the creek."

Sawyer was a lean thin man with a dark saturine face. "We are viewed with suspicion," he said dryly. "Nobody on this creek will say anything about the trouble with the cattlemen."

"They are afraid to talk," Bruce replied. "Strangers don't come here to fish—too far from the railroad and a lot of good streams far nearer. The natives are afraid you might be men employed by the big ranches, cattle detectives or gunmen."

"Do we look like gunmen?" Barnard asked.

"They don't want to take chances. Did you come by way of Redrock?"

"Yes. We stayed there two days." He added, after a pause: "We talked with a good many residents of the town. They express opinions more freely there than here."

"Not in the danger zone," Bruce said.

He did not ask them with whom they had talked nor what their reaction was to what they had heard. They were probably close-mouthed men and would give nobody a line on their findings before reporting at Washington.

"If people knew why you were here they would talk fast enough—both sides," Bruce suggested.

"We've just decided to give out that information," Barnard said. "I can't see that it will do any harm."

"You will have to take with a few grains of salt whatever any of us tell you," the ranchman told him smilingly.

Bruce realized that as soon as the cattlemen learned that the campers were government men the two investigators would be invited to the big ranches and treated royally. This might have an important bearing on their findings, but it was something that could not be helped.

One good angle to the publicity would be a temporary cessation of hostilities. As long as Barnard and Sawyer were in the vicinity there would be no hostile actions committed by either faction.

17. Shots from Ambush

BRUCE RODE UP A DRAW to the bench above. His wary gaze checked every shrub and land crease behind which an enemy could hide. Of late the price of life for him had been constant vigilance, and though by this time the big ranches must have heard that government men were in the neighborhood investigating, one of their overzealous riders might be irresponsible enough to cut loose at him.

Shadows from small clouds drifting in the deep sky tessellated the floor of the draw. The roan waded through blue and yellow flowers, and occasionally Bruce saw clumps of dainty columbines and a flash of red Indian paintbrush. His mount humped up the last steep rise to the ridge marking the boundary of the park.

From here the rider could look across an undulating stretch of wooded and open country to the snowclad peaks of the distant range. A thin silver thread back of a willow fringe showed him where the creek wound its way to the box cañon down which it would go tumbling over rocks and rapids.

Patiently Bruce scanned the country in front of him through field-glasses. There were cattle grazing on a hillside half a mile from him, and though he meant to ride to them presently his immediate attention was concerned with any sign that might show a fellow-traveler on the tableland. What he looked for was a puff of dust or some moving object. He knew he could not make sure he was the only human being

70

on this wide landscape. All he could do was to take what precautions he found possible.

He worked along the lip of the park toward the stock, searching carefully the broken terrain below him. When he was opposite the cattle he moved down the slope to get closer. If they carried the Quartercircle D C brand, he meant to push them out of the park to a grazing ground nearer his ranch. This was Diamond Tail range, no safe spot for his stuff, unfenced government land claimed as a priority right on account of long use.

A long look through the glasses assured him that this was his bunch, and he rode along the hillside to round up the animals. From a gulch not fifty yards away a man on horseback appeared. Rod Randall, with a rifle across the saddle hull in front of him. He was as much surprised as Bruce at the meeting, but he gave no overt sign of it. The men checked their mounts almost knee to knee.

"So you're pushin' your stuff onto our range," Randall snapped.

Even then, with no certainty how far the man's reckless gusty temper would take him, Bruce took note of how well the Diamond Tail rider's appearance matched his arrogance. His long beautifully proportioned body showed at its best in the saddle. From the wide strong shoulders a well-poised head rose gracefully as that of the Praxiteles' Hermes.

"Driving it back to Bear Creek," Bruce corrected.

"So you say."

"If my fences hadn't been cut, they wouldn't have strayed," Bruce mentioned.

The chill dark eyes of Randall flashed anger. "You can talk yoreself out of anything, you damned sandlapper." It was in the mind of Rod that this was no time to force a decision. Not with the government men here making an investigation. Moreover, he was more than half of the opinion that Sherrill was telling the truth. He would not run the risk of driving his stock up here to graze. The grass lower down was just as good. This logical conclusion annoyed Rod.

The watchful eyes of Bruce did not lift from those of his challenger. Except for a muscular hardening of the jaw there was no evidence of tenseness. The lean whip-cord body was motionless. The fingers of the right hand resting on the thigh did not tighten. Rod Randall was a man of unpredictable impulses. He might let a blaze of passion fling reason overboard. Bruce had to be ready, yet appear to be at ease.

"Would I be fool enough to drive my stock up here and leave them at the mercy of your punchers?" he asked quietly.

Randall flung out a hand in an impatient frustrated gesture. "Get 'em off of here," he ordered.

71

Without another word Bruce swung his horse around that of Randall and started to circle the grazing cattle. He did not look back, and it was not until he turned to head a steer toward the rim that he caught sight of the Diamond Tail man again. Rod was watching him from the mouth of the draw out of which he had first ridden.

Bruce gave his attention to moving the cattle up the slope and was for a few minutes fully occupied. When he looked again Randall had disappeared. The stock were restless, half inclined to bolt. He edged them up gently, not urging the animals to travel fast. As soon as he had them over the lip of the park he knew they would be in a compact group and would accept guidance more readily.

The sound of a rifle shot whipped across the hillside. From a clump of young pines a small billow of smoke puffed. Bruce hung low in the saddle and raced for the shelter of a deep gully. The Winchester cracked again as the roan plunged into the water-gutted cut.

The gully led to the summit. Bruce followed it without an instant's delay. The origin of the shots puzzled him. It was possible that Randall had ridden to the pines and fired from there. But that explanation did not make sense. He could have picked off his victim better from the entrance to the draw. If it could be done without too much risk, Bruce meant to find out who had tried to kill him.

The floor of the gully was filled with stones and rubble, and the hoofs of his horse advertised his progress with a clatter of shifting rock. The sound might not carry to the would-be assassin. In any case he had to risk it.

He came out of the gully at the rim of the park and took a swift survey of the ground in front of him. No other rider was in sight. He reasoned that if his ambusher tried to escape without being discovered, he would get out of the park as soon as he could, in which case he would appear on the rim in front of him within the next minute or two. There was a chance the fellow would elect to stay where he was until he thought it safe to move to another clump of pines deeper in the park. By following that plan he would probably get away without detection.

Bruce tied his horse to a stunted pine and went forward on foot, his senses keyed to the tensest wariness. Excitement hammered in his veins. He was the hunter, but it was in the cards that he might also be the hunted.

The sound of a rider moving up to the ledge reached him. He heard the sound of a hoof striking against a stone. Presently a cowpony clambered into sight.

The man in the saddle was Wally Jelks. He swung his mount in the direction of Bruce and pulled up abruptly. A rifle jumped to his shoulder and the roar of the gun crashed along

72

the ridge. The sound of Sherrill's gun was close enough to have been the echo of the first shot.

The rifle dropped from the hands of Jelks. He caught at his left forearm with an oath and slumped forward against the horn.

"Hold it!" ordered Bruce, and stepped forward.

Jelks snatched at the reins, but under the menace of the lifted rifle stopped. The sleeve of his shirt showed a growing patch of crimson.

"Get down!" Bruce said sharply.

The cowboy swung from the saddle. "You've busted my arm, damn it," he complained angrily.

"Sit down by that tree," Bruce told him. "I'll look at it."

The man sat down, still holding his arm. His surly face showed fear. "All the blood in my body is drainin' out," he yelped.

The Pitchfork rider watched Bruce draw the revolver from his holster and toss it into the brush before he made and set the tourniquet to stop the bleeding. The amateur surgeon was still at work when another rider came along the ridge. Bruce looked up, to see Rod Randall swinging from his horse. He grounded the reins and joined the others.

"He shot me," Jelks whined.

Rod looked down at the wounded man contemptuously for a moment before he gave judgment, "You damned yellow-belly!" He had seen the first shots fired and could guess the rest of the story.

"I got to have a doctor quick," Jelks pleaded. "I'm bleedin' to death."

Bruce stood up, his job finished. A cold anger burned in him. He spoke to Randall, his eyes stern and hostile. "Take the assassin. He's yours."

Dark blood poured into the cheeks of the Diamond Tail man. Anger sharpened the handsome face and brightened the eyes.

"No more mine than yours," he flung back. "I don't deal with bushwhackers. I can kill my own snakes—in the open."

Bruce thought of Quint Milroy, and a thin satiric smile rested on his lips. Rod might not be responsible for the man, but he was backing his father's campaign, and the chances were great that some day soon the old man would send the killer out on a murder mission. It was true, of course, that Jelks was not a Diamond Tail man. Probably he had not been commissioned to rub out Sherrill, but he had acted on the assumption that the big cattle interests would be glad to see him dead, a supposition that was one hundred per cent correct.

"You're easily satisfied," Bruce said, contempt in the sneer. "Take him or leave him. It's all one to me."

73

He turned away, to walk back to his horse. Randall let him go a dozen yards before he called.

"Wait a minute."

Bruce stopped and looked at Rod without answering.

"Get this, fellow," Randall said. "You're leaving this fool to die. You shot him, and you're not going to shift him on me."

"You mean to ride away and leave him?"

"Just that. I've nothing to do with him."

Jelks begged them not to go away and desert him. He was not much older than a boy, though he had trodden evil paths for years, and he was afraid.

If left alone the man would probably die, Bruce thought. He needed nursing, rest, and the attention of a doctor. To reach the Pitchfork he would have to travel a rough trail for more than fifteen miles. The Diamond Tail was even farther, and the nearest way there was down Bear Creek past the Quartercircle D C. Reluctantly Bruce admitted to himself the wounded puncher ought to be taken to his ranch. But he was not going to give in without a return concession.

"Looks bad for your friend," he said callously, adding as if by an afterthought, "unless you'll throw in for once with a damned nester and help save the scoundrel."

"How?" demanded Randall.

"Help me get him to my ranch, and then send one of your riders for a doctor."

Rod did not like any part of this. He did not want to join his enemy even on a humanitarian mission. But he had to admit that Sherrill was going more than halfway in offering to take in the man who had just tried to murder him. Hard though he was, young Randall had his own standards. He could not ride away and leave a wounded man to die.

"Let's go," he said harshly.

They helped the wounded man to his saddle and rode with him between them. When they came to the upper stretch of the cañon the trail in places was too narrow for even two horses. Bruce turned his roan over to Randall and walked beside Jelks, lending a hand to support him when necessary. The cowboy thought it a hundred miles before they reached the ranch.

Ramrod came from the house to meet them, amazed at what he saw.

"You've read about the wolf and the lamb dwelling together," Bruce said with a satiric smile. "Here you have it. Nothing but loving-kindness in our hearts."

"And smoking guns in our hands," Randall added.

Rod stayed until the wounded man had been put to bed. He wanted a word with Bruce.

"You understand that what I told you last time we met still

goes," he said. "This happy little incident is over, and by my way of it you're still a one-gallus windjammer trying to be cock-a-doodle-do."

Bruce had come out to the porch to remind him about sending for the doctor. He said, "You're entitled to your opinion. I hope you won't forget to send for Doctor Bradley."

"I won't forget," Randall replied curtly, his dark stormy eyes on the other. "When you know me better you'll find out I don't forget my promises."

"That's too bad. Sometimes a hasty promise gets a man into trouble."

"Or a hasty shot." Randall's white teeth showed in a smile that held no friendliness. "Afraid you've got yourself into a jam, Mr. Sherrill. These government men are guests at our ranch for a few days. It will break my heart to have to unload this story to them."

"I'm sure it will," Bruce agreed. "You intend to edit the facts, I gather."

"Slightly. I got on the scene just in time to see you drop Jelks while he wasn't looking, and I had to throw a gun on you to keep you from killing him. Then I made you bring him down here. Too bad, but we cattlemen can't afford to let wrong impressions get out just now."

"You don't mind hitting below the belt, then," Bruce suggested.

"Not in a free-for-all fight with nesters ruining the country."

Bruce called to Ramrod and asked him to bring out to the porch his rifle and that of Jelks.

"Do you need rifles—right now?" Randall asked, narrowed eyes on his foe.

"For evidence." Bruce turned to Ramrod. "Examine both guns and tell us how many shots have been fired from each."

Ramrod reported. "Three from Wally's gun, one from yours, if the magazines were loaded to start with."

"*If* is a big little word," Randall sneered. "How the hell you going to prove Jelk's rifle was full up?"

He walked to his horse and swung to the saddle. "I'll send Doc Bradley," he said. "Don't throw any more slugs in poor Wally before he gets here."

They watched him ride down the road, his straight flat back to them a symbol of insolent arrogance.

"He's got a lot of front window," Ramrod said angrily.

"And plenty of goods to back the display," Bruce replied regretfully. "He's one tough *hombre*."

18. A Difference of Opinion

BEN HAD WANDERED DOWN to the corral, had gathered the eggs for Linda from the barn, and was now lying on a stave hammock on the porch. He still tired easily, though he was improving daily.

Linda brought him out a glass of milk with an egg beaten in it. "Drink that," she ordered.

He drank it obediently. "There's a guy riding up the road," he said. "Funny how many punchers come to ask you have you seen a stray buckskin pony with white stockings on the front legs, and seeing as I'm here, Miss Lindy, how about saving me a quadrille at the dance Friday night." He tilted a grin at her over the edge of the glass.

She looked down the road at the approaching rider. "The trouble with this country is that there aren't enough girls in it. There are so few of us that every goose looks like a swan to them."

"How right you are about the first part of what you said." He sat up at sudden attention. "It's Rod."

"I've know that for several minutes," Linda said.

Rod swung from the saddle and dropped the reins. "How you doing, Ben?" he asked after a word of greeting.

"Fine as silk. This girl's nursing could cure a dead man."

"Thought you weren't allowed to come here," Linda said, the sting of a fine whiplash in her voice. She was carrying a chip on her shoulder for Rod.

He laughed. The girl's sarcasm did not reach him. He knew it was not necessary to explain to her or to anybody else that he did not ask any man's permission to do anything in the world he wished.

"I couldn't be in the doghouse, could I?" he asked. "You sound a little edgy, cousin dear."

"How could I be anything but pleased to have you remember me?" she replied. "With so many more important things on your mind."

His spurs jingled as he came up the porch steps and found a chair. He leaned back and laced his fingers behind his head. "About those more important things?" he inquired.

"Entertaining men from Washington. And saving Wally Jelk's life from a desperate ruffian."

"Remarkable how fast news gets around." He slanted an amused look at her. "I still have time to drop in on my sick brother and his sweet-tempered nurse."

Ben interposed with a question. "What about that Wally Jelks business, Rod?"

76

His brother replied with a Yankee answer. "What was it you heard?"

"We heard you stopped Sherrill from killing him after he was wounded."

"Well. Don't you like that story?"

"Was that the way of it?"

"That's the official version."

"I don't believe it," Linda said flatly.

Rod gave her a long smiling scrutiny. "Just between us, I don't believe it myself," he agreed. "Not exactly."

"I knew it," the girl cried.

"How did you know it?"

"I just did."

"I see. Woman's intuition. You were right this time. Sherrill wasn't thorough enough to finish the job. What he intended to do was to walk away and let the man die. I wouldn't have it that way."

"Were both men shooting?" Ben asked.

Rod took time to phrase his answer carefully. "I'll say only this—that Jelks is a no-account skunk."

"He started the shooting," Linda said with sharp decision.

"Anyhow, he deserved what he got. Let it rest at that. The point that sticks out like a hurt thumb is this—Sherrill shoots a cowboy right while the government men are here investigating. He can't lift that load off his sore back."

"Do you think that is fair fighting, when you know Wally Jelks started the shooting?" she demanded indignantly.

"Were you there?" Rod wanted to know, with mock deference.

"I said, do you think it's fair to hold back part of the truth?"

He gave her his point of view, with the tolerant patience a parent uses toward an unreasonable child. "This isn't a sporting game we are playing. It's war. I play the cards dealt me, for all they are worth. I'm not such a jugheaded fool as to be soft with our foes. I'll hit them as often and as hard as I can, and I don't care a hang about the rules. When I slam a blow in it is meant to go where it will hurt the most."

Linda objected to an assumption he had made. "It isn't war—yet. But it will be soon if we don't come to our senses. Do you have to be so hard, Rod—to hate Bruce Sherrill so much?"

"You're wrong about that, girl," Rod corrected. "I don't waste my time hating him. If he weren't such a trouble-maker I think I could like him. The fellow has sand in his craw. But that's nothing. He's our enemy, trying to tear down all we have built up. I'll fight him to a fare-you-well, since that is what he wants."

"Legally?"

He flung that aside with an impatient gesture. "Any way."

"With bullets?"

"If he hasn't sense enough to get out of our road."

Her troubled eyes searched his unhappily. "You are as mad as your father," she said in a low voice. "To kill a man does not prove him wrong."

"It keeps him from pestering you any more," he said bluntly.

His dark intent look held steadily to her vivid face. He thought it beautiful, desirable for what it withheld as much as for what it offered. She was not like the bouncing daughters of other ranchmen in the neighborhood. In her there was the deep pride of reticent self-respect. Except when she was excited her voice was low and husky, rich with sweet undertones. The timbre of it excited him far more than the inviting giggles of pretty girls with come-hither eyes. She could be gay and friendly yet free in spirit, mistress of her own soul. He sensed in her a gallant courage she carried like a banner. This both attracted and irritated him. Her independence was an unconscious challenge to him. Women ought to accept the standards of their fathers or their husbands. The girl he married must merge her individuality in his and take his judgment as final, not critical of anything he thought or did.

"Yes, it keeps him from troubling you," she agreed, bitterly. "God gives life—and any fool can destroy it."

Both of them were trying to save the strong attraction, never put into words, that drew them together as a magnet does steel filings. They had to find a common ground or suffer the hurt of knowing there was a barrier between them they could not cross.

Ben guessed at the emotional stress lying beneath their words. He rose from the hammock, deciding that they could get along better without him. "If you're going to discuss theology I'll take a walk," he said lightly.

They watched him stroll away. Rod brought his gaze back to the girl.

"When a problem comes up a man has to make up his mind what to do," he told her. "It's not a woman's place to tell him. She must feel he is right and support him. It may be something he hates to do, and yet the job is there waiting for him. He can't shirk it, and nobody can stand between him and it, least of all the woman who loves him."

"You think she should stay at home and pray that he will be successful and won't get killed himself when he starts out to be judge, jury, executioner, and God," she cried.

"A man can't run away from facts that face him," he replied, his tone still quiet but with no yielding in his stern face. "Sherrill nearly killed Ben. He wounded Jelks. His next victim won't be so lucky." He stopped a moment, to choose words for his next point. "There are worse things than killing, Lindy. Take Sherrill as an example. He was with the Rough Riders in Cuba. It was his duty to kill. If he picked off a Spanish sharpshooter, was he doing wrong?"

"That's not the same at all, Rod," she protested. "He was fighting for his country. There was no decision for him to make. He would be risking his life to do his duty. But if he kills somebody now for his own personal benefit he will be a murderer."

"Meaning that I will be one if I am forced to shoot him. You use harsh words, Lindy—and think harsh thoughts." He looked at her a long time, his grim eyes drilling into hers. "I thought we were friends."

"I thought so too." She could not keep her voice quite steady. "And now we seem miles apart."

For the first time he put into words a recognition of the tie that had bound them. "A woman must trust the man she loves, not judge him. She must understand that what he does is right for him and not oppose it. If she loves, she doesn't criticise."

Linda knew there was no use arguing or trying to explain. They had come to a fundamental difference of viewpoint.

"I'm sorry," she said dismally.

"Is that all you can say?" he demanded.

"I can't change the way I think, Rod. If I let a man I loved do what I thought wrong, because I was afraid to tell him so, I would despite myself."

"You think nagging him would do any good?"

"No," she admitted, her voice flat and hopeless. "Nothing would do any good if their views were as far apart as ours are."

He walked to his horse, swung to the saddle and without once looking back rode away. The girl watched him go, her eyes blurred with tears. She went slowly into the house and upstairs to her room. Linda had never wanted to marry him. A deep instinct warned her that she was too independent to live with a man like Rod. Clashes and frustrations would fret her soul. Yet she had come near loving him. Something warm and exciting had gone out of her life.

19. Conspirators Whisper

BILL CAIRNS TIED AT THE FAR SIDE of the Diamond Tail corral and walked around it as quietly as he could, keeping an eye alert to make sure no rider of the outfit saw him. The lights in the bunkhouse were already out. It was nearly eleven, and in the ranch country men go to bed early. The night was dark, neither moon nor stars showing, but on his way to the house he kept in the shadow of the outbuildings as much as he could. He did not know why old Jeff Randall had sent for him, but his instructions were to keep from being seen if possible. The old schemer had some deviltry afoot, of course. He would presently find out what it was.

The big house was dark too, except for a lamp in the room Jeff called his office. Cairns tiptoed across the porch and knocked. When he opened the door he saw the ranchman's shapeless body slumped down on a chair. He had been reading the Redrock *Beacon* by the inadequate light of a cheap little kerosene lamp.

"Sit down, Bill," the old man invited, and pushed a chair with his foot toward the visitor. "Anybody see you?"

"Hell, no. It's the middle of the night."

"Good." Jeff shoved a bottle and a tumbler in the direction of his guest, who poured the glass half full and drained it. "I see by the *Beacon* that Hal Bonsall announces he's going to run again for county clerk. He's a good man and deserves re-election."

"Did you have me ride twelve miles to tell me that?" Cairns growled.

"Don't push on the reins, Bill," his host said amiably. "Rest yore weary bones and taken another drink. We got all night before us."

The Pitchfork foreman reached for the bottle and had another. "Maybe you've got all night," he complained "I've been in the saddle most of the day and I've got to get back to the ranch while it's still dark. You've shot my night's sleep to pieces, but that makes no difference to you. When you whistle you expect us to come on the jump."

"Nothing like that, Bill," Jeff demurred. "I've a piece of business to talk over, and I thought it best not to tell the whole world. What people don't know won't hurt them."

"All right. Shoot."

Randall took a little time to come to the point. He thought he had Cairns sized up correctly, but if he was making a mistake it would be a very serious one.

"I'm giving you a chance to make a hundred dollars, Bill, with very little trouble," he said.

"That's fine," jeered the foreman. "Right generous of you."

He knew that when Jeff Randall gave something for nothing, it would be time to be looking in the woodpile for what was concealed there.

"Fact is, we've got to do something to make these government snoopers see what skunks the sodbreakers are. Maybe you don't know it, but they are moving over to stay two-three days at the Pitchfork."

"So I've heard. What about it?"

80

"My idea is to give them a sort of an object lesson, one they won't forget. Jolt them, kind of."

"Talk turkey," Cairns said impatiently. "This ain't a guessin' contest, is it?"

Randall tapped the table with the edge of the folded newspaper. "Let's suppose somebody slashed Pitchfork wires, then went in and shot down a bunch of cattle, say about a dozen. Wouldn't that convince them, so they would give hell to the nesters in their report?"

Cairns started at the humped-up ranchman with unbelieving eyes. "Goddlemighty!" he cried. "I'm foreman of the outfit. You askin' me to do this?"

"I'm not suggesting you throw down yore boss, Bill. This would be the best thing in the world for him if you would do it." The voice of the cattleman was suave and wheedling. "What are a dozen steers to a man who has thousands? It won't mean a thing to him. But it will mean a whole lot to Daly to have these two birds get the right idea about these nesters. You can see that."

"Why don't you shoot some of yore own stuff?" Cairns wanted to know. "You got more than the Pitchfork has."

"It ain't in human nature, Bill, for a man to destroy his own stuff," Randall explained, his manner making a virtue of it. "I thought of it, but I just couldn't do it. But if I pay you a hundred dollars Daly and I will be bearing the loss together. That's reasonable, isn't it?"

"Ask Daly if he thinks so," Cairns barked. "You're proposing I sell my saddle—for a hundred plunks. I can lose that much at the wheel in twenty minutes. Every man may have his price, but I'm not going to throw down my outfit for chicken feed. You must figure me cheap."

Randall moved noiselessly to the door, flung it open to make sure nobody was eavesdropping, shut it, and shuffled back to his chair. "Keep yore voice down, Bill," he admonished. "I'm not advertisin' the contract for this job." The old man leaned forward and wagged his thick forefinger at the Pitchfork foreman. "Listen. If this report goes to Washington the way I want it there is going to be a new shuffle of the deck out in this neck of the woods. Quite a few homesteaders are bound to throw up their hands and quit. I don't claim to be a prophet, but it wouldn't surprise me if one or two of them were missing about that time, *if you know what I mean.*"

Cairns nodded. He knew very well. "Go on," he said. "Finish sayin' yore piece."

Randall's voice fell almost to a whisper. "How would you like to own the Quartercircle D C? It's a fine little ranch. The right man could get along fast on it. He could run a nice bunch of cows and have plenty of feed and water for them."

"I'd like it down to the ground." The dull eyes of Cairns

held fast to the gross face of the ranchman. "But far as I know it isn't for sale."

"It would be—if anything happened to Sherrill. He has no near relatives. It would be flung on the market and sold for a song."

"And who would buy it?" Cairns answered his own question. "Cliff Applegate, of course. He needs it bad."

"It wouldn't suit me to have Cliff get it." Randall's strong jaw clamped. There was a vindictive glare in his eyes. "I'll see it goes to a man I can trust—like you. Don't worry, Bill. I know how to pull the strings to get what I want."

The foreman did not doubt his last statement. The question was whether he would want Cairns to have the ranch. He had sons of his own he could put on it.

"How about putting it on paper, just as a sort of reminder to us both?" the Pitchfork man asked

"That's a fool thing to say, Bill. Sherrill is still alive. You don't want to hang us both, do you?"

"Why don't you get Quint Milroy to pull off this cattle-killing?" Cairns asked suspiciously.

"A fair question. I'll tell you why." The bullnecked old man's face was twisted for a moment to an expression of amused contempt. "When Quint was a boy his father ran cattle. Now get this, Bill. The doggoned fool is sentimental. He likes cows. Rubbing out a man is just business, but pumping lead into a bunch of stock is gosh-awful. He isn't tough enough for that."

Cairns rubbed his unshaven chin with the palm of his hand. It helped his slow brain to think. "If there was a scoundrel who was dangerous to you, who went around dusting off men on our side, maybe Quint's conscience wouldn't keep him from doing a little drygulching," he suggested.

"I think Quint could be persuaded," Randall answered. His eyes were as cold as glacier ice.

There was no longer need to tell Cairns to keep his voice down. Both men were talking in whispers. Each looked at the other with unwinking eyes that searched for assurance. Neither trusted his fellow conspirator as far as he could throw a rope. But their interests marched together, at least for the present.

"Of course, like you say, I would be doing Daly a service if I helped bring this fight to a head in his favor," the foreman said.

"Sure you would." Randall realized the man wanted to be persuaded of this in self-justification. "No doubt about it, Bill. You have to take a long view in a matter like this. Everybody but you and me would think the nesters had shot the stock." An idea struck him. "Why not build up some evidence of that? We could have Flack snitch some personal thing Sher-

82

rill wears—his hat or pocketknife or anything that could be identified as his—and leave it on the ground near where the cattle are killed."

Cairns thought that a good idea. He developed it further. "You could have Flack warn us of the raid and I could lay a trap for the night riders. I could have some of our boys stationed near, and they could show up after the shooting. It would look as if Sherrill had to make his getaway so fast he couldn't stop to pick up the hat he had dropped."

"Fine," Randall approved. "You could work that easy. There's no moon now. Not the least bit of danger for you."

"Easy for you to say that, with you sitting here reading the *Beacon* while I pull off the job," Cairns grumbled. "Yo're always gettin' other fellows to pull yore chestnuts outa the fire. And coming down to cases, when would Quint get busy taking care of Sherrill?"

"Soon as it is safe. We'd better wait till those men go back to Washington and turn in their report. Don't worry about Sherrill. He's as good as buried right now."

"I've heard that brag for some time," sneered Cairns. "But the cocky devil still struts around steppin' high as a bull elk in the rutting season. He has been the leader of these sodbusters from the first. If my guess is good—and it's the same as yours —he pulled the wires that got these snoopers out here. You and Daly and the other big cattlemen are the fellows he and his friends are putting the kibosh on. I'm just a hired hand, but so far I'm the only one in any of yore outfits has shown any fight. I'm the guy who put a slug in him, to keep him from finishing Ben. I hunted him down and would have caught him if Cliff Applegate's girl hadn't double-crossed me. At Redrock I killed his horse and would have got him only he stayed holed up in the sheriff's house till it was safe. You claim to be the big mogul around here. Why the hell don't you do something except load it all on me?"

In his excitement the foreman's voice had risen to a higher pitch than the whisper he had been using. The old man lifted his hand in warning to be more careful.

"You don't have to hire a hall, Bill," he murmured. "And you don't have to tell me what this scoundrel has done. I know it same as you do." His narrowed eyes were slits of shining menace, his mouth a thin cruel gash in the large face. "You've done well, but I'll do better. Just let me play my hand. I know when to wait and when to strike. It's not only getting rid of this fellow. We have to rub him out in a way that there won't be any come-back on us. You do this chore and I won't ask anything more of you. And get this. If it's the last thing I do in this world I'll make sure Sherrill lies under the daisies in a wooden box."

"Yeah, and what guarantee have I got that you'll fix it for me to have his ranch and not grab it yourself?"

Randall showed distress at being mistrusted. "I would not do that, Bill." He knew that a declaration of good faith would not be convincing and went on to give reasons. "Fact is, I couldn't even if I wanted to. No use pretending the other cattlemen aren't jealous of me. I'm pretty aggressive. But a man can't hog everything in sight. It will be all I can do to see Cliff doesn't get the Quartercircle D C. I won't let him have it after throwing me down. I want a man on it who is on my side and owes me support. You're the one I have picked. Naturally if I buy it for you I'll have to put a mortgage on it, but you can pay it off on easy terms. We'll work together fine, Bill."

Since Cairns wanted to believe this, he accepted old Jeff's reasoning. It was true there would be a lot of adverse criticism if he raked in the ranch for himself. To have there a man indebted to him would be wiser, since the other cattlemen resented greatly his greedy dominance.

They talked over in detail plans for the raid, after which they shook hands as allies. Cairns took another long drink and clumped out into the night. His mind was not quite easy, but he was not in a position to make surer that the old fox would play fair with him.

20. A Hat Is Found

NED DALY, OWNER OF THE PITCHFORK, lay on a sofa and smoked a cigar, his eyes fixed on the visitor who sat uneasily on the edge of a chair. The ranchman was tied fast to the house by reason of a broken leg due to a fall from a pitching horse.

"You say they mean to pull this off tonight?" Daly asked.

"That's right, Mr. Daly. They're coming in through the north pasture." Flack was not happy about what he was doing. He did not know the object of it. Since he was a timid man he liked to play safe, and he had a feeling there might be danger here for him somewhere. But he had his instructions from Jeff Randall and had to carry them out.

Cairns walked heavily into the room.

"I sent for you, Bill, to listen to a story this man has brought me," Daly said. He waved his cigar toward the homesteader. "Go ahead, Flack."

What Flack had to tell was no news to the foreman, whom he had met in the willows by the creek less than an hour ago. He parroted the story old Jeff had rehearsed with him, that Sherrill had come to get him to join this raid on the Pitchfork.

Ramrod and another Quartercircle D C rider would be with them. And there was to be a fifth man. Sherrill had not decided who yet.

Daly did not doubt the story. There was no apparent point in this rat-faced spy coming to him with a cock-and-bull yarn that would prove untrue in a few hours. Yet it seemed strange for Sherrill to play into the hands of his enemies while the investigators were actually staying at the Pitchfork, or even while they were still in the district. Perhaps he was trying to get even because Wally Jelks had shot at him.

The owner of the Pitchfork was a big heavy-set man in his early fifties. Honest blue eyes looked out of a frank face tanned by wind and sun to a deep brown. He was an impetuous man, irascible at times, easily led, subject to strong prejudices.

"What do you think?" he asked Cairns.

"We've got the fool sure as God made little apples," the foreman exulted.

Daly looked at his watch. "It's dinner time, Flack. I don't reckon you want to eat with the boys. It might not be too pleasant for you. Go into the kitchen and tell the cook I said for him to fix you up to eat there."

As soon as Flack had gone, Daly flung out a question. "Do you trust that treacherous skunk, Bill?"

"I've got no use for him," Cairns answered. "But he is in Randall's pay. He wouldn't dare try to put anything over on us. I think his story is true. Don't you?"

"I reckon so. We'll have to fix up a trap for Sherrill." He added fretfully, "Too bad I've got this busted leg."

"Don't worry. I'll get him."

"No killing, Bill. Surprise them and take Sherrill prisoner. The others too, if you can. My guess is that they will come down the cañon and enter the pasture about where Bear Creek strikes it. If you keep the boys hidden in the willows they will ride right into you."

"That's so," agreed Cairns. "There's no way for them to hit the north pasture except by the cañon."

For an hour they discussed the problem. Daly was insistent that there should be no bloodshed. If Cairns could not capture any of the raiders without that he must let them escape. It was important that the cattlemen show clean hands just now.

Before the Pitchfork riders left that night, Daly had them into the room and made it clear they were out to capture the raiders but not kill them. Anyone disobeying this injunction would be fired at once and would get no help from the ranch if the law wanted them.

Barnard and Sawyer were in the room and heard the instructions given the men. Both of them were troubled at being caught in such a situation. They realized that it would have been better not to have visited the ranches, but the mistake could not be helped now. Barnard said a few blunt words. He warned the cowboys that the United States government had become interested and would not tolerate any lawlessness.

The night was dark and cloudy. The riders could see only a few feet in front of them, but Cairns knew every acre of the rough terrain and led his party with a sureness the younger men respected. They traveled an hour and a half before reaching Bear Creek. The foreman chose a spot with plenty of shrubbery on the bank of the stream and concealed the cowboys at strategic points, each man not to close to his nearest neighbor. He warned them that there was to be absolutely no talking back and forth. The success of the trap would depend upon the raiders being caught completely by surprise. Cairns chose for himself the place at the lower end of the line.

It must have been about twenty minutes later that a burst of firing startled the men in ambuscade. Eight or ten shots rang out, not more than a few seconds apart. They had been fired a few hundred yards below them, from around a bend in the stream.

The Pitchfork punchers came out from cover and gathered into two groups which presently merged into one. They milled around, uncertain what to do.

"Where is Cairns?" one of them asked.

None of them had seen him. A redheaded youth raised his voice and shouted the name of the foreman. Two more shots sounded.

The voice of Cairns reached them. "This way, boys," he shouted. "Hurry up!"

They found him, his horse beside him, looking down at a dead steer. Two others had been shot and lay on the ground not far away.

"I got a crack at one of the scalawags," he said. "But they were lighting out fast as they could. Don't think I hit him."

"We didn't get a crack at one of the whole doggoned bunch," a puncher cried, slapping his hat against his leathers in vexation.

"How about giving them a chase?" another asked.

"Might try it." Cairns' voice sounded very dubious. "Not much chance. They were getting outa here hell-for-leather. Listen."

No sound of horses' hoofs came to them. Evidently the raiders had made a clean escape. There would be small chance of finding them, since they could ride in almost any direction.

"They've killed two steers and a heifer," one lad announced.

The moaning of a wounded animal came to them.

"Hit in the head," a cowboy called out after he had knelt

and examined the steer. "Have to kill it, I reckon. Take a look, Cairns."

The foreman's gun cracked and the head of the steer fell down.

"Look what I've found," a man shouted.

He joined the others, an old white wide-brimmed hat in his hands. Cairns took the hat and stared at it. "It must of fell off one of their heads, and he dassent stop to pick it up," the foreman said.

He handed it back to the man who had found it. "We'll keep that, Jack. It might be evidence."

"How?" someone asked. "The fellow ain't gonna advertise in the *Beacon* he has lost a hat."

Jack gave an exclamation of excitement. "His initials are stamped in the band. See here." He struck a match to read them. "B. S. Why it's Bruce Sherrill's hat."

They crowded around. Somebody struck another match. The initials were stamped on the sweatband plain to read.

"He's left his calling card," Jack cried jubilantly. "I'll bet he's sweatin' blood right now wondering who will find the hat."

"Mr. Sherrill was sure careless," Cairns said. "But you'll see he will have some kind of explanation. Maybe he sold his hat some time to one of you boys."

Cairns congratulated himself on the smooth way he had worked this. He had let one of the boys find the hat and identify its owner. There had not been a slip-up anywhere. The whole affair had been pulled off with perfect timing. There was not a possibility he could be suspected.

They rode back to the ranch house and reported. Late though it was, Daly and his two guests were still up. They had been too interested and too anxious to go to bed. In an expedition of this sort there was always a chance that somebody would be killed. Even though no raider had been captured, Daly was more than satisfied. The hat found on the scene was a mute witness Sherrill would find it hard to refute.

21. At the Pitchfork

CAIRNS CARRIED THE NEWS HIMSELF to the sheriff. He was not going to lose the opportunity of exulting over him. Humphreys was disturbed to hear of the raid and particularly to learn that there was evidence implicating Bruce Sherrill. But when he took the story home to his wife Jessie scoffed at his fears.

"Bruce isn't such a fool," she told him stoutly. "And I

wouldn't believe a word that scoundrel Bill Cairns says, not after he stood out among the trees there and shot Bruce's horse. I wouldn't put it past him to have done it himself just to get Bruce into trouble."

"That's possible," the sheriff agreed. "But Bill Cairns did not find the hat, he says. The boy who found it was Jack Peters. He seems to me a nice straightforward lad. I think I had better ride out to the Pitchfork and look around. Daly too has the reputation of being an honest man. I don't think he would cook up evidence. I would like to talk with him."

"What about Bruce?" she asked. "He is in town. As he passed an hour ago he waved at me. Are you going to tell him?"

"I think so. If he has a defense I want to hear it before I meet Daly."

The sheriff found Bruce at Doan & Devon's store. He drew the ranchman aside and told him what he had heard.

"Looks like a frame-up," Bruce said at once. "I didn't leave the ranch Thursday night."

"Can you prove that?"

"Only by Ramrod. Mark and Neal went to a dance and didn't get back till morning."

"That's bad. They claim Ramrod was with you. And what about that hat they found? Could it be yours?"

"I don't see how it could. There's an old hat of mine around the house. But how could Cairns get hold of it?" Bruce came to a swift decision. A gleam of mirth sparkled in his eyes. "You say you are going out to the Pitchfork. I'll side you and be your deputy, Tim."

Humphreys reminded him that he was under suspicion. "You can't laugh this off, son. It's a serious charge."

"Can't I whistle in the dark?" Bruce wanted to know. The smile was wiped from his face. "Fact is, I can't let a lie like this stand without facing it, not with Barnard and Sawyer out at Daly's ranch having the wool pulled over their eyes."

The sheriff understood the urge of Bruce to clear himself. He was not sure whether Bruce had been involved in this raid, though it did not seem in character. He was bold enough to do anything, but Tim had thought him too wise to prejudice the case of the homesteaders by such a piece of folly. Nor was Sherrill the kind to shoot down cattle wantonly, unless his friend's judgment of him was wholly wrong. It was possible of course that another of the raiders might have done the killing before he could be stopped.

It would not be a bad idea to let Bruce confront his accusers. Sometimes in the heat of talk the truth slipped out unexpectedly. But there was another angle to this. Cairns was not the only Pitchfork man who had made threats after the wounding of Wally Jelks. According to the story told the riders. Wally had been shot without warning. If they believed Bruce the leader of this raid, they would think of it as an outrageous defiance of the ranch.

"I don't think you had better go out to the Pitchfork now," the sheriff said. "It has quite a score piled up against you. Some of its warriors are a little quick on the trigger."

Bruce brushed the danger aside as negligible. "Like Wally Jelks," he said dryly. "When I am not looking for trouble. Out in the open all they will do is scowl."

"Aren't there any buildings or ditches at the Pitchfork from which a man could take a crack at you?" Humphreys asked.

Sherrill chuckled. "I'll be under protection of the sheriff. When do we start?"

"All right. All right." The sheriff threw up his hands in surrender. "Be ready to start in fifteen minutes. Meet me in front of my office. And don't forget that Cairns is in town. At least he was an hour ago."

The mention of the name was like a stage cue. The foreman straddled into the store and ordered a cigar. His glance picked up Humphreys and Sherrill.

"You arresting that scoundrel, sheriff?" he demanded.

"Take it easy, Bill," Humphreys advised. "When the time comes for an arrest I'll make it."

"I wonder," Cairns replied insolently.

"Now, gentlemen. If you please. Let us not have any trouble here." The placatory voice was that of Clem Doan, one of the owners of the store.

Bruce said nothing. This was the sheriff's business, and he judged him competent to handle it.

"There won't be any trouble, Clem," Humphreys said quietly. "Bill is one of my constituents and wants to be sure I do my duty."

He turned his back on Cairns and walked out of the store with Bruce beside him. Ten minutes later the two men were jogging out of town.

Near the summit of Wind Break Pass, Humphreys looked back over the zigzag trail they had followed and caught sight of a horseman a few hundred yards behind them.

"I believe it is Cairns," he said. "On his way to the Pitchfork."

Bruce nodded. "I think we'd better stop and admire the view, Tim," he proposed. "I'd rather have him in front of us than behind."

The foreman did not draw up, but as he passed he flung a jeer at the officer. "You make a fine front, sheriff, for criminals to hide behind."

"I gather you don't approve of me, Bill," Humphreys answered blandly.

"What do you care, since the crooks who elected you do?" Cairns snarled. "I judge a man by the company he keeps."

He rode past them, his thick body still in the saddle. At intervals they caught sight of him in front of them every mile of the way to the ranch.

They reached the Pitchfork in midafternoon. The ranch house lay in a circular bowl slashed by openings through which a small stream ran in and out. From the rim, before the road dropped, the valley was a checkerboard of brown and green, the pattern set by pasture lands of native grasses and alfalfa fields. The big house, as the main building was called, stood out of the cluster of structures huddled beside the creek in a grove of cottonwoods. Except for a wide porch extending across the front and one side, it was plain and unadorned.

A man came out of the bunkhouse and caught sight of the two riders moving down into the valley. He watched them until they were close enough for identification before waking to excited activity. He shouted something through the door behind him, then broke for the big house at a run and disappeared in it. Men poured out of the bunkhouse like seeds squirted from a squeezed orange. The sound of their voices drifted to the approaching horsemen. One gave directions and the men scattered to posts at different parts of the yard.

"Mr. Cairns has been fixing up a welcome for me," Bruce drawled. "Where do we go from here, sheriff?"

Humphreys held his pony to an even road gait. "To the front porch. Cairns isn't with them. I don't think they will start anything, at least until he shows up. Not with me here."

"Nice to have the law so close," Bruce said, his smile a trifle stiff. "Hope none of the boys forget who you are."

"Don't make any cracks," Humphreys warned. "I'll do any talking that's necessary."

"I'll be quiet as an undertaker," Bruce promised.

A man stood at a corner of the blacksmith shop, two at the stable, a fourth in front of the bunkhouse. An older man, baldheaded, had moved to the house porch. Bruce noticed that all of them watched him steadily. That they had itching trigger fingers he felt sure.

The sheriff waved a hand in greeting and dismounted. Bruce was careful not to hurry, not to let an alarmed glance sweep the yard.

"Howdy, Baldy," Humphreys said evenly. "You head of the reception committee."

"What's that killer doing here?" the baldheaded man demanded.

"You mean Sherrill. Why, he's here with me. Don't make a mistake."

A slim girl of about fifteen with long dark-lashed eyes came

90

out of the house, quite unaware that this was an explosive moment. "Father says for you to come in," she told the visitors, and looked with shy curiosity at Bruce. His friendly smile surprised her. It did not match his hoof-and-horns reputation.

The self-invited guests followed her into the big room where her father was lying on a lounge. The foreman stood near him bristling at Sherrill, his shallow bleak eyes filled with venomous hostility.

Daly said angrily, "You have yore nerve to come here, Sherrill, after what you did the other night."

"I brought him with me, Mr. Daly," explained Humphreys. "Thought we ought to get both sides together and figure out the right of this."

"Goddlemighty!" the cattleman exploded. "What do you mean figure on it? Has he a right to shoot down my stuff?"

"Sherrill claims he did not leave the ranch that night."

"He's a damn liar. Probably he'll claim he didn't shoot Jelks either." Daly turned to his daughter. "Janet, ask Mr. Barnard and Mr. Sawyer to come here. And don't come back yoreself."

The government men joined the party. They had met and talked with the sheriff during their stay at Redrock.

"First-off, Humphreys, let's get this clear," challenged Daly. "Is this fellow yore prisoner?"

"I haven't made any arrests. I'm here to investigate this raid. I've wondered how your men happened to be on the ground just as it was being pulled off."

"Can't tell you that," Daly answered bluntly. "We were warned. That's all the information you'll get from me on that point."

"Warned that Sherrill was leading a raid on your place?"

"That's right."

"You can't leave it that way, Mr. Daly," the sheriff remonstrated. "If you have evidence against him you'll have to come clean with it. He has a right to demand that."

"I don't care what he demands. I'll tell what I please. Bring me that hat, Bill."

Cairns brought him a hat from the table and Daly handed it to the sheriff. "One of my boys found it right near where the cattle were killed."

The officer looked the hat over, read the initials stenciled on the sweat band, and handed the Stetson to Bruce.

"This yours?" he asked.

Before the hat reached his hands Bruce knew that it was his. "Yes," he said.

"Any idea how it got here?"

"No." Bruce looked for a long moment at Cairns. His gaze shifted to Daly and shuttled back to the foreman. "But Cairns can tell you."

"You're right I can," the wagon boss replied, heavy triumph in his voice. "Jack Peters picked it up thirty yards from where you killed our stock. I was cutting loose at you, and you couldn't stop to pick it up when it fell."

"You recognized me?"

Cairns hesitated. His original story had not included this detail, but he had slid in later that he felt sure one of the retreating raiders was Sherrill.

"Practically."

"How far was I from you?"

"Not more than thirty yards."

"And on a black night, without moon or stars, you identified me at thirty yards." Bruce turned contemptuously away. He addressed his words to Barnard. "This is a frame-up. I don't know yet how Cairns got my hat, but I am sure he planted it where one of his boys would find it. Do you think I would be so foolish as to raid this ranch while you are here investigating this trouble?"

"Somebody raided it, Mr. Sherrill," Barnard said.

"I think it was an inside job, done to prejudice you against the homesteaders. The story smells to high heaven. I have ridden for years and never saw a cowboy lose his hat unless he was on a pitching horse or there was a heavy wind blowing. My boys will tell you that I haven't worn that old hat for months."

"How do you think it reached the place where the cattle were killed?" Sawyer asked.

"Cairns can tell you that. He must have got somebody to smuggle it out of my house to him."

The Pitchfork foreman exploded angrily. Barnard raised a hand to stop his profane denial.

"There's another charge against you, Mr. Sherrill," the government man said. "Only a few days ago you shot a cowboy."

"After he had fired at me three times."

"That's not the way we heard it from a bystander."

"Randall told me he was going to doctor the facts to suit him. I don't know whether you commissioned Jelks to kill me, Daly. If so, don't blame him. He did his best. While we're on the subject. I wish you would send a wagon to pick up your killer. Doctor Bradley says he can be moved safely. I don't want the fellow around my place any longer."

Daly flushed angrily. "With Rod Randall on the spot as a witness you'll have trouble getting anybody to swallow your lie that Jelks was my killer. You've got so much gall you think you can talk yoreself out of anything."

The sheriff cut into the quarrel. "Thought I was to do the talking, Bruce," he said.

The accused man nodded. "All right, Tim." He knew he had lost ground with Barnard and Sawyer. The weight of evidence was against him. "I'll say just one thing more. If the Pitchfork expects to prove I was leading a raid against its cattle, Daly will have to uncover the witness he claims brought him warning of it."

"Right," agreed the sheriff. "Now if you are all through I'll take charge. I want to talk with each one of the boys who went out to stop the raiders. I'll do all the questioning. You and Mr. Sawyer may be present, Mr. Barnard. Also Daly and Sherrill."

"You're trying to cut me out of it," blustered Cairns. "I won't stand for it."

"I want only one man on each side present," Humphreys said. "If you would rather leave and let Cairns stay, Daly——"

"I'll stay," Daly interrupted. "You can go, Bill. That's fair enough. Get the boys in soon as you can."

Cairns left, sulkily. Humphreys talked with the cowboys one at a time. He got from each one his story of the night's adventure. Before he had finished certain facts stood out. None of them had at any time seen any of the raiders. Nor had they heard the sound of their horses. The only evidences of their presence, outside of the hat, were the sound of the shots and the dead cattle. One other material point came out. When the shots were heard, Cairns had not been with them. They found him a short time later at the scene of the shooting.

After the testimony had all been heard, Daly flung an angry question at the sheriff. "Are you trying to prove, Humphreys, that I got Cairns to shoot my own cattle?" he demanded.

"I'm trying to get at the truth," the sheriff replied. "But I'll say this. Cairns could have killed the stock before the boys got there. If he did, I don't think you had a thing to do with it."

"That's a crazy idea. Why would Bill do that?"

"I don't say he did it. He might have done it—to prejudice these gentlemen against the homesteaders."

"No decent cattleman ever did such a thing," Daly protested.

The sheriff agreed that was true. Neither did any decent homesteader.

"You are not going to arrest Sherrill?" Daly said.

"Not unless you will let me hear the story of the man who warned you of the raid," Humphreys told him.

"He'd be in danger of getting shot if I did," the cattleman urged.

"Not if you let me talk with him privately. He would not be known."

"I'll see if I can fix it," the cattleman said.

Bruce had a suggestion for the sheriff's ear alone. "Come over to the ranch and talk with Jelks. Bring these two men with you."

Humphreys thought that would be a good idea.

22. Cash on the Barrel Head

CAIRNS MADE IT HIS BUSINESS to see Jeff Randall the night of the day the sheriff visited the Pitchfork. He was getting disturbed at the course of the investigation into the raid. It had not occurred to him that he would fall under suspicion. Flack was the danger spot. Rumors had reached him that the homesteaders distrusted the man. Sherrill was no fool. He knew that somebody had brought the hat to the Pitchfork, and it would not take him long to decide on Flack as the man. Under pressure the spy would break. The foreman had no doubt of that. If the fellow confessed to his part in the conspiracy, Cairns knew he would be through, not only at the Pitchfork, but in this whole district. A man could not throw down his own outfit without being ruined.

From Randall the worried man got at first small comfort. The owner of the Diamond Tail was concerned only for his own safety. If the truth came out, it would be very damaging to him. Not only would it influence the report of Barnard; his position as leader of the cattlemen would be lost forever.

"You've sure made a mess of it," Jeff snarled. "I might of known you'd put yore clumsy foot in a hornet's nest."

Cairns flared up. "*You* botched this job. It was yore idea. It was foolproof, you claimed. Flack is not my man. You picked him. I'll say this right now. If they hang the raid on me, you'll be in it up to yore neck."

Randall did not waste any time arguing this. His mind moved directly to a consideration of the obvious way out. He sat slumped in a chair before the office table, his thick fingers making circles on a cheap pad with the blunt point of a pencil stub. Before he raised his flinty washed-out blue eyes to the Pitchfork foreman, he knew exactly what he meant to do.

"Leave this to me. I'll take care of it." In his voice there was the rasp of harsh command. "Keep yore chin up. Daly won't suspect you. He's the kind of fool who would never believe one of his own men would throw him down. If anything comes up, stand pat on the story you told. Don't give way an inch."

"What are you going to do?" Cairns asked.

"None of yore damn business." There was more than a

94

touch of contempt in the old man's manner. "And for God's sake don't get goosey. I'll see you through."

After Cairns had gone, he sat for a long time huddled in the chair, no expression in his gross hard face. At last he rose and shambled over to the cabin where Quint Milroy slept alone. He tapped on the door, gently. The gunman's voice answered almost at once.

"Who is it?"

"Jeff Randall. Want to talk with you, Quint."

"In a minute." Milroy had been asleep, lightly as usual. He rose, put on his trousers, and buckled the belt around his waist with the butt of the forty-five close to his hand, after which he lit a lamp and opened the door, standing well back of it as he did so.

Randall walked in. "Sorry to waken you, Quint," he said. "Something has come up unexpected."

Milroy closed and bolted the door. He waited in silence, cold eyes fixed on his midnight guest. Long ago he had learned to be sparing of words. More than one of his victims had talked themselves into a grave. No curiosity and no questions showed in his dark saturnine face. He could be as patient as an Indian.

The old man sat down and motioned the other to a chair. "I've got a job for you, Quint," he said bluntly.

Still Milroy waited, silent, watchful.

Old Jeff lowered his voice almost to a whisper and talked for several minutes. When he had finished, the killer made one comment.

"It will be five hundred dollars," he said.

The ranchman's face showed a pained protest. "Have a heart, Quint. You never had an easier job. No danger and no possible come-back. Everybody will think the homesteaders did it for throwing them down."

"If it is so easy and safe, do it yourself," Milroy suggested, his low voice studiously polite.

"Now—now. You know I can't do that, Quint. For you it is just like shooting tame trout in a pond. You are an expert. There isn't a man living I would trust to do this quick as I would you."

"The price is still five hundred dollars," Milroy mentioned gently. "Payable in advance."

Randall threw up his hands. "You win. One thing, though. This has to be done quick."

"How quick?"

"I'd like it done tonight. I know that's rushing you, but it is a hurry-up job."

Milroy rose from the chair, his lithe slender body straight as a ramrod. "Get the money while I saddle," he said.

95

The old-timer shuffled to the door, then turned for another word. "You'll have time to get back before morning. It won't do for you to be seen—or to be away at breakfast time."

The gunman said nothing. He did not need any advice from amateurs.

23. Flack Dreams

FLACK FINISHED WASHING THE DISHES and drew the window curtain. Nobody lived within three miles of him. There was not a chance in ten thousand that anybody would be watching him, but he was a careful man and did not believe in taking avoidable risks. After bolting the door he pushed aside the cot, removed a loose board in the floor, and from a recess underneath took a tin box. This he carried to the table and opened. Inside it were a cheap notebook and a small number of bills with a rubber band around them. Most of these were ones, but there were a few fives and two tens.

Out of a hip pocket he drew several more crumpled bills. Lovingly he smoothed them out and put them with the others. He opened the notebook and jotted down a memorandum.

July 16. That old fox J. R. has trapped B. S. Looks like they have got B. wriggling in a cleft stick.

He replaced the box and its contents in the hiding-place, then settled down to read a two-weeks-old *Beacon* by the light of a small coal-oil lamp.

The house in which he lived was a one-room log cabin and a good deal of the furniture was home-made. But the place was meticulously neat. Though he was living in the cheapest possible way, Flack was no careless housekeeper. He liked to know that everything was in its place ready for use when he wanted it.

He looked twice at his fat silver watch, and at exactly eight-thirty rose to make preparations for bed. By nine o'clock he was sound asleep. He dreamed that the tin box was bulging full with bills, many of them of one-hundred-dollar denomination. When he took them to the bank at Redrock, the president, Dean Kilburn, told him they were all counterfeit and that he would send the sheriff to arrest him. Hardly had he reached home before Humphreys came knocking at the door. He could hear the knocking now, not loud but persistent.

To the sound of that knocking he woke up.

Flack sat up in bed, not fully restored from the unhappiness of his dream. "Who's there?" he quavered.

96

"Quint Milroy," a voice answered. "I'm bringing a message from Jeff Randall."

"From Jeff. What's he want—at this time of night?"

"He wants you to take a trip for him. Something has come up unexpected, he told me."

Flack put on his trousers and opened the door. "Come in, Quint," he said.

Milroy entered and delivered the message. It roared from the barrel of a forty-five and the homesteader collapsed to the floor. The killer struck a match and made sure another shot was not necessary. From a vest pocket he took a paper and pinned it to the nightshirt of the dead man. On the note some words were printed roughly by a pencil.

The messenger rose, looked at his victim for a long moment, and left the cabin. He closed the door behind him, then walked to a small pine where his horse was tied.

He had earned his five hundred dollars.

24. The Sheriff Reads a Diary

WHEN SHERIFF HUMPHREYS talked with Wally Jelks in the presence of the two government men, the cowboy had nothing to say except a repetition of the statement that he was not going to talk. He had been in a sullen, suspicious mood ever since reaching the Quartercircle D C. It was not pleasant to be staying in the house of the man he had tried to kill. His first fear of retaliatory violence had subsided. He could not complain that his physical needs were not met. What irked him was the cold contempt of the men who waited on him. If Neal brought him breakfast, he put the food down and walked out without a word. Any necessary speech with him was made as brief as possible. Though he was now able to sit down at table with the others, he was served alone. "Like I was a skunk or a rattlesnake," he told Ramrod bitterly, and for once got an answer. "A rattler gives warning before it strikes," the foreman replied scornfully. This treatment of him, as though he were something vile, had got under his skin. He found some compensation in acting mulish with the sheriff.

His attitude raised a doubt in the minds of the government agents. An innocent man did not armor himself in sullen stubbornness. Rod Randall was a prejudiced witness, and it was possible he had not told the truth.

From the ranch on Bear Creek, Humphreys crossed the ridge to Squaw Creek. He wanted to see Flack. Daly had given him the man's name, under a promise that he would not let the homesteaders know the fellow was acting as a spy for the cattlemen.

The sheriff dropped down from the top of the hogback to Squaw and followed the trail toward its headwaters. It was a rough path and grew worse the farther he went. A cañon brought him to the park where Flack had homesteaded. He looked down from the lip of the saucer on the cabin, stable, and mountain corral of the steading. No smoke was rising from the chimney, but the nester's big pony horse was in the corral.

Humphreys rode down, tied to a sapling, and walked to the cabin. It was probable that Flack was not at home, but he could leave a note for the man. He knocked on the door, and receiving no answer opened it.

What he saw shocked him. Flack was lying on the floor, face up, arms flung wide. A crimson stain above the heart showed that he had been shot. Since he was wearing a nightshirt and was barefoot, the presumption was that he had been killed before daybreak. On his breast a paper had been pinned. Without touching it, the sheriff knelt and read the words written there.

The dirty spy was betraying us and got what was coming to him.

There was no signature. That he had been rubbed out because he had become involved in the feud was clear. The implication of the note was that the homesteaders had shot him in revenge for his betrayal of them.

Though no detective, Humphreys was an experienced man of strong common sense. He was glad he had discovered the body instead of arriving after a dozen others had tramped down any evidence the assassin might have left. Without knowing in the least what he was looking for, he made a thorough search of the cabin. If Sherrill was right in his suspicion, Flack probably had money hidden. There was no sign that the murderer had looked for this. The homesteader's new suit and hat were hanging in the home-made closet. His old leather trunk had apparently not been disturbed. The papers and clothes in it were neatly arranged.

Humphreys went through it carefully and gathered no information of value. He knew some of the ways of solitary men and searched the rafter angles without success. The crevices between the logs of the walls concealed no hidden cache. His eyes scanned the floor foot by foot for a loose board. Not finding one, he pushed the cot to one side. All the planks seemed to be nailed down, but by testing them he found that in one shorter nails had been used that did not reach the two-by-four supporting the floor. In the space below he found a tin box. The key to it was in Flack's pocket.

The box contained bank bills and a notebook that had evidently been used as a sort of diary. Flack had jotted down data that seemed important to him, the high spots in the monotonous life of a homesteader. The first pages Humphreys skimmed over rapidly. They dealt with his taking up the land, the shifts he was put to in stocking his place and getting enough food to keep alive. There were stretches when he had nothing to eat but beans and oatmeal, except for the fish he caught and the game he shot. Sherrill's name appeared several times. Once he had brought him a side of bacon and a pound of Arbuckle's coffee. A week later he had loaned Flack five dollars, to be turned over to Prop Zang as a first payment on a horse he was buying on time. In February he had been to Redrock and persuaded Doan & Devons to let him have a load of groceries on credit, Sherrill having guaranteed payment. His muley cow had strayed, but a line at a later date mentioned that he had found it grazing on Slab Hill with Malloy's stuff.

Under date of April 3 the sheriff found an item he thought significant. On the valley road the hillman had met Jeff Randall driving a buckboard. To his surprise the old man had stopped to talk with him and had made a proposition. Flack had not set down what it was, but there was a comment that showed he was justifying to himself his future coarse. *When a fellow is pushed to the wall he has to look out for himself.*

From that time only initials were used to represent the leading characters in the story that was developing. Days and weeks were skipped with no record. An entry dated June 7 read:

Got $15 on acc't from J. R.

The fortunes of the nester improved after this. The sheriff read:

June 12. Saw J. R. and Bill C. at the Cross Roads store. Gave them tip of wirecutting and got $25 for the info.

The raid in which Ben Randall was wounded occurred on the night of the twelfth, Humphreys recalled.

June 26. Met B. S. at Redrock. I hadn't ought to of bought the suit yet, but think he swallowed my story. Notified J. R. I saw him.

July 15. From J. R. $40 for story to D. and for swiping hat to give Bill C. Am not easy abt this. The boys on the creek look funny and quit talking when I show up. Malloy bawled me out yesterday. Was afraid he would jump me. He made threats.

July 16. That old fox J. R. has trapped B. S. Looks like they have got B. wriggling in a cleft stick.

There were no more entries. The last one must have been made a few hours before the death of Flack. The man had evidently begun to get anxious lest his treachery be discovered, but he had not guessed that retribution was so near. The sheriff knew that his visit to the Pitchfork had precipitated the murder. It had developed the fact that somebody was betraying the homesteaders. Suspicion had fallen on Flack. Perhaps his neighbors already had evidence implicating him and this had been the last nail in his coffin.

Humphreys had spent the night at the Quartercircle D C. Sherrill himself had not left the ranch unless it had been after midnight, but one of his riders might have crossed the hogback with word of Flack's treachery. It had to be that way, if the killing had resulted from his share in the conspiracy to discredit the homesteaders by faking a raid. Unless Daly had sent them word who his informant was—a supposition absurd on the face of it—nobody but Sherrill had been present at the Pitchfork investigation who could have spread the news, except himself and the government men. The sheriff did not like the conclusion to which this was driving him, but he could find no escape from it.

Cal Malloy was named in the diary. He might be the actual killer. Malloy was a plump tubby man with a round moon face, well thought of by his neighbors, ready to divide with any of them what he had. But back in his amiable kindliness there was a steely nature with a vindictive streak. He gave loyalty, and he expected it in return. How far his anger would take him Humphreys did not know, but at present the sheriff made him his number one suspect.

Back of the murder—the real cause of it—ran the sinister plotting of Jeff Randall. That was quite clear to the officer. The old schemer could not be touched by the law, but if he had not been trying to get the better of his enemies by foul means, Flack would still have been alive. The diary would have to be offered in evidence at the trial of the man or men against whom proof of guilt piled up. Whether it hurt them or not, it would certainly ruin Randall's influence with the cattlemen whom he now led.

25. Bruce Asks a Question

BRAND APPLEGATE BROUGHT THE NEWS to the Bar B B that Flack had been found dead in his cabin by Sheriff Humphreys.

"Who did it?" his father asked.

"They don't know yet. Some of his own crowd. There was a note pinned on his breast saying they had shot him because he was betraying them."

Linda was dishing up the potatoes for dinner. She stopped, to ask a question of her father. "I suppose Flack was the one who told in advance of that raid when Ben was shot," she said.

The cattleman nodded. "No harm in your knowing now. That was the way of it. The little scoundrel was selling his saddle."

"And they found out?"

"Must have. Those things get out in the end. You can't keep a secret known to half a dozen people."

"Who does Tim suspect of killing him?" she asked.

Brand took the dish of potatoes from her and helped himself liberally. "He doesn't say. But it came out while he was at the Pitchfork that somebody was giving information to Uncle Jeff. Bruce Sherrill was the only one of the other side there."

"So they think he did it?" Linda inquired quickly.

"Search me," her brother answered. "He might have passed the word on and had somebody else do it."

"Or he might not be guilty at all."

Brand agreed. "I can give you a dozen names to put in a hat. Pick out any one, and it might be right."

Nonetheless Linda's heart was heavy with dread. Sherrill had been in the raid. That was known, by reason of his hat found on the scene. It was logical to think he must have had something to do with the killing of the man who had betrayed them.

After dinner Ben saddled two horses and Linda rode with him to the Cross Roads store. A few supplies were needed at the ranch, not enough to justify a trip to Redrock.

"Do you think Bruce Sherrill killed this man?" she asked her cousin after a long silence.

"He might have," Ben replied. "A man does crazy things. Look at how I came close to killing Pete Engle."

"Yes, but this is different. Whoever did this went up to the man's cabin to murder him. It was a cold-blooded killing."

When they rode up to the store half an hour later, a man came out of the building to the hitch rack where his horse was tied. Linda felt a queer excitement pulsing through her body. The man was Bruce Sherrill. He waited for the cousins to dismount, uncertain of the greeting he might receive.

Ben nodded to him, stiffly, but did not speak. He answered silently with a slight bow.

Linda said, her eyes drilling into his, "I hear a friend of yours has been killed."

He retorted quietly, "No friend of mine."

"An enemy, perhaps," she challenged.

He brushed aside indirection. "What are you driving at, Miss Applegate? Say it plainly."

She knew the urgent impulse in her had carried her too far, but she had to go on now. "Do you know who killed this man Flack?"

His steady eyes mocked her. "No. Do you?"

"He was a spy. Somebody must have found it out. He was killed in revenge."

"You're wrong." His voice was hard and cold. "He was killed because somebody was afraid of him."

"Afraid of him?" she repeated, not understanding what he meant. "Why would people fear him?"

"He knew too much, and under pressure he would have talked. He had to be destroyed before he told what he knew."

She shook her head. "That doesn't mean anything to me. What did he know, except that he was betraying his side?"

"He knew there was no raid on the Pitchfork pasture Thursday night, that he had been paid to tell a cooked-up lie to Daly—and to give Cairns an old hat of mine to show I had been there."

"But there *was* a raid," she flung back. "Several Pitchfork steers were killed."

"By Cairns probably—to prejudice the government men against us homesteaders."

Linda turned puzzled eyes on her cousin. "Does that make sense to you—that Mr. Daly would kill his own stock?"

"I know Daly wouldn't," Ben told her. His hostile eyes fastened on the owner of the Quartercircle D C. "He's up against it, Lindy, and has to find a story that will shift the blame to our side. So there wasn't any raid, and his friends weren't sore at Flack for double-crossing them, and it was the Pitchfork that was in a jam and rubbed out the spy. He didn't think up a good enough yarn to get away with it. That one is too thin."

Bruce knew the facts must be as he had said. He had been up and down the creeks and talked with every homesteader within a range of a dozen miles. That none of them had anything to do with the murder of Flack he was convinced. But he realized that unless proof of guilt was established elsewhere few would believe in the innocence of the small settlers. The obvious explanation of the spy's death was that he had been blotted out by some of his angry neighbors in punishment for what he had done.

It was of slight importance to Bruce what Ben Randall thought of him, but the desire was strong in him to set himself right with Linda Applegate. He put a blunt, sharp question at her.

"Do you think I murdered Flack?"

The words, the stern eyes, the clean pride of the man shown in the fine set of head and shoulders, were a challenge not only to her judgment but to her emotions. A heat flamed up in her as when a match is put to tow. There was a sudden gladness in her, the quick music of joy bells ringing in her heart. She knew, beyond any need of evidence, in spite of any testimony that might be piled up against him, that good was in him and not evil.

She said, her low husky voice a little tremulous, "I'm sure you didn't.

Her answer took Sherrill as much by surprise as it did her cousin. She had been a great deal in his thoughts since she had come into his life at its most dangerous hour to save him from imminent death. The girl was a lovely creature, slim and tall, with a light free step that reminded him of the meadowlark's song in spring. What was it in a woman's eyes and lips, the turn of her head, the powdered freckles beside her nose, that set her apart from all others of her sex? And deeper yet, what was that electric spark which drew a man and a girl together, in close kinship of the spirit, regardless of their will to hate and of circumstances that made them enemies?

Ben said, with flippant irony, "Flack probably shot himself by accident while he was cleaning a gun, then after he was dead went out and flung the gun in the creek."

"Or it might be this way," Bruce suggested. "The man who hired him as a spy was afraid he might not stay hired and thought it a good idea to get rid of him before it was too late."

"Maybe you would like to name this man who hired him and later killed him," Ben prompted, his voice low and even.

Bruce shook his head. He knew that he and young Randall were thinking of the same man, but he did not intend to go out of his way to start premature trouble. "Not now," he replied. "All I could do is guess—and my guess might not be any better than yours."

"Or as good," Ben told him scornfully. "Come on, Lindy. What are we waiting here for?"

Linda looked at Bruce, trust and trouble in her shining eyes, then turned and followed her cousin into the store.

26. Bruce Argues His Case

TIM HUMPHREYS WENT TO MERRITT CHARLTON, the county prosecuting attorney, with the information he had gathered about the killing of Flack. Charlton listened to the story and read the diary. He shook his head. There was no evidence pointing to the actual murderer, though it was a fair guess that one of the creek settlers had shot him on account of his spying. The sheriff had looked into the threat made by Malloy. Two or three men had been present at the time, and they agreed that it had been a warning rather than a threat.

"It may be one of his neighbors killed him, but I don't see how we are going to find out who unless those in the know start talking," the lawyer said.

"I asked Sherrill to drop in to your office," the sheriff said. "He ought to be here any minute."

"Does he claim to have evidence?"

Humphreys told what he had found out about the raid while at the Pitchfork. The assertion of Bruce that there had not been any raid was backed up by what Flack had written in the diary. If this was true, Bill Cairns had a potent reason for closing the mouth of the man who might have ruined him. One of the ranch riders had mentioned casually, with no idea of the fact's possible importance, that on the night of the sixteenth he had seen the foreman slip into the corral, saddle, and ride away. The cowboy had supposed he was going to see a woman.

Bruce walked into the office, greeted the men, tossed his hat on the table, and sat down. He grinned cheerfully at Charlton. "Not guilty, Mr. Prosecutor," he said.

"Can you say as much for all your friends?" the attorney asked bluntly.

"I'm sure I can," Bruce answered. "We wanted Flack alive very much. Inside of twenty-four hours we could have proved by him the raid on the Pitchfork was a fake. They beat us to him and rubbed out our witness."

"You say he was your witness. That may be just a bluff. If the other side had him in their pay, why would he go back on them?"

"Because when we got after him he would not have had the sand in his craw to stand out. Flack was a weak sister."

"Can you prove Flack was a spy?"

Bruce had to agree he could not. But he believed that Daly would admit it now the man was dead. In point of fact he had to be a spy or the contention of the cattlemen that the creek settlers had killed him in revenge fell to the ground.

"He was a paid spy," Humphreys admitted. "We have evidence of that, and we feel sure that you suspected it."

"I did. But he was not worth killing. We shut him out of our confidence. Think this through, Charlton. This last raid was a frame-up to get us in bad with the government men. When Tim began making inquiries about the raid, somebody got frightened for fear the truth would come out. There was one way to prevent that, by getting rid of Flack."

That might be true, the prosecuting attorney assented, but on the other hand the homesteaders had a grievance against Flack and one of them might have taken this way to settle it. Bruce pointed out that these covered-wagon settlers were not violent people. They had come from communities where law prevailed. They did not carry guns, as many of the cowboys did. Nor were they used to making their own law, as cattlemen had been forced to do in earlier days and to some extent still did. Living in older districts as tenant farmers had tamed their insurgent impulses.

Charlton shrugged his shoulders. He had observed that the most subdued man in the world was sometimes capable of murder. Blandly he suggested that Bruce was at that moment carrying a six-shooter.

"I belong to another breed of cats," Bruce told him.

"That's not a fair argument, Charlton," the sheriff said. "The cattlemen feel very bitterly toward Bruce, and their riders hold this feeling too. While we were at the Pitchfork the other day some of the boys from its bunkhouse very nearly got to shooting. Bruce would be foolish not to carry a gun for protection."

"I'm not accusing him of killing Flack," answered Charlton. "Fact is—not for publication—I would pick a man on the other side. But that's only a guess."

"You mean Bill Cairns," Humphreys prompted.

"I'm not saying his name."

"If you happen to be looking in the direction of Cairns, you might take a glance at the Big Mogul behind him," Bruce said. "At the man who pulls the strings and makes his puppets jump."

Charlton leaned back in his chair and gazed at the ranchman wearily. "Give me some evidence and I'll look at him."

Bruce turned to the sheriff. "It might be interesting to find out if Quint Milroy has a good alibi for the night Flack was killed."

"If he were to tell me he was asleep in his cabin, would you have any way to prove it wasn't true?" Humphreys asked.

"Just a shot in the dark," Bruce admitted. "He may be innocent as Mary's little lamb."

The owner of the Quartercircle D C had not expected the sheriff to welcome Milroy as a suspect with any enthusiasm.

Tim would do his duty. If there was any lead pointing to the man, Humphreys would look into it thoroughly, but he was not going to antagonize Milroy on an unsupported guess.

The prosecuting attorney raised a point. "Could Flack have got your hat without anybody seeing him around your place?" he asked.

"Easily," Bruce told him. "We are often all away from the house hours at a time. Not far away. Say down in the pasture. He could have slipped in without being seen."

Humphreys rose. "Well, I've got to get back to my office. By the way, Bruce, Mr. Barnard wants to see you before he leaves. He is starting for Washington tomorrow. He'll be at the hotel here tonight."

"Has he given you any line as to how he feels?" Bruce inquired.

"No. He is close-mouthed. I had a long talk with him today. He asked a lot of questions about Jeff Randall. You might as well know. Flack left a diary. He was Randall's man and got forty dollars for stealing your hat and telling Daly you were going to raid his ranch."

"That helps," Bruce said eagerly. "It helps a lot. Randall is in this now. He has a motive for killing Flack."

Charlton spoke a word of caution. "The diary doesn't say Jeff Randall. It says J. R."

"Same thing. Does Barnard know about the diary?"

"Yes. He and Sawyer have read it. Would you like to see it?"

"Very much." Bruce read what was written in the notebook and returned it to the prosecutor. "Thanks a great deal, Charlton.

"I don't know that I ought to have shown it to you," the lawyer replied. "But I don't think you had anything to do with this killing."

Bruce had a long talk with the two government men at the hotel that evening. They questioned him closely on every angle of the trouble between the cattlemen and the homesteaders. What they wanted were facts, and they offered no opinion of their own. One point struck Bruce as favorable. A great many of their queries had to do with Jeff Randall, his relation to the other cattlemen and his attitude toward the small settlers as shown by his actions.

27. Birds of a Feather

THE DECISION OF THE ADMINISTRATION AT WASHINGTON was a stunning surprise to those of the cattlemen who had fenced government land. It came in the form of an order to take down within thirty days all fences enclosing land belonging to the federal state. Messages flew back and forth between the offending ranchmen and their Congressmen. Senators called on the President and received no satisfaction. Jeff Randall went back himself, met the man in the White House, and did not help his standing with him by getting into a passion in which he said bluntly he would be damned if he would take down the fences. He had a title to the use of the land established by long custom and he was not going to be euchred out of it.

Jeff came home in a towering rage. It did not improve his temper to discover that Daly, Applegate, and the other stockmen who had been his allies in pre-empting illegally were busy tearing down barb-wire in obedience to the order. To find them very cool to him was a shock. Humphreys had shown them the notebook left by Flack. They had long resented the ramrod ways of the owner of the Diamond Tail, and it was more than they could stomach to learn that he had killed a friendly neighbor's cattle and hurt rather than helped their cause with the authorities. He realized that his influence over them was gone and that now he was practically a lone wolf in the community.

Cairns showed up at the Diamond Tail the day after Randall's return. He had been discharged by Daly after a severe tongue-lashing and had spent the time while Jeff was at Washington in heavy drinking at Redrock. The two men quarreled bitterly, but ended in burying their resentment and entering into a treaty of offense and defense. Each of them needed the other, since both were in bad odor. So the former foreman of the Pitchfork went on Randall's pay roll.

Rod remonstrated with his father about the hiring of Cairn. He knew the old man was bent on revenge and that Cairns would egg him on to folly that might ruin him.

"You can't afford to take Bill on," he urged. "The fellow is completely discredited. It is generally believed that he murdered Flack. Why tie him around yore neck when you are in bad yoreself?"

"I'll take on anyone I like," Jeff stormed. "You may be a quitter like your brother Ben, but I'm going through to a finish."

"What's the sense in being bullheaded when you know you're licked?" Rod asked. "No man can fight the United

107

States government. And to hire Cairns now is like waving a red rag in front of a wild bull. All the neighbors will resent it."

"Let 'em. I don't care a cuss how they feel." He glared at his son. "Or anybody else."

Rod was one man on the ranch who was not afraid of Jeff. He said, casually: "You can't quarrel with me, because I won't have it that way. And when you get hell-in-the-neck like you have now I'm not going to pussyfoot and tell you it's fine. That man in the White House is just as tough as you are. Knuckle down before it is too late."

"I wouldn't give up if I knew he was going to send me to the pen for the rest of my life," the old man roared. "I'll not pull down a single rod of fencing. If he doesn't like it he can lump it."

"He'll like it fine," Rod said dryly. "All he'll do is sick the law on you. I like a good fighter, but I don't see any sense in one trying to butt his head through a stone wall."

But old Jeff was beyond caution. If he could not rule he would ruin. He felt that even his own family had turned against him. He could not settle scores with all those who had fought him and those who were now deserting him, but at least he could destroy the one whom he thought the originator of all his troubles.

The bitter bile so filled him that he wanted his enemy to know the destruction of all his hopes, the defeat of his plans, before the man went out himself in the crash of his fortunes. Jeff was no longer sure of all his men. Even tough reckless cowboys became sensitive to the pressure of public opinion. His hatred of Sherrill they could understand and respect. What they could not forgive was the raid he had engineered on a friend's stock. One of his riders had quit. Two or three others were sullen and critical. He would have to move adroitly to involve them in his schemes. Quint Malloy he could depend upon. The man had a dour loyalty to the one that paid him. And since Cairns now had nobody else to whom he could turn he would go through if he could do so without too much danger. There was a big brutal quarterbreed called Rudy who would do anything for money, and a sidekick of his named Fox who always followed Rudy. Jeff could not count his son Rod in to obey orders. That young man's reactions were unpredictable. He was violent enough. Given what he considered sufficient cause, he might stand up and shoot it out with Sherrill. But he had standards he would not violate. It did not make Jeff any happier to know that Rod's code had been his once, before the lust for power had grown stronger than his principles.

One afternoon Rod met Linda and her brother Brand in the hills driving a bunch of strays back to Bar B B range. The girl was wearing old levis, high-heeled boots, and a dusty sombrero droopy with age. But the boy's clothes she wore could not conceal the grace of her slim, lithe figure or the beauty of her vivid face. Rod had not seen her since the day he had broken with her at the Applegate ranch. It gave him a stab of pain to find her so lovely, but no sign of this touched his immobile countenance.

They stopped to chat. All talk in this cattle country now came shortly to the one absorbing topic, the order of the government to tear down fences illegally built.

"I hear Uncle Jeff is standing pat," Brand said.

"Yes, he's hell-bent to get into a federal prison. No arguing him out of it." Rod smiled, ruefully. "I don't know whether he thinks he's too big a man for the law to make an example of, or whether he is just so bull-headed he is going to ram-stam it through. He has got the idea that all the rest of us are quitters. Since I told him what I thought he doesn't talk with me about it any more. He and that scoundrel Bill Cairns sit with their heads together cooking up trouble."

"What kind of trouble?" Linda asked.

Rod looked at her. "He did not tell me what kind."

Her heart sank. "It's too bad he has taken in Cairns," she said. "Folks think the fellow killed that man Flack."

He lifted his shoulders in a shrug. "Does it matter who killed Flack? He was selling his friends down the river."

"Whoever did it is a murderer. That matters, doesn't it?"

Rod agreed. "Yes. That was no way to kill a man. But since Flack was what he was, I'm not going to get into a sweat about who rubbed him out. He's better dead."

He spoke with sharp decision. Linda did not argue the point. He might be right. In any case there was no profit in disagreeing with him.

She and her brother picked up the cattle again and pushed them down to their own range. She was worried. With Cairns beside him to whisper revenge in his ears Jeff was not likely to sit with folded hands waiting until the government made him a prisoner. He would settle the score with at least one man first.

The day was hot and the air filled with the dust stirred up by the moving cattle. Linda had offered to help Brand because she felt restless. It was sometimes a relief to get on a horse and face the sweep of the wind against her body. But today was an exception.

After a long silence she said, "I'm glad Rod stood up to Uncle Jeff."

"Rod is all right." Brand added an explanation. "Uncle Jeff is like an old bull who has been boss of the herd a long time. He starts snorting and pawing up the ground when competition shows up, and nothing will convince the old-timer he isn't still tops but a whale of a licking. That's what Uncle Jeff is pointing for right now."

Linda realized this, but the worst of it was that before the old man was made harmless he could do damage beyond repair.

28. The Applegates See Red

LINDA SWUNG FROM THE SADDLE and handed the reins to Brand. "I'm so hot and dirty I'm going down to the swimming hole," she said.

"You're in luck," he replied. "I won't have time till dark."

She went into the house and got a towel and soap, after which she found fresh underwear, a petticoat, dress, and shoes. These she carried with her. The swimming hole was about three hundred yards from the house. Before undressing she ran up a white flag to the top of a pole her father had put there. When the flag was flying, all the men on the ranch knew that Linda was using the pool and gave it a wide berth.

She dived from a big flat rock into the cool water and swam leisurely across to the trunk of a dead tree on the opposite side of the creek. Here she relaxed, taking it easy. Holding to the stub of a branch, she splashed water with her feet. Not far away a meadow lark was flinging out its full-throated song. She floated lazily, and peace began to flow into her soul.

The sound of a breaking twig startled her. The girl's glance swept across the stream. Bill Cairns was stepping onto the big rock from which she had dived.

His tobacco-stained teeth showed in a wide lewd grin. "In case you don't know me, I'm Bill Cairns, the fellow you have never thought about," he said.

From her brothers she had heard the man had been drinking hard since his disgrace, and she could see that though he might not be drunk now he was under the influence of liquor.

"You had better go away quickly," Linda said. She was holding to the broken branch of the tree, sunken in the water up to her throat.

"Why, I've just come, my dear," he jeered. "Rode a long way, and got a nice eyeful. If you want to hit me again come right out and do it. Remember last time I was here? Lookin' for that wolf Sherrill, and you having him hid in yore bedroom all the time. You ain't got him under the water there now, have you?"

"Go, you fool!" she ordered. "You know what my father or my brothers will do if they come."

He sat down on the rock, fingering her clothes with his hairy hands. "But they're not coming," he exulted. "We're here alone, you and the man who isn't good enough for you to spit on."

"If you don't go I'll call for help," she warned.

"I wouldn't do that," he mocked. "I'm toting a gun, and they'll come running without any—if they hear you at all."

"Haven't you any sense? Don't you know you'll be hunted down like a coyote and shot on sight if you don't stop bothering me?"

"Now let's talk that over. I haven't lifted a finger to you. I'm just sittin' on a rock by a creek enjoyin' the beauties of nature. It's a free country. A fellow can go and come as he pleases." He broke off, struck by the change in her. She was looking past him at something that held her eyes fixed. "What's the matter, girl?" His eyes slewed around, and his jaw dropped.

Brand Applegate was standing not five yards from him, a revolver pointed at Cairns.

"Don't kill him," Linda cried.

Her brother's eyes were hard and ice-cold. "I'll teach him to play his dirty tricks on you," he said. "Get up, you rat, and keep your hands away from that gun."

"He's drunk, Brand," the girl urged. "Remember that. Don't shoot him."

Brand stepped forward, drew the man's revolver from its holster, and flung it into the creek. "I won't kill him this time," he promised. "I'm going to hammer him with my fists till he can't stand. Get along, fellow. We're heading for the house. You haven't a thimbleful of brains, or you wouldn't have left your horse where I could run on to it."

Cairns was frightened. "I wasn't aimin' to hurt her any, Brand," he wheedled. "You know that. Jest havin' a little fun."

The forty-five prodded into his back. "Don't talk!" Brand snapped. "Get moving."

As soon as the men had gone, Linda swam back to the rock and dressed hurriedly. She left the discarded boots, levis, and shirt where they lay. Cairns was a big muscular fellow, twenty pounds heavier than her brother, and a notorious bruiser. He might beat Brand badly and shoot him with his own gun. She ran toward the house.

While she was still a hundred yards away, she caught sight of the fighting men. They were not standing toe to toe slugging it out. Brand was too wise for that. He was a good boxer, and he was making the most of it. Though not as strong as his foe, young Applegate was hard as nails. He had not flung away his stamina in dissipation. Hard punishing blows sank into the bully's belly and made him grunt. Slashing right- and left-handers bruised his face and cut it. Cairns was breathing fast, his wind already gone. His flailing fists went wild, landing mostly on Brand's arms and shoulders.

Linda had to pass near them to get into the house. Since she was no longer worried about her brother, she had stopped running. But only for a moment. Cairns broke away from the fight, to get Brand's revolver lying on the porch. The girl beat him to it and whipped the gun from the floor as she ran.

The big man turned, to meet Brand crowding close.

"I've had enough," he bawled. "I give up."

The younger man's fist struck his nose and set blood trickling. "I haven't started yet," Brand told him.

Cairns covered up to protect his face. The jarring blows pounded his stomach. His knees bent and he sank to the ground.

"Get up," Brand snarled.

Nothing less than an earthquake would have brought the beaten man to his feet. He lay there cowering. Brand glared at him disgusted.

Linda caught her brother's wrist. "No more, Brand—please."

"All right." He pushed the toe of his boot into the fallen man's ribs. "Get up and light outa here. Don't ever show your face on this ranch again."

As Cairns rose heavily to his feet, Cliff Applegate and his younger son rode into the yard. The ranchman's gaze took in the ruffian's battered, bleeding face, his cowed manner, and the harsh anger of Brand. He swung from the saddle and moved forward, a quirt dangling from his wrist. His eyes demanded an explanation from his son.

"Lindy went down to the swimming hole after we got back," Brand told him. "I found him sitting on the rock deviling her."

"She was swimming?" Cliff asked.

"Yes. I brought him back here and whaled him."

"He's just leaving, Father," the girl said hurriedly. "I think maybe he was drunk."

"Go into the house, Lindy," the cattleman ordered, his strong fingers closing on the handle of the quirt.

Linda turned and went into the house, closing the door behind her. She heard the frightened protest of the victim, followed by a howl of pain, and she hurried to the back of the house to escape the sounds of the whistling quirt and the yelps of the unhappy wretch enduring it.

Presently there was silence. She looked out of a window. Young Cliff was bringing the horse of Cairns from the place where he had left it. The beaten man stumbled to the horse and clung to the horn to support himself. He tried two or three times to lift his foot to the stirrup and could not make it. When at last he got his boot into it, he had hardly the strength to drag himself to the hull. Slowly he rode away, shoulders bowed and both hands fastened in a tight grip to the pommel.

Linda went into the kitchen and sank down into a chair beside the table. She knew by the surging inside her that she was going to be sick.

Bud Wong noted her white face and colorless lips. "Missy not feel well," he said.

Through a window he had seen the last part of the fight and the subsequent quirting. He guessed that somehow she was involved in the trouble.

"I'm sick," she told him. "Go away, please."

She was moving to the sink as he vanished.

After a time she felt better physically, but the whole incident was something dreadful to remember. She was unhappy and much distressed. The picture of the coarse scoundrel fingering her clothes and gloating over her nakedness sent waves of shame through her. Why were men such beasts? And why did her father and brother feel it helped to beat the fellow into a state of whimpering cowardice?

She knew that Cairns had got off lightly according to the code of the frontier. If Brand had shot him down few would have censured him. There was no sympathy for the fellow in her thoughts, only a sense of somehow having been soiled.

29. Old Jeff Sympathizes

CAIRNS LAY ON A HILLSIDE above the Diamond Tail ranch house until long after dark. He waited until the light in the bunkhouse went out and only one was left in the main building. Everybody had gone to bed except old Jeff. He could go down now unnoticed.

He was very stiff and sore. The least movement would send pains jumping through his body. When he had looked at his legs a while ago, he had been sorry for himself. They were ridged with purple wheals where the quirt had wound around them like a rope of fire.

Though the clothes rubbing against his flesh made walking painful, he could not face the torture of getting into the saddle again. Leading the horse, he went down a draw to the house. From the back of the root house he watched to make sure nobody would see him. His vanity could not endure witnesses to his humiliation. He would have to let old Jeff see him, but nobody else.

Jeff was muddling over his accounts when Cairns opened the door of the office. He looked up, and was startled at what he saw.

"Great Caesar's ghost!" he exclaimed. "Have you been tangling with a panther?"

"Gimme a drink," Cairns said hoarsely.

Jeff got a bottle and a glass. The battered man poured out and drank enough for three men.

"Who in Mexico did that to you?" Randall asked.

Cairns lied. "The Applegates jumped me, all three of them. They pounded me till I couldn't stand, then the boys held me while the old devil wore himself out quirting me."

"What for?"

"I happened to drap down to the creek while that little vixen Lindy was taking a bath. Brand covered me with a gun. He made out I was down there spying on her. After he got me to the house they all jumped me."

Randall took the story with several grains of salt, but he did not intend to say so. He was going to be a good Samaritan and tie the humiliated man to him by sympathetic kindness.

"They're a high-handed bunch of lunkheads, Bill." He shoved a chair in the direction of his visitor. "Sit down and tell me about it."

"I can't sit down," Cairns explained angrily. "My thighs hurt like hell. I'll have to go to bed and stay there for a week."

Jeff suppressed a chuckle. "Too bad. I've got some ointment might help them."

"I'm not going to the bunkhouse. You'll have to let me stay at the house." Cairns ripped out a furious oath. "This has got to be kept quiet. I won't have your riders getting funny with me. I'll gun any one of them that does."

"I'll fix that," Jeff said in a soothing voice. "You can have the room next ours. Nobody will need to see you except Mary and me. Better tell me all about it now, so that if anything gets out I'll know what to say."

Cairns went into details, suppressing some and inventing others that would put him in a better light. The ranchman nodded his head, a sly wise smile on his face.

"She could have saved you, Lindy could, if she'd had a mind to do it. All she needed to say was that you had drapped down to the creek to wash up, account of its being so hot a day. And why didn't she? Because you made that crack about Sherrill in her bedroom. Now don't misunderstand me. The girl is straight as a string. But I've heard she is crazy about that fellow. You made her mad, and she let her men folks beat you up. You can blame Sherrill for that."

"I don't have to blame anybody but the Applegates, and you bet I'll take care of them some day." Cairns replied with bitter venom.

114

"You're not lookin' at this right, Bill," the older man told him. "The Applegates aren't going to spill a word of what happened, account of it might embarrass Lindy to have folks talking. But if you do any one of them a meanness the whole story will come out. You know how popular the girl is with all the young fellows. One of them sure would fix your clock. Listen. You want to pay her back for what she let them do to you, don't you? There's one sure way. Hit her through the man she is in love with."

Randall did not stress this any further at the moment. He had sown a seed in the man's mind that later might germinate. Cairns was a jealous cantankerous brute, and also revengeful. The old man thought he could prod the fellow's urge to kill in the right direction.

Cairns was up and about in two days but he looked, as one of the boys in the bunkhouse said in an aside, "like a harrow had run over his face." The sarcastic comment of his neighbor was that it was an improvement at that. Bill was too overbearing to be a popular citizen. Jeff had given the boys as an explanation of his new employee's plight the story that he had been thrown by his mount in rocky ground. The Diamond Tail riders had accepted this in skeptical silence, broken by a big tough fellow called Rudy. His comment was, "I reckon his bronc must of picked him up again after it throwed him and then jounced him up and down on the other side of his face."

One of the cowpunchers asked Cairns which horse in his string had piled him, but Bill flew to anger so swiftly that others decided not to try questions with a sting to them. Of late they had revised their opinion of Bill. The fellow had thrown down his outfit and they felt contempt for him. But he was a big cranky bully who could use his fists and there was no use inviting trouble with him. The men at the bunkhouse knew that somebody had given him a terrible beating and they discussed among themselves who it could be. "If I knew who he was the guy would be right popular with me," Rudy drawled. "Maybe he has got Mr. Cairns so tame I won't have to knock his ears down myself."

Rod returned from Redrock and reported to his father a rumor he had heard. A fellow had told it to him just as he was leaving town. There might be nothing to it. The country was full of all sorts of wild guesses these days. This might be just a pipe dream. The story was that the sheriff had uncovered a witness who had actually seen Flack murdered.

While he repeated the rumor Rod watched the old man, for there had been moments when he suspected his father of knowing too much about the killing of Flack. But the old man did not bat an eye. He made a casual comment, then asked his son how the market for beef stuff was standing up.

But inside of the hour Jeff was having a private talk with Quint Milroy. The killer told him not to worry. He was satisfied that nobody had seen him either going or coming. Any fool could start a story of that sort to make himself momentarily important. Jeff agreed that was true, but he could not keep a small worry from gnawing at his mind.

30. Sherrill and Applegate Ride Together

PROP ZANG CAME to Sheriff Humphreys with an odd story. He had recently employed to help him at the corral a young cowpuncher named Sid Tepley who had been riding through this country on the chuck line. An old-timer who did odd jobs when he was not drunk had been sleeping in the hay at the barn of the Elephant one night and awakened to hear voices in one of the stalls below. One of the two in conversation was Tepley, the other a range rider he had known in Montana. Next day old Libby came to Zang and told him what he had heard.

In strict confidence Tepley had let out to his friend that he felt sure he had seen the murderer of Flack a few minutes after the killing. The night of the crime he had camped on the creek a couple of hundred yards below Flack's cabin. He had been riding all day and reached the park late. Before he reached the house, the light went out. He decided to wait until morning, then drop in on whoever lived there in time to join him at breakfast.

Later in the night he had been awakened by the sound of a horse's hoofs on the trail a few yards from him. The traveler was heading for the cabin. Tepley was not interested and settled himself to go to sleep again, but before he could do so the sound of a pistol shot startled him. He heard presently the noise of an approaching horse, probably the same rider returning. The itinerant cowboy was curious. He was not exactly disturbed, but he was at least interested. He crept close to the trail and crouched back of a thick clump of bushes. The mounted man passed within four feet of him.

When it ought to be breakfast time, Tepley saw no smoke rising from the cabin chimney. The owner might be a late riser. After a time, warned by his stomach that he needed food, the puncher rode closer and halloed the house without result. He opened the door and found a man lying dead on the floor.

It did not take Tepley long to get out of the park, and not only the park but that part of the district. He was a stranger and might easily become suspect. The best course was to keep his mouth shut. This he had done until the night he met an old friend upon whom he could rely.

The sheriff and the prosecuting attorney put Tepley through a stiff questioning. At first the cowboy denied the whole tale, but after he had made sure they held no thought of his own guilt, he threw up his hands and admitted its truth. He had been close enough to get a good look at the man who was probably the killer and thought he would recognize him if they met again.

Humphreys decided to tour the district with Tepley and give him a chance to look over the inhabitants. But first he had to make sure this new development was kept secret. Five men in addition to Tepley had heard the story. That was too many. The weak link in the chain was Libby. The sheriff considered flinging him in jail for a few days as a vagrant, but he could not bring himself to hurt the harmless old fellow's feelings. He warned him earnestly not to tell anybody what he had learned. Unfortunately the old toper drank too much that night and babbled his story to a room full in a saloon. It was the first time in years he had been given a chance to be important.

With Tepley posing as his deputy, Humphreys had left town that afternoon and did not find out that Libby had broadcast all he knew. The two men talked with every homesteader on Squaw Creek and crossed over the hogback to the Quarter-circle D C. There they spent the night. In the morning they rode to the Bar B B, in time to see its riders before they set off to work. Nobody they had yet met was the horseman Tepley had seen riding from Flack's place.

The Applegates were pleased to have Humphreys drop in and Linda insisted he and his companion stay for dinner. The sheriff was sorry he had not time. They had to get on to the Diamond Tail to talk with Randall. It was more than an hour after they left that Bruce Sherrill rode up to the house on a horse that had been ridden hard.

Linda came to the door. "You!" she cried, surprised.

He had scarcely time to say good morning before blurting out, "Is the sheriff here?"

"No, he left a little while ago," the girl told him. "Has something happened?"

"It may, if I don't reach him in time. Can I get a fresh horse?"

Linda's father came to the porch from the house. "Why don't you come at night?" he asked. "Then you could take one without a by-your-leave, as you did last time."

"I'm sorry, Mr. Applegate," Bruce answered. "This is urgent. I'm afraid there will be a killing, unless I can head off Humphreys."

"What do you mean—a killing?" the ranchman demanded. "Who is going to get killed?"

"Maybe nobody. Maybe I'm worried about nothing. But I don't think so. An hour ago a man just back from Redrock dropped in at the ranch. He says the talk is buzzing all over town that the young man Humphreys has with him, the one he claims is his deputy, is a witness to the killing of Flack. They have been all up and down Squaw and Bear creeks, over to my place, and then here. This Tepley claims he would know the man again if he saw him. That's the story they are telling. Tim is giving him a chance to look us all over."

"What's wrong with that?" Applegate wanted to know. "It will suit me fine if they find the scoundrel and arrest him."

"They won't arrest him. They'll be shot down. Humphreys doesn't know it has got out that Tepley is a witness to the killing. He'll be knocked off without a chance for his life—he and Tepley too."

"You're assuming he'll run across the guilty man," Applegate differed. "Chances are ten to one he won't."

Bruce looked at him hard and long. "He'll find the man if they go to the Diamond Tail. The murderer has to be one of two men—Bill Cairns or Quint Milroy. Do you think either one of them would let Tepley get back to Redrock alive if it is true he can identify the killer?"

Cliff Applegate's eyes held fast to those of the younger man. He was thinking this out, and Bruce could see he did not like the thoughts trooping through his mind. The ranchman had read the diary Flack had left. He knew that the latest raid on the Pitchfork had been framed by Cairns and Jeff Randall, that Flack might easily become a dangerous witness against them. Cairns was the kind of man to commit a cowardly murder to save himself, but it would be like him to involve somebody else in it too if he could. Applegate no longer had any dealings with old Jeff, but after all the man was his brother-in-law. It shocked him to think Randall might have let himself get trapped in so evil a business. If Quint Milroy had any part in this, it had been at the instigation of the man who employed him.

The cattleman spoke to his daughter sharply. "Tell Grant to saddle Buck for me. I'm going over to the Diamond Tail. Have him rope Nugget for Sherrill."

He went into the house for his Winchester. Bruce walked beside Linda to the stable, leading his spent horse.

She said, "Do you think Uncle Jeff had anything to do with this?"

"I don't know," he answered. "I believe the killing was hatched at the Diamond Tail, but if Cairns did it he might have played a lone hand."

"I hope you catch Mr. Humphreys before he reaches the

Diamond Tail. It isn't safe for you there, nor for Father either."

Bruce told her he did not think old Jeff hated Cliff Applegate that much.

"It's not Uncle Jeff. It's that Bill Cairns." Embarrassment brought a deeper color to her cheeks. "Something happened here the other day. The man—overstepped himself. Father gave him a terrible beating. We weren't going to talk about it, but—I wish he weren't going to the Diamond Tail while the fellow is there."

"I'll keep an eye on Cairns while your father is around," Bruce promised. "With so many of us about he can't do anything."

"Thank you." Her face still flushed, she tried to explain away the appeal she had not quite put into words. "I don't know why I ask this of you, since you have so many more enemies there than he has. And anyhow, you are not one of us. I have no right to expect you to watch out for him."

He said, his voice low and gentle: "Not long ago a girl looked out for me, an enemy of her family. She saved me from my foes, who were ready to pounce on and kill me. She fought for me against her father and her brothers. She dressed my wound and she nursed me. And more than all that she believed in me when others didn't."

Linda felt a queer sense of weakness, of stilled pulses, followed by a clamor of the blood, by a warm gladness flooding her bosom. She did not dare to look at him. When she spoke, her words were an evasion, the first irrelevant ones that came to her lips.

"I'm glad we have two horses in the corral and won't lose time running some up."

She watched the two men ride away. Her father's manner was still stiff toward Sherill, as though he wanted it understood that they might be allies for the moment with no friendship involved. But at least Applegate no longer cherished bitter enmity. The situation had changed, and he was adapting himself to it. Linda thought perhaps he held a reluctant admiration for Bruce, a feeling he certainly would not admit.

What Linda felt was a little frightening. When Bruce looked at her she had a sense of being drawn to him irresistibly. Her will became fluid. Probably if he whispered "Come" she would run to him. When she was alone at night she chastised herself for being such a fool. But she knew the truth, that if anything happened to him the light would go out of her life.

31. The New Deputy

HUMPHREYS GAVE HIS PSEUDO-DEPUTY INSTRUCTIONS as they came down the hill to the Diamond Tail ranch house.

"Listen, Sim," he said. "If the killer is either of the fellows I think it is, he is too dangerous to arrest here. I wouldn't get away wit hit. One in particular is a notorious bad man, a dead shot and chain lightning on the draw. Don't let him know you have ever seen him before. I'll get him to town somehow and arrest him there. You can let me know he's the one we want by giving that bandanna round your neck a pull to straighten it."

The moment Jeff Randall saw them the bleached blue eyes in the weathered face narrowed warily. Not an hour earlier a messenger had reached him with a story confirming what Rod had been told and adding that the sheriff and the new witness, a wandering cowboy named Sim Tepley, were traveling through the district to identify the guilty man.

Quint Milroy was out in the big pasture helping to drive home a bunch of calves, but he might get back at any minute. It was very important this Tepley should not meet him.

"Have to excuse me just a minute, Humphreys," the cattleman said. "I got to tell one of my boys how to fix up a horse got cut by bob-wire. Be back in a minute. Make yourselves at home."

The sheriff was suspicious of this explanation, but he could see no ground for his mistrust, even when he saw through the window the old man talking with Cairns.

Randall rejoined them and suggested a drink. Humphreys declined. He was a teetotaler. Tepley took two fingers of whiskey and washed it down with water.

The ranchman asked how the Flack case was coming on. Had the sheriff made up his mind who had shot the man? Not yet, the officer admitted. There was not much evidence on which to go. Randall said his best guess was that scoundrel Sherrill. He was a bad character and had plenty of reason to want to get rid of the spy.

From his seat the sheriff saw Cairns ride out of the yard and wondered where he was going. His mind was not easy.

They discussed the fencing order.

"Mine stay up," the cattleman announced bluntly.

"Afraid you'll have trouble," Humphreys commented. "I think the President has his dander up and means to go through."

The door opened and Quint Milroy walked into the room. He had a bunch of mail in his hand.

"Didn't you see Bill?" Randall asked sharply.

120

"No. Is he looking for me? I swung across the pasture to pick up the mail as I came back."

Tepley was busy adjusting the bandanna around his throat. The sheriff said: "Quint, meet Sim Tepley. Sim, this is Mr. Quint Milroy."

Taken by surprise, the cowboy stared at the newcomer unhappily. It was disturbing to discover that the man whom his testimony might send to the gallows was the most notorious gunman in the Northwest. To find this out sent a shock of alarm through him. If the killer became aware of what he knew, his chances of living long would be slight. He made a gesture as if to step forward and shake hands, but Milroy did not meet the advance. The killer never shook hands. Once he had seen a man shot down by another while his right hand was held fast.

"Tepley is the sheriff's new deputy," Randall explained.

With the still hard-eyed wariness that distinguished him, Milroy looked the young man over. Tepley was probably only a cipher in his life, but since he was a law officer he was worth attention. There was always a chance that they might come into conflict. It amused him to see how the mere mention of his name had startled the young fellow. He was used to that look on the faces of those who met him for the first time. His reputation inspired awe. They did not talk with him casually and freely, but chose their words carefully in order not to give offence.

"New in this neighborhood, aren't you?" Randall asked Tepley.

The young man said he was, and privately thought it would be a good one to leave. He added that he had been working on the 3 D ranch near Miles City, Montana.

"But you thought you'd rather come here and be a deputy sheriff," the old man suggested.

"Well, it wasn't quite thataway," Tepley answered. "When I got to Redrock I was riding the chuck line. I happened to meet Mr. Humphreys and he took me on for a tryout."

"I see." The old man rubbed his unshaven chin with the palm of his hand, faded eyes fastened on the unhappy youth. "And do you like being a man-hunter?"

The sheriff smiled. "That's a kind of big word, Jeff, for a little job. Nine-tenths of a sheriff's work is just routine. I brought Sim along on this jaunt so he could get the hang of it."

Randall tittered. "Not to get the hang on someone here, I hope."

Humphreys laughed obligingly at the pun. "Well, I reckon we better be drifting, Sim," he said.

The cattleman had other ideas. "You're going to stay for dinner," he announced flatly.

This left the sheriff no choice. The custom of the ranch country was that anybody dropping in before a meal time stayed to eat. Without discourtesy he could not decline.

While Milroy and the two guests were washing up for dinner a half-hour later, using the tin basins on a bench outside the house, Cairns came into the yard at a road gait. He pulled up to stare at them in surprise. Before he could say a word, Jeff called him sharply to the porch. The man swung from the saddle and joined his employer. As Humphreys dried his face, he noticed that Randall was giving Cairns murmured instructions.

Cairns gobbled his dinner fast and left. A few minutes later Milroy also departed. There was nothing unusual about this. Riders in the ranch country went to the table to eat and after they had finished withdrew from the room. Dining was not a formal function. But Humphreys felt a bell of danger ringing in him. It was time to get away from here, he thought, if not already too late. Yet his mind could give him no justifiable reason for this apprehension.

While the sheriff and his companion saddled, they saw nothing of Cairns and Milroy. Over a hill trail Rod dropped down to the ranch. He had been checking the feed on the bench land above with a view to pushing some more stock up from the valley pastures. The presence of the departing guests surprised him. He exchanged greetings with Humphreys and took a long look at Tepley.

"Tim's new deputy," Jeff explained. "Just giving their ponies a workout." His son caught the sarcasm in the old man's words.

Rod did not answer. His eyes had shifted to the road that ran down from the ridge to the ranch house. Two riders were descending it.

"Looks like Uncle Cliff," he said. Astonished, he cried a moment later, "And the man with him is that fellow Sherrill."

"Sherrill! What's he doing here?" Old Jeff's voice held the rasp of anger.

"I reckon we're going to find that out," Rod said quietly. The riders drew up at the porch.

"Nice to see you again, Cliff," Jeff snapped ironically. "I see you brought a friend with you."

"No friend of mine," Applegate dissented. "He had a little business with the sheriff, and I thought maybe I'd better come along."

"Brought yore rifle in case you met a bear on the way," Jeff snorted.

"I don't know exactly why I brought it," Cliff replied, "except that fire works seem to go off when Sherrill is around."

Rod said to Bruce, "Your business with the sheriff to give yourself up for gunning Flack?"

Bruce retorted, looking him steadily in the eye, "Private business."

Jeff exploded. "Don't bring yore private business here, damn you, unless you want yore head shot off."

The sheriff interposed. "We're just leaving, Bruce. Unless you want to stay, you can ride with us."

"That will suit me fine," Bruce said.

"It will suit us too," Rod added.

Jeff was searching the reason for this visit and the effect it might have on plans he had made. His brother-in-law and Sherrill had come, of course, to help the sheriff in case any protection was needed. Word must have reached them that Tepley was the witness who had seen the killer of Flack, and they believed that the murderer was connected with the Diamond Tail outfit. It pleased Jeff to have Sherrill ride back with Humphreys. Given good luck, the men lying in wait for Tepley would get him too. But he did not want Applegate to be one of the party. If Cairns had a chance, he would certainly shoot Cliff down too. For two reasons that would be bad medicine. The owner of the Bar B B was too big a man in the community. His death would stir up a tremendous row. And though Jeff had been angry at Cliff, still was in fact, his anger did not run to a deep hatred. He expected some day to patch up the quarrel with him.

"Since you are here, Cliff, you'd better get off and rest yore saddle," Jeff said. "I haven't had a chin with you for a long time."

Cliff was surprised at the invitation. It was as near an apology as one could expect from Randall. But Cliff was stiff-necked, with a proper sense of pride. He felt that Jeff had grossly insulted him, and he did not intend to show any eagerness to resume cordial relations. He was not going to let Jeff get the idea that he could be kicked out and picked up again easily.

"Some other day, Jeff," he said with some constraint. "I'm too busy to stop now."

"You weren't too busy to ride all the way over here with this scalawag Sherrill," Jeff told him, bristling.

"I didn't want him to come alone," Cliff said bluntly. "If your invitation holds we'll come over some other time."

"Don't bother," Jeff flung out angrily. "It's now or never."

"Just as you say," Cliff turned to the sheriff. "If you're ready we'll start, Tim."

Jeff watched them go, then turned abruptly and shambled into the house. Half an hour later he hunted up Rod.

"Boy, slap a saddle on yore bronc and ride after your uncle," he said. "I'm scared something will happen to him. Bill Cairns may have seen him come and be watching to get him. Cliff gave him a terrible quirting the other day and he's hell-bent to get even."

"Why didn't you tell me sooner?" Rod demanded, heading for the corral.

"I kept gettin' more worried, thinkin' it over. Likely there's no sense in worrying. Still, if that fool Cairns did take a crack at him there would be hell to pay."

Five minutes later Rod rode out of the yard at a gallop.

32. A Two-Way Trail

SHERIFF HUMPHREYS WAITED till they had topped the ridge at the lip of the valley and were out of sight of the ranch house before he burst out with the indignant question he had been holding back.

"What have you to say to me, Bruce, so danged important it brought you busting into the Diamond Tail where you are as welcome as a hydrophobia skunk?"

Applegate answered for Sherrill. He was annoyed because he had let himself be stampeded into going to his brother-in-law's place when there was no need of it. "He got goosey for you, Tim. Word came from Redrock that yore new deputy is an important witness in the Flack case, and that you had brought him along to identify the killer. He was so het up I got to worrying too. I ought to have had better sense."

Bruce explained, apologetically. "I was playing a hunch, Tim, that the fellow who killed Flack lives at the Diamond Tail. If he does—and if word had reached him that you were bringing Tepley to identify the murderer, I thought you two wouldn't be good insurance risks."

The sheriff stared at him, but his eyes were looking at details that began to piece themselves together in his mind. The whisperings of Randall and Cairns. Bill riding out to intercept Milroy and missing him because he had detoured to get the mail. The look on old Jeff's face when Milroy walked into the room. His keeping the two visitors for dinner. The hurried departure of Cairns and Milroy.

What had been a vague sense of danger sharpened to a certainty. Somewhere on the road to the Bar B B, gunmen were now lying in the thick brush to close forever the mouth of the witness.

Humphreys said sharply, "You're right, Bruce. If you hadn't warned us neither Tepley nor I would have reached the Bar B B alive."

"Now you've gone crazy with the heat too, Tim," scoffed Applegate. He did not want to believe a cold-blooded killing could have been planned at the Diamond Tail.

"Tell him your story," the sheriff said to his deputy.

The cowboy repeated what he knew. He was willing to take oath that Quint Milroy was the man he had seen riding from Flack's cabin just after the shot had been fired.

Applegate was unhappy. He did not doubt that Tepley was telling the truth, and he was sure that if Milroy had killed Flack, it had been done at Jeff's order. He understood now why Randall had tried to detain him at the ranch. Even though he had quarreled with Cliff, he did not want him to be trapped in an ambush set for others.

"If they mean to bushwhack us, what spot would they pick?" Humphreys asked.

"The only good place would be at the gulch the other side of Tucker's Prong," Applegate answered. "The ground is hilly, with plenty of brush, and a trail winds up the gulch by which they could get back to the Diamond Tail without being seen."

"That trail leads two ways," Bruce drawled.

The cattleman caught his meaning. "So it does. If we strike it above us here, it will take us to the gully where they are lying, assuming that it is true they are out to get you and Tepley, Tim."

"You mean we could surprise them and capture Milroy now," the sheriff said.

"That's what I mean," Applegate replied. His eyes were hard and chill. There was a cold lump in his stomach. What he was going to do might bring disaster to a man who was a relative by marriage and had once been his close friend. But he had to find out the truth. Mingled with his heartache was anger. He was not going to condone the drygulching of a friend.

"I'll have to swear you in as deputies," Humphreys said.

Bruce remembered his promise to Linda and regretted his suggestion.

"Three of us will be enough," he said. "I don't think Mr. Applegate need go. Randall will regard this as a personal fight on him, and we don't want to start trouble among relatives."

Cliff turned on him, resentful antagonism in his bleak eyes. "If you will kindly let me run my own business, sir," he said.

Bruce had nothing more to say. He knew his attempt to exclude Applegate had been crude, but it was the best he could think of at the moment. The ranchman was justified in thinking it presumptuous.

They passed through a gate into a Diamond Tail pasture. This they crossed, ascending by a grade that got steadily sharper to the plateau above. After leaving the pasture, they struck a trail and followed it. This was ground that Applegate had covered fifty times. He knew it as a man does the palm of

125

his hand. It was still open range, and his cattle mingled with the Diamond Tail stock to feed on it.

They rode for miles along the rim of the plateau, at times close to the edge from which they could look down into the valley below and across at the sandstone cliffs that defined the opposite limit of the floor, and again farther back in the rolling park country they were traversing.

Applegate drew up in a cluster of pines and swung from the saddle. They were on Tucker's Prong, which jutted out into the valley from the adjoining rock rim like a folded thumb from the knuckles of a fist. The other three dismounted, tying their horses to young trees as Cliff was doing. He led them into the upper neck of the gulch that dropped down to the road below.

"No talking," he ordered. "And don't make any noise. When we get far enough down so that I can see them, I'll give you a signal. The gulch opens up near the bottom. There's a lot of brush. You'll have to be very careful how you move. We'll spread out. Lie low till you hear me give the order to Milroy to drop his gun. I don't know how near we can get to them without being seen."

The sheriff added a word. "We are here to capture Milroy. If we can do it without any shooting, fine. We must not hurt either Milroy or Cairns except in absolute self-defense."

"If they make a break to escape when I throw down on them, don't kill them," Cliff said. "Shoot their horses."

Though his eyes scanned the cañon below him carefully, Applegate took the first quarter of a mile at a steady walk. As he got lower he moved more slowly. One of the Diamond Tail men might be stationed higher than the other, to make sure a chance range rider did not drift down on his way to the road. At a bend in the gulch he raised a hand in warning. The others joined him. Below them the cañon opened to a greater width, the floor of it covered with a thick tangle of bushes. If their guess about the ambushers was correct, the men were concealed somewhere in that deep carpet of vegetation.

"We'd better separate here," the sheriff directed. "You creep down close to the left wall, Tepley. I'll be next you, with Sherrill on my right. Then Applegate. We must try to keep abreast of one another. We're going to have a heck of a time getting through the brush without being heard."

The shrubbery was thicker in the center than it was closer to the walls. Bruce knew they were near the mouth of the gulch and that the road could not be far below them. Somewhere in the next hundred yards they would sight the ambushers. He moved very carefully, not taking a step without scanning the terrain in front of him. Each time he set down a foot he had to be sure a dead branch did not snap, and as he

126

parted bushes to make way for his rifle and his body he had to know there would not be a rustling to betray his presence.

Back of a rock slab projecting from the wall he caught sight of horses. A guard was with them. Bruce reocgnized the man, Mose Fox, a Diamond Tail cowboy. Since he was here, the rider of the fourth horse was probably his pal Rudy.

A rifle crashed, and the echo of it went roaring down the gulch. The trigger of Sim Tepley's rifle had caught on a twig. There was an agitation in the bushes below, the parting of branches as men scurried through the thicket to reach better cover.

Cliff Applegate rose from back of a rock, rifle in hand. "Stay right where you are, Milroy," he ordered. "I've got the drop on you."

The head and shoulders of the sheriff appeared above the scrub oak. "Don't make any trouble, boys," he shouted. "The law wants Milroy."

It flashed through the mind of Bruce that this was a fool-hardy thing for both of them to do, though he realized that Humphrey's hand had been forced by the cattleman, who in turn had been pushed prematurely to show himself by the accidental discharge of the deputy's gun.

The challenge brought the Diamond Tail gunmen to activity. A bullet from a Winchester whipped up the gorge. Applegate swayed on his feet and went down back of the boulder. Bruce fired at the spot from which the smoke came. A man running low dodged from the brush and made for a pile of rocks near the wall. As Bruce raised to fire again he recognized Cairns. The man flung himself back of the boulders, apparently not hit.

The cañon was filled with the sound of gun explosions beating against the cliffs. Bruce caught a glimpse of Applegate's head and rifle lifted above the sandstone outcrop behind which he crouched and heard the smash of the slug against stone.

Tepley cried, "I'm hit."

A voice, shrill with panic, shouted, "We'd better get outa here." Cairns, Bruce decided. A moment later he saw the man edging among the rocks toward the horses.

Applegate fired. A horse gave a shrill whinny of pain and sank to its knees. The other ponies, wild with fear, tore through the brush toward the road. Cairns caught the bridle of one, swung to the saddle, and crouched low on the neck of the animal as it galloped through the slapping scrub oak.

Fox ducked out from the pocket formed by the rock slab to follow Cairns. A bullet from the sheriff's rifle stopped him. He stumbled and fell.

"I give up," he cried, repeating the words several times.

Bruce became aware of bushes rustling to the left, not far

127

from the wall. The foliage moved. Somebody was creeping up to reach Tepley, somebody who wanted to finish a job he had started, one very important to him.

Sherrill wormed his way back of the sheriff, traveling on hands and knees, hitching the rifle forward as he went. He was in a hurry.

Humphreys murmured, "They've got Applegate and Tepley."

"One of them is coming up to make sure of Tepley," Bruce answered in a whisper.

A bullet whistled past him just as he reached the cowboy. Since he could not see the fellow who had sent it Bruce guessed the man had fired on the chance of a hit.

"I'm wounded," Tepley said.

Bruce nodded. "He's on the way up now to get you. You hit bad?"

"I dunno. In the side. Don't leave me."

"I won't. We'll get to that big rock."

Tepley edged along, supported by Bruce. Another bullet whined through the shrubbery. Bruce did not fire but kept going. He did not want the sharpshooter to know their exact location.

The cowboy slumped down, exhausted, back of the boulder. Bruce waited, crouched beside him, his rifle half-raised.

There was a lull in the shooting, broken by a shot from the draw, not far above the road. That would be Rudy, Bruce guessed. Cairns was galloping away from the danger zone, Fox was wounded and out of the battle, and Milroy was crawling up through the underbrush to destroy the witness who could hang him. Since there had been only four horses, there could be only four of the ambushing party. Tepley alive was a danger to one of them, and that one was Quint Milroy.

33. Bruce Takes a Prisoner

A HEAVY SCREEN OF FOLIAGE burgeoned out beside the rock that gave cover to Sherrill and the wounded cowboy and through this Bruce could check on the man stalking Tepley. Once or twice he caught sight of a part of an arm or leg. Yet he did not fire. He was convinced that Milroy did not know he had joined Tepley and had not spotted the exact position of his victim.

An idea was buzzing through the head of Bruce. The gunman was moving directly toward their rock. It might be possible to capture him alive. Bruce whispered to his companion not to make the least sound. The enemy was scarcely forty feet distant.

Humphreys saw the moving bushes and flung a bullet at what they might conceal. The desperado must have realized the brush was not dense enough to give him cover. He fired once in the direction of the shot and made a dash for the boulder.

Bruce could have killed him, but he waited. Milroy was delivering himself into his hands. The Diamond Tail gun fighter clawed his way up a short steep bank below the rock and flung himself on hands and knees behind it. For one startled fraction of a second horror stared out of his eyes. Before he could lift a finger the barrel of a rifle crashed down on his head. The limbs and body of the man relaxed instantly. He was out. Bruce took the bandanna from his throat and tied securely behind his back the hands of the captive.

He called to the sheriff, "I've got Milroy."

Humphreys came across the hillside, looked down at the unconscious man, and then at Bruce.

"You had a chance to kill him," he said.

"Thought you said you wanted him alive."

"So I do, but I said that before they shot up our friends . . . How is Sim?"

"I haven't had time to look." Bruce knelt beside the young man, took off his coat, and unbuttoned his shirt. Luck had been with Tepley. The bullet had made only a flesh wound. It had struck a pipe in his pocket, been deflected, and plowed through muscular tissue without piercing the rib.

"I'll leave you to take care of him, Tim," Bruce said. "Want to get across and see how Applegate is."

"Go carefully," the sheriff warned. "One of them may still be down there ready to plug you."

"Better take a look at Milroy before he wakes up. I may not have tied his hands tight enough."

Humphreys drew handcuffs from his pocket and fastened them on the prisoner.

No shots from below interfered with the passage of Sherrill across the gulch. It was probable that Rudy had either caught one of the horses or was making his escape on foot.

Bruce found the cattleman sitting behind his rock shelter, the rifle across his knees. "Hell in Georgia for a while," he mentioned grimly. "Tim and his deputy all right?"

"Tepley was hit. In the side. A glancing bullet. He ought to make it all right. How about you, sir?"

"One in the shoulder, kindness of Cairns, I think."

"Yes, I took a crack at him as he ran for the rocks, but I don't think I hit him." Bruce suggested he had better look at the wound.

"All right. That fellow Fox is down just below us. Every time he hears a shot he yells for me not to kill him."

129

While Bruce examined the shoulder he told Applegate that they had captured Milroy.

"Wounded him first, I reckon?"

"No. He got too close to where I was hidden and I knocked him out with the barrel of my rifle."

A voice hailed from the road. It asked if Cliff Applegate was there.

"Reinforcements, for our side or theirs," Cliff decided. "Ask him who he is and what he wants."

The man below replied that he was Rod Randall. His father had got worried and sent him.

"Tell him I'm here, and for him to come up if he is alone," Cliff said.

Bruce shouted the message. Voices from the road drifted to them. Rod called up that he had been alone, but the Applegate boys had just joined him.

"You all right, Father?" someone asked.

"That's Brand," the cattleman told Bruce. "I reckon Lindy got worried and sent the boys when they got home."

The three young men came up through the mouth of the gulch and joined them.

"You're hurt," Brand cried, after one look at his father.

"I'll make the grade," the cattleman told him. "This fellow patched me up fine. There's a Diamond Tail rider near the rocks who has been shot up some. One of you better look after him."

"Do you know who these scoundrels attacking you are, Uncle Cliff?" Rod demanded angrily.

The ranchman looked at young Randall with no friendliness in his frosty eyes. "I know three of them and can guess at the fourth," he said sourly. "If you want to make sure who he is, better ask Jeff."

Rod said, "You ought to know Father wouldn't try to do you any harm." He added, to back his claim. "When he found Bill Cairns missing, he was scared the fellow meant to waylay you and sent me to warn you."

"Good of him," the cattleman told Rod bitterly. "I'm certainly grateful to him. Did he send Milroy and this crybaby Fox with you?"

Bruce cut in. This was no time for angry argument. "We have three wounded men on our hands—maybe four—two of them prisoners. First thing is to get them out of here to some place where a doctor can look after them."

"The Bar B B is nearest," Brand said, looking doubtfully at his father. "But we're not prepared to take care of that many."

"You won't have to," Bruce explained. "Tim can take Milroy to town with him in a wagon—and Tepley too. I don't know how badly Fox is hurt."

"He has been making enough fuss," the cattleman said scornfully. His gaze fastened on Rod. "If he has a friend here he had better go look after the fellow."

Rod answered stiffly. "I'm particular who my friends are. I don't include dry gulchers any more than you do. But I'll take a look at him."

Randall turned and walked to the wounded cowboy. He was both angry and unhappy. The explanation his father had given him did not cover the situation. Cairns might have lain in ambush to attack Cliff Applegate, but the other three men would not have been with him without orders from old Jeff. He understood why his father had sent him to warn Cliff. Warped though his standards had become, he could not let his former friend, the uncle of his children, walk blindly into a trap set for others.

What was he to do? Milroy would probably keep his mouth shut, but if pressure was put on Fox he might tell all he knew. Rod had to save his father if he could. The first thing he must find out how deeply Fox could implicate Jeff.

The cowboy was shot in the right thigh. There was a good deal of blood around the wound, but no arteries had been cut. While Rod was giving first aid, he questioned the man. He learned that Jeff had not talked with Fox before the party set out to intercept the sheriff. Rudy had got him to come, and Rudy's instructions had reached him through Quint Milroy and not direct from the boss. It might be worse, Rod reflected. If Cairns and Milroy did not blab, the old man might have an out, though of course he would be suspected.

One detail of the story Fox told him gave Rod a gleam of hope. The first shot had come from the sheriff's party. Rod drilled into the wounded man the point that this was an anchor post upon which to tie the defense. His party had been pushing Diamond Tail stock down the gulch when somebody began shooting at them. This had started the battle. He must stick to that regardless of the pressure put upon him. If he held fast to that, Rod promised to see he had a good lawyer and money to fight the case. If he did not, the ranch would cut loose from him and leave him to his fate.

After Rod had done what he could for Fox, he crossed the gulch to have a talk with Milroy. The gunman would expect the Diamond Tail to get him out of this trouble and Rod wanted to assure him that it would stand back of him. There was a better chance to see the prisoner alone now than there would be later. Young Cliff had gone up to the top of the Prong to bring down the horses left in the grove. Brand was on his way to the Bar B B to get a wagon. He noticed that Sherrill was hovering around their father, perhaps to protect him against the possible return of Cairns, with an occasional eye directed toward Fox to prevent any attempt at escape.

Humphreys asked Rod how badly wounded were Applegate and Fox. Randall thought they would both pull through and inquired about Tepley. The sheriff and Tepley had been lucky.

Rod thought all the wounded were fortunate. "About a pint of lead spilled and not a coroner's case in the lot," he said, and then pointed a question at Humphreys that was meant to make a suggestion to the prisoners. "How come you to start shooting at our boys while they were driving stock down the gulch?"

"So that's going to be your story," the sheriff replied.

"Am I wrong?" Rod persisted. "Didn't you fire first?"

"One of our guns went off by accident."

Rod's skeptical smile was grim. "By accident? That sounds strange to me, sheriff. You start shooting and four men are wounded. Then you claim an accident. I say it's a damned outrage, and to top it you have Quint handcuffed. For defending himself, I reckon."

"Milroy is under arrest for the murder of Flack," Humphreys answered. "Before anybody was hurt, I told your men I had a posse to capture him. That started the fireworks. Cairns shot down Applegate."

"If Cairns did that, he is through at the Diamond Tail. But I'll have to get more than your word for it, Humphreys." Randall spoke with a cool arrogance that admitted no doubt. "And as for that nonsense about Quint shooting Flack, no unbiased person will believe a word of it. I don't suppose Quint ever spoke ten sentences to the man."

"Not five," Milroy corrected, his voice even and low. Inside the man was boiling with rage, but this showed only in the bleak deadly menace of the eyes. His anger was at Sherrill, who had brought him to this humiliating pass.

He knew that Rod was giving him assurance of support at his trials, but this was not enough. He did not intend that there should ever be a trial. Long before that he meant to be free and out of the country.

"Like to have a word alone with Quint," Rod said to the officer.

Humphreys had expected this. He nodded consent. "Walk over to that fault in the wall—after you have left your gun here, Rod. No shenanigan. I'll drill a hole in Milroy if you make one false move."

"I'm not a fool," Rod retorted irritably, and laid his revolver on a rock.

He walked beside the prisoner the seven or eight steps to the cliff. The two men spoke in whispers.

"I'm not going to lie cooped up in jail," Milroy said flatly. "Tell Jeff he has got to get me out right away."

The words were a threat. Rod realized that. If Jeff did not rescue him he would talk.

"We'll get you out, if I have to tear down the jail," Rod promised.

"See you do," Milroy ordered. "Soon as I'm free I mean to kill that devil Sherrill and light out from here."

Rod did not comment on that.

34. Quint Milroy Takes a Walk

ROD SLAMMED AN ULTIMATUM at his father straight from the shoulder. "You're in one hell of a jam," he said. "You're bucking the government, and the law at home here. All your friends have quit you. The homesteaders have got it in for you, and the stockmen won't support you an inch of the way. I don't want to hear how deep you are in the Flack killing. But I can tell you this. You've come to the end of your rambunctious bullheaded course. The rest of your life will be spent in the penitentiary—unless you show some sense. Either you do what I say or I fork my bronc and get out of here for good."

Jeff looked at his strong reckless son and knew he dare not let him go. The old man looked ten years older than he had a few weeks earlier. Everything had gone wrong for him. He could no longer find comfort in his family or his possessions. The position he had held in the community was lost. The doors of a prison were opening for him. His nerves were jumpy, and he could not sleep nights.

"What do you want me to do?" he asked.

"First, kick Bill Cairns out and tell him never to show his face on the place again. Next, give orders to the boys to begin tearing down the fences on government land tomorrow. You have only a week left to get them down."

"You give them the orders," Jeff said. "I just can't do it. If I've got to back water let me save face. But what about Quint? You know I've tried to get them to let me go bail, and they won't do it."

"I'll take care of Quint." Rod looked through the window and saw Cairns crossing the yard. He leaned out and called the man. "Come here, Bill."

Cairns stood in the doorway. "Want me?" he asked.

Rod looked the man over contemptuously. "Pack yore things, then come and get your time. You're through here. Get out and don't ever come back or I'll set the dogs on you."

The big ruffian's face turned purple with rage.

133

"You boss of this outfit?" the man demanded, and slid an ugly look at the old man.

"Don't talk back," Rod ordered. "Get going."

"Jeff can still talk, can't he? He hired me. It's up to him to fire me, if that's what he wants."

"I told you to let Cliff Applegate alone," Jeff snapped. "But you were hell-bent on getting even with him for the quirting he gave you. When a man works for me, he can't grind his own corn in my mill. What Rod has told you goes."

"Fine," Cairns retorted bitterly. "I do yore dirty work for you and lose out at the Pitchfork. I'm to get the Quartercircle D C ranch after you have bumped off Sherrill. Instead I get the boot. You're a fine character, Jeff. By God, you would double-cross yore mother. But you won't get away with this. I'll spill everything I know—and that's plenty."

The big man backed away hurriedly as Rod advanced toward him. "Don't you!" he cried. "Don't you dare touch me."

He was close to the edges of the porch when Rod's fist lashed out and caught him just under the chin. His head snapped back, and he went off the porch, shoulders and buttocks hitting the ground together. For a few moments he lay there, jarred and shaken, before he got heavily to his feet. He glared at his assailant furiously. The man's fingers almost touched the revolver butt at his hip. Rod was not wearing a coat. Cairns could see he was unarmed. Now was the time to send a slug into the flat stomach of the arrogant fool.

But Cairns could not do it. Not with the fearless eyes fixed on him scornfully. And presently the urge to kill subsided. It would be a crazy thing to do. He would never get off the ranch alive.

"I'll remember this, Jeff," he said to the ranchman grinning in the doorway back of his son. "You can't do this to me and get away with it. Sure as God made little apples I'll fix you for this."

He turned and walked to the corral. Fifteen minutes later he rode out of the yard. A bilious hatred boiled in him, of Jeff far more than of his son. Rod did not owe him anything. What he had done had been for his father. But the old man was in his debt plenty. In serving Jeff he had lost a good job and become an outcast. Now the ranchman was repudiating him to save his own skin.

Cairns did not go to Redrock. If he hung around there on a drinking spree, Humphreys would probably arrest him. He went to a hog ranch he knew twenty miles down the river where he could get drunk without interruption and plan revenge.

Rod decided not to tell his father what his scheme was for freeing Milroy. He meant to play a lone hand, and it was safer to take nobody into his confidence. After breakfast the day following the departure of Cairns, he left for Redrock on a bay horse he had recently bought, one that did not carry the Diamond Tail brand. His first call was at the office of the sheriff, to get a permit to visit Milroy with a view to discussing with the prisoner the retaining of an attorney for the defense.

To this Humphreys could not very well object, though he told Randall he would have to search him to make sure he was not carrying a weapon. They decided that since it was a little late Rod should see Milroy the following day.

The sheriff walked with Rod to the jail next morning and personally took the young man to the cell where Milroy was confined. He did not offer to unlock the cell, since the men could talk as well with the bars between them. But he did leave them alone for a private talk.

Milroy let Rod do most of the talking. He fixed his dead heavy-lidded eyes steadily on the young man and listened.

"It ought to work," he said at last.

"Looks to me almost foolproof," Rod answered, "Cairns would probably find a way to bungle it if he was in your place, but you won't. It is safe and easy. You get out without hurting the jailor. That's important." The eyes of Randall held steadily to those of the bad man. "Schmidt is married and has three kids. If you kill him you are sunk. I'll help see you never get away alive. But there needn't be any shooting. He'll give up soon as you cover him."

"Don't threaten me, Rod. I won't take it." Milroy spoke in a soft even voice like the purr of a cat, one as chill as a blizzard-laden north wind.

"Use your head, Quint," Randall said impatiently. "I know your record. What I said was for your sake as well as for Schmidt."

"I don't get jumpy and kill when it isn't necessary," Milroy reminded him.

Rod opened his vest and unwound from his body a long length of string. He handed it through the bars to the prisoner, who at once concealed it under the mattress of his cot.

"The best time for the break would be tomorrow morning early if you can make it then," Rod suggested. "There aren't many folks around before church time Sunday."

"Schmidt brings my breakfast about seven. That would be all right with me."

"Good. The horse will be in that clump of cottonwoods about a hundred yards south of the jail. You'd better make straight for the Colorado line, Quint."

The dead-pan face of the killer was blank of expression. "I'll consider your advice," he said.

Humphreys came back into the room. "You boys finished your talk?" he asked amiably.

Rod grinned at him with friendly impudence. "We're going

135

to get Tom Black of Denver to defend Quint. He'll knock hell out of your case, Tim."

"It's not my case, Rod," the sheriff corrected. "I'm through when I make the arrest."

It was nearly midnight when Milroy heard the hoot of an owl outside. He rose from the cot and went to the barred window. Neither moon nor stars lit the night. A man was standing below. Quint lowered one end of the string that had been given him. Presently there came a tug. He drew up the string carefully and took from it a revolver.

Before he put it under his pillow he discovered that there were no cartridges in the cylinder.

The early morning sun was shining through the window when Schmidt arrived with his breakfast. While the tray was still in the jailor's hands the prisoner covered him with the revolver.

"Take it easy," Milroy warned. "Don't shout. Don't try to run. Put the tray on the floor and unlock the door."

Schmidt did as he was told. Milroy tied his hands behind him with the string and gagged him, using the man's own handkerchief to stuff into his mouth, then locked him in the cell.

The prisoner walked out into the pleasant sunshine and across to the cottonwoods. Two men were moving down the street toward him less than a hundred yards distant. He did not hurry. If they showed any interest in him, he could get to the saddled horse in plenty of time. When he reached the grove he tested the stirrups to make sure they were the right length. The men passed the jail without giving him a second look. He rode from town through its straggling outskirts into open country. But the road he took was not one that would lead to Colorado. Unfinished business in Wyoming claimed his attention before he hit the long trail.

Near the point where Squaw Creek ran into the valley, he met a young Diamond Tail puncher named Dick Spears. The cowboy opened his eyes at sight of Milroy.

The gunman stopped his question. "Never mind how I got out, Dick. Point is, I'm here. I want you to take a note to Jeff Randall."

"Sure," Dick said.

Milroy knew he was dependable, but after he had scribbled a few lines he stressed the need of secrecy. He was to give the note to nobody but Jeff and was to keep his mouth shut afterward.

Looking into the man's cold eyes, Dick knew he would do no talking.

35. A Debt Is Paid

BEFORE JEFF RANDALL REACHED THE LINE CABIN he knew that somebody was there or had been recently. A thin trickle of smoke rose from the stovepipe. Likely it was Jim West, one of the Diamond Tail riders. The old man jogged forward and pulled up in front of the shack. He lowered to the ground the sack of provisions he was carrying and started to swing his ungainly body from the saddle.

"Stay where you're at," a harsh voice ordered.

Bill Cairns stood in the doorway, a rifle in his hands. It was plain that he had been on a long hard spree. He was unshaven, red-eyed, and slovenly. The expression on his face shocked Randall. The usual sullen ugly look had sharpened to one of cruel triumph.

A cold knot of fear tied up the old-timer's stomach. He knew that never in his long turbulent life had he been in greater danger. Hatred of him was surging up in this fellow's heart. The week's debauch had blurred his judgment. But Jeff never had been a coward. There was no change in his granite face, none in his slumped figure. He had to talk fast, and what he said had to be good.

"Nice to meet you again, Bill," he replied, his voice cool and even. "I wasn't expecting to see you here."

"You didn't come then to kick me off yore ranch again?" Cairns jeered.

Jeff played for time. "I reckon I was a little hasty, Bill. We can fix everything up fine, you an' me."

"Sure. You can fix anything, damn yore lying tongue. You fixed for me to have the Quartercircle D C. Just leave it to you. You fixed me out of a good job and then double-crossed me. I was sittin' pretty till you fixed it to ruin me."

The voice of Cairns rose almost to a scream. He was working his nerve up for the kill. Jeff realized the passion of the man was getting out of hand. Death was crowding close to him.

"I aim to satisfy you, Bill," he said, still apparently confident that they were going to arrive at a friendly understanding. "No reason why we should fuss after all these years. Now listen. I've got a plan——"

"Take it to hell with you," Cairns interrupted furiously. "You've come to the last step of yore last rotten mile."

The rifle roared. Jeff's gray head fell forward. Slowly the heavy body slid to the ground. Cairns moved toward him. He drew a revolver and fired it into the huddled mass at his feet.

Cairns stared down at what he had done, fear already beginning to seep through him. Even though he got away at once, Rod would suspect him. He told himself that nothing could be proved, not if he escaped unseen. Far up in the range was an old trapper's cabin. Few knew of its existence, since cattle never ranged so high. He still had left half a jug of whiskey. By stuffing a few more provisions in the gunny sack he could have food enough for a week. After that he could light out for parts unknown.

From a draw where he had left his mount he brought the animal and saddled it. Panic was starting to rise in him. He must get from here at once. His hurried glance swept the cabin, to make sure he was leaving no evidence that would betray him. Those who found Randall's body would know somebody had eaten a meal here, but they would have no way of telling who it was. He tied his roll and the sack of food back of the saddle and climbed into the hull.

Not until he had disappeared into a draw leading to the foothills did the crawling fear inside his belly subside. Give him another mile or two and he would be deep in the folds of the land waves. He came out of the draw to the ridge above, and a wave of sickness swept through him. Linda Applegate, on horseback, was watching him as he came up from the gully. After the murder was discovered, she would be a witness to prove he had been on the spot.

His first crazy impulse was to kill her. He had his Winchester half-raised before caution stopped him. She probably was not alone. His second thought was to turn and run. But this would convict him if he ever came to trial. Slowly he rode forward, his fear-filled eyes stabbing right and left in search of any companion she might have.

The girl remained where she was, motionless. He tried to smile, and his mouth twisted to a horrible grimace. His throat was so dry that when he spoke the words that came were a croak.

"Are you alone?" he asked.

The look on his face warned her. Back of the fawning smile was something dreadful and cruel. She knew he had started to kill her and had stopped.

"Of course not," she answered, her gaze holding fast to his. "My brothers are just over the hill rounding up strays. Do you want to see them?"

His frightened eyes swept the brow of the hill. "No, miss. I jest happened to be here—on my way to the Diamond Tail. Came up from down the river."

Linda felt sure he was lying and could see no reason for it. She still had an urgent sense of imminent danger, unreasonable though it was. He reminded her of a wild beast ready to pounce, held by some restraining fear. Her heart died within

138

her. She had to fight down a rising terror. She must not let him know she was frightened.

"You'd better go," she warned him. "If my brothers see you it will be too late."

The lids over his eyes narrowed. "You wouldn't lie to me."

She had to go through with her bluff. "I don't have to put up with this," she told him contemptuously. "I'll call them."

"Don't you!" he snarled, and tried to cover the threat with an apologetic grin. "I'm kinda out of sorts, Miss Lindy. Been traveling without food all day."

Linda turned her horse up the hill and rode away. She did not look back, though she was dreadfully afraid he would shoot. As soon as she was over the brow she put her horse to a gallop. To deceive the man she tried to shout "Brand— Cliff!" but no sound came from her frozen throat. The horse was wet with sweat when she pulled up at last, a clammy perspiration on her forehead.

If she had known it, Cairns was driving his mount just as fast in the opposite direction. He cursed the luck that had brought her there just at this moment. He would stay at the trapper's cabin over night, but no longer.

The fugitive moved in and out among the hills, working steadily toward the blue range at the horizon's edge. When he reached the cabin Pierre Renaud had built twenty-five years before, darkness was beginning to settle over the hills. He dismounted before the door, now sagging from its leather hinges, untied the sack, and went into the cabin.

While his eyes adjusted themselves to the semi-darkness, he stood near the door. Some stir of movement startled him. A pack rat, no doubt. But a wave of terror swept over him. The dim figure of a man was taking form.

He dropped the sack. "Who is it?" he cried, nerves jumpy.

"Take it easy, Bill," the answer came low and cold.

An instant relief swept away his panic. "Goddlemighty!" he yelped irritably. "That you, Quint? What's the sense in scaring the living daylights out of a fellow? How come you here?"

"I'll ask the questions," Milroy said curtly. "That grub?"

"In the sack. That's right."

"You didn't know I was here? So Jeff didn't send you."

Cairns hesitated. He had to be careful what he said. "I haven't seen Jeff for a while. You expecting a message from him?"

Milroy did not intend to give out information till he knew where Cairns stood. "Why haven't you seen him? Isn't he at the ranch?"

"I reckon he is. I been on the dodge. Humphreys got to crowdin' me, account of my wounding Applegate."

139

That sounded reasonable enough, but there was an unease in the manner of Cairns that told Milroy he was concealing something. He never had trusted the big bully and he was full of doubts now. Was it possible Cairns had turned traitor and was buying his own safety by betraying Quint?

"Where did you get that grub?" Milroy demanded.

"Bought it at the Cross Roads store as I came up. Figured I would hole up here till I could make a getaway." He dallied with the impulse to tell the truth, but decided against it. Milroy evidently still had a tie-up with the Diamond Tail.

Quint pushed his suspicion into the background of his mind. There was nothing at all fishy in the story of Cairns. Yet he meant to be on his guard every minute.

"If you have grub enough for two-three days it will save me a trip to the south boundary cabin," he said. "Since you are here, you had better fix us up some supper."

Milroy mentioned that he was a little short of ammunition and helped himself to a dozen cartridges from his visitor's belt. After he had loaded his revolver, he read a copy of the Redrock *Beacon* the former foreman had brought with him. With one watchful eye on the cook he read the story of the Tucker's Prong battle and an editorial praising Sheriff Humphreys. When Cairns called, "Come and get it," he moved to the table. As they ate they sat opposite each other.

"Seen or heard anything of that fellow Bruce Sherrill?" asked Quint.

"No, and I don't want to," answered Cairns sourly.

His companion's reply was soft but chill. "Different here."

When the meal was over and Cairns had washed the dishes at his host's suggestion, Milroy mentioned that they would have separate bedrooms in order not to disturb each other by snoring. He would stay in the cabin and Bill could choose any place he liked under the starry sky.

Cairns grumbled at this, but did not press the opposition beyond saying that Quint was acting mighty funny. They both kinda had their tails in a crack and had ought to trust each other and pull together.

He picketed his horse at a grassy spot back of the house. For his own sleeping camp he chose a place nearly a quarter of a mile away from the house. He did not know of any reason why Quint should have a chip on his shoulder, but since he felt that way a fellow had better fix it so the killer could not pump lead in him while he slept.

36. Visitors at the Bar B B

ROD WAS SITTING ON THE HOTEL PORCH sunning himself when Tim Humphreys and his wife passed on their way to Sunday School. Randall lifted his hat to the lady and fired an innocent question at her husband.

"What's this I hear about a prisoner walking out on you, sheriff?"

Deacon Humphreys lost his temper and temporarily his religion. "For a thin dime, you blasted scamp, I'd throw you into jail to take Milroy's place," he exploded. "I ought to have known better than to trust a hellion like you out of my sight. I don't know yet how you did it, but I'll find out and when I do——"

Rod was as grave as a judge. "What have I done, sheriff? He was in prison, and I visited him. Isn't that what your Bible teaches you to do?"

Jessie Humphreys giggled at the young man's effrontery. Her husband flung a withering look at her, and decided not to discuss the issue at present with the jaunty reprobate on the porch. He was afraid that if he stayed any longer he would not be in the right frame of mind to teach his Sunday School class.

Randall strolled down to the Elephant corral and hired Prop's flea-bitten gray. As he swung to the saddle he was still smiling at his passage with the sheriff. He did not get many laughs nowadays, and this prison break was a double-jointed joke. One on the sheriff, and one on Milroy when he broke the revolver and found no cartridges in it.

On his way home he turned in at the side road leading to the Bar B B. He wanted to find out how Cliff was getting along and to drop a hint for relay to Sherrill.

A rider cutting across the pasture waved a hand at him. He pulled up to wait for Linda. She had been down to the box to get the mail, she said, and had ridden a few miles farther for the fun of it.

"Have a good ride?" he asked.

After a second's hesitation she told him it had been all right. She did not want to tell him or any of her family that she had met Bill Cairns and had a harrowing experience with him. The last meeting before this one had nearly resulted in the death of her father.

They found a horse tied at the hitch rack in front of the house. Linda recognized the pony and her pulse began to quicken.

"Mr. Bruce Sherrill paying a neighborly call," Rod drawled.

This suited him, since his visit had to do with the owner of the Quartercircle D C.

Cliff Applegate was lying on the sofa in the parlor talking with Bruce when they came into the room. Linda said, her voice casual, "I think you know Rod, Mr. Sherrill."

"We have met," Rod said dryly.

Bruce laughed. "We have what you might call a shooting acquaintance. Every time we meet, his friends are making a target of me."

"Not friends of mine," Rod differed, eying Sherrill with cool insolence. "My friends fight in the open. Not that I'd wear any mourning if one of these brush skunks shot straight for a change."

Cliff Applegate brought his fist down on the seat of a chair standing beside the sofa. "It's time we ran the scoundrels out of the country, Rod. This fight about the fencing is over. We lost it when the government made its decision. These bush-whackers are paying off private grudges. The good citizens of the country won't stand for it. Either these assassins quit or we hunt them down like wolves."

Rod's next remark seemed on the surface to bear no relation to what Applegate had said. "By the way, there was a jailbreak this morning at Redrock," he mentioned.

Though he tossed the news out lightly, all of those present guessed its significance.

"Quint Milroy?" Linda asked.

"Right first time," Rod answered.

Bruce was not much surprised. He had not expected the man to be a prisoner long. "How did he pull it off?" he wanted to know.

"Threw down on Schmidt with a six-shooter when he brought him his breakfast. Somebody must have slipped him a gun. He locked Schmidt up, walked out of the jail, and found a saddled horse waiting for him in some cottonwoods near. Maybe somebody rode in to go to church and just happened to tie it there."

"Five blocks from any church," Bruce commented.

"Same fellow who gave him the gun left the horse," Cliff said with decision. "Whose horse was it?"

"Horse not yet identified." Rod smiled blandly. "Glad I'm in the clear. I dropped in on Quint yesterday to talk over getting him a defense lawyer to fight the silly charge he killed Flack. Humphreys is a suspicious soul. He searched me before he would let me see Quint."

"Surely nobody would suspect you," Bruce said, without a smile.

"Does anybody know where Milroy went after he got away?" Linda asked. "He wouldn't come back here, would he?"

Rod rolled and lit a cigarette. "When I talked with him the day before the getaway, he didn't mention his destination." The dark eyes slanted toward Sherrill. "But he did say something about unfinished business in this district."

A cold wind blew through Linda. "What did he mean?"

"That's anybody's guess," Rod answered. "What do you think he meant, Sherrill?"

"How would I know?" Bruce replied, his gaze locked to that of Randall. "I'm not in his confidence."

"No, I don't suppose you are." The smoker let out a fat smoke wreath and watched it drift to the ceiling, thinning as it moved. "He's a little annoyed at you for some reason. Maybe he doesn't like being slammed over the head with a rifle barrel. Quint is a proud man. Nobody ever got the best of him before. It got under his skin to be lugged off to jail like a drunken cowboy. He doesn't blame Humphreys. That is what a sheriff is paid for." Rod took another drag at the cigarette and said, as if he were meditating aloud, "I don't think I would like to be the man he has it in for."

"If I were the man I would be grateful to the one who had told me," Bruce said carelessly.

"If you were the man," Randall returned, his voice as casual as that of Sherrill, "it would be a good idea to stay under cover until Quint had said a permanent good-bye to this part of the country."

Linda knew that Rod would not take the trouble to warn Bruce unless the danger was urgent. In spite of the fear his information had drummed up in her, the girl wondered at Rod. He had of course contrived to free Milroy, yet he had stopped to get her father to warn Bruce of his peril. The man had unpredictable impulses. She guessed some instinct for fair play in him had been the motive. If he had been a little different—if it had not been for the occasional willful streak of ruthlessness in him, she might have fallen in love with him.

Instead, she had given her heart to this man who had been an enemy of them all. The two men were much alike. Both were strong and fearless and independent. Each followed his own way of life with little regard to what others thought. Neither of them was cut to a pattern. But there was one essential difference. In spite of his recklessness Bruce was dependable, knew right from wrong and made the better choice.

Bruce rose and said he must be going.

"I'll ride with you far as the junction," Rod suggested.

Cliff would not hear of it. "You'll both stay for supper."

While they ate, Cliff proposed that Sherrill remain at the Bar B B for a few days and help with the stock. One of the boys could ride over and tell Ramrod he would not be home.

Bruce shook his head. He was sorry, but he had to get back to the ranch. He had ridden over to find out how Applegate was getting along, but just now they were too busy at the Quartercircle D C for him to be gone long.

This was the answer Linda had expected, but she could not let it rest as final. She made a chance to be with him alone.

"Why don't you stay with us?" she asked. "You know Rod wouldn't have said what he did if he weren't sure this Milroy means to kill you."

" 'The best-laid schemes o' mice and men gang aft a-gley,' " he quoted. "Milroy is just a man, the same as I am."

"He's a terrible man. He won't give you a chance. If you stayed here you would be safe."

"Safe and shamed," he said.

She flung up a hand in a small gesture of impatient despair. "You men are all alike. As if you were little boys being egged on to fight. You are afraid someone will think you afraid."

"Maybe," he agreed. "But I can't skulk here in hiding from any man and keep my self-respect."

"Why not?" she urged. "You have given proof you are not a coward. To set yourself up for a mark to be shot from ambush isn't bravery. It's foolhardiness."

"What would you think of your brother Brand if he crept into a hole because somebody thought perhaps a desperado was looking for him?"

"There isn't any perhaps about this, Bruce. Milroy told Tim Humphreys he would get you soon as he was free. He must have told Rod that too. They say he has killed a dozen men. He'll sneak up on you like an Indian. Don't go and let yourself be killed."

They were standing on a vine-covered porch in the vague light of those few minutes when dusk is giving way to darkness. The fine planes of her face, the fear in the dark shadowed eyes, gave her the ethereal look that in the semi-darkness sometimes make even a plain woman beautiful. And Linda had never been to him anything but lovely. He had an absurd conviction that if he held her close, if he kissed those tremulous lips, their souls would fuse and become spiritually one.

"I'm not going to be killed," he promised. "I never had as much to live for as now."

His hand found hers in pledge of what he said, and the pulse of her fingertips went through him like a drink of strong wine. The throbbing life in them was a symbol of the vitality of her slim warm body and vivid personality. He could remember afterward that when he drew her to him she gave a little contented sigh as her arms went around his neck.

It might have been a minute later, it might have been ten, when young Cliff's voice brought them back to earth.

"Where is Sherrill at?" he asked. "Rod is ready to go."

His father answered, "He and Lindy stepped out somewhere."

144

Still in her lover's arms, Linda whispered quickly, "You won't go now."

"I've got to go," he told her.

"Not now that we have just found each other," she pleaded.

"I don't like it, but this is the way it has to be. I'll be careful. You needn't worry."

Her fingers bit into his arms. "I won't have it," she cried softly, passion in her voice. "You can't go. It's senseless—and insane. All he has to do is wait in the brush and shoot you."

"I'll be watching for him every minute."

"I thought you loved me," she protested. "If you do, you are part of my life. I have a right to help decide what you will do."

"Even you can't come between me and what I think right," he told her, his low words asking for understanding.

Her fear was accented by what she had gone through a few hours earlier. "Listen, Bruce," she urged. "I didn't mean to tell you, but I must. This afternoon I met Bill Cairns on the ridge above the south line of the Diamond Tail. He raised his rifle to kill me—and didn't fire because he was afraid I wasn't alone. I told him my brothers were just over the hill gathering strays. That saved my life. But nothing would save yours if Milroy got the drop on you."

He stared at her, greatly disturbed. "He must have been bluffing, unless he has gone mad. Why in God's name would he hurt you?"

"I don't know why, except that Father and Brand gave him a terrible beating. But he wasn't bluffing. I read murder in his awful face."

He could feel her body trembling in his arms.

"Don't ever leave the ranch until I've settled with him," he ordered hoarsely. "Stay near the house. Never go riding."

"I won't, if you'll stay here too until Milroy is captured."

"I can't do that. Don't you see I can't, Linda? No use talking. I've got to go."

Her anxiety, the futility of its demand, broke loose in anger. "I'm to do as you order, but it doesn't matter how much I worry when your silly pride tells you to go out and be murdered."

She walked down the porch and into the house. Without a moment's hesitation Sherrill repeated to her father what Linda had told him of her afternoon's danger. He could feel the girl's anger beating on him for the betrayal of her confidence.

"You knew it was a secret," she said in hot scorn.

The shocked horror of Applegate found a vent in temper. "A secret when a villain threatens your life! Are you crazy, girl? It's our business to see he never gets another chance. It would have been a fine how-d'ye-do if Bruce had left without warning us."

After Rod and Bruce had gone, Linda turned on her father, a stormy challenge in her eyes.

"I suppose you think it's right for him to strut around and get killed and wrong for me to stick my nose out of the house," she cried.

Cliff looked at her gravely. He guessed her emotions were involved and wondered how deeply.

"Sherrill is a man and you're a girl. He has to play his cards the way they are dealt. Out in this country a man has to fight his own battles. He can't call in the police to protect him. With a woman it is different. It's our job to see she is safe."

Linda went upstairs to her room, bitterly resentful. A woman was of no importance. She must take orders like a forty-dollar-a-month cowboy. If she married, she must be her husband's slave for life. When he came home, having nothing more interesting to do at the moment, she must be a good contented squaw and meet him with a smiling face. He would let her make decisions about when to set the hens and buying a new dress. But if it was anything that counted, his will must be law.

She paced the room, eyes bleak and heart troubled. Her distress lay far deeper than her anger, which was for the hour only and not too serious. Not long ago she had argued with Rod that when a woman loved a man she must make him see what was right to do. Now she realized that she could not be a conscience for Bruce Sherrill any more than for Rod Randall. A strong man would be guided by his own code and standards, not by hers.

And as she thought it out, she discovered that did not matter vitally, if the principle that governed him was decent and honest. She would have to trust her husband's integrity. The real ache in her heart was the fear that she might never see him again alive. Somewhere she had read that to part is to die a little. How true that was if the parting was with somebody one loved as wildly as she did Bruce! For the first time she understood how the women in the Civil War days must have felt when their lovers and husbands went gaily to the battlefields.

37. Rod Finds a Charred Envelope

BRUCE SHERRILL AND ROD RANDALL jogged down the valley not too comfortable in each other's society. They had been enemies and still felt a sharp animosity. Scarcely more than a month ago Rod had warned Bruce to mend his ways or be shot. But since that time the feud had been stopped by the intervention of the government. Though they would probably never be friends, in their feeling was a mutual substratum of respect and even admiration.

Upon one subject they were agreed. Bill Cairns must be run out of the country or killed. Neither of them was sure that he had really intended to shoot Linda. He was a bully who liked to see others afraid of him. He might have been trying only to frighten her. Since he had evened the score with her father by wounding him, there did not seem to be any point in the wanton murder of Cliff's daughter. But whatever his intention it would not do to let him ride around terrifying women.

At the Cross Roads they separated, Bruce to take the foothill trail and Rod to continue to the Diamond Tail.

Rod noticed there was no light in the office of his father. Usually the old man spent his evenings there working out his accounts. When Ned came out of the house to meet his brother, Rod flung at him a careless question.

"Where's the old man?"

Ned explained that he had ridden down to the south boundary cabin in the morning with a sack of provisions and that he ought to have been back before supper, but had not arrived. It was odd, Rod thought, that his father had taken the supplies himself instead of sending one of the riders. It might be because he wanted to get away from the house, where he could see his men tearing down the wire on the government land above the valley. To see this tangible evidence of his defeat galled the stiff old-timer's pride.

Out of the gloom a saddled horse without a rider moved toward them.

"It's Nig!" Ned cried. "Father was riding him."

He ran forward and caught the bridle of the horse. To quiet the animal he laid a hand on its neck in reassurance. The boy looked at his hand, eyes dilated. There was blood on the palm and fingers. He stared at his brother, the heart pounding fast against his ribs.

"There has been an accident," he said, with a catch in his throat.

Rod's mind worked in flashes. This was no accident. If his father had been flung from the horse there would be no blood on Nig's neck. What he saw in imagination was old Jeff shot in the saddle, probably in the head. His body must have fallen forward, face against his mount.

The older brother snapped out crisp orders. "Tell Yorky and Cash to saddle for a ride. Have Bud hitch the wagon, and put some straw in the bed, and drive to the south boundary cabin. Say for them to be quiet about it. We don't want to worry Mary till it is necessary."

147

Ned got a six-shooter from the house and saddled a pony for himself. His brother made no objection. In a few minutes they were on their way. Bud would follow with the wagon.

They found Jeff Randall's body lying in the dust outside the cabin. He had been shot through the forehead just above the eyes. There was a second wound in the body, from a revolver fired at close quarters into the heart. He had been dead a good many hours.

Yorky lit a lamp in the cabin and the brothers carried the body inside and put it on a cot. Ned covered the face with a handkerchief.

The hut was one used by line riders caught by night too far from the ranch. It was kept stocked with provisions for them. Somebody had eaten a meal there that day. Unwashed dishes and scraps of food littered the table. On the stove were a greasy fry-pan and a coffee pot half filled.

"Father must have fixed him a dinner," Ned said.

"Not Father, somebody else," Rod differed. "The man who ate here saw him coming and killed him before he got off his horse."

Ned, white-faced and shaken, looked at his brother. "While I was driving the calves up this morning I saw a fellow riding across the pasture. The horse was a bay. It was heading this way."

"Could you tell who the man was?"

"No. Too far away. I kinda thought the horse was one I knew. But I guess not." He would have said more, but his brother was not listening.

Rod had picked up a paper, burnt at one end. It was part of an envelope twisted into a spill, no doubt to light a pipe. Part of the address was still on the charred paper, the letters at the right-hand side.

> ns,
>   nch,
>   oads,
>   ming.

The young man frowned down at the scrap of writing, trying to complete the words. "Someone on a ranch who gets his mail at Cross Roads," he murmured. "What ranch, do you reckon? Might be ours."

Ned peered around his shoulder. "One of our boys might of left it a week ago."

"Yeah, so he might." Rod spoke slowly, thinking aloud. "Or the killer might have left it today. Dick Spears slept out here night before last. You know how neat he is—always cleaning up before he leaves." A startled look jumped to Rod's face. The letters had made words in his mind. "Whose horse was it you thought was crossing the pastures?" he asked.

"I sort of thought for a minute it was that big bay of Bill Cairns'," Ned replied. "But I might easy have been wrong."

"You weren't wrong," Rod told him, his face harsh and grim. "The man was Cairns, and the murdering fool has left his calling card to tell us he was here." From his pocket Rod took a letter, and on the back of the envelope wrote an address:

Mr. William Cairns,
Diamond Tail Ranch,
Cross Roads,
Wyoming.

Cairns had probably lit the spill after he had eaten, before the arrival of Jeff. He had stamped it out and dropped it. At that time it did not matter whether anybody knew he had stopped here for a meal. The custom of the country was that a traveler helped himself to food at a line cabin and chopped enough wood to replace what he had used.

But after Cairns had shot the ranchman from his horse, it became vitally important nobody should know he had been in the neighborhood. Rod had no doubt that the fellow had been in a panic to get away without being seen. The charred spill escaped his mind entirely.

The gunny sack with the provisions had vanished. The killer must have taken it with him. If he was getting out of the country he would want to travel light, yet have supplies enough to get him far out of the district without having to ask for food at a ranch house. He might strike south for Colorado, but Rod did not think he would head for a fairly thickly settled farming country. More likely he would try to reach the Hole-in-the-Wall where a nomadic population of outlaws still skulked between raids in unknown mountain pockets. A fugitive could lead a furtive life there for months untouched by the law.

Rod knew now that Linda had not exaggerated the danger when she met Cairns. He had wanted to kill her because he had not dared to let her stay alive, a witness who would testify he had been on the spot where the murder was committed. Only the girl's quick wit had saved her. Everybody knew that Linda sometimes rode with her brothers after stock. If they were near he dared not shoot.

After Bud arrived with the wagon, they took the body of the ranchman back to the Diamond Tail. Rod sent riders to the adjoining spreads with the news of the crime. He did not wait for the sheriff, but armed and saddled his men as quickly as he could. His mind was made up to shoot Cairns down as soon as he could find the ruffian.

Before they started, Mary brought out to Rod a note she had found in the coat pocket of her husband. Evidently it had been left by a messenger. It read:

Jeff, I'll be at the old Renaud cabin tonight. Bring me grub and cartridges for my .45. Do this yourself or send Rod. If you can't make it to Renaud's leave the stuff at the south boundary cabin. Keep mum about my being here. I am not forgetting the job you want done. Burn this.

Quint.

This was the explanation, of course, for old Jeff's trip to the line cabin. Rod had another angle in the tragedy to worry over. Had Quint Milroy been a party to the killing? If so, by setting the killer free, Rod had helped seal his father's doom. The note might have been a decoy. He could not see what Milroy had to gain by the death of a man bringing him food to assist in his escape, but there might be factors in this Rod did not know.

He was inclined to acquit Milroy of complicity. Since his father had wanted to get food to the man, he felt he ought to carry out the old man's wishes. Rod decided to take some to the Renaud cabin himself and have a talk with Milroy. That might clear his mind as to the fellow's guilt. It had been fifteen years since his father had shown him Renaud's Roost while they had been hunting. It was in a wild and not easily accessible region, but he felt sure he could find the place again.

As Rod rode into the hills with his men, a sentence in Quint's note jumped more than once to mind. *I'm not forgetting the job you want done.* He wished he could forget that. It was not a pleasant memory of his vindictive father to carry through the years. Rod was quite sure he knew what the job was.

38. At the Old Trapper's Cabin

BRUCE HAD NOT BEEN ASLEEP AN HOUR when he was awakened by the barking of the dogs and the voice of somebody outside calling to him. Through the window he saw a man on horseback, who turned out to be Dick Spears from the Diamond Tail. He was rousing the settlers on the creek to tell them to be on the alert for Bill Cairns who had murdered Jeff Randall at the south boundary cabin. The cowpuncher brought a special message from Rod to Bruce. It was that the killing must have occurred just before Cairns met Linda on the ledge above the cabin. Bruce drew the same deduction that Randall had. Linda had missed death by a hair's breadth. The miscreant had been afraid the sound of a shot would bring her brothers over the hill to avenge her.

"Rod thinks Cairns will make for the Hole-in-the-Wall," Dick explained. "We're combing Squaw Creek and the country north of here. He thought you might cover Bear and its headwaters. Bill took enough grub from the cabin to last him several days."

The assignment suited Bruce. He decided to take Mark and Neal with him, leaving Ramrod at the ranch. While they were loading a pack animal with supplies, he consulted with the old-timer as to where the fugitive was likely to hole up. Ramrod thought that was anybody's guess. The fellow might have got over the passes already, or he might be lying low until the hunt for him spent itself. If he had crossed the divide, it would be up to Humphreys and other sheriffs to cut off his retreat, but if he was still on this slope there was a good chance of one of the posses jumping him up. He would have to be within reach of water, and in a place where he could find concealment for his horse. The foreman suggested several spots for a camper on the dodge, among others Renaud's Roost.

Bruce had heard of the old cabin, but did not know exactly where it was. On a piece of wrapping paper Ramrod drew a map for him. When he reached the fork he was to follow the branch known as Sunk Creek till he came to a small park into which a grove of aspens ran down from a draw at the northeast corner. This draw led to a walled cañon. Near the upper end of the gorge was a break in the south wall. If he followed this defile it would bring him to a rough region of wild and rocky scarps. He would see three bunched pines standing alone to the left of the rim. The cabin was in a hollow back of them. Ramrod had never been there but once, and then he had been guided to the spot by Cairns, who had mentioned casually that it would be a good hide-out for a fellow in a jam.

Though there was no chance of running across Cairns during the night, the Quartercircle D C men traveled for hours, working deeper into the high hills back of the ranch country. There was a sliver of a moon, and the stars were out. Even in the rough country over which they moved, the ponies were surefooted as cats.

About three o'clock Bruce called a halt. They lit a fire, thawed out, and rolled up in their blankets. When they awoke, the sky was lightening with the promise of coming day.

Bruce thought there was only a slender chance of finding the hunted man at Renaud's Roost, but he felt he ought to check on the place rather than by-pass it. He left the two cowboys, arranging to meet them later near the headwaters of Bear Creek. Neal suggested that perhaps he ought to go with Sherrill, but Bruce vetoed the offer. He did not think two men ought to waste hours on a detour of so little promise.

He struck Sunk Creek at the fork and followed its winding course through the hills to a grassy meadow from the yonder end of which aspens marched up a gulch to the rim. He skirted the edge of the grove and rode into a box cañon. It brought him to a gorge that slashed through the south wall to the floor of the ravine. Up to this point in the journey Ramrod's memory had served him perfectly.

The gorge was steep and narrow. Its bed was filled with rubble and with boulders flung from above through many centuries. He emerged at the upper entrance, to see in one sweeping glance a tangle of tossed-up hills in the hollows of which a hundred men might have hidden. The three twisted pines Ramrod had promised were bunched on the rim of the mesa a few hundred yards from him.

To one of the pines he tied his horse. From the rim he looked down into a pocket out of which ran four or five draws. A small stream from the mesa watered it and disappeared in one of the outlets. On the bank of the brook was an old log cabin. Screened by bushes, Bruce watched that cabin and its surroundings for several minutes. He could see no sign of occupancy.

In the near end of the cabin there was no window. Bruce moved down cautiously, keeping to the fringe of bushes bordering the stream. A man in the house could not see him unless he came to the door and looked up the creek. If anybody had appeared in the doorway, Bruce would have been greatly surprised. His opinion was that there was not another human being within miles of him.

Yet he did not take a step without scanning the terrain closely. Though he was coming up on the blind side of the shack, Cairns might be crouched back of the sagging door watching him through the wide crack between it and the jamb from which the hinge had broken loose. He covered the dozen yards between the creek and the blank wall at a run. When he peered around the corner there was still no movement about the place. On tiptoe he stepped forward and crouched back of the rotting door. A moment later he was inside the cabin. Nobody else was in the room.

But what he saw startled him. On the home-made table were cans of tomatoes, a slab of bacon, a package of Arbuckle's, and a small sack of flour. A skillet and a can with coffee grounds in it stood on the chimney hearth. The ashes in the fireplace were cold. Whoever was staying here had not yet breakfasted this morning. But it was an easy guess that the owner of the provisions would be back soon. He took a step toward the door—and stopped abruptly. Somewhere in the stretch of space outside a pistol shot rang out, and two more before the sound of it had died.

39. Man-Stalking

HALF AN HOUR before Bruce reached Renaud's Roost a man came out of a draw and walked toward the cabin with breakfast in mind. The man was Bill Cairns. He stopped abruptly. His eye had fallen on a horseman coming down from the rim. Quickly he ducked back into the land fold from which he had emerged. The one man in the world he least wanted to meet was Rod Randall.

A hideous fear welled up in him. He was trapped. His horse was picketed back of the cabin, and he could not reach it without being seen. A fugitive afoot in this wild country was as good as dead. He did not know what had brought Randall straight to the spot where he was hiding, but it was sure that he would not be in the hut three minutes without learning from Milroy that Cairns was here. His best chance was to get Rod now, while he was not expecting trouble. It took all the nerve he had to announce his presence, even by a shot from ambush. If he missed, that young devil Randall would probably succeed in rubbing him out.

Rifle in hand, he came out of the draw to try his luck. The distance was about two hundred yards. Rod had dismounted and grounded his reins. He was moving toward the house. Milroy was in the doorway, and they stood talking for a moment.

Cairns tried to steady his shaken nerves, but as soon as he had pulled the trigger he knew that he had failed. At sound of the shot Rod bolted into the cabin. Cairns turned to run.

Milroy and Randall looked at each other.

"Must be Bill Cairns," Milroy said. "But why? What has he got against you?"

"Don't you know why?" Rod asked, with steady, accusing eyes.

"How would I know?" Milroy asked. "I haven't seen anybody to talk to except you since I was locked up."

"When did Cairns get here?"

"Last night. I somehow mistrusted him and wouldn't let him sleep in here."

"He didn't tell you that he had killed my father?"

The amazed look on the desperado's face gave him a verdict of acquittal from Rod. "He told me he had not seen Jeff for days, that he was on the dodge account of wounding Applegate."

153

"I had Father kick him out. He has been lying around drunk ever since. Yesterday he killed Father at the south boundary cabin when he took a load of food there for you."

Milroy came clean. "I sent a note to Jeff by Dick Spears. Asked him to get me food and send it either here or to the line cabin." In the bleached narrowed eyes of the bad man was a hard glitter. "Who told Bill Cairns your father might be at the line cabin?"

"I think Cairns was riding the chuck line," Rod answered. "He knew there was always some food there and figured he could bum a few meals." The young man brushed aside explanations. He had a job to do. "I've got to see he never gets away from here alive."

"I'm with you," Milroy said. He did not mention that by killing the boss of the Diamond Tail Cairns had robbed him of five hundred dollars he had expected to collect from Randall for destroying Bruce Sherrill. "His horse is picketed near here. Bill has to have it for a getaway. He will sure make a break for it, and he dare not wait long."

They decided that they would move their own horses to the spot where Cairns had left his mount and that Rod would wait to cut him off when the man appeared. Milroy was to swing around behind the fugitive and drive him forward from his cover. Cairns would reason that the two men had come out to hunt him and he would attempt to reach his horse. It was his one chance of escape.

"Your forty-five loaded?" Rod asked.

Milroy remembered the trick Rod had played on him when he brought the pistol, but that was water under a bridge now. "With Bill's bullets," the desperado said grimly. "Nice if I can give one of them back to him."

Rod frowned. He did not like this set-up. There was a faint lingering doubt of Milroy in his mind. He might go out to find Cairns and throw in with him. But if he was on the level with Rod, a six-shooter was no weapon with which to go hunting a desperate man with a rifle. Yet the spot where the horses were picketed was the focal one. Randall did not intend to leave it.

"You'd stand a fat chance against a Winchester with a forty-five," he suggested.

"He won't even see me if this works out right," Milroy said. "All I need to do is to fire a couple of shots from cover and push him back this way. You're the one entitled to rub him out, not me."

Rod could not think of a better plan than the one they had made and he let it go as arranged. He waited in the brush forty or fifty feet away from the place where the nearest horse was picketed. As long as he had the three mounts in sight, Cairns was tied to the neighborhood.

154

Milroy crept up the creek, making the most of the willows and the wild plum trees that grew on the banks. Unless Cairns exposed himself at the entrance of the hill fold where he was hiding, he could not see the stream, and Quint's judgment was that the man he stalked would keep out of sight as long as he could. The gunman stayed with the stream till it left the valley and cut into the hills.

He left the brook, to take a fold that led to a clump of aspens above. These he skirted to a rise from which he could look down on another dip. On the opposite slope of this were more aspens. He watched them, patient as an Indian, and observed a shivering of the branches more sharp than that made by the breeze. Somebody was crawling through the young trees.

Presently his keen eyes focused on a moving object. The distance was about a hundred yards. He took aim with his forty-five and fired, with no expectation of scoring a hit. The foliage of the aspens was violently agitated. He fired two more shots. Cairns broke from cover, appeared for a moment silhouetted against the skyline, and disappeared over the brow. Milroy charged down the slope in pursuit and up the hill on the yonder side. From the top his glance swept the panorama below. He saw Cairns running toward the hollow where the horses were picketed.

Rod's voice came to him sharp and clear, from too great a distance for the words to reach him. Cairns fired. There came an answering shot from Rod. The hunted man dropped into a gully and raced for the house, evidently with the idea of holding it against attack. He reached the cabin.

What occurred then was a total surprise to Milroy. Cairns stopped, abruptly as if the loop of a rope had pulled him up. He flung up his rifle and fired. Quint knew there must be a fourth man in the Roost.

40. "Both of Them Are Better Dead"

THE SOUND OF THE PISTOL SHOTS held Bruce frozen for a moment, so unexpectedly had they broken the deep silence. He stepped to the door and looked in the direction from which he thought they had come. In the pleasant sunshine the scene was peaceful as Eden before the serpent incident. A meadow lark on the branch of a willow lifted its head and flung out a full-throated burst of joy. Yet with the sixth sense that men who lived on the frontier sometimes acquired Bruce knew there was something sinister in those three tightly packed shots.

His rifle he laid against the door jamb. He did not want to

be hampered with it if trouble came quickly at close quarters. He did not draw his revolver yet, but the thumb hitched in the sagging belt was scarcely four inches from the butt of the weapon projecting from the pocket of his chaps.

The landscape looked as deserted as when he had arrived. He walked as far as the corner of the hut, to sweep with his eyes the view from that side of the house. What the shooting was about he did not know, but for the present he meant not to venture farther from the cabin. Cairns might not be alone, and in case of attack he might need a fort of refuge.

Once more the stillness was shattered, this time by the whip-like reports of two rifles much nearer than the pistol shots had been. He heard the slap of running feet coming toward the house.

Bill Cairns burst round the corner of the shack and stopped with shocked alarm at sight of him. The killer could not take time to aim. He jerked up his rifle and fired, almost from the hip. A fraction of a second later a revolver slug slammed into his belly. The big man gave a great gasp of pain. He half-lifted the Winchester for another shot, but a second bullet tore through this throat. The weapon clattered to the ground. The spread fingers of Cairns's hairy hands pressed in against his stomach. He lurched forward a step or two before the hinges of his knees gave way and let the heavy body slump to the ground.

Bruce watched him, not moving from where he stood. A trickle of smoke rose from the barrel of the revolver in his hand. During the past brief seconds there had been no time for fear. Every sense had been keyed to intense concentration. He had to kill or be killed. But as he looked at the sprawled body, a moment ago filled with malevolent life and now stilled forever, a kind of horror grew in him. By no desire of his own a crook of his finger had destroyed a human being. He had neither remorse nor regret, only a feeling of dismay that some quirk of fate had made his the hand to put an end to this evil force.

The pure sharp song of the meadow lark lifted again.

He became aware of somebody moving through the brush a hundred yards from the cabin. As the crouched figure crossed an open spot he recognized Rod Randall.

Bruce shouted his name, and Rod came forward. He looked at the prone body and then at Sherrill.

"So you got him," he said.

"He didn't have a chance," Bruce explained. "When he showed up round the corner he wasn't expecting me. It startled him, and he fired too fast."

Rod looked down again at the outstretched figure. "Both your shots were bull's-eyes." On his grim face a sardonic smile showed. "Might have been me instead of him, the way I felt

156

about you a month ago. It's a damned uncertain world. Then you were an infernal nuisance. Now you'll be the boy for this country's money. I'll say this, Sherrill. You're turning out quite a lad."

"Because I was forced in self-defense to kill a murderer?" Bruce shook his head. "Nothing to be proud of in that. I wish you had done it."

"I wish so too. I had a crack at him and missed. You landed solid both times. How in Mexico did you happen to show up here?"

Bruce explained. Before he had finished Rod interrupted. "Hell's bells! I had forgotten. You had better light a shuck out of here, Sherrill. Quint Milroy is just over the hill."

"You're not kidding?" Bruce looked at him sharply.

"No. That's why I'm here. To bring him grub."

"Yes." Bruce spoke after a moment's thought. "I'd better go."

"Unless you would like to turn hunter." There was in Rod's eyes a gleam of impish mirth. "He has only a forty-five, and if you're careful you can pick him off with a rifle at no risk."

Coldly, Bruce replied, "I'm not a murderer."

"He'd get you any way he could," Rod mentioned.

"He would. You wouldn't." Bruce spoke harshly.

Rod laughed. "All right. I didn't expect you to take good advice. Better be hitting the trail sudden, fellow."

"My horse is back on the rim," Bruce said.

"If you hurry he won't know who was here until you've gone. Dust along."

Bruce showed no signs of haste, perhaps because the desire to get away fast was so strong in him. It hurt his pride to run away from any man, even though he knew that a pistol duel with Milroy was as unfair as it would be for him to shoot down the other with his rifle. He counted himself a good shot, better than average, but he had never known anybody else who possessed the swift deadly accuracy with a revolver Milroy was reputed to have.

"Get going, you lunkhead," Rod snapped. "He'll be here soon."

"Be seeing you," Bruce said.

He retrieved his rifle and walked back to the fringe of bushes along the creek. By keeping close to the shrubbery he might reach the rim without being seen. There was one stretch of about forty yards where he would have to come into the open, but by that time he would be near enough to his horse to reach it in spite of Milroy if the man appeared in the pocket.

On the rim a wind was blowing. It picked up the dust of disintegrated sandstone and swept it across the bluff in a small cloud. Bruce looked across at the three twisted pines. A warning stirred in him sharply. Back of the trunk of one was something that had not been there thirty minutes ago. He stopped, the rifle half-raised.

The blast of a forty-five sounded, and the hat was lifted from his head. His heart began to pound. There was a tightness in his chest. He felt the icy crawling of fear along his spine. Quint Milroy was here before him.

From that first bullet the distance and the wind had saved Bruce. Before he could move, a second slug struck the rifle barrel and glanced off in ricochet. A cold anger brushed away all fear and scruples. Milroy was an assassin trying to ambush him, a desperado entitled to no more consideration than an Apache in covered-wagon days. He raised his rifle, took deliberate aim at the crouched figure, and fired.

That he had hit his foe Bruce knew, but the chances were that the wound was not a fatal one. He drew back a dozen yards to be out of range and made a half-circuit of the pines, watching the center of the circle every foot of the way.

Milroy broke from cover, reached the horse, pulled the slipknot, and swung to the saddle. He fired, body bent low, just before he jumped the cowpony to a gallop. He headed straight for Sherrill, evidently aware that if he tried to escape he would be a mark too plain for a good rifleman to miss. As he charged, his revolver barked again.

The man was less than twenty yards from Bruce when the rifle bullet tore through him. His body slumped. The frightened horse swung away at a sharp angle and the rider pitched out of the saddle at the feet of Bruce. The fall jerked the weapon from the slack fingers of its owner. The glaze of death was already in the eyes of Milroy. He gave a strangled cough, and his frame shrank in collapse. The killer had gone out to the sound of roaring guns, as so many of his victims had done.

Bruce followed his horse down into the pocket and found that Rod had caught the animal.

"You killed Milroy?" Randall asked.

"Yes." Bruce had fought down the wave of sickness that swept him after the battle. "I saw him back of one of the pines. He had to try a long shot, and the wind was blowing. He knocked my hat off. I wounded him with a rifle shot and circled around to get him from behind. He made a break for it on my horse—came right at me, his gun blazing. I couldn't miss."

"Both of them are better dead," Rod said bluntly.

"Maybe," Bruce agreed bitterly. "But who am I to play at God and decide that?"

Rod grinned. "For a tough hard rannyhan you're too soft, fellow. They both asked for what they got. What else would you figure on doing when a pair of wolves start for you?"

Bruce had no answer for that, but he knew that what he had done made him heartsick and wretched.

41. The Quartercircle D C Finds a Mistress

ROD RODE OVER TO THE BAR BB with Bruce. The story of what had occurred at Renaud's cabin had preceded them. For the first time the voice of Cliff Applegate was warm when he spoke to his neighbor of the Quartercircle D C.

"What in Mexico you trying to do, son?" he asked. "Clean up all the riffraff so the sheriff won't have anything to do but sit on his behind?"

"I hope to God I'm through forever," Bruce said fervently. "They came at me smoking, and nothing but gilt-edged luck brought me through."

Linda had just come into the room. "Or Providence," she amended. "Maybe God thought it was time for them to die."

Their eyes met. They had things to say to each other that could not be said before an audience.

"Who wants to ride down and get the mail with me?" she asked a few minutes later.

Rod jumped up, mischief in his eyes. "You're speaking to me, Lindy?"

"I want to talk with you about yore plans for the Diamond Tail, Rod," Cliff interposed. "Is Mary expecting to stay there with the children after the funeral?"

"Sure. It's their home. I reckon I'll run the ranch." Rod waved a hand at Linda. "If you ask him pretty please maybe you can get Bill Hickok here to ride down with you."

"I'll do the asking," Bruce said. "Miss Linda, will you—?"

"Yes," she interrupted.

Rod looked up at the ceiling innocently and began to hum "Here comes the bride——"

"Oh you!" Linda scolded, her cheeks a deep pink.

After they were on their way to the mail box, Bruce mentioned that it was nice of Rod to propose for him.

"I thought you had already proposed," Linda said happily.

"So I did, but it didn't turn out a very good job. If you remember, I was in the doghouse before I left."

"Maybe we had better start all over again."

"I think so." The road had dipped into a hollow through which a small stream ran past a clump of cottonwoods. He pulled up his horse, dismounted, and lifted her from the saddle. "How do you think this place will do?" he asked.

"Any place that suits my lord will do," she murmured.

"Hmp! That sounds to me. I'll probably be the most hen-pecked husband in the county."

If he thought so it did not seem to worry him much. After much warfare and many troubled days, they had come together at last, and out of this nettle danger they had plucked something much dearer than safety.

CLATTERING HOOFS

Contents

1 A Hostage for Pablo

Sandra sat at the table making out a list of groceries to be bought for the ranch. Later in the day she and her brother Nelson would drive over to the cross-road store and get them.

"The sugar is plumb out too, Miss Sandra, an' in two-three days I'll be scrapin' the bottom of the flour barrel," Jim Budd said. "Beats all what a lot of eatin' is done on this here ranch."

"When the wagon goes tomorrow it can pick up the flour," Sandra decided. "We can bring the other supplies. You haven't forgotten anything?"

"I disremember havin' forgot a thing," Jim replied, and flashed a set of shining teeth in a face black as the ace of spades. The huge cook found it easy to grin at his young mistress. He thought her the loveliest human under heaven, and he adored her. In his warped life few people had been kind to him. At the Circle J R ranch he had found a home.

Into the kitchen burst a redheaded boy, eyes popping with excitement. "You know what, sis?" he cried. "They've just brought in Rod Spillman. He's been shot."

Sandra stared at her brother, the grocery list banished from her mind. After a moment of shocked silence she asked a question. "Who shot him?"

Nelson shook his head. "I dunno. They're taking him into the bunkhouse. Wouldn't let me see him. Told me to scat."

The girl ran out to the porch. She moved with the light grace of youth and perfect health. From the bunkhouse a man walked toward the stable. Sandra intercepted him.

"Buck, is it true about Rod?" she asked.

The cowpuncher stopped. "Yes'm. They sure enough got him."

"You mean he's . . . dead?"

"That's right. We found him near the mouth of French Gulch."

"Who did it?"

"Rustlers. We dunno who for certain. They run off a bunch of our beef stuff. Looks like Rod must of bumped into them while they were making the gather."

John Ranger stepped from his office to the porch. He carried a rifle in his hand. "Hustle up the mounts, Buck," he ordered. "We want to get started."

"You are taking out after the men who killed Rod?" his daughter asked after she had joined him.

"Yes. The boys are notifying the neighbors. We're meeting at Blunt's."

"Buck says you don't know who did it."

"We think it was Scarface and his gang. They were seen last night in the valley."

"You'll be careful, Father."

Ranger was a large hard-muscled man who looked able to take care of himself. "Don't worry about me," he said. "Those scoundrels aren't fighting. They are running."

"Is there anything I can do, Father?"

"Not a thing, honey. It's a bad business. They must have shot Rod so he couldn't tell who they were."

Five minutes later the owner of the J R and three of his men cantered down the road, leaving a cloud of dust in their wake.

Though still under nineteen, Sandra had managed the house since the death of her mother two years before. Her slim body looked slight, but there was in her a toughness of fiber given by life on the frontier and the responsibilities it had thrust upon her. The death of Rod shocked her, yet she did not let it interfere with the work of the house. By the time she had changed the bed linen and swept the rooms Jim Budd had dinner ready.

"When do we start for the store?" Nelson asked her as he finished a second helping of rice pudding.

"As soon as you have hitched up Chance to the buggy," she told him. "I promised to stop and see Elvira on my way back."

"Good. Mebbe we'll hear at Blunt's whether they have caught the rustlers."

They took the short cut through the brush, following a trail just wide enough for the buggy. Shoots of mesquite and cactus slapped at the wheels. The girl had chosen this road to escape the clouds of yellow dust that travel on the main highway would stir up.

Chance was a short-coupled, round-bellied buckskin with no ambition to break records. He preferred to walk, but when Nelson tickled his flank with the whip he would reluctantly break into a slow trot.

At Bitter Wells they met a horseman, Miguel Torres, a middle-aged Mexican who owned a ranch in the vicinity. He had been their neighbor ever since they could remember, and Nelson pulled up to exchange news of the pursuit of the rustlers.

The road dipped to the flats, and for the next mile they moved along a jungle of cholla, prickly pear, and occasional

8

huisaches. Cattle runs cut through here and there. Once they crossed a dry wash of burning sand over which heat shimmered.

Four Mexicans rode out of the brush and drew up on the road in front of them, evidently to discuss the direction they wanted to follow. They wore the tight trousers, sombreros, and short decorated vests of vaqueros in their native land. One of them caught sight of the buggy and raised a shout.

Sandra did not know the men, but at first she was not at all alarmed. She had been brought up in a land where there were many Mexicans, and she knew them for a gentle friendly race. These riders were armed with rifles. It occurred to her they might be a detachment looking for the rustlers.

They pounded toward the buggy at a gallop and dragged their mounts to a halt.

"Oho!" one of them cried in Spanish. "We have flushed a plump little quail in the desert."

Both Sandra and her brother were frightened. These men were a villainous-looking lot, and their mocking laughter was not reassuring.

"What do you want?" Nelson demanded. "John Ranger is our father. Please get out of the road and let us go on."

"So you are children of the great John Ranger," a bearded ruffian said. "That is good. Pablo will like that. He will keep you for hostages."

It came to Sandra that he meant Pablo Lopez, the notorious bandit whose name was a terror to the border. He lived in Sonora, but several times his band had swept into Arizona to burn and pillage ranches and to drive cattle across the line.

"If you will let us go my father will pay you anything you ask," Sandra promised.

"Si, señorita, he will pay, but we will not let you go."

Nelson let out a cry for help. Fear choked up in his throat. Pablo Lopez was a villain without conscience, and it was a pleasure to him to kill gringos. He recruited his band from the riff-raff of the border, and he preyed on his own race too.

"Come, little quail," the bearded ruffian jeered, still in Spanish. "Come to the loving arms of Pedro."

He reached forward, and his hands closed around the waist of the girl. Nelson struck at him with the whip. Another outlaw brought the barrel of a forty-five down on the boy's head. Though Sandra struggled, she was dragged across the wheel of the buggy. Her fingers clawed at the dirty brown face of her captor.

"Que diablo" he cried, pinioning her wrists with the fingers of one hand. "This is no quail, but a hawk. Be still, chiquita, or Pedro will slap that pretty face."

She screamed, with no real hope that any friend might hear.

Miles of desert lay between her and any who might come to the rescue.

Sandra was held close to the thick body of the bearded outlaw, face toward him. Vainly she tried to wriggle out of his encircling arm, then with unexpected suddenness stopped fighting. Over the man's shoulder she had seen a horseman at the top of the rise from which the buggy had just descended.

For an instant the newcomer sat there, silhouetted against the horizon, a lean long-bodied fellow with a rifle in his hands. His horse jumped to a gallop, and he charged down the slope. Sandra had no time to guess who he was or why he was coming. She was too absorbed to breathe. It was afterward that she likened that headlong rush to the flight of an avenging angel.

2 A Tough Hombre Trapped

Out of a gash in the hills two men rode warily to the edge of the mesa and searched with their eyes the torn valley below. Seen from above, its floor was as wrinkled as a crumpled sheet of brown wrapping paper. The surface was scarred by lomas, washes, and arroyos running down from the bench back of it.

A brazen sun beat down on baked terrain sown with cactus and greasewood. In this harsh desiccated region the struggle to live was continuous. Vegetation was tough, with clutching claws. Reptiles carried their defensive poison. The animals that at rare moments flitted through the brush were fierce and furtive.

But no more savage than the men whose gaze squinted up and down the basin at their feet. The skin of the cholla was less tough than theirs. When cornered they could strike with the swift deadliness of the sidewinder. Across their saddles rifles lay ready for instant use. The butts of revolvers projected from the pockets attached to the shiny leather chaps they wore. Into every fold and wrinkle of their clothes the dust of long travel had filtered.

"Filled with absentees, looks like," one of them drawled.

His companion added dryly, "I hope."

The first speaker, a long dark man with a scar across his left cheek from ear to chin, lifted a hand in signal. Cattle dribbled out of the cut through which they had just come, pushed forward by a heavy-set squat man bringing up the drag. The animals moved wearily. It was plain they had been driven far and hard. The bawling of the beasts for water was almost incessant.

Anxiously the scarfaced man slanted a look at the westering

sun. "Come dark we'll be in the clear—if night ever gets here. Once we reach the pass they'll never find us."

"Likely we had a long head start." The squat man's glance swept the valley slowly. In the tangled panorama below him he could see no sign of human life. "No use gettin' goosey, I reckon. Loan me a chaw, Sim."

Sim was the oldest of the three and the smallest, with a face as seamed as a dried-up winter apple. He drew a plug of tobacco from his hip pocket and threw it across to the other and watched the sharp teeth at work. "You don't have to eat the whole plug," he remonstrated. "If I was you, Chunk, I'd buy me two bits worth of chewing some time and see how my own tobacco tasted."

They turned the leaders into a draw that dropped down to the valley and presently the herd was in motion again. A cloud of fine dust, stirred by the tramping feet, rose into the air and marked their progress. The cattle smelled water and began to hurry. Scarface tried to check them, fearing a stampede, but the cattle pounded past him on a run. They tore down to the creek, which was dry except for half a dozen large pools, and crowded into the water. Those in the rear fought to get forward, while the leaders held stubbornly to the water until they had drunk their fill. The herders had their hands full moving the watered stock out of the way to make place for the thirsty steers.

They were getting the last of the cattle out of the bed of the creek when Chunk looked up and gave a shout of warning. Four armed men had just topped a knoll two hundred yards away and were coming up the valley toward them. The heavyset man whirled his cowpony and jumped it to a gallop. Scarface took his dust not a dozen yards in the rear. It took Sim a moment to understand what was spurring his companions to flight. He was on the side of the herd nearest the approaching riders, and he lost more time circling the closely packed cattle.

A voice called to him to halt, but Sim had urgent business elsewhere. He stooped low in the saddle, his quirt flogging the buckskin he rode. The crack of a Winchester sounded, then another. The body of the little man sank lower. He clutched at the horn of the saddle. His head slid along the shoulder of his mount toward the ground. As he plunged downward, the fingers of his hand relaxed their grip on the horn.

Three of the pursuers went past him without stopping, the fourth pulled up and swung from the saddle. The body of the little man lay face down in the sand. He turned it over. Though the lips of the rustler were bloodless and his face grey, he was still alive. He recognized John Ranger, the man at his side.

"Who got you into this mess, Sim?" the cattleman asked.

The outlaw shook his head. His voice was low and faint.

11

"You've killed me. Ain't that enough?" he murmured.

They were his last words. He shut his eyes. A moment later his body relaxed and seemed to sink into itself.

Rustlers and cowmen had disappeared over a rise, but to Ranger had come the sound of shots, four or five of them, the last one fainter as the distance increased. He remounted and rode after his friends. The reason why the thieves had fled without a fight was clear to him. They were not so much afraid of a battle as of having their identity discovered. A rustler caught in the act had either to get out of the country or be killed. Since these fellows were not ready to leave they had to avoid recognition.

Near the end of the valley Ranger pulled up, uncertain whether the riders had ridden to the right or the left of the great rock which rose like a giant flatiron to separate the two cañons running out of the flats to the hills beyond. A rifle boomed again, far above him to the left. The explosion told him which gulch to follow. Before he reached the scene of action he heard other shots.

The cañon opened into a small park hemmed in by a rock wall, at the foot of which was a boulder field. In one swift glance Ranger's eyes picked up his companions. Two of them were crouched behind cottonwoods and the third back of a fallen log, all watching the rock pile lying close to the cliff.

"Got a coon treed, Pete?" Ranger asked.

"Y'betcha. He's skulking in the rocks." The voice of the speaker was flat and venomous, his foxlike face sour and bitter. Peter McNulty was his name. He ran a small spread up by Double Fork. "Darned fool hasn't anything but a six-gun. We'll smoke him out soon."

The man behind another cottonwood had a suggestion. "Can't get at him from here, John. How about you riding up the gully and potting him from the bluff? He'll have to throw in his hand then."

"All right, Russ. The fellow you knocked off his horse down below has cashed in. He was old Sim Jones."

Russell Hart frowned. He was a quiet and responsible cattleman. It gave him no pleasure to know that he had killed a man, and particularly as inoffensive a man as Sim Jones. Wryly, by inference at least, he justified himself. "That's what bad company does for a man," he said. "If he hadn't thrown in with Scarface he would have gone straight enough. Sim was trifling, but there was no harm in him."

Ranger swung his horse round and guided it into a sunken channel that had been cut by floods from the ridge above to the park. At the summit he dismounted and tied the pony, then moved forward cautiously to the edge of the precipice.

The trapped man was kneeling back of a boulder, revolver in hand. Other rocks protected his flanks.

The cattleman took careful aim and fired at the flat plane of one of the rocks. Startled at this attack from the air, the man below looked up. The face turned toward Ranger was bearded but young.

"Throw up your hands and walk out of there," ordered Ranger.

The man with the revolver knew he was beaten. His forty-five would not carry accurately to any of his foes. Ranger was quite safe on the bluff, but from where he stood he could send bullets tearing into the body of the other.

"What's all the shooting about?" demanded the stranger. "Why should you fellows jump me when I'm riding peaceably about my business?"

"Don't talk. Drop that gun and get going."

"All right. Call off yore wolves and I'll go out."

Ranger shouted to the others that the fellow in the rocks was surrendering. Hands up, the man walked out from the boulder field. Two rifles covered him as he moved forward. When he was eight or ten paces from the men carrying them he dropped his arms. He was a slim young fellow, coffee brown, in cowboy boots, levis, and well-worn Stetson. His blue-grey eyes were hard and frosty. In his motions there was a catlike litheness. The muscles of his legs and shoulders rippled like those of a panther.

"I'll listen to yore apologies," he drawled.

Pete McNulty tittered, his small eyes gloating. "He's gettin' fixed to saw off a whopper on us. I'll bet it's good."

"What is this—a sheriff's posse?" the prisoner snapped.

"If any questions are necessary, we'll ask them," Hart answered harshly. He did not like the job they had agreed to do, and he was hardening his heart to it.

The man in levis was a stranger to them, but that meant nothing. Drifters came and went. That Scarface had picked up some scalawag on the dodge to help on the raid was very likely.

"I think we finish this now." The man who had been behind the log shuffled around the end of it and joined the others. He moved ponderously, his short heavy legs supporting an enormous torso. Leathery folds hung loose on cheek and jaw. His deepset, peering little eyes looked shortsighted. Altogether, he resembled a rhinoceros. Though his name was Hans Uhlmann, his intimates called him Rhino. "Nice and quick, then get started with the cattle."

The cornered man tightened his stomach muscles. He braced himself to meet what might be coming, deep-set eyes fierce as those of a trapped wolf. For he knew Uhlmann of old, and that knowledge set a passionate hatred churning in his

13

heart. He owed the man a deep and lasting grudge, one he had waited long years to satisfy. That the ranchman did not recognize him was understandable. The big man had seen him last a pink-cheeked boy of nineteen, smooth-faced, thin as a rail. Now he was bearded. His body had filled out. The bitter intervening years had etched harsh lines in his face, given it an edge of lean sternness. Even a casual observer could not have missed the steely hardness, the defiant challenge of one at war with the world.

"You've made a mistake," he said. "I'm not the man you want."

Uhlmann showed bad teeth in a cruel grin. "You're the man we'll hang. Right now. Do the job and get on our way."

The brutal ruthlessness of the man's words angered the captive. They had made up their minds. They were not going to pay any attention to his story.

"What am I supposed to have done?" he asked.

Hart spoke, ignoring the question. "I reckon Scarface met up with you recently. You're a stranger here."

"Right. My name is Cape Sloan. Never heard of this Scarface."

McNulty laughed, with heavy sarcasm. "He doesn't know Scarface—wasn't rustling stock with him. He was just riding along peaceable when we went gunning for him."

"Get your rope, Pete," Uhlmann said.

Sloan could read in the faces of McNulty and Uhlmann nothing that gave him hope. That of the former was full of cruel mirth. The German's was set as an iron mask. Toward Hart and Ranger he pointed his appeal.

"You haven't told me yet what my crime is," he said quietly.

"You know damned well what it is," McNulty broke out. "No sense in talking more. Let's get this business done."

"I started this morning from Redrock," the stranger said. "Last night I stayed at the road house there. That I can prove. All day I have traveled alone."

McNulty showed his yellow teeth in an ugly grin. "Didn't I tell you boys he would spread the mustard good?"

"I stopped at a Chink restaurant on Congress Street in Tucson for breakfast. A deputy sheriff named Mosely sat opposite me at the table. We talked about the Apache Kid."

"So *you* say," jeered McNulty. "Why don't you claim you sat opposite John L. Sullivan?"

Sloan kept his eyes on Ranger and Hart. McNulty he ignored completely. "If you write to the road house at Redrock or to Mosely you'll find that what I say is true."

"We ain't gonna write anywhere. We're gonna string you to a tree."

"Don't push on the reins, Pete," Hart counseled quietly.

"We'll listen to what this man has to say."

"Where do you hail from?" Ranger asked.

For a half a second Sloan hesitated. "From Holbrook, I drifted west from Vegas."

"Cowboy?"

"Yes."

"With what outfits have you ridden?"

"I've worked for the Bar B B near Holbrook and for the A T O in New Mexico."

"When did you work for the A T O?" Ranger inquired.

"Couple of years ago."

"The A T O has been out of business for four years," McNulty shouted jubilantly. "That cooks his goose."

The stranger knotted his brows in thought. "That's right. Time jumps away so fast you can't keep up with it. I drew my last pay check from Tidwell 'most five years ago."

"What does Tidwell look like?" Hart queried.

"He's a fat bald man with only one good eye—wears a patch over the other."

"What's that got to do with the question? This guy might be Tidwell's brother for all we care. Point is, he's a rustler caught stealing cows. That's enough." McNulty tossed the loop of the rope in his hand over the head of the suspect, who promptly released himself from it.

"What are you doing in this country?" Ranger demanded.

Again there was a little pause before the young man opened his lips to answer. Before he could speak McNulty slid in an answer. "Why, that's an easy one, John. He's stealing our stock."

"I asked him, not you, Pete," mentioned Ranger.

"Just seeing what's over the next hill," Sloan answered. "You know how punchers move around. Thought I'd pick up a job riding for some outfit."

Uhlmann took the rope from McNulty and shuffled a step or two closer to the victim. "What's the use of talk? We caught him stealing our stuff. No use wasting time."

The cowboy choked down the dread rising in him. "I tell you I'm the wrong man," he said evenly. "Let me prove it."

3   *Pablo Lopez Takes a Hand*

"Fellow, this case is closed," McNulty retorted. "You been tried and convicted. By facts. Like Rhino says, we caught you in the act."

Cape Sloan talked, for his life. But he didn't let his desperation sweep him away. His voice was quiet and steady.

"If I was driving off your stuff, where are the other fellows that were with me? They didn't come up this gulch."

"You say Scarface didn't come up here?" Ranger asked.

"Nobody passed me between here and the foot of the hill—neither this Scarface you are talking about nor anybody else."

Ranger put a question to Hart. "You saw Scarface take this turn at the Flatiron, didn't you?"

"Not exactly," Hart admitted. "Someone on a horse was moving up the gulch ahead of us. Naturally we thought it was one of the birds we wanted."

"It was, too," cut in McNulty. "It was this fellow."

"There must be some other trail they could have taken," Sloan protested. "They didn't come up here."

"There was the other fork," Ranger agreed.

"Looky here, boys," McNulty urged. "We got the dead wood on this man. They weren't out of our sight hardly a minute—just when they dipped down into the bend before the Flatiron. Then we see him again, riding hell-for-leather up the cañon. Only by that time he ain't the one we want, by his way of it. Me, I don't believe in fairy tales. This vanishing stuff don't go with Pete."

"There must be tracks where they took the other fork," Sloan said.

"Might be," Hart nodded. "Though there was a lot of loose rubble on the ground there."

"I don't want to make a mistake about this," Ranger said. "We'll take a look."

"There's a cottonwood over there handy," Uhlmann grumbled. "No trees at the foot of the hill. We're wasting time."

John Ranger stood six feet two, a man in the prime of life. He wore a short thick beard, and the eyes above it were strong and steady. No man in the neighborhood was more respected.

"I can afford to waste a quarter of an hour to make sure I am not hanging an innocent man," he replied curtly, and turned his horse down the cañon.

At the fork Uhlmann guarded the prisoner while the others examined the ground for the tracks of horses. There were marks where hoofs had slipped an inch or two on the loose rubble, but since there had been no rain for weeks there was no way of telling how recent they were. The three men moved up the hill looking for tracks that might tell a more convincing story, but when they returned ten minutes later none of them was sure.

"All bunk what he claims," McNulty shouted to Uhlmann. "They didn't come this way."

"We don't know that," Hart differed. "Horses have been up this cañon, but we can't tell when."

16

"I say hang him right damn now," the foxfaced man voted. "Rustling is one disease you can't cure a fellow of except with a rope."

The blue-gray eyes of Sloan flamed hot with anger. "You're tough as bull neck rawhide when you're talking to an unarmed man with a gun in yore hand and two-three other men to back yore play," he said scornfully.

"You can't talk that way to me," blustered McNulty angrily.

"I am talking that way to you. I'm telling you that you're a yellow-bellied coyote, or you wouldn't want to hang an innocent man who can prove he wasn't in this raid if you give him time."

Before he could be stopped McNulty slammed the barrel of his rifle against the side of the stranger's head. Sloan swayed on his feet and would have fallen if Hart had not supported him.

"Proving what I've just said," he told McNulty hardily.

"Exactly that," Ranger agreed. "If you lay a hand to this man again, Pete, I'll wear you out with my quirt. We may have to hang him, but I'm not going to have him abused first."

"I reckon he's guilty," Hart said, after he had tied his bandanna around the bleeding head of their prisoner. "But I don't want to live regretting today all the rest of my life. I think we ought to go back to Blunt's place and let the other fellows have a say in this."

"You're shouting when you say we've got to hang him, Russ," Uhlmann replied roughly. "But what's the sense of taking him back to Blunt's? We're the fellows who caught him and we're the ones that ought to have the say-so. What more do you want? We caught him in the act."

"I wouldn't be riding on a raid without a rifle, would I?" Sloan asked.

"You threw it away to help your alibi," McNulty chipped in sourly.

"I've seen this guy before somewhere," the German scowled. "Wish I could remember where. Maybe with Scarface some time. He ain't so much a stranger as he claims he is."

"You can hold me till you find out whether my story is true," Sloan told them.

"No," Uhlmann growled. "What's the sense of being soft? Before we started we agreed to hang any of them we caught. They shot up Spillman, didn't they?"

"He'd likely bust out of any place we put him," McNulty grumbled. "Thing to do is to finish this while we've got him."

"Even though I'm innocent," their prisoner added.

"You're guilty as the devil," the German flung out bluntly. "All right. Let's go back to Blunt's. There are no trees there, but we can prop up a wagon tongue for him."

17

Near the sandy bed of the Creek they drew up beside the body of Sim Jones.

"I wish it hadn't been Sim I got," Hart said, looking down at the weak, rather kindly, face of the dead rustler. "He had no business running with Scarface. I reckon if I had worked hard enough I could have won him away from that crowd. We all treated him as if he was unimportant and kinda laughed at him. So when Scarface buttered him up it flattered him."

"Sim got what he asked for," Uhlmann spoke up coldly. "When he started running off other men's stock he might have known he had this coming. Anyhow, he didn't amount to a hill of beans. I'll say though"—he glanced across at the prisoner callously—"that I'm glad we caught another waddy to keep company with Sim and help him from feeling lonesome where he's gone."

They roped the body to the mount of McNulty back of the saddle and continued down the valley. Uhlmann kept guard over the captured cowboy while the others drove the recovered cattle.

Sloan's thoughts were somber. His reckless feet had carried him along dangerous trails and they had brought him at last to this. He would be lucky if he escaped from the plight in which he was. Cowmen intent on setting an example to warn other rustlers did not usually take two or three days to investigate the story of a man caught on the spot.

While they were passing through a cut in the hills that jammed them close together he overheard a few words that passed between Ranger and Hart.

"He isn't much more than a boy," the former said. "Though he has the look of a man who has lived in hell."

"Nits make lice if you leave them be," Hart answered.

The pressure of the cattle brought Sloan knee to knee with Ranger for a few moments.

He said, stiffly: "I'm not asking mercy because I'm young, Mr. Ranger. For eight years I've been a grown man. I don't want pity but justice. I wasn't trying to steal yore cattle. I don't know any of the men who were. All I ask is decent fair play. Wire to Mosely at Tucson. Describe me. Ask if he didn't eat breakfast with me today. I'll pay for the message."

"There's no place within thirty miles from which to send a telegram."

"What's thirty miles when a life is at stake?"

"Nothing. I'll do my best for you, but the feeling is intense. There has been a lot of night raiding and we have lost many cattle. This time they killed a cowboy named Spillman who saw them making the gather. You can't blame the boys for being excited."

"How can I?" Sloan flung back bitterly. "If they are excited, it would be unreasonable for me to object to their hanging me even if I am innocent."

Ranger had no answer to that. It was not quite just, he reflected, to expect a man whose life was at stake to make allowances for those judging him.

From a hogback they looked down on an undulating brush country of greasewood, mesquite, and cactus. To reach it they passed through a grove of sahuaros struggling up the hill, their trunks pitted with holes made by woodpeckers.

Ranger's gaze rested on their captive, a worried frown on his face. Whatever else might be said about him, the fellow was a cool customer. He had a hard tough look, in his eyes a reckless, almost arrogant challenge, the defiance of one with plenty of fighting tallow. The cattleman half believed his story, but he had a feeling that Sloan was holding something back. It was not wander-lust that had sent him into this part of the country. He was no footloose puncher moved only by restlessness. A definite reason had brought him here. The man rode at loose ease in the saddle, but there was in him a banked explosive force that differentiated him from the average drifting cowboy.

Moving to the top of a loma, Sloan caught sight of windmill blades flashing in the sun. McNulty made it a point to ride close to him.

"Blunt's," he explained, pointing to the windmill, his mean eyes exulting. "Its cross-bars will be better than a wagon tongue."

Sloan did not answer. He did not want to give him the satisfaction of a reply. Uhlmann, he noticed, did not appear to be guarding him closely. This was an invitation for him to attempt escape. He knew that if he tried it the German would shoot him down before he had covered forty yards. This was a hopeful sign. The fellow would not be tempting him to make a break for liberty if he was quite sure the conference at Blunt's would vote for an immediate hanging without waiting for his story to be verified or disproved.

The voice of Hart rang out. "Look!" he cried.

Out of an arroyo a rider appeared. He was flogging his mount with a quirt. They could see that he was swaying in the saddle. With one hand he clung to the horn.

"It's Bill Hays," McNulty announced. "What's the matter with him?"

The man headed straight for them. They could hear him shouting, but could not make out what he was saying. He skirted the edge of the herd and pulled up not a yard from Sloan. Uhlmann caught him as he slid from the saddle.

"Pablo Lopez' raiders," he gasped before sinking into unconsciousness.

There was a stain of blood on the front of his shirt still wet and soggy.

"By Moses, here they come!" McNulty shouted. "I'm lighting outa here."

"No," Ranger snapped. "They'll get you sure. We'll move back into the wash we just crossed. They may take the stock and not attack us."

McNulty was close to panic. His frightened eyes clung to the dozen riders charging toward them. Bullets whistled past him.

"They'll murder us," he yelped.

Uhlmann pushed into his hand a rifle and the reins of the horse he had been riding.

"Git a-holt of yoreself, fellow," he snarled. "This is a fight you're in." The German stooped and picked up Hays, then strode toward the wash.

McNulty reached there long before any of the others. He was in a panic of terror. In his haste he had dropped the rifle of the German and released his horse. Back of the two-foot bank he lay trembling. The reputation of Pablo Lopez was well-known. On raids across the line from Mexico his bandits killed gringos right and left.

Hart and Ranger stayed to protect Uhlmann by covering his retreat. Their Winchesters flung back an answer to the shots of the outlaws. All of them came safely to the bed of the dry stream.

Uhlmann put the wounded man in the sand and turned to McNulty. "Where's my rifle?" he demanded.

"I . . . slipped . . . and it dropped," the poor wretch quavered.

The German caught him by the coat collar and dragged him to his knees. His hard horny hand slapped the colorless face.

"Fight, damn you, or I'll put a bullet through your belly now," he said savagely.

The big man did not wait for an answer. He went lumbering back through the brush to get the rifle. Bullets whipped past him, but he paid no attention to them. The Mexicans were riding fast and could fire with no accuracy. A few seconds later he was back in the wash with his weapon.

"What's become of the rustler?" he asked.

"I saw him fork Bill Hays' horse," Hart said. "Thought he was bringing it here."

"He must either have lit out or got shot," Ranger guessed.

"Cut his stick? That's what he's done. Bill's bronc is faster than his." There was shrill complaint in the high voice of McNulty. "Left us here to be killed while he slips away. I knew we'd ought to have hanged him right away."

"We're not going to be killed." Ranger's voice was cool and

resolute. "We're going to get a few of these murderous devils. They never could shoot straight."

The sound of Ranger's rifle echoed back and forth between the banks of the wash loud as the roar of a cannon. One of the Mexicans pitched headlong from his horse. Those behind him pulled up hurriedly and broke for cover to right and left.

"Good work, John," encouraged Hart. "Number one rubbed out. We'll be all right yet. They'll hear the firing at Blunt's and some of the boys will come moseying this way to help us." He caught a glimpse of a head peering above a hummock and blazed away at it.

4 Sloan Interrupts

The intervention of Lopez' raiders came to Cape Sloan as a chance for escape to be seized at once. A man hard and resolute, under other circumstances he would have stayed with the cattlemen to help stand off the attack of the bandits. But he saw no percentage in remaining, since if he survived the battle there would still be the likelihood of being hanged later.

He swung to the saddle from which the wounded man had fallen and made off at a right angle through the brush. His captors were too busy looking after their own safety to pay any attention to him. Though he put the horse to a gallop, he rode crouched, his body close to the back of his mount, in the hope of using the mesquite as a screen between him and the outlaws. It was a comfort to see Hays' rifle close at hand in the scabbard beside his leg.

Life on the frontier, lived recklessly, had made of Sloan a hard-bitten realist. If possible, he meant to make a clean getaway. First, he had to avoid being shot down by the raiders, and afterward to make a wide detour of the Blunt ranch in order not to be stopped by any of those hunting the Scarface depredators. In spite of his keen watchfulness against the immediate danger, he felt a sardonic amusement at the development of the situation. The foray of one band of rustlers had imperiled him; that of a much more malignant one had brought him rescue.

A stranger to the chaparral would have found difficulty in picking a way through the dense growth, but Sloan wound in and out without once pulling to a walk the cowpony he was astride. The yucca struck at his legs with points of steel. Strong spines of the cholla and the prickly pear seemed to be clutching for him. But he was so expert a brush rider that he could miss the needles by a hair's breadth without slackening his pace.

21

Back of him he heard the firing of the guns drumming defiance. They told him that the first charge had been broken and that for the time at least the battle had settled down to a siege. Later Lopez' men would probably get tired of that and try another attack in force unless a rescue party from the ranch interfered with them.

The noise of the explosions sounded fainter as the distance between him and the wash increased. He had been traveling back into a hill country, but after a time he pulled up to decide on a course. By now he must be well south of the Blunt place and could swing around it if he kept to the brush. There was no longer any danger of pursuit by the Mexicans. Whether they had seen him at all he did not know. If so, they had let him go and concentrated on the men in the wash. He guessed that after finding that they could not rub out Ranger's party without loss they might drive the cattle away, not stopping to exterminate the owners. Sloan had heard that though Lopez was ruthless he liked to run as little risk as possible.

There was no longer any need of haste. The young man moved down into the flats, holding the buckskin to a walk. Technically he had become a horse thief, but that did not seem important at the moment. When he did not need the animal any longer he could turn it loose and it would return to the home ranch. The rifle he would keep, at least until he had reached a place of safety.

The sun had slid down close to the jagged horizon line. Inside of two hours darkness would sift down over the land. After that he would be in little danger. During the night he could get forty miles away from here. His plan had been to stay, for reasons he did not yet want to make public. But until he had cleared up this matter of the rustling that would be madness. Even before this mischance, he had known that every hour he spent here would be perilous.

He came to a road that cut through the mesquite, not a main-traveled one. It was narrow, and in places young brush had grown up in it. The wheel tracks were faint. Upon it the wilderness brush was encroaching. Greasewood and ocatillo reached out across it and whipped at the flanks of his horse.

As he came into the road he heard the creaking of wheels and at once drew back into the chaparral where he would not be seen. A buggy came around the bend, driven by a boy of about fourteen. There was a hole in the lad's straw hat and through it a tuft of red hair had pushed into the open. Beside him sat a girl several years older.

Cape Sloan had read of golden girls, but he had never before seen one that fitted the mental picture he had formed. This one had honey-colored hair twisted around her head in strands. Her eyes were deep sky blue, and her cheeks had a soft peach bloom. A slant of sunlight was pouring straight at her, as if a stage had been set to throw her young beauty into relief. She was laughing, and he glimpsed a double row of shiny ivory teeth. Though slenderly modeled, there was promise of strength in her straightbacked supple body.

The buggy dipped into a draw and after it had disappeared Sloan took the road again and followed. Before he had gone fifty yards he heard a jangle of voices, a whoop of jeering laughter, and a boyish treble raised in frightened protest. Trouble of some sort, he decided, and was sure of it when the scream of a girl reached him.

Swiftly he rode to the top of the rise and looked down. He saw four men surrounding the buggy. The girl was in the arms of one of them, flung across the saddle in front of him.

"We take you to Pablo, señorita," one of them called to her. "Maybe he hold you for a nice fat ransom. Or maybe—"

He finished the sentence with a ribald laugh. There was cruel gloating in the sound of it. Sloan knew that these men were not of the kindly smiling Mexicans who made a picturesque background to this desert land. They were members of the band of Pablo Lopez, the dregs of the wild turbulent borderland.

Sloan touched his mount with the spur and charged down the slope. He knew it was a mad business, but gave that no thought. During the two or three seconds while the horse pounded down the slope his mind moved in swift stabbing flashes. The boy's head lay against the back of the seat. He had probably been pistol-whipped. That was a game two could play—if he ever got the chance.

One of the bandits turned, shouted a startled warning, and fired wildly at the man on the galloping horse. Another bullet whistled past the ears of Sloan. A third outlaw fired just as Sloan dragged his mount to a halt.

The rifle in Sloan's hands swung up and crashed down on the head of the man who had first seen him. The rider went out of the saddle as slack as a pole-axed bullock. A second raider spurred his pony against the cyclonic stranger. A knife flashed in the sun. The head and body of Sloan swerved, but too late to escape entirely. A red hot flame ripped through his shoulder. He drew back the Winchester and fired it from his hip.

An agonized expression distorted the face of the attacker and the knife dropped from his hand to the sand. Wide-stretched fingers caught at his stomach. The muscles of his back collapsed and he slid head first to the ground.

Cape Sloan lifted his voice in shout. "Come on, fellows. We've got 'em."

The remaining two bandits wanted no more of this. One flung a hurried shot at Sloan and dragged his horse around to escape. The other dropped the girl and raced down the road at the heels of his fellow.

Sloan swung from the saddle, grounded the reins, and stepped forward to see how badly the boy was hurt. Groggily the lad stared at him.

"He hit me with a gun," the boy explained, the world still swimming before his eyes.

The girl climbed into the buggy and put an arm around him. "Are you all right, Nels? I mean—are you much hurt, dear?"

Her brother felt his head gently. "Gee, I'll say I am."

Sloan examined the lump above the temple. It had been a fairly light tap. The skin was not broken and there was no blood. If there was no concussion Nelson had got off easily.

"He'll have a headache, but I don't think he is much hurt," Sloan decided.

Cape had kept an eye on both of the prostrate bandits. Now he examined their wounds. The one he had shot was dead. His companion showed signs of life. Sloan stripped both of them of their weapons.

"Where are the other men—the ones you called?" the girl asked.

"There are no others." Cape smiled. "Thought I'd encourage these scoundrels to light out before they had massacred me."

"I haven't seen you before, have I?" she said. "You don't live around here."

"My name is Cape Sloan." He added, "I'm a stranger in these parts."

The horse of one of the raiders was grazing close to the trace. No sign of the second one could be seen. The animal had probably run down the road after the departing outlaws.

Sloan unhitched the horse from the buggy and removed the harness. The girl's eyes followed him as he moved.

"My name is Alexandra Ranger," she said. "This is my brother Nelson. We live at the Circle J R ranch."

"If your father is John Ranger I think I've met him," Sloan answered, his eyes grim.

She looked down at the dead man and shuddered "It's . . . dreadful, isn't it? Who can they be? What did they want?" Her voice was low and held a moving huskiness. It stirred in him a queer emotion he did not understand. Except for diversion women had not meant much in his young life. It had been many years since he had exchanged a smile with one.

"They belong to Pablo Lopez' gang. A mess of them are raiding this district today." He did not mention that he had last seen a dozen of them trying to kill her father. If there was bad news waiting for her she would learn it in time without his help. "We've got to get out of here *pronto*. I don't know how far away the rest of the gang are. Your brother can ride

24

this horse. You'll have to take that one." He indicated the one the dead man had been riding.

"Yes," she replied, taking orders from him without comment. The color had washed out of her cheeks, but she gave no evidence of hysteria. "Can you help Nels up?"

He lifted the boy to the back of the buggy horse.

"You're all right, aren't you?" he asked. "Not lightheaded?"

"Sure, I'm all right. Where are we going?"

"I don't know yet. Just now into the brush." He turned to Alexandra. "You'll have to ride astride."

"Yes. Will you help me up, please? It's such a high horse."

He put a hand under one foot and lifted. She swung into the seat and tried to pull her skirts down, but a long stretch of slender shapely leg showed.

For anything that his wooden face registered she might have been a wrinkled Indian squaw. His eyes apparently took no note of the small firm breasts or of the long curves of her gracious figure. His job was to save them and himself. He wasted no time on amenities. He whipped up his left arm and said curtly, "This way."

Though fear was still knocking at her heart, she was full

of curiosity about him. The horse he was riding bore a

brand. What was he doing with one of her father's mounts? Why had he stiffened at mention of her name? He was a man who unconsciously invited the eyes of women, not less because of his obvious indifference to them. There was strength in the bone conformation of his face and a sardonic recklessness in the expression. The motions of his body showed an easy grace, due to the poised co-ordination of mind and long flowing muscles. She had never seen one more sure of himself.

They cut into the chaparral, Sloan bringing up the rear. In silence they traveled for at least a mile before he halted the little procession.

"How far is the nearest ranch?" he inquired.

"About three miles, maybe," Nelson answered. "The Blunt place. Wouldn't you say about three miles, Sandra?"

Sandra thought that might be right.

The men hunting the rustlers were to rendezvous at Blunt's. Cape guessed that would be the safest point for which to strike.

"Let's go," he said.

"Wait," Sandra cried, pointing to a red stain on his shirt. "You're wounded. Where the knife cut you."

Sloan brushed aside her concern impatiently. "A scratch. It will wait."

5 A Reunion at Blunt's

The battle of the wash had developed into a snipers' contest. This suited the defenders. Time was running in their favor. Lopez had to get the stock across the line before his retreat was cut off. Soon he would decide that was more important than killing two or three gringos. Moreover, there was always the chance that cowmen riding to the rendezvous at Blunt's would hear the firing and come to the rescue.

"All we have to do is sit tight and hold the fort," Ranger said. "I've been in a lot worse holes than this."

"What I'd like is to get a bead on old Lopez himself and watch him kick," growled Uhlmann.

"What I'd rather see is the whole caboodle of them high-tailin' it away from here," McNulty differed. Though he did not feel comfortable he had settled down and was behaving better.

The words were hardly out of his mouth before the attackers began to evacuate their positions. Those in the wash could see the dust of moving cattle. There were still occasional shots from the brush, but it was an easy guess that a few men were posted to hold them until the stock could be pushed a mile or two toward the line.

It was half an hour later before the cattlemen dared leave their cover. Very cautiously they moved, fearing an ambuscade. But the raiders had cleared out.

There was no thought at present of attempting to recover the cattle. Bill Hays had to be got to a place where his wound could be properly dressed. Blunt's ranch was the nearest.

Ranger thought the wounded man could not get that far on horseback. "One of us could go get a buckboard," he suggested. "The rest of us could carry him out to the cow trail that runs up to Coyote Creek."

Uhlmann offered to ride to Blunt's.

"Keep away off to the north," Hart advised. "I figure Lopez is skedaddlin' for the line fast as he can push the cattle. But keep yore eyes skinned every foot of the way."

"Better take my horse," McNulty said. "He's fast."

The others waited for some minutes after Uhlmann had gone before starting with Hays. They half expected to hear

26

the sound of shots and were relieved that none broke the stillness. By this time the German must be safely well on his way.

Two of them carried Hays, taking turns. The third walked forty yards in advance, his eyes searching the bushes, a rifle in his hands. Pablo might have left a couple of sharpshooters to pick them off when they were not expecting an ambush.

At Coyote Creek Hart and McNulty waited while Ranger went back to the wash to bring up the horses. He had not rejoined them more than a few minutes when they heard the sound of wheels and presently of voices.

Hart shouted a challenge and Uhlmann answered. Three armed men and the driver of the buckboard were with him. One of them was Joe Blunt. He drew Ranger aside.

"I don't want to frighten you, John," he said. "But just before I left the house I heard something that worries me. Miguel Torres met yore boy and girl in a buggy about two hours ago near Bitter Wells. They were headed toward our place, to see Elvira, likely. But they haven't got there, or hadn't when we left."

Ranger's heart died within him. Lopez would probably pass Bitter Wells on his way back to the border. Two years earlier he had been condemned to death for the murder of a settler's family and had broken prison a few days before the execution hour. Other charges were piled against him. If he met the young people neither fear nor pity would have any weight with him.

"Did you send anyone out to—to make inquiries?" the father asked.

"Soon as we heard Pablo was on the loose Torres gathered a posse and started back toward Bitter Wells. He's a good man, John, both game and smart. He'll do his best."

"Yes," Ranger agreed. But there was no confidence in his assent. Darkness was falling over the land, and there would be small chance of finding the raiders in the night. Even Torres, good trailer though he was, could not cut sign without light.

"Chances are Pablo's men haven't run into Sandra and Nels at all," Blunt continued.

Again Ranger said "Yes" without conviction. If they had not been stopped his children would have reached the Blunt ranch long ago. "I'll take Uhlmann and Hart and Sid Russell with me. We'll pass by the ranch to make sure the children haven't been heard from, and from there we'll strike south."

"They may have learned Lopez was raiding and turned back to yore ranch."

"I'll check on that."

Heavy-hearted, Ranger rode into the night. With any luck either his posse or that of Torres might strike the cattle drive

27

before it reached the line. But there would be danger to Sandra and Nelson in a fight. Lopez was a merciless devil. Rather than give them up he might in sheer malice shoot them down. The best way would be to bargain with him, if that was possible.

They traveled fast. Ahead of them they could see the lights of the ranch house. They struck the main road, and after about a mile deflected from it to the private one running up to the white ranch house.

A sentry challenged them. Ranger's answer was a sharp question. "Anything heard of the children yet?"

"Not yet, Mr. Ranger."

"Blunt will be back in half an hour. How many men have you here that you can spare me?"

"Lemme see. Tom Lundy could go. I can. And Buck Ferguson."

"Slap on yore saddles. We can't wait. Join us at Bitter Wells. Bring all the men you can."

"If Lopez is driving a herd we can beat him to the line."

To them there came a sound of a horse hoof striking a stone. Ranger's body stiffened. He stared into the gathering darkness, shifting the rifle in his hands to be ready for instant action. "Who's there?" he demanded sharply.

The vague bulk of riders came out of the night.

"Halt where you are," Ranger ordered.

The high boyish voice of Nelson Ranger rang out. "That's my father." He slid from the back of his mount and ran forward.

John Ranger took the boy in his arms. "Your sister?" he cried.

"I'm all right," Sandra shouted. She was already out of the saddle and flying toward him.

One of her father's arms went around her shoulders. "Thank God!" he murmured shakily. To the boy he said a moment later: "You've been hurt."

"You bet." The youngster was half laughing, half crying. He was excited and a little hysterical. The dangerous adventure had shaken him, but he was proud of his wound, though only an inch of skin had been scalped from his head. "One of Pablo Lopez' men did that. We left him lying in the road."

A third rider had moved forward out of the shadows. Uhlmann shuffled toward him and gave a triumphant yelp. "By jimminy, it's the rustler. Don't move, fellow, or I'll pump a slug into you."

"I'm a statue of patience on a monument," Sloan jeered.

Sandra's relaxed muscles grew taut. She broke from her father's embrace. "Put that gun down," she ordered Uhlmann. "He saved us from Lopez. He's wounded."

28

The German's heavy jaw dropped, but his gaze clung to Sloan and his rifle still coverd the young man. "He's a cow thief just the same."

Ranger strode swiftly after his daughter. "You hard of hearing, Hans?" he sanpped. His hand closed on the barrel of the rifle and pushed it down.

Sloan swung out of the saddle hull heavily. The fingers of one hand held tightly to the horn to steady himself. His head felt strangely light, and the earth tilted up to meet the moonlit sky. For the first time in his life he felt as if he were going to faint.

But white teeth flashed in a smile defiant and derisive. "Thought I'd better drop in at the rendezvous," he said. "McNulty and the Dutchman can't have their hanging without a hangee."

6 *A Chip on His Shoulder*

Ranger took first things first. "Let's get into the house and look at your wound," he said. "Can you walk?"

"Learnéd twenty-six years ago come Christmas," Sloan replied, a thin grin on his sardonic face.

He gave up the support of the saddle horn and moved forward jauntily. But his step faltered.

Sandra slipped an arm around his waist. "Lean on me," she told him.

Her father took the other side. "Don't walk. We'll carry you."

He would not have it that way. "Just a li'l knife rip in the shoulder. Nothing to make a fuss about."

But he let them steady and help him to the steps, up them, and to the lounge in the parlor, where he promptly fainted from the loss of blood. Life in this rough brush country developed many accidents. John Ranger had doctored broken limbs, gunshot wounds, and knife gashes. Now he gave competent first aid to Sloan.

"Will he be all right?" Sandra asked him while he was washing his hands in the tin basin outside the house.

"Ought to be good as new in a few days," her father said. "A fine clean muscular specimen like he is builds blood fast." He dried his hands on a none too clean towel. "Now I'll listen to your story, honey."

Nelson had joined them. The two saw that the tale lost nothing in the telling. The stark fact stood out that Sloan had charged four desperadoes, killed one, slammed another unconscious, and driven the other two away.

"He's got sand in his craw," the cattleman admitted. "All the time Pete and Hans were wanting to hang him he was as cool as if they were talking about another fellow."

"Hang him!" Sandra cried aghast. "What for?"

"We trapped him up a cañon where we had driven Scarface. He claims he isn't one of the gang. I'm beginning to believe it. I hope he is telling the truth."

"Of course he is," his daughter cried in hot indignation. "He's wonderful, Father. He came down the hill like a tornado. It was all over in ten seconds. I was terribly frightened, but I needn't have been."

"He just banged one of 'em over the head and shot another through the belly quicker 'n scat. The others lit out like the heel flies were after them." The eyes of the boy were big with reminiscent excitement. "Gee! He could of licked a regiment."

"You aren't going to let anybody harm him, are you?" Sandra asked. "After what he did for us."

"No." John Ranger spoke with crisp decision. "I'll have a talk with the boys. There won't be any trouble."

"He isn't a thief," Sandra announced loyally. "And if he was I wouldn't care."

The cattleman wished he was as sure Sloan was innocent. But innocent or guilty it was not going to make any difference with him.

Blunt and his party reached the ranch. Bill Hays was put to bed and his wound dressed. One of Ranger's riders started on the fifty-mile ride to bring a doctor. After supper John gathered the men around him at the corral.

He told the story of how this man Sloan had saved his children from the raiders. There was a long silence after he had finished.

Blunt spoke first. "He has guts. That's sure."

"But he's a cow thief just the same," McNulty added.

Ranger looked at him with contempt in his steady eyes. "I don't think it. We'll know in a couple of days whether his story is true. But right now I'm serving notice that whether it is or isn't nobody is going to harm this man."

Uhlmann protested sourly. "Now look here, John. We can't turn a cow thief loose because he's game. He would be a menace to the community. Take Scarface. They don't make them any gamer than he is, but by jiminy, if I get my gun sights on him he's going to die."

Ranger said, spacing his words deliberately: "We're not talking about Scarface, but about a man who has just saved my children at great risk to himself, a man who had got away scot free and came back because he had to make sure that they would get home safe. I'm talking about the man lying wounded in that room."

"But if he's a rustler—" began Blunt unhappily.

"If he is a rustler we'll drive him out of the district. But that will be all." Ranger did not lift his voice, but there was an icy threat in his words. "Anybody who lifts a hand against him will have to settle with me."

Blunt shifted ground. "John is right, boys. I'd feel the same as he does if it had been my Elvira. Guilty or not guilty, we'll have to take a chance on this young fellow."

Uhlmann grumbled that he had cattle in the bunch taken by the rustlers. They were on their way to Mexico now. If he lost them, he'd be damned if he was going to let anybody be generous at his expense.

"When you know how many you have lost, make a bill and send it to me," Ranger told him scornfully. "I'll pay it unless it is shown that Sloan was not one of Scarface's men."

"Don't think I won't send it to you," Uhlmann retorted. "Get soft with cow thieves if you like. I won't."

Within twenty-four hours the truth of Sloan's story was confirmed. He had spent the night of the raid at a roadhouse in Redrock. The following morning, while the raiders must have been chousing the stolen stock across the flats to the hills, he had eaten breakfast at a Chinese restaurant in Tucson, just off the old plaza. He had sat opposite the deputy sheriff Mosely while they ate their flapjacks and steak and had discussed the depredations of the Apache Kid a dozen years earlier.

Some days later Sloan was sitting on the porch of the Blunt house in the warm sunshine waiting for a wagon that was to take him to the Circle J R. Two men rode up the lane to the house and swung from their saddles. They were McNulty and Uhlmann. Blunt was shoeing a horse and they stopped for a minute to talk with him. While they were still talking, a wagon driven by Ranger rolled into the yard.

The owner of the Circle J R pulled up in front of the porch. The bed of the wagon was filled with hay to make the riding easier.

"Ready to go?" Ranger asked Sloan.

"Yes, sir. But there's no need of my bothering you. I'm doing all right here. In a couple of days I'll move on."

"You won't bother us. We all want you to make a long visit at the ranch. The children won't let me rest until I get you."

McNulty and Uhlmann clumped forward from the outdoor blacksmith shop with the awkward gait of men who wear tight high-heeled cowboy boots. Pete went up the porch steps to Sloan, an ingratiating smile on his face. He held out a hand.

"Put her there, pardner," he said. "Looks like the joke is on we'uns. You can't hardly blame us, of course. The story you pulled was the thinnest darned one I ever did hear. But, as the old sayin' is, all's well that ends well."

Sloan did not seem to see the hand. He looked coldly at McNulty. When he spoke his voice was icy, without a trace of passion. "What I said about you the other day still goes. I wouldn't want to live in the same township with a mean-hearted scoundrel willing to hang a man without giving him a chance to prove his innocence."

An angry flush swept McNulty's face. Blunt had come from the forge and was standing beside Ranger, a pleased smile in his eyes. He did not object to hearing the little scamp told off. But Pete resented public castigation.

"If that's the way you want it, suits me," he blustered. "Since you're askin for it, I'll say I'm not satisfied yet. By my way of it, you're still a cow thief."

"For that, next time we meet I'll flog you within an inch of yore life," Sloan promised, a silken threat in his low voice.

"You can talk tough now, because you claim you're a sick man," Uhlmann said sourly. "But when you're well don't try to ride me, unless you want to come with your gun a-smokin'."

"Enough of that, boys," Ranger interrupted hurriedly. "Mr. Sloan has a right to be annoyed. If you two had got your way, we would have hanged an innocent man. You ought to be mighty pleased he's living. It's a lesson to all of us not to go off half-cocked. If you're ready, we'll go now, Sloan."

Cape Sloan rose, a wiry brown man with a dynamic force in him that was arresting. His gaze traveled with leisurely contempt over McNulty and rested on the pachydermous face of Uhlmann. He stood apparently at careless ease, a thumb hooked in his sagging belt.

"In a moment, Mr. Ranger." His steady narrowed eyes were still on Uhlmann. "It was my left shoulder the greaser cut," he mentioned, slurring the words gently. "My right arm is good as ever, if anybody wants to find out."

Ranger stepped swiftly between the German and Sloan. "Cut out that kind of talk, both of you," he ordered sternly. "You're grown men, not kids. You fellows let each other alone. The difficulty is settled now."

Sloan's smile was grim. "You in particular stay away from me, McNulty," he said. "My promise still stands. You can't call me a rustler and get off scot-free. If we meet again I'll wear a quirt on you."

He turned his back on Pete and climbed into the wagon.

7   Jim Budd and Sloan Agree
to Bury the Past

The Circle J R ranchhouse was a long low rambling building
that had been constructed bit by bit, new wings being added as
the owner grew more prosperous. Deep porches ran around
the front and sides, with vines climbing trellises to give protection from the broiling heat of midday. The house was
furnished comfortably and with taste. There was a piano in
the sitting room, and along the walls were well-filled bookcases.
The tawdry bric-a-brac one usually found in parlors was
notably absent. In the bedroom to which Nelson took the guest
cheerful chintz curtains had been hung. The armchair beside
the window was deep and built to give the body rest.

As soon as Sloan had washed away the dust of the journey
he was called to supper. He was starting to sit down when a
huge black man in an apron came in from the kitchen carrying
a platter of fried chicken. The Negro's staring eyes goggled
at him. It was a bad moment for Cape Sloan. His stomach
muscles tightened. For a second or two he missed what Ranger
was saying, but he picked up the sequence and answered
before the cattleman noticed. During the rest of the meal he
gave his surface mind to the conversation at the table. His
deeper thoughts were concerned with Jim Budd and the consequences of this unfortunate meeting.

Since he was a convalescent, Sandra insisted that he retire
early. He protested only formally, for he was tired from the
jolting journey in the wagon. While he was undressing a knock
came on the door of his room. It was Jim Budd who tiptoed
in after his invitation to enter. He had expected Jim would
make him a visit.

Sloan looked up at him from the bed where he was sitting.
He wondered what winds of mischance had blown the Negro
here.

"And to think I had to bump into you," he said, with obvious distaste.

"Yassuh," Jim agreed. "We sure done come a long way to
meet up."

"Do they know who you are?"

"They don' know where I wuz."

"How do you happen to be working at the Circle J R?"

"Why, when they turn me loose I kinda jes' started driftin' east, as you might say. Mister Ranger was looking for a cook. Me, I was workin' in a restaurant at Benson where he come in, an' we fix up for me to do the cookin' here."

"If they knew you had been in the pen they wouldn't keep you a day."

"I reckon that's c'rect. But I wouldn't know. Mister Ranger sure a fine man, an' the little missis sho the finest lady in de land. Mebbe they might keep me." His face took on a look of humble pleading. "You wouldn't go for to tell them, Mister Webb."

"The name is Sloan." He frowned at the honest dish face of the cook. "I don't know. I'll have to think about that."

"I ain't any bad man. I never wuz. That fellow Candish I gouge was a mighty bad killer. He jump me, jes' because I was a colored man."

Sloan knew that was true. Budd had been railroaded to prison. He had wounded Candish in self-defense. The chances were that he would live peaceably the rest of his life. No doubt he was devoted to the family for whom he was now working. The ranch guest felt a wry sense of sardonic amusement at the way he had inverted their roles. He was the one who would be in danger if the truth were known. For he had escaped before his sentence was finished and if discovered would be dragged back, flogged, and lose his time for good conduct.

"Mister Webb——"

"Sloan," interrupted the ranch guest.

"All right, Sloan then. You wuz Webb when you wuz in the pen at Yuma with me, but if you say Sloan that all right with me. What I wanna say is that I done served my time in prison for wounding Candish. I hadn't ought to of been in there a day. When they turned me loose I came 'way out here to make a fresh start. I'm doing fine. I'm with good folks I would do a heap for. I never done you any harm. Whyfor do you want to stir things up and get me flung out on my ear?"

"I don't want to throw you out of a good job where you are giving satisfaction, Jim. But I want to play fair with the Rangers too."

There was a faint gleam of grinning irony in Jim's reply. "I reckon then you'll want to tell them all about yo'self too, Mister We— Sloan."

"No, Jim, I don't want to do that. I'm here just for a short visit. I don't want them or anybody else to know about my stay in the pen at Yuma." Sloan came back to Jim's case. "We all knew there that you aren't a bad man, Jim. You ought never to have been convicted. I don't see how it can hurt the Rangers for you to stay here. You really like them?"

34

"I ain't got any folks of my own—never did have. My wife run away with a yaller nigger, and that busted up what li'l' home I had. Here's where I wan' to stay the rest of my life. They good to me. Never was any people I like as well. I feel like they're mine, kind of, if you understand me."

"That is fine, Jim. We'll call bygones bygones. What about me? Can you keep that big grinning mouth shut and not let anybody know you've ever seen me before?"

"Sure I can. Listen, Mister Webb-Sloan."

"Sloan," corrected the other. "Be sure to get that right."

"Yessir. Well, I think a powerful lot of Miss Sandra. When you rode in hell-for-leather and saved her from a whole passel of bandits you ce'tainly made me feel a powerful lot of respect, Mr. Sloan. My big mouth is done already padlocked."

8 Sandra Speaks Out

At the Circle J R the guest took life easier than he had done for many a day. Sandra did not let him get up with the family, but saw that Jim prepared a breakfast for him long after the others had eaten. He lounged about the place and let the sunny hours slip away in pleasant indolence. Sometimes he strolled down to the bunkhouse and chatted with a rider who had broken an ankle when his horse stepped into a gopher hole; or he sat on the corral fence and watched the cowboys top young horses they were breaking to the saddle. Occasionally he sat in a rocking chair on the porch of the big house and read a book called *The Three Musketeers*, dealing with the remarkable and improbable adventures of an amazing chap called D'Artagnan.

Nelson hovered around him a good deal. The boy was passing through an attack of hero-worship and was drawn to Sloan as a moth to the lamp. The young man had what it takes to win a boy—a touch of recklessness, cool courage, an easy indifferent grace, and back of him a life lived dangerously. Moreover, he knew exactly how to treat a boy. He never talked down to him, and he had a flair for "joshing" the youngster without making him conscious of the inferiority of the teens.

Of the Golden Girl he caught only glimpses during the day as she went to and fro about her work. Having been since her mother's death sole mistress of the ranch, she had charge of buying supplies not only for the main house but for the boys at the bunkhouse as well. Sloan was surprised at the efficiency with which she did her job. He did not at all wonder at the deep liking and respect, amounting almost to reverence, she won from the tough, tanned young men working for her

35

father. In the case of Jim Budd the devotion he showed was almost pathetic. If it would have helped her he would have chopped the fingers from his hand.

After supper Sandra always joined her father and Sloan on the porch. During the past hour cool shadows from the hills had blanketed stretches of the valley and lifted the heat from its dusty floor. The stark bare mountains glowed with jewels, their brilliancy softening to violet and purple lakes in the crotches between the peaks, filling them with mysterious dark pools. After the sun had set, magic began to fill the desert night.

Cape Sloan was very much aware of the girl sitting near him, though she spoke seldom. The young man was inclined to let Ranger carry the conversation, but the cattleman drew him out and forced him to take a share. Sandra observed that their guest was no ignorant cowboy. He could talk well, on many subjects. He had traveled a good deal, not only in the West but as far as Rio de Janeiro and the cattle country of Brazil. But she noticed that his wary and reticent remarks covered a good many elisions about his life. His youth he told about when questioned, and he did not avoid the wanderings of the past two months. But before that there was a gap of five or six years concerning which he said nothing.

Also, there was some secret understanding between him and Jim Budd. She had seen Jim's startled astonishment at their first meeting and the momentary discomposure of Sloan. When she had talked with Jim about it he denied ever having met their guest before—and she did not believe him. There had been something in the past that both of them wanted to conceal, some dark and unhappy memory rising to plague them now. An evil ghost from Cape Sloan's wild and turbulent youth had come to life again.

Sandra felt a hint of wariness about his indolent ease. It seemed to her a mask worn by a man always alert and even suspicious. She found confirmation of this view in an incident that occurred the third day of Sloan's stay at the ranch.

Late in the afternoon a man rode into the yard and dismounted in front of the house. Sandra chanced to be with their guest on the porch. She had just brought out a pitcher of lemonade and a glass for him.

The horseman tied his mount and came up the steps. He was heavy-set, middle-aged, with bleached blue eyes in a deeply tanned face. Scores of tiny wrinkles went out from the outer corners of the eyes like spokes from a hub. His cowboy boots were old and scuffed, his Stetson faded and floppy. Dust had sifted into the creases of the corduroy trousers and coat. The checked shirt had been washed so often that all the life had gone out of the color.

He said, smiling at the girl: "My throat's dry as a lime kiln, Miss Sandra. Does that rate me a drink of yore lemonade?"

She nodded. "It's ice-cold. I'll get a glass for you. This is Mr. Sloan, sheriff." To Cape she said, "Sheriff Norlin."

There was the slightest steely hardening in Sloan's eyes. She would not have noticed it if she had not been watching. The men looked at each other steadily as they shook hands. What they said had nothing to do with what they were thinking.

Norlin mopped his face with a bandanna, after he had murmured "Pleased to meet you," and mentioned that it was nice to get in the shade after being cooked by a blistering sun for four-five hours. The younger man remarked that he didn't ever remember it being hotter at this time of year.

Sandra went in for a glass and when she returned Norlin was telling Sloan that Lopez had been forced to abandon the stolen herd just this side of the line. A troop of cavalry had come on the raiders by chance and sent them scuttling into the brush. That was good, Sloan said. And how about Scarface? Had they heard anything of him?

"No." The sheriff rubbed the palm of his hand across an unshaven face meditatively and slanted a searching look at Sloan. "Looks like he has holed up and pulled the hole in after him. I reckon if anybody could give us information——"

He dropped the sentence there. Sloan was of no help.

"Maybe someone who knows him might give you a line on where his hangouts are," Cape said smoothly.

Norlin admitted to himself that he was unduly suspicious. He had in his pocket a letter from the deputy sheriff Mosely describing the young man who had sat opposite him at breakfast the morning after the raid. It fitted very accurately this youth who called himself Cape Sloan. The fellow could not have been in two different places at the same time. Yet he did not act just like an innocent man. There was a touch of challenge in his manner that was almost insolent, a sort of a "You-be-damned, prove it if you can" air.

"I've brought some sugar," Sandra told the sheriff, "in case you like your lemonade sweet."

He sampled the lemonade and said it was just the way he liked it. "Cooler up in the mountains," he suggested, cocking an eye at the other man.

Sloan recognized this as a trial balloon. "Should think it would be," he agreed.

"Did you say you came by way of Globe?"

"I didn't say." Cape's voice was cool and indifferent. It invited no further discussion of the subject. "I'll throw in with the sheriff about the lemonade, Miss Ranger. Best I ever drank."

"It tastes better because the day is so hot." She looked into the pitcher. "There's a dividend left for you."

"No, no. I've had my share. You drink it."

Sheriff Norlin had an elusive little notion flitting through his mind that he had seen this young man before. There was something faintly familiar about his voice, or was it in his manner of speaking?

"Not yore first visit to this part of the country, Mr. Sloan, I take it," he said.

"You think I don't look like a tenderfoot, sheriff." There was a slight drawling derision in the tone. "I reckon that's a compliment coming from an old-timer."

Sandra was a little annoyed at Cape Sloan. She knew he was taking an impish pleasure in sidestepping the sheriff's questions even though a frank answer would involve him in no trouble. For some reason he had built up a defense so quick to assert itself that it was almost belligerent.

"I had a letter from Mosely today," Norlin said. "You'll be glad to know it clears you, Mr. Sloan."

"Since I knew it would, I won't throw my hat up in the air and cheer about it," the young man answered dryly.

After the sheriff had left, Sandra's guest offered a drawling comment. "If I'd known my *pasear* into your country was going to upset so many citizens, I reckon I would have brought a letter of introduction from the governor."

Sandra's honest eyes met his directly. He had raised the question. She would tell him the truth. "I think you are a good deal to blame yourself. You act like a small boy with a chip on his shoulder. If you were more frank and friendly——"

"Friendly with the fellows who want to hang me for something I didn't do?" he inquired with his sardonic smile.

"Sheriff Norlin isn't trying to hang you," she said sturdily. "I don't want to find out anything you don't want to tell. I'm on your side anyhow. But since I'm not a complete fool I can see you are holding something back." She raised a hand quickly to head off his interruption. "You have a right to your secrets. That's not the point. You were dodging Sheriff Norlin's questions just to irritate him. What difference does it make whether you did or didn't come through Globe?"

"No difference," he admitted. "But Norlin had just one legitimate point of interest in me, my connection with the Scarface gang. When he discovered I hadn't any he ought to have been through. But after he got Mosley's letter he rode twenty miles to see me."

"To make sure you fitted the description Mr. Mosely gave of you. That was his duty."

"After he saw me he still wasn't satisfied."

"Because of your . . . evasions."

He brushed the sheriff out of the picture. "In spite of those . . . evasions . . . you are still for me. Isn't that what you said?"

His cool hard eyes drilled into her. She felt a pulse of excitement begin to beat in her throat. No balanced judgment would ever decide her feelings toward this man. It was not only that he had done her a great service at much risk to himself. Something reached out from that lean body with the whipcord muscles, from the strong reckless face, that drew her irresistibly to him.

She said, in a low voice: "I think you have been wild and lawless and that there is something . . . shocking . . . in your past. But whatever you have done, you are not evil. A man's actions, at some crisis, and what he really is, are two different things. I don't have to be told what is troubling you to know that I am on your side."

Swiftly she turned and walked into the house. The man's gaze followed her. He was astonished at what she had said, at the insight which had probed through the incriminating facts to the essential truth. She lived on the other side of a gulf he could not cross. None the less a warm glad excitement filled his breast.

He beat it down, almost savagely. His way of life was chosen. It was one that probably would include violence and bloodshed. There was no room in it for a woman like Sandra Ranger, nor for any of the pleasant and kindly friendships that might temper his ruthlessness. He was in a tight spot from which he did not expect to get out alive. But he had set himself to a task. He meant to go through with it unless his enemies destroyed him first.

9 *Concerning a Gent on the Make*

The name of Jug Packard came up one evening while the Ranger family were sitting with Cape Sloan on the porch facing the shadowy outlines of the Huachucas. The ranch guest had dropped a casual question to which he knew the answer.

"Yes," replied John. "There's right smart ore there. Copper, and some gold."

"In paying values?"

"You must have heard of the Johnny B—near the mouth of Geronimo Gulch."

"Seems to me I have. Is it locally owned?" Cape kept his voice indifferent. Nobody could have guessed by hearing him that he was doing more than making talk to pass time.

"Jug Packard holds a controlling interest."

The young man stifled a yawn with his forefingers. The obvious lack of interest was fraudulent. He had not heard the name for years, but the sound of it set a pulse of excitement strumming in him. "Lives in New York, with an office on Wall Street, I reckon," he suggested.

"No, sir. Lives at Tucson, when he isn't at the mine. Mostly he stays right at Jugtown, where the works are. His family put on considerable dog at Tucson, but the old man dresses like he did when he didn't have a nickel. A tramp wouldn't say 'Thank you' for anything Jug wears."

"I see. An old-timer, a diamond in the rough."

"An old-timer all right. He's been here since Baldy was a hole in the ground, but I wouldn't call him exactly a diamond or rave about his heart of gold."

"A millionaire?"

"He's got money enough to burn a wet mule." Ranger added, after a moment: "Jug is a crabbed old tightwad. Hangs on to a dollar so hard he squeezes the eagle off it before he turns it loose."

"But otherwise an estimable citizen," Sloan commented. His sardonic face was in the shadow of the vines and told no tales.

"Hmp! Not unless rumor is a lying jade," returned Ranger. He was a man who spoke his mind, and he did not like the mine owner. "I wouldn't trust him farther than I could throw a bull by the tail. Some nasty stories about Jug have floated around. By the way, your friend Uhlmann used to be a foreman or pit boss or something or other for him."

"Did he mention that he was my friend?" the younger man asked with frosty irony.

Ranger leaned back in his chair, drew on his pipe, and released the smoke slowly. "Jug came in as a mule skinner for a freight outfit," he said. "The pachies ambushed the party on the Oracle road and would have got the whole caboodle if Bob Webb and two-three of his boys hadn't happened along and drove them off. Jug was wounded, so Bob took him to Tucson and looked after the bills till he got on his feet again. They say Mrs. Webb nursed him. Anyhow, later Bob took him down to the Johnny B and gave him a job."

"Mr. Packard seems to have made good there," Sloan said dryly.

"Jug is one of those fellows born to make money. If he sees a dime around that isn't nailed down he gets it. No doubt he saw right away that there was a fortune in the Johnny B. Jug is mighty competent, the kind that is bound to get to the top. Webb was kinda easy-going. He relied on Jug a lot. In three-four years he was superintendent and had a small interest in the mine. All he needed was that toe-hold." The cattleman

40

stopped talking. He put his boots on the porch railing and relaxed.

His daughter prodded him. She was in the lane of lamplight that streamed from the window of the parlor. "Well, go on," she urged.

It was her eyes, Sloan decided, that quickened a personality interesting and exciting. They were shining now like pools of liquid fire. He did not know that she had divined intuitively that this story somehow concerned him greatly.

"Webb was killed when a charge exploded unexpectedly in one of the drifts," her father continued. "After that Jug took charge, though Mr. Webb still owned most of the property. He organized it into a stock company, and by that time he held the next biggest interest to Mrs. Webb. The mine ran into a streak of bad luck. They lost the pay vein, and none of the drifts seemed to have much ore. For a couple of years the Johnny B shut down. The stock went down to almost nothing. Jug bought it right and left, a good deal of it from Mrs. Webb, who had to get money to keep herself and her two kids. When the mine opened up again Jug owned nine-tenths of the stock. Almost right away they struck a bonanza."

"Fortunate for Packard," Sloan remarked.

The girl looked at him quickly. He was covering up carefully, but back of his arid reserve she read a deep bitterness. "You think Mr. Packard just happened to hit pay ore?" she asked.

"That's his story. You can take it or leave it." Ranger's resentment at the man exploded into words. "No, I think he pulled off some kind of shenanigan. Maybe he knew the ore was there and shut down to get control."

"Who kept the mine books?" Sloan asked abruptly.

"I don't know. Why?"

"He might have been looting the mine before it shut down— pocketing the profits so as to have enough to buy up the stock later."

"I wouldn't put it past him. Anyhow, he has the Johnny B, however he got it."

"And Mrs. Webb—what did she do about it?" Sandra asked.

"What could she do?" Ranger answered. "Jug had been too slick for her."

"So the story ends there."

"No. After a while young Webb came back and raised a row. He was a wild young coot, I gather. Got off on the wrong foot and killed a fellow named Giles Lemmon, who was one of Jug's men. They gave him twenty years in the penitentiary."

"Which made it nice for Mr. Packard," Sloan drawled. "Showing how all things work together for good to them that love the Lord."

"How dreadful!" Sandra murmured. "For him and his poor mother, if she was still living."

"She was then," Ranger replied. "She isn't now. Two years after he went to prison I read in the paper of her death."

"And the son—he's still in the penitentiary?"

"I reckon so, Sandra. Maybe he deserved what he got. When a man kills he can't kick if he has to pay the price. But one thing is sure. Jug Packard brought about that killing. He was more to blame than the boy."

"Men with as much money as Packard don't go to prison," Sloan said, a cynical bitterness in his face.

"Oh, I hope that isn't true in this country," Sandra cried.

"In the land of the free, where all men are born equal," the ranch guest mocked.

"It isn't true, Sandra," the girl's father said. "Though I'm afraid it is true that a rich man can often buy delays and even avoidance of punishment that a poor one can't afford. In Packard's case there was no evidence that he had committed a crime. I've said too much. I don't know he slickered Mrs. Webb out of her mine. That's only my private opinion."

Sloan rose and said he thought he would be turning in for the night. Sandra was shocked at his face. His mouth was a thin tight slit and there was something wolfish in his tortured eyes.

10   Sandra Guesses a Secret

Jim Budd was transferring a box of grocery supplies from a wagon to the kitchen when Sloan drifted across the yard to meet him. The cook stopped in the doorway, box in front of him, and gave the ranch guest a morning greeting.

"How is you this fine day, Mr.—Sloan?"

"Fine as the wheat, Jim. Go ahead. I'll come into the kitchen."

Budd deposited the groceries on the table and turned to find out what the other wanted to say to him. Sloan wasted no time.

"I understand a colored boy who cooks at the Johnny B mine will probably drop in to see you this afternoon," he said.

"Yessuh, he 'most generally does on his way to town. Miss Sandra tell you Sam wuz comin'?"

"She said he might. Do you know how long he has worked at the Johnny B?"

"More'n ten years, he tole me."

"I want you to do me a favor, Jim. Find out from him if you can where Stan Fraser is now. Years ago he used to run the engine at the mine. Put it sort of careless. Make out you once knew him. And whatever you do, don't let him know you're asking for me."

"Okay, Mr.—Sloan."

Sandra came into the kitchen and Cape explained his presence with an apologetic laugh. "I've got so little to do that I go around gassing with everybody and interfering with their work. But you'll be rid of me tomorrow. I'll be on my way."

"Where are you going?" she asked.

"I'm not dead sure. Think I'll try to pick up a job on some ranch."

She said nothing more about it, but she made up her mind not to let him ride for any outfit in this part of the territory if she could help it. She believed he was in great danger here. He ought to go away to a place where he was unknown, where he was not surrounded by enemies. It would be madness for him to stay here, especially so since he was brooding over some dark purpose of revenge. That he was the son of Bob Webb she felt sure. Either he had been released from prison or he had escaped. If he got into fresh trouble, even though he might be out on parole, he would be dragged back again without a trial.

The intensity of her feeling was disturbing. When they met, excitement flooded her breast and left her a little breathless. She wondered if this were love, and told herself she hoped not. There could be no happy consummation to such madness. How could one walk through life happily beside a man who strode with such reckless feet along perilous trails? A silly question, she put it to herself severely, about a man who was showing not the least interest in her.

She took to her father the problem of Cape Sloan's future. He was in the room he used as an office, checking a bill from a hardware store. Sandra waited while he finished adding a column.

"Aren't you ashamed, Mr. Ranger, to have an ex-convict here as a guest?" she asked.

He frowned at her. "What nonsense have you in your head?"

"I'm talking about Mr. Sloan, alias Webb. I'm not sure he is a released convict. He may be an escaped one." She added, with a smile: "In which case of course you are an accessory and will have to go back with him."

"You mean that this man is Bob Webb's son?"

"That's what I mean." She gave up abruptly the playful approach she had adopted. She found herself too distressed for foolery. "He says he is going to get work on some ranch near here. I know he is back looking for more trouble. You must make him get out of this part of the country as quick as he can."

"What makes you think he is Webb?"

43

"I watched him last night while you were telling about how Jug Packard got the Johnny B. He sat back where you could not notice his face. But I saw it—so hard and bitter and savage."

Ranger marshaled stray impressions of his own. "You may be right. Come to think of it, he looks some like Bob Webb did. Or would, without that beard. The same bony structure of face. If he is young Webb, he ought not to be in this neck of the woods. Why would he come back?"

"I don't know. But he didn't come to shake hands with Jug Packard. There's another thing. Do you know whether he might have been turned loose on parole? If not—"

"There was a prison break at Yuma a few months ago," Ranger said. "I read only the headlines in the paper. Three or four men escaped. Webb might have been one of them." He stroked his short beard reflectively. "I think we'll have to call Sloan in for a show-down."

"What if he admits he is Webb?"

"Nothing to do but urge him to leave Arizona."

"If he has made up his mind to stay he won't go."

"Now that he is smoked out he'll probably go."

Sandra glanced through the window, said quickly, "Here he is."

Sloan stood in the doorway and looked from one to the other. "Excuse me," he said to Ranger. "I didn't know you were busy."

"Come in," his host invited. "We have something to talk over with you."

Again the guest's glance slid from the cattleman to his daughter. "About how to get rid of a guest who outstays his welcome, I reckon," he said. "I'll relieve yore minds. I'm traveling this afternoon. And since we're together, I'll tell you right now how grateful I am for all the kindness you have shown me."

Ranger flushed with embarrassment. He did not find it easy to broach the subject in his mind.

"We're in your debt more than we can ever repay, Mr. Sloan," he began. "You're welcome to stay here till Christmas if you like. But, the fact is, the way things are with you, if we've guessed right—"

The ranchman bogged down. He could not bluntly tell this man they thought he was a convict and a murderer.

"Just how are things with me?" Sloan asked, his voice murmurously ironic.

"We are wondering if you aren't Bob Webb's son," Ranger gulped out.

Sloan smiled, after an instant's pause. "Miss Ranger has quite an imagination, hasn't she?"

44

Color crept into the cheeks of the girl. "You're right to blame me," she admitted. "My father would never have thought of it."

"She mentioned it to me because she was afraid you are stacking up trouble for yourself," Ranger corrected.

"For argument's sake, let us say I am Bob Webb's son." The steely eyes of the young man held fast to those of the girl. "And an escaped convict. What do you propose to do about it?"

"We think this is the most dangerous spot in the world for you," she answered, her words low and husky. "Whatever purpose has brought you here can bring only trouble, unless you give it up. They'll discover who you are, just as we have done. You must go far away from here at once."

"My brother has a cattle ranch on the White River in Colorado. It's a fine country, but thinly settled. He would find a job for you if we asked it." Ranger finished with direct advice. "I would go tonight. Any delay might be disastrous."

"I'll go part way at least tonight," Sloan promised with a sardonic grin. "Whatever happens, you'll have done yore full duty by me—and some more. I'll never forget yore kindness to me."

"You don't mean to leave Arizona at all," Sandra charged. "You mean to stay and—and—"

There was the beginning of panic in her eyes. She did not know the conclusion of her sentence, only that it would be something dreadful.

"I'll leave as soon as I've finished my business."

"What business?" she demanded.

"Personal and private." His cynical smile denied her any knowledge of it or any part in it.

The repulse was a slap in the face. But she cared nothing for that. Her mind was too intent on saving him.

"Stay around here and you'll leave with handcuffs on your wrists!" she cried.

"Sandra!" her father warned sternly.

The young man disregarded Ranger and spoke to the girl. In his eyes she saw again the reckless defiance of consequences. "I don't think so. One place I'm not going to is Yuma."

From a white miserable face she stared at him. He meant that he would be killed rather than go back to prison. All his thinking was warped by the horrible experience he had endured. When he first went to the penitentiary he must have been just a boy. She had read stories written by released prisoners who had been shut up by society like wild beasts. It had twisted and embittered their lives. That was how it was with Cape Sloan. Existence had narrowed down with him to a determination to get revenge. And there was no way to show

45

him that he was making a fatal mistake, that today might mark the beginning of a new life if he could escape the mental miasma in which he moved.

When he rode away next morning Sandra watched him from the window of her bedroom. She had already said a smiling good-bye to him at breakfast, but there was no smile in her eyes or on her lips now. She was convinced that he was going to his death—perhaps not today or this week, but soon—and she believed he knew it. Yet he rode flatbacked and lightly, a sardonic recklessness in the gray-blue eyes set so challengingly in the coffee-brown face. It was dreadful to fear that all the virile strength of him might in a moment be stricken from that superb body.

This morning Cape Sloan was not thinking about anything so grim as death. The warm sun was shining. A gentle breeze from the Huachucas stirred the mistletoe in the live oaks. It was the kind of day to make a man glad he was alive. Sloan's thoughts were of the girl he was leaving behind him, though he did not let these deflect him from giving wary attention to the country through which he was traveling. He had been for months a man on the dodge. More than once he had shaved capture by a hair's breadth. Since the hour of his prison break there had been scarcely a day when he had not walked with danger at his side. But meeting Sandra had set the sap of hope stirring in him again. He would beat it down savagely later, but for the time he let its sweet madness flow through him.

There were ranches in the valley, but he circled them carefully, to meet as few people as he could. The morning was old when he struck the San Pedro river and followed it to the little village of Charleston drowsing in the sun. The river swept half way round the town, a row of fine cottonwood trees on the bank.

Cape loosened the revolver in its holster, to make sure of free action in case he had to draw. The chances were he would not be molested, but a man who rode as wild a trail as he did could not take any chances.

11 Stan Fraser Buys Chips

It was high noon when Cape Sloan rode into the little town of Charleston and tied up at the hitch rack in front of the Raw-hide Corral. He strolled through the big gate and stopped beside a small man in jeans who was greasing a wagon.

"Mr. Stan Fraser?" asked Sloan.

"Yes, sir," the owner of the name answered crisply.

He had a lean sun-tanned face much wrinkled around the eyes, which were steel-blue and looked at his questioner very steadily. Fraser was nearer fifty than forty, but the years had not tamed a certain youthful jauntiness in him. His pinched-in Stetson was tilted to one side and the bandanna around his leathery throat was as colorful as an Arizona sunset.

The muscles of Sloan's face stiffened. He spoke slowly, choosing his words carefully. "You cussed old cow thief, I might have known I'd find you in this rustler's town where honest men are as scarce as hens' teeth. I'm sure surprised the law hasn't caught up with you yet in spite of all the deviltry you've done."

Fraser's eyes grew frosty. "A man who talks like you are doing has come to pick a fight. Before you start smokin' mebbe you'll tell me what the trouble is about. After that I'll accommodate you if you'll give me time to get a gun."

The features of the younger man relaxed to a smile. "Not fighting talk if I grin when I say it," he denied. "Don't you know who I am, you old one-gallus brushpopper?"

Astonishment rubbed the anger from the face of Fraser. Recognition came slowly, after a long half-minute of eye searching. "By criminy, you're young Bob Webb," he cried. His gaze swept over the corral fence, and up and down the street. "What in heck you doing here, boy? You'd ought to be holed up in Mexico."

"Thought I'd drop in and shake hands with an old friend. But you don't need to shout about it. There might be someone here with the idea that I ought to be holed up in Yuma and the two hundred dollars reward money jingling in his pocket."

The owner of the corral lowered his voice. "You're dead right about that. This place is infested by lowdown scalawags who would sell their brothers for a dollar Mex. They claim that in Curly Bill's time there was some honor among thieves. If a fellow was a crook he was safe here or at Galeyville or anywhere in this corner of Cochise County, safe from the law anyhow. But not now. Plenty of rustlers and bad men drop in here to get corned up. They are particular though to keep a saddled bronc in the alley to fork for a quick getaway."

"Since I rate as a crook I'd better do that too," Sloan said.

Fraser flushed. "Quit talkin' foolishness, boy. You're the son of my old boss, who was the whitest, straightest man who ever threw a saddle on a horse. You've had bad luck. I know thirty fellows walking the streets today who have killed for one reason or another. None of 'em ever served a day for it. You were just a kid, and they socked you twenty years. The scoundrels railroaded you. Everybody knows you got a raw deal."

"And do nothing about it," Sloan added cynically.

"What can we do, boy? We got up a petition to the governor

for a pardon. Jug Packard blocked it. He's a political power in the territory now. If I was you, I'd lie low with me till night and then ride hell-for-leather till you had crossed the line into mañana-land."

"Don't worry about me," the young man advised carelessly. "Nobody is going to drag me back to Yuma, not while I'm alive. I came to have a talk with you, Stan. After that I'll vamoose."

Stan Fraser looked at the hard bony bearded face, lips close shut, eyes cold and steely, at the smoothly-muscled shoulders and the poised confidence of the man's carriage, and he realized that it would be hard to recognize in him the loose-jointed gangling boy who had been convicted of killing Giles Lemmon more than seven years ago.

He shrugged his shoulders. "You're just like yore father. No use telling him anything. He'd go his own way. When I said Jug Packard was a cold-blooded traitor without an ounce of decency or gratitude in him, Bob wouldn't listen to me. He got hot under the collar." The boss of the wagon yard hesitated a moment before blurting out what was in his mind. "I can't prove it, but it's my opinion yore father was killed by foul play. When we brought his body out of the drift I saw Hans Uhlmann and Jug whispering together. Hans was the only fellow except Bob down on that level at the time of the explosion."

"You think Uhlmann was paid by Packard to get rid of my father?"

"I've told you all I know," Fraser replied. "You do the thinking."

Sloan nodded. "I know that talk like that is dangerous. As for its going any further, you can be sure nobody else will ever know you said it." Recalling subsequent events the eyes of the convict grew bitter and the muscles of his jaw stood out like ropes. "I don't suppose you ever heard that after my father's death Packard proposed to divorce his wife and marry my mother. She was terribly angry and put him in his place. Then he decided to take the Johnny B lock, stock, and barrel. That way he got my share too."

"And there's not a thing you could do about it."

"Not then."

The older man slanted a sharp look at Sloan. "Or now. Don't you start getting any crazy ideas in your head, boy. You tried it once and it ruined yore life."

"Yes," the escaped prisoner agreed. "I didn't know enough then to fight a man like Packard. I blundered in like a fool and was framed. The story I told at my trial was true. Both Packard and Uhlmann gave false testimony. When the firing began I was near the middle of the room, with Uhlmann on one side of me and Lemmon on the other. I ducked under the desk, and by chance Uhlmann's bullet caught Lemmon in the throat. Packard made Uhlmann stop shooting. He figured it would look better not to kill me, but to send me to the penitentiary."

"I knew it was some kind of frame-up, but I thought they deviled you into killing Lemmon." The mind of Fraser picked up something else the young man had said. "You didn't know enough then, and now they have the cards stacked against you. No use trying to fight Packard. Even if the law wasn't waiting to drag you to Yuma you couldn't do a thing. He's had time to get everything fixed. The way it is now you haven't a dead man's chance. First move you make, they throw you back into a cell. Be reasonable, son. You're young yet. Get out of this country and make a new start. Forget Packard. One of these days he'll get his."

Sloan ignored that. "Uhlmann didn't have a nickel when he was working at the Johnny B. They say he has a pretty good ranch now. How did he get it?"

"I've got quite a bump of curiosity myself, and I once looked into that. He claimed an uncle died and left him fifteen thousand dollars. That's not true. Jug set him up in business, took a mortgage on the place, and a year or so later released it. I'll bet Rhino never paid a dime of it. He knew too much, and Jug had to square him."

"Of course that was the way of it," Cape Sloan assented. "They'll stand together. I couldn't get anything on them that way."

"Nor any other way."

"A fellow named Newman used to do the bookkeeping for the mine. Is he still there, do you know?"

"No. He quit long ago. Works in the Southern Pacific railroad offices at Tucson." Fraser added further information. "Funny thing about that. I met him soon after he had quit Packard and asked him why he had left the Johnny B. He gave me a quick look and shut up talking right then. Looked to me as if he was scared to say anything."

"Think I'll drift over to Tucson," Sloan mentioned.

Fraser slapped down on the tire of the nearest wheel the dabbler with which he had been scraping grease on the axle. "I can see you are lookin' for trouble, Bob," he yelped excitedly. "Haven't you got a lick of sense? Jug Packard is in the saddle. He'll rub you outa his way soon as he finds out you're around. If you don't pull yore freight he'll pull you in a wooden box or have you slapped back in jail. Jug is the cock-a-doodle-do around here."

A fiery wave seemed to pass through the younger man. He might make wreckage of his life, if there was any of it left that had not already been shattered, but he would stand up and fight to a finish.

"You think this man murdered my father. So do I. He robbed my mother and broke her heart when his lies put me in the penitentiary. With me locked up, he left my little sister alone in the world. What kind of a weak-kneed quitter do you think I am?"

His friend gave up trying to dissuade this bitter reckless man. Bob Webb's son would walk unafraid into desperate peril if need be, as his father had more than once done before him. He was as tough as ironwood and as unrelenting as a wolf. It flashed across the mind of Fraser that he would not like to be in the shoes of Jug Packard as long as this enemy was alive.

"All right," the little man said quietly. "I'll side you. The best friend I ever had was yore father."

The convict shook his head. "No, Stan. I'm playing a lone hand. They'll probably get me. I'll not drag you down too."

Fraser flared up angrily. "Hell! Do you think you're the only darn fool in the world? I've got no wife or kids. You can't make up my mind for me. I'll ride the river with you, fellow."

"Whether I want you to or not?" Sloan asked.

"Y'betcha! This is a free country. You can't stop me from going where you do any more than I can prevent you from doing what you've a mind to do."

"But this is my job, Stan," the younger man explained. "It's not yours. I have a right to risk my own life. The way I'm fixed it's not worth anything anyhow. But I can't lead you into trouble."

"Who's leading me?" The old-timer bristled up to Sloan. "Not a young squirt like you. I'm trailin' along to dry-nurse you."

Cape Sloan knew that his friend was game as a bulldog. He had been brought up in the outdoor school of the frontier which kept in session twelve months of every year. It was a rough and tumble school where there was no law to protect a man except the Colt strapped to his side. Stan was a small wiry bundle of energy. There was an old saying in the West that all men are the same size behind a six-gun. Cape could guess by the quick excitement in the eyes of the corral keeper that he was eager to escape from his present humdrum existence and turn back the clock to face the perils of a renewed youth.

"There may be trouble," Stan reminded him.

"Sure there'll be trouble. Ain't that what I keep tellin' you?"

"My idea is to move lawfully, getting evidence against Packard that will stand up in court."

"That's fine with me."

"But it won't be with Packard. If it looks like I'm getting anywhere it's a cinch that guy will start to smoke."

Fraser opened his eyes with mock astonishment. "You don't

think that good old mealy-mouthed Jug would start anything like that?" he demurred with obvious sarcasm.

"How would I feel if one of their bullets got you instead of me?" Sloan wanted to know.

"They have not molded the bullet yet that will get me," the little gamecock retorted. "I'm sittin' in, boy. Done bought chips. Where do we go from here?"

"We go and have dinner first if there's a restaurant in this burg."

"Best place is Ma Skelton's. I eat there. Let's go."

They strolled across the street to an adobe house that had been plastered once on the outside but was beginning to scale.

"Remember that my name is Cape Sloan," the man who claimed it warned the other.

A few moments later Fraser introduced the stranger to Ma Skelton. She was a large angular woman in the late forties with a hard leathery face and brusque manner behind which was concealed a warm and generous heart open to all in distress. More than one cowboy with a broken leg had convalesced at her home in spite of the fact that he had not saved a nickel to pay for food, lodging, and rough nursing. No matter how tough an *hombre* the invalid might be, that was always one debt he paid later if his span of life was not cut short. In case he was inclined to be forgetful, Ma's other guests prodded his memory forcibly.

12   *Sloan Renews a Promise*

"Dinner's ready," Ma Skelton said. "Sit down. Any place."

Sloan and Fraser stepped across a bench that ran along the table close to a wall and sat down. Several others joined them at the table.

A long dark man came into the room and closed the door behind him. He stood there for a moment, poised and wary, his gaze sweeping the place in a check-up of those present. Cape Sloan understood that look. It was both furtive and searching. He had himself acquired one much like it from months on the dodge. The man had a livid scar across the left cheek, stretching almost from ear to chin.

The newcomer circled the table and sat down with his back to the wall beside Cape. From where he was he could see instantly anybody who came in either from the outside or the kitchen. The forty-four at his side pressed against Sloan's thigh. Without a word of greeting to those present he reached for the platter of steak the waitress had just brought, chose the largest portion, slid a half dish of fried potatoes to his plate, and began to eat voraciously.

"Anything new up San Simon way, Scarface?" Fraser inquired amiably.

The disfigured man slanted a resentful look at the corral owner. When he came to town he did not care to have his name bandied about. For though the local residents knew him there might be law officers around who had never met him. He growled out that nothing ever happened in his locale.

Since Sloan had half guessed that this man was Scarface, his poker face betrayed no least interest in the rustler. The business of eating appeared to absorb his full interest. Under other circumstances he might have felt it his duty to help arrest the fellow, but he was himself a fugitive and had been for years wholly on the side of the hunted lawbreaker rather than the pursuing officer.

Dinner was nearly over when the door opened to let in four men who quite evidently had been lined up in front of a bar prior to adjournment for eating. The one in the van was a big redfaced man in the clothes of a town dweller. He gave the hostess a placatory smile.

"I reckon we're a few minutes late, Ma," he said airily.

She stared at him with a wooden uncompromising face. "At this house dinner is served at ten minutes past twelve, as you very well know."

"Now, Ma, we had a little business to finish and couldn't get here any sooner," he protested. "You wouldn't deny food to hungry men?"

"Yore business was at O'Brien's saloon," she told him bluntly. "This is the third time in ten days you've pulled this on me, Rip Morris. You know my rule, and I've warned you before. Get here on time—or stay away."

"Two cowboys got in here after one o'clock yesterday and you fed them," Morris reminded her.

"So I did. They had been on a cattle drive since five in the morning and not idling before a bar. That was an exception. This isn't."

One of the others who had just come in spoke up sourly. He was a mean-looking fellow with a face that would have curdled cream. "So we don't get dinner," he snapped. "Is that it?"

"Not here you don't."

A snarling oath slid out of the corner of his thin lips. "We'll take our trade where it's wanted, Rip," he sneered. "There are other places to eat beside this."

"Then go to them, Pete McNulty," Ma Skelton snapped. "And never show yore face in this house again if you don't want to stop a flatiron with yore ugly mouth."

52

Uhlmann was another of the four. At sight of him and McNulty the escaped convict had become at once watchful. He observed that both of them had nodded a greeting to Scarface with no evidence of animosity. This was surprising. A few days ago they had been clamoring for his blood. He had stolen their stock and killed the rider of a neighboring cattleman.

As McNulty turned sullenly to go, Scarface murmured out of the corner of his mouth. "Be seeing you later."

Uhlmann's glassy eyes fell on Sloan. "Look who's here, Pete," he snorted.

McNulty glared at the young man. "Blast my eyes, Rhino," he cried, "if it ain't our friend the rustler again."

The hard gaze of the convict bored into the man. "Wrong on both counts," he said very quietly. "Not yore friend and not a rustler. This makes twice you've called me a thief."

"Caught you in the act, didn't we?" shrilled McNulty.

Scarface looked suspiciously from the little ranchman to Sloan and back again. "What's eatin' you, Pete?" he wanted to know. "You got anything against rustlers? Or is it just this one that annoys you?"

"He claims I was helping you run off a bunch of stolen stock the day of the Lopez raid," Sloan explained.

"I never saw you before," Scarface retorted. "I don't get what this is all about."

"We trapped him in Two-Fork Cañon with our stuff and he tried to play he was innocent and you guilty," McNulty explained. His frown was meant to warn Scarface that he would tell him all about it later. "Course Rhino and I knew better than that."

Sloan said, still without raising his voice, "When I meet you in the street later, McNulty, if I do, I'll wear you to a frazzle with my quirt."

Ma Skelton addressed herself sharply to Sloan. "Young man, we won't hear any more out of *you*. Nobody can bring quarrels to this house and unload them here. I won't have it."

"I've said all I'm going to say, ma'am," Cape promised, and busied himself with his pie.

"If you fool with me, fellow, I'll let daylight through you," McNulty warned.

He retreated hurriedly, for Ma Skelton was striding toward him. Two of his companions clumped out of the boarding-house at his heels. Uhlmann lingered a moment, the little eyes in his leathery face fastened on Sloan.

"I've seen you some place before that time we met in the gulch," he said, a puzzled frown on his forehead.

"Maybe at Delmonico's in New York," Cape suggested ironically.

"One of these days I'll remember when and where, fellow."

"Then we'll sing about auld acquaintance."

"Don't get funny with me," Uhlmann snarled.

Sloan looked up at Ma Skelton, a grin on his face. "No comment to make. All I'll talk about is the weather."

An angry animal growl rumbled from Uhlmann's throat as he lumbered out of the room.

"A nice pleasant gent to keep away from," Fraser commented lightly.

Nobody else had any remark to add. As the corral owner had suggested, Uhlmann was a good person to let alone. Presently Scarface rose, paid for his dinner, and departed.

Fraser and Sloan walked out into the dusty unpaved street and stood on the wooden sidewalk the planks of which were falling into decay. The buildings were of adobe and frame, the latter all with false fronts upon which the lettering was faded. In the days of John Ringo and Curly Bill, Charleston had been a riotous little town, but its hour of glory was now in the past.

13 *McNulty Has a Bad Five Minutes*

"What the Sam Hill is this about you being a rustler?" Fraser asked.

His friend smiled grimly. "Mr. McNulty had a rope around my neck the other day. They were set on hanging me to the nearest tree. Their story was that I belonged to the Scarface gang, which had just raided a bunch of cattle and killed one of John Ranger's cowboys."

"I heard something about that, but I didn't know you were the man they caught. John was with them when they caught you, I was told."

"Yes. He and Russell Hart. All four of them thought I was one of the rustlers, but Ranger and Hart were willing to wait and make sure. Uhlmann and McNulty wanted me hanged right then. At the time I thought they were just a pair of cold-blooded ruffians, but I'm not so sure now. They claimed they wanted to get Scarface and were full of threats against him. It doesn't look now as if they are so crazy to get him. In the dining room they acted as if they had some kind of understanding. Scarface told them he would be seeing them later. Why, if they are honest cattlemen and he is stealing their stock?"

"Doesn't look too good, does it? Ten-fifteen years ago Pete McNulty had a bad name. His neighbors thought he was stealing their stuff but couldn't prove it. Maybe he is up to his old tricks."

"There were one or two of his and of Uhlmann's animals in the drive," Sloan said. "But that might be a blind. These fellows might be along with the hunters to make sure they didn't get the thieves. And when they caught me that suited them fine. They could hang me and go home, leaving Scarface to slip away. I'll bet that's how it was."

"You certainly get around where the trouble is," the old-timer commented with a grin. "It ain't enough for you to have a reward out for you as an escaped convict. You've got to get into a jam for rustling too and escape the noose by a miracle. On top of that you build up a nice little feud with McNulty and Uhlmann. For a guy who is supposed to be not lookin' for notice you sure gather a lot of attention. You don't really aim to quirt this bird, do you?"

"Not if I don't meet him."

"There ain't two hundred people in town. If one of you don't light out *pronto* you're bound to meet. Try to give this fellow leather, and he'll plug a hole in you."

"I don't think so. He's yellow."

"That makes him more dangerous. He's liable to get scared and let you have it."

"Well, it's too late to help that now."

"With yore past you're in no shape to go around with a chip on yore shoulder. The thing to do is sing small. My idea is to light out of here this evening. I'll get Mose Tarwater to look after the corral while I'm gone."

"Why go at all?" Sloan asked. "You're under no obligation to go butting into my grief."

"That's done settled," Fraser told the younger man irritably. "We'll go sit in my office where you won't be noticed."

"All right. In just a minute. I want to get some Bull Durham."

Sloan stepped across the road to the store on the corner. He passed two saddled horses tied to a hitch rack. They were drowsing in the sun. A quirt hung looped over the horn of the saddle nearest him.

Out of the store McNulty came. He stood lounging against the door jamb, his head turned over the left shoulder. He was talking with somebody in the store.

Sloan stepped back and flicked the quirt from the horn. A moment later McNulty caught sight of him. The rancher jerked a Colt forty-five from its pocket in his leather chaps.

"Don't you come any nearer me," he yelped, his voice shrill with alarm. "Not a step, or I'll plug you."

Cape's stride did not falter. It brought him forward evenly and deliberately. "Not you, McNulty," he said quietly. "Not while I'm looking at you." On his lips was a contemptuous smile, but the man in the doorway found no comfort in it. The implacable blue-gray eyes shook his nerve, told him with dreadful certainty that he was delivered into the hands of his enemy. That his own boasting had brought punishment home to him made it no easier to face. The hand holding the gun trembled. Under his ribs the heart died within him. He could not send a message from his flaccid will to the finger crooked around the trigger.

"Rip—Rhino!" he shrieked. "Here's that Sloan lookin' for you. Hurry!"

Uhlmann's huge shapeless body appeared back of his companion. Sloan was not five feet from the wavering revolver. He said, still with no excitement in his steady voice, "A private matter to settle between me and McNulty, one you're not in, Uhlmann."

Cape plucked his victim from the doorway with his left hand as the lash whipped round the wrist holding the weapon. McNulty let out a cry of pain, and the forty-five clattered to the sidewalk.

The German put his hands in his pockets and grinned. This was no fuss of his. He did not like this stranger who had come into his life, and he knew that if they continued to meet there would be trouble some day. But he lived by the code of the outdoor West, at least when he was in the public eye.

"Hop to it, Pete," he encouraged. "Knock hell out of him. Whale the stuffing outa the brash fool."

The quirt in Sloan's hand wound itself with a whish around the thighs of McNulty. It rose and fell again and again. The tortured man cursed, threatened, screamed. He tried to fling himself to the ground to escape, but Cape dragged him back to his feet. The lash encircled Pete's legs like a rope of fire. He howled for help from Uhlmann and begged for mercy.

Sloan flung the writhing wretch from him and dropped the whip. He looked around, to find himself the focus of a score of eyes. They were watching him from doors and window, from the road and the sidewalk. Uhlmann's big body still filled the doorway, one thumb hitched in the sagging belt at his side.

Fraser put a hand on his friend's arm. "Come on, boy," he said. "Show's over."

"What was it all about?" somebody asked.

Rip Morris laughed. He shared the opinion of many others about Pete McNulty, that the fellow was a rat, and he had enjoyed seeing him brought low. "Pete said this fellow Sloan was a cow thief, and I reckon he objected."

The breast of the thrashed man was still racked by sobs he could not control, but he made a feeble attempt to save face. "He had a quirt—and I slipped."

"That's right," Uhlmann retorted scornfully. "All you had

was a gun, except yore fists. You certainly showed up good, Pete."

"You're a fine friend, Rhino," whined McNulty. "Stood there and let him use a whip on me, when I was kinda stunned and couldn't fight back."

Uhlmann's beady eyes were cold and expressionless. "You're a grown man, ain't you? Toting a forty-five in your hand. Whyfor would I interfere? If you can't back yore play, don't call a man a thief." The German turned to the owner of the corral. "You a friend of this bird who goes around hunting trouble?" he demanded.

"No, I don't reckon Pete would call me a friend of his," Fraser answered.

"I'm not talking about Pete, but this bird Sloan here."

"Why, yes, I've known Bob some time."

"Bob? Thought his first name was Cape."

Fraser hastened to cover his error. "So it is. But when he was a kid some of us called him Bob. Kind of a nickname."

"Well, whatever you call him, tell him from me that I don't like the color of his hair, nor his face, nor anything about him. Tell him if he wants to stay healthy to keep outa my sight."

Sloan said his little piece. "And tell Mr. Uhlmann from me, Stan, that he's got me plumb scared to death. If I could find a hole handy I would certainly crawl into it."

Fraser grinned cheerfully. "Now, boys, let's not start a rookus. A pleasant time has been had by all, except Pete. Why spoil it now? Come along, Bob."

Sloan turned and walked across the street with Fraser. They picked their way along the sidewalk, in order not to tread on broken boards. Stan slid a look compound of irritation and admiration at Bob Webb's son.

"I've sure enough tied myself up with a wampus cat," he said reproachfully. "I wonder how near that yellow wolf came to filling you with lead. Don't you know better than to walk up to a forty-five pointed at you?"

"It wasn't pointed at me most of the time," Sloan defended apologetically. "The point of the gun was wandering all over Cochise County."

"Yeah, in the hands of a man scared stiff. That kind is most dangerous. I looked to hear his gun tear loose any moment. If that's the way you expect to fight Jug Packard and his gunmen you won't last longer than a snowball in hell."

"This fellow wasn't Packard or one of his warriors. He was just a rabbit."

"You're the luckiest fighting fool I ever saw. If McNulty didn't happen to be a guy everyone despises you would never have got away with it. I could see that Rhino was half a mind

57

to butt in, but he wanted to see Pete get what was coming to him. When he got nasty later I wasn't surprised."

"Nor I. But I figured him out right—guessed he would decide, the way we all do out here, that a grown man has to fight his own battles."

"Hmp!" grunted Fraser, "Uhlmann has plenty of sand in his craw, but he hasn't any code you would dare bank on. The fellow would just as soon shoot you in the back as not, if nobody saw him."

"He didn't recognize me anyhow."

"No, but he's edging close. One of these days he will. You have some of your dad's ways, and it will come over him all of a sudden that you are young Webb. I didn't help any when I called you Bob twice."

"I'll try to keep out of his sight after this."

They had reached the Rawhide Corral. In one of the stalls they found a big bay horse that had not been there when they left.

"That is Scarface Brown's horse," Fraser said. "When he is in town he usually leaves it here. He's coming over from the store now."

The rustler had shiny leather chaps over his jeans. He wore a faded hickory shirt and a big white sombrero that drooped down on his face. Though his brows were knotted in a scowl, there was a reluctant good will in the eyes turned on Sloan.

"Fellow, you ain't got sense enough to pound sand in a rat hole, or you wouldn't of been crazy enough to walk up to Pete's gun thataway." A gleam of mirth twitched at his dark face. "You sure gave him the leather a-plenty. He's a mean little polecat. Nobody likes him. You ought to be popular with the boys." After a slight hesitation he added: "But you're not with some of them. Take Uhlmann now."

"I gathered that he is a little annoyed at me," Sloan replied dryly.

"Annoyed is not the word. He has figured out who you are. Something about the way you walk told him."

"And who am I?"

"You're Bob Webb, he claims. Rhino is fixin' to do something about it."

"What does he mean to do?"

"He didn't exactly say. But I reckon it will be sudden. Don't make any mistake. You can't monkey with him the way you did with Pete."

Sloan nodded. His cool appraising eyes rested on the rustler. "I'm much obliged, sir. But I don't quite see where you stand. I notice things. The other day Uhlmann and McNulty thought hanging was too good for you. They did considerable talking. They don't seem to be so eager now."

The rustler's frown carried a warning. "Strictly their business and mine. Don't make it yours."

The smile on Sloan's sardonic face was friendly. "I can wonder why you are telling me this if you are tied up with Uhlmann, can't I?"

"Hell, I don't have to give reasons," Scarface growled irritably. "Just because a man does business with another doesn't mean he has to back every play he makes. You did me a favor the other day without meaning to when I was being crowded some. That'll do for you, won't it?"

"If I nearly shoved my neck into a rope loop it wasn't out of kindness to you," Sloan said. "You've got a better reason than that. It sticks in yore craw to see a man murdered without a chance for his life."

"Uhlmann played you a rotten trick once, I've heard. I never did like the brute. If you can slip across the line into Mexico that will be all right with me." Scarface turned to Fraser. "I'll be hittin' the trail now, Stan. I'm headin' south a ways. Maybe yore friend will join me till our trails divide."

"I appreciate the offer," Sloan told the outlaw. "But I'm riding in another direction."

"If I was in yore shoes it would be south," Scarface reiterated. "But you're playin' the hand."

He rode away with a wave of the hand, a dangerous sinister scoundrel, but one Cape much preferred to his associates Uhlmann and McNulty.

Sloan remained at the corral while Fraser hunted up Mose Tarwater to take over for him during his absence. Cape was not happy about what he had done. He recognized ruefully the liabilities of his temperament. What if McNulty had called him a thief? Hard names break no bones. He might have let the little sneak go. To use a whip on a man was degrading to both parties. After Cape had flung down the quirt he had felt for a time physically sick. One had no right to treat another human being with such contempt. Wasn't there something in the Bible about a man being made in the image of God? Already he had paid bitterly for his hot temper. If he had any sense at all by this time he would have learned to curb and control his anger.

Though still a boy when he was taken to the penitentiary, he had already become embittered at the injustice of a social system that permitted the innocent to be robbed by a smoot scoundrel using the law to cover his theft and to ruin the life of a lad framed for a killing he had not committed. The endless days in prison, every minute regulated by armed guards who treated him like a chained wild beast, had intensified the sour resentment churning in him.

A clean fastidious streak in his character had saved him

59

from the underground vileness propagated by some of his fellow convicts. He lived within himself, apart from the prison politics, too proud to cater to those in authority or to join in the plots of those in his cell block. It had been only by sheer chance that an opportunity had come for him to join in the jail break organized by others.

During the days that followed he had lived like a hunted wolf, ready to kill or be killed at a moment's notice. Then Sandra had come into his life. The friendliness and the kindly consideration with which she and her family had treated him had gone to his heart as water does to the roots of a thirsty plant. He had fought against the softness beginning to undermine his hatred. In Sandra's way of life he had no part, he told himself.

14 The Half-Pint Squirt Says His Piece

Fraser came hurrying back almost on a run. "Slap yore saddle on, son. We're gettin' outa here quick. Something cooking over at O'Brien's. Uhlmann has three-four of the boys in a huddle, and that spells nothing good for you."

They left by the back gate of the corral to avoid notice. More than once they looked back, half expecting to see men mounting in pursuit. Except for a few horses tied to hitch racks the street was as deserted as one in a Mexican village during the hours of siesta.

Sloan laughed. "I'm not so important as you thought I was," he said. "Nobody cares whether I go or stay."

"Don't fool yoreself," the little man barked. "This country is gonna be plenty hot for you. Rhino will see to that."

They did not follow the road to Tombstone but cut across the hills. Below them they could see a wagon moving along the winding road to the quartz mill of the Tough Nut Mining company, but nowhere was there visible on it a body of riders who might be looking for an escaped convict with a reward on his head.

Fraser noticed that though young Webb, or Sloan as he now called himself, gave evidence in his actions and bearing of a desperate recklessness, born of the assurance that he would some day pass out to the sound of crashing guns as slugs tore into his body, he none the less scrutinized vigilantly the terrain they traveled, just as his wary eyes an hour ago had probed into the enemies he was facing. He had set himself a task, and until he had finished it he meant if possible to stay alive.

60

"We'd better not reach Tombstone till after dark," Fraser suggested. "There's a reward notice for you posted at the post office and at Hatch's saloon. We'll slip in kinda inconspicuous and put up at a rooming-house I know on Allen Street."

They unsaddled in a hill pocket and lay down beneath a live oak which protected them from the heat of the sun. Cape fell asleep within five minutes. He had been hunted so long that he had learned to snatch rest whenever he could do so with safety. The sun had set when Fraser awakened him by throwing a chunk of dead wood at his legs.

Sloan came to life suddenly, gun in hand. He glared at his friend a moment, then grinned at him sheepishly.

"Force of habit," he apologized.

"That's why I threw the chunk at you," Fraser explained. "I reckoned you might be jumpy if you were roused by hand, and I'd hate to have you sorry about puncturing me."

It was after dark when they slipped into Tombstone and left their horses at the O.K. Corral, which a few years earlier had been the scene of the famous gun battle between the Earp brothers and the McLowry-Clanton faction. They walked up Fremont Street to Fourth and ate in a small Mexican restaurant. There was better food at the Can-Can, but they decided against going there on account of its popularity. Best to meet as few people as possible. Before sun-up they expected to be on the road for Tucson.

For the same reason they avoided the Grand Hotel and put up at a cheap rooming-house just outside the business district.

"You stay put right here, son," Fraser ordered. "I'll drift uptown and look around. Maybe Uhlmann has sent word that you may be in town tonight. If there's any news floating about, I'll pick it up."

He sauntered up Allen Street and dropped in at the Crystal Palace. Back of the bar, near one end of it, was a blackboard on an easel upon which were tacked notices of an ice-cream social at the Methodist church, of a school entertainment, and of the new bill at the Birdcage Theater. Beside them was a poster offering two hundred dollars reward for the arrest of Robert Webb, who had escaped from the penitentiary at Yuma on the night of June 22, together with Chub Leavitt and Oscar Holton, both of whom had since been recaptured. He was described as a man of twenty-six years of age, weight one hundred and sixty pounds, wiry and athletic, not likely to be captured without a struggle. Blue eyes. Thick brown hair. Height, five feet ten. Disposition, morose. Was clean-shaven at the time of the prison break.

Fraser put a foot on the rail and ordered a drink. After supplying him, the bartender nodded toward the easel.

"Saw you reading that poster," he said. "Funny about that.

61

I hear he was in Charleston today, but I don't believe it. If you ask me, he's probably in Mexico. Say, somewheres around Mazatlan or Monterrey. He's had plenty of time to light out. He wouldn't be fool enough to stick around here."

With that opinion Fraser agreed. "Sure, unless he's a plumb idjit. Who says he was at Charleston?"

"Fellow by the name of Uhlmann. Claims to have recognized him. He was in here a while ago. Uhlmann, I mean. With some of his cronies. He was lookin' for Webb."

"Well, I haven't lost him," Fraser drawled. "I'll say this. I knew Giles Lemmon, the fellow he was sent to the pen for killing. Anybody who has served seven years for bumping off that curly wolf has done paid the account with a hell of a lot of surplusage."

The man with the apron put his hairy forearms on the bar and leaned forward. "I was in Prescott when young Webb was tried," he said. "Never saw him. But I've met Jug Packard, and I've heard plenty about how he robbed the Webbs and fixed it so this boy had to go to the pen. Just between you and me and the gate post, brother, they sometimes put the wrong man behind the bars."

"You've talked a mouthful." Fraser finished his drink and turned to go.

Before he reached the swing doors several men pushed through them and came into the room. A wry twisted little smile showed on the face of the corral owner. He knew that there would be trouble ahead unless he lied convincingly. For the first man through the door was Uhlmann. Behind him trooped Morris, McNulty, and a big fellow from the San Simon Valley who called himself Cole Hawkins.

" 'Lo, boys," Fraser invited. "Have one on me."

"Where is yore friend Webb?" demanded Uhlmann.

Stan's wide hat was tilted jauntily. He put an elbow on the bar and looked at the huge man with affected surprise.

"Why, I wouldn't know exactly. He went south with Scarface. My guess is that he ought to be crossing the line about now."

"That's a lie. Scarface left Charleston alone—before you and Webb did."

"That's right. About fifteen minutes before us. Webb and I separated outside of town. He went south, to catch up with Scarface."

"I don't believe it," Uhlmann growled angrily. "He's here in town somewhere."

"What makes you think that?" Fraser asked. "He's not a plumb jackass. When Scarface came to the corral he told us you had recognized Webb. Bob figured that spelled trouble, so soon as I had fixed him up with some grub he hit the trail for mañana-land."

Uhlmann mulled that over in sullen silence. It seemed altogether likely. Scarface had told him bluntly he ought to let young Webb alone. Nothing was more probable than that he had warned the man in danger, and if so the only sane thing for Webb to do was to get to the safety of Mexico as fast as a horse could carry him.

But this was not a satisfactory solution for Uhlmann. He wanted to believe that the man he had injured was within reach so that he could strike again.

"If he was going with Scarface, why didn't they start together?" McNulty asked suspiciously.

Fraser gave the man his studied attention. "I've mentioned the reason. Webb stayed while I rustled him some grub. You interested in meeting him—again?"

"One for you, Pete," Hawkins said, grinning.

Uhlmann pushed to the forefront of the talk. "*I'm* interested in meeting him, if you want to know, Fraser. Seems you're a friend of this jailbird. That's yore business, since you want to run with trash like that. But—"

"You've done said it, Rhino," interrupted the little man. "I pick my own company without advice from anybody else."

"Yeah, then listen, fellow." Uhlmann's voice rumbled anger. "I don't let any half-pint squirt pull any shenanigan on me. Get between me and Webb, and I'll tromp you down like I would a beetle."

There was a clean strain of fighting tallow in Fraser. He had ridden the Texas brush country when those who dwelt there fought the raiding Kiowas and Comanches. He had followed the cattle trails to Dodge and Ellsworth regardless of stampedes, blizzards, and bank-full rivers. It was a chief article in his creed to back down for no man.

"Interesting," he murmured, as if to himself. "I've read that the bigger they are the harder they fall—and they are sure easier to hit."

Hawkins slammed a heavy fist joyously on the top of the bar. "The li'l bantam rooster crows fine. Damfidon't take him up on his offer. Line up, boys. Mr. Fraser's treat."

Reluctantly Uhlmann accepted the drink. There was no percentage in quarreling with Fraser. The owner of the Rawhide Corral was a privileged character. He was an honest man in a community where rogues abounded. He did not interfere with them, and they in turn let him go his own own way. Perhaps it was his blunt fearlessness that made him popular.

"Just the same, if you know what's good for you, Fraser, you'd better cut out siding with Webb," the German grumbled.

"That's what I say," agreed McNulty.

"I reckon Rhino is mighty glad to have yore backing, Pete," Fraser said gently. Since he was not looking for a quarrel with the big ruffian he ignored his threat.

McNulty looked at him angrily, started to speak, and changed his mind. Every time his trousers rubbed against the thighs beneath them he was given a painful reminder of the possible penalty on free speech.

15 *The Rangers Make a Call*

When Sandra drove with her father to Tucson by the old mission road, the day after their hunted guest had ridden from the ranch, it was ostensibly to get material for a new dress. But there was another more urgent reason for the trip. This she broached to John Ranger at the end of her shopping spree. They were eating supper at a Chinese restaurant on Commerce Street.

"Jim Budd told me that Mr. Sloan's sister lives in Tucson," she said, as her father lit his post-prandial cigar. "I'm not very happy about him. He risked his life to save Nels and me. We were able to do so little for him. I'm wondering if we couldn't meet his sister and maybe help him in some way."

Ranger shook the light from his match and considered this. "It's not our fault that we didn't do more, Sandra. He has his neck bowed to go his own way."

She sighed. "Yes, I know. But it wouldn't do any harm to get in touch with his sister. She's married, Jim says."

"How does Jim know so much about her?"

The girl decided to speak out the suspicion in her mind. "I think he was in the penitentiary with Cape Sloan."

"What makes you think that?"

She gave her reasons. They were not convincing, but they might very well be true, the cattleman reflected.

"If you're right about this, I suppose I'll have to let Jim go," he said regretfully.

"Why will you?" she flared up. "Jim is one of the nicest colored men I ever knew. He is devoted to us. I know he is. Just because he has been in prison—"

John smiled indulgently at the cook's champion. "I won't be hasty about it. We'll find out why he was in, and all about his record. Maybe he is entitled to another chance. I like him too. And about Webb—"

"We'd better call him Sloan," she suggested. "Or we'll make

64

a mistake and call him Webb when somebody else is around."

"All right, Sloan. I'm willing to look his sister up. Do you know her married name?"

"No. Jim had never heard it."

"We'll have to move carefully, so as not to get anybody wondering why we are looking for her." He took three or four puffs at his cigar while Sandra waited. "I'll speak to Phil Davis. He's on the *Star* staff and knows everybody in town, more or less. He and I are good friends. He'll keep his mouth shut."

Ranger walked to the office of the *Star* to have a talk with Davis, recently promoted to managing editor. The newspaper man was rotund, middle-aged, and very deaf. At sight of the caller his eyes lit. A good many years earlier they had been in a small party that had stood off a bunch of Apaches for two days.

He jumped up and slapped the ranchman on the back. "You blamed old skeezicks! Where have you been all these years? You come to town and never look me up. Why not?"

"I'm looking you up now," Ranger shouted in his ear. "It was just three months ago I saw you."

They sat down at the desk. The owner of the Circle J R drew a paper pad toward him and scribbled a line. Davis read, "My business is private. Mind if I write it?"

The editor nodded. "Hop to it, John."

Ranger wrote: "I want to find the sister of Bob Webb, the man who was sent to the pen for killing Giles Lemmon. She has been married since, I've been told."

"Young Webb broke jail two-three months ago," Davis murmured.

The cattleman used the pad again. "I know that. It's his sister I'm interested in just now. Thought you might help me locate her."

Davis moved over to a long table with a *Star* file of the previous year. After leafing the bound volume for five minutes he found what he was seeking. It was a story half a stick long telling of the marriage of Joan Webb to Henry Mitchell. He turned to the town directory and ran down a column of names beginning with M.

"They live at 423 Fourth Street, or did when this was got out," he said. "Fortunate you didn't ask for the address of her brother. I'd have had to tell you, somewhere in Mexico."

"Much obliged," Ranger scrawled. "I'll be pleased if you'll forget I asked you."

"Sure. If there's a story in it, let me know when it can be published."

"There isn't, Phil." Ranger crumpled up the sheet of paper he had used and put it in his pocket.

They talked of other things for a few minutes. When a printer in his shirt sleeves brought in a galley of proof John departed.

He was a little troubled in mind by a feeling that his daughter was emotionally involved in the fate of Bob Webb. If so, she was bound to be unhappy until the fancy had spent itself. He thought of taking this up with her but decided it was better not to do so. Her good sense would tell her that there could be no possible future for her with this man, and he did not want to embarrass either himself or her.

The heat of the day still hung over the town as they walked to the address given in the directory. The man who came to the door was a blond good-looking young fellow with a frank open countenance. He identified himself as Henry Mitchell and said that his wife was at home. As he ushered them into the parlor he was plainly a bit puzzled. He had never seen these strangers before. The girl was one of the loveliest he had ever met, and her father—if the man was her father—was evidently a solid cattleman of importance.

Joan Mitchell was a very pretty dark-eyed young woman not very long out of her teens. When Ranger mentioned her brother's name she showed instant signals of alarm. He reassured her at once. They were friends, he explained, and told her the whole story, as far as he knew it, of Bob Webb's adventures since their first meeting.

"So you see we are very much in his debt," Ranger concluded. "We want to put ourselves at your service to help in any way we can."

"But I don't know where he is," Joan said. "I wish I did. Since he escaped I have had one letter from him. He did not tell me his plans. I want so much to see him."

Her husband added an explanation. "Joan understands that Bob could not come here. The place is watched. I think the letter that reached her had been opened and sealed again. Fortunately there was nothing but the postmark to give away Bob's whereabouts, and of course he had left there long before word could be wired to find and arrest him."

"Bob did not kill Giles Lemmon, though if he had it would have been self-defense," Joan cried. "He told me so before he was tried and again after he was convicted. It was a crazy idea for him to try to talk Mr. Packard into doing justice to mother. I expect Bob got excited. Lemmon and another man named Uhlmann started shooting at him and by accident Uhlmann killed Lemmon. So they got rid of Bob by lying him into the penitentiary." Her voice broke to a sob. "And now they are hunting him like a wild beast. I suppose they will kill him."

Sandra moved to Joan's side and put an arm around her. "I

don't think so. He isn't a boy now, but a strong and clever man."

"Why doesn't he get out of the country?" Joan asked piteously. "He can't dodge around Arizona forever."

John Ranger and his daughter were of that opinion too, but they did not voice it. Some day Webb would ride into a town to buy provisions and he would be arrested or shot down while trying to escape.

"He is hoping to get evidence that Packard got the Johnny B crookedly," Ranger told her. "I don't think he can do it. Jug must have covered his tracks long ago."

"I haven't seen Bob for over a year," his sister said. "I suppose he is still very hard and bitter."

"He lives in a shell," Sandra answered. "Beneath that he is as kind and gentle as any of us, though he doesn't want anybody to know it."

As the Rangers walked back to their hotel, Sandra said hopelessly, "There's nothing we can do for him—nothing at all."

"Not just now," her father agreed. "There may come a day when we can help him."

They passed the dark entrance of a store in which a man was lurking. Neither of them glanced at him, though they were near enough to have reached out and touched him. He was the man who called himself Cape Sloan.

16   *Chandler Newman Talks*

An hour after the Rangers got back to their hotel the son of the proprietor came up to announce that a man in the lobby was inquiring for them.

"Says his name is Fraser. I was to mention Guaymas to you."

The eyes of the cattleman warmed. "Must be Stan Fraser," he told his daughter. "Before you were born I got in a jam at a fandango at Guaymas. It looked like kingdom come for me when a young fellow I had never seen before threw in with me. We went outa that hall side by side with our guns smoking, and quick as we could fork our broncs pulled our freight to hide out in the brush. For several days soldiers hunted us, but we made it back across the line finally."

Sandra's eyes were wide. "Did you kill anybody?"

"No. We winged a couple. I didn't start the trouble. A big Mexican crowded me." John turned to the boy. "Tell Mr. Fraser to come up."

After the greetings were over Fraser explained his presence. "Henry Mitchell told me you were in town and staying here. He said you hadn't been gone ten minutes when I dropped in."

"You know Mr. Mitchell?" Ranger asked.

"Never met him before. I took a message from Bob Webb to his sister."

"He isn't here—in Tucson?" Sandra questioned.

Stan smiled at her. "Maybe you'd better not ask where he is. It's supposed to be a secret. Bob does not want to implicate his friends."

"Then he's here," she cried quickly.

"I didn't say so. But I know how friendly you feel toward him. Mitchell said you would do anything for Bob you could. There's a way you could help, if it wouldn't embarrass you."

"Of course we'll do whatever it is," Sandra promised.

"A man named Chandler Newman lives here—works in the Southern Pacific offices. He used to be bookkeeper for Jug Packard at the Johnny B mine. I'm pretty sure he knows something about the dirty work Packard pulled off in getting control of the mine and freezing out the Webbs. If he does, he has kept his mouth padlocked. Afraid of Jug, my guess is. The point is, could you get him to talk, John?"

"My opinion is that Webb—we'd better call him Sloan even among ourselves—must give up this idea of getting even with Packard if he hopes to escape," the cattleman said.

"That would be any sane man's opinion," Fraser agreed. "But Sloan won't have it that way. He's got his neck bowed and means to go through. He figures not only that Packard has ruined his life but is responsible for the death of his mother. I think if he could pull Packard down he would be content to pay with his life."

"We'd better see this Newman," Sandra decided. "Maybe if he has nothing to tell us Mr. Sloan will give up this crazy idea."

"I'd go see Newman myself, but if I was seen talking with him they might track me back to Bob," Fraser told them. "We don't want Packard to get the idea that anything is stirring."

"If you have his address we'll call on Newman tonight," Sandra cried.

John Ranger did not want to take his daughter with him, but she insisted so strongly on it that he gave way. The ranchman could see that she wished to have a part in anything that might help Sloan.

Chandler Newman was a thin colorless individual, pale and narrow-chested. He was not mentally equipped to stand up to as ruthless a villain as Jug Packard. But he had in him a clean core of honesty. He had broken with Packard because he would not have anything to do with so flagrant a steal as his employer was putting across on the widow of the man who had befriended him. But farther than that he did not intend to go. Knowing Packard, he was going to do nothing that would invite his anger. He had the obstinacy of a weak man, and Ranger faced that barrier at once when he mentioned why he had come.

"Nothing to say," the bookkeeper insisted, and repeated the words when Ranger refused to accept that as final.

Not until Sandra saw that her father was going to fail did she have any part in the talk. They were sitting in a small parlor with their host and his wife. Mrs. Newman was younger than her husband, plump, with bright beady eyes and quick birdlike motions. As they talked, her gaze shifted from one to another quickly.

"I watn to tell you something, Mr. Newman," Sandra began. "You've heard about the raid of the Lopez gang not long ago. Maybe you don't know that four of the ruffians captured me and my young brother. One of them wounded him and another dragged me from a buggy to his horse. I knew something dreadful was in store for me. Just then a man topped a rise in the road and saw us. He came at a gallop, slammed one of the bandits down with the barrel of his rifle, shot another dead, and drove the others away. I never saw anything so daring. It's a wonder he escaped alive."

"We read something about it," Mrs. Newman said, her shining eyes fixed on this eager lovely girl.

"That man was Bob Webb," Sandra explained. "So you see we have got to save him."

Mary Newman saw more than that. This golden girl was in love with the escaped convict. Nothing less could account for the rapt look in her blue eyes. "Yes," she agreed. "If you can."

"Bob Webb did not kill Giles Lemmon. He says so, and we are sure he is telling the truth. It suited Jug Packard to have him sent to prison, and he fixed the testimony so that the boy was convicted."

Mrs. Newman looked at her husband. You've always thought that, Chan."

"You keep out of this, Mary," Newman snapped.

"But why?" Sandra cried. "If he isn't guilty we ought to find out and try to get him freed. You wouldn't want an innocent man to spend half his life in prison to satisfy a scoundrel's grudge?"

"What I think doesn't matter," Newman replied doggedly. "All I've heard is rumors. Why come to me?"

"We came to you to find out something you do know," the girl said, her husky voice tremulous with emotion. "You kept the books for the Johnny B. All the time Packard was engineering his steal of the mine from Mrs. Webb you were right there. You must know how he did it. Was he robbing her of the ore? He closed down for two years to make the stock worth nothing. Had he struck a rich vein before he did that?"

Mrs. Newman did not speak, but she looked steadily at her husband, compulsion in her eyes.

"All that is a closed book," the man blurted out. He was unhappy at the position in which he was placed. He knew that his wife had never been wholly satisfied at his silence, but she had persuaded herself that to speak would do no good and would surely endanger Chandler. "No use trying to reopen it. Jug has the mine now, and nobody can do a thing about it."

"Bob Webb doesn't think so," Ranger answered. "It is the one chance he has of saving what is left of his life. For Heaven's sake, speak out if you have any proof of Packard's chicanery."

"There was a fire at the mine," Newman said. "The books were burned."

"Go on, Chan," his wife insisted in a low voice.

"It wouldn't do Webb any good for me to speak, but one of Jug's gunmen would get me sure." The words seemed to be dragged out of Newman's mouth.

"It isn't for us to say whether it would do Mr. Webb any good," Mary differed. "Perhaps it might. Anyhow, now the question has come up again I think you ought to tell what you know."

"You know what will happen to me if I do," Newman protested. "I wouldn't live long enough to tell the story in court."

"You're overestimating Packard's power," Ranger told him. "I've been threatened several times in my life, once by a notorious killer and another time by a bad outlaw gang. I'm here. They have gone. The dangers we foresee rarely harm us. If we walk up to them, they usually aren't there."

"This is different. I'm no gunfighter. You are an outdoor man, used to weapons, and known to be game. And you are a prominent citizen, with a bunch of cowboys back of you, whereas I am nobody. There wouldn't be much of a fuss made if I was shot down."

"Couldn't we get protection for Mr. Newman?" Sandra asked her father.

"If he tells his story to the district attorney and swears to it before a notary it would not do Packard any good to hurt him," the cattleman said. "In fact, it would greatly prejudice his chances in court."

"That would do me a lot of good if I was dead," Newman retorted, with a bitter laugh.

Sandra realized that the man would have to be given some assurance of safety. It was all very well for her father to talk about walking through danger and seeing it vanish like mist before the sun. But John Ranger had always trod the way of the strong, whereas Chandler Newman was a bookish timid man with too much imagination, one who had never taken a risk that could be avoided. A plan sprang to her mind that might be feasible. Ranger did a lot of shipping over the Southern Pacific and was on friendly terms with the manager of the western division.

"You have been talking about getting a bookkeeper to bring your books down to date and to clean up a lot of back correspondence," the girl suggested. "Maybe Mr. Compton would give Mr. Newman a leave of absence for three or four months to come to the ranch. He and Mrs. Newman could live in our old adobe house. It's very comfortable. They would be quite safe there."

"I could certainly use you to advantage," Ranger admitted, speaking to the clerk. "You could stay with us until this whole thing is settled one way or another. If Packard wins out I'm sure Compton would place you in Los Angeles or San Diego."

A flush of pleasure came into the face of Mary Newman. "We've talked so often of moving to California," she reminded her husband.

Before yielding he felt it necessary to defend his past inaction. "When I saw what Packard was doing I wrote an unsigned letter to Mrs. Webb," he said. "As soon as I could do it I gave up my job at the Johnny B."

"Right," commented the cattleman. "You felt you could not work for a scoundrel."

"Packard did not want me to leave. He made it plain that if I did any talking he would settle with me. Twice since I left him he has sent for me to come to his house here. Each time he gave me a quarter of beef, but I felt the threat back of his interest in me."

"His threats can't harm you if you are at the Circle J R," Ranger promised.

Newman was nervous as a caged wildcat, but he made a start in his story at last. "I discovered he had struck a rich vein when I saw by chance two sets of smelter returns from the same shipment. One was very rich; the other didn't pay the expenses of smelting. Packard must have given the manager of the smelter a percentage to help him in his crookedness. My idea is that before he shut down he made enough to buy up the stock when it went off to a low price. I kept copies of the duplicate returns and have them yet." In answer to questions Newman gave the name of the smelter. The manager had been discharged a year later for robbing the company. Newman had heard he was now living in Phoenix.

"Someone else must have known what was going on,"

Ranger hazarded. "There must have been at least one book-keeper in with the superintendent to falsify the returns."

Newman agreed that must have been the case.

"If we can find out who it was we may be able to bring pressure on him to talk," the ranchman said. "At any rate we can try."

He arranged with the Newmans to see Compton at once to get a leave of absence. As soon as it was granted the bookkeeper and his wife had better move to the ranch. On that last point Newman was heartily in accord with him. He wanted to be in a safe shelter when Packard discovered what was afoot.

17   *In a Lady's Bedroom*

Henry Mitchell came back into the dark hall and reported that all was clear. Joan clung to her brother with clenched fingers, as though her physical grip on him could hold him from the danger pressing close.

"If you would only forget what has happened and ride out of the country," she cried. "Leave us to clear all this mess up. You have good friends now who will help."

Bob Webb, alias Cape Sloan, gently opened her fists and freed himself from her. "Everything will be all right now," he promised. "I'll not throw down on myself. *Adios, muchacha.*"

As he kissed her good-by he tasted the salt tears on her cheek. To his mind there jumped a picture of a small girl with pigtails sitting on their father's lap listening to a good-night story of a mired calf rescued from a quicksand. Memories of the old days flooded him. He was moved and took care not to show it. She belonged to that vanished chapter of his life when he had thought the future was his to shape as he wished.

Stan Fraser came out of the darkness to meet him.

"Everything dandy out here," the little old-timer said. "Long as nobody knows you are in Tucson and you keep under cover you'd ought to be all right. What I'm worried about is Uhlmann and his crowd. McNulty talked like they might drift over this way. My idea is for us to get out now and camp on the mesa, then soon as it is day be on our way."

Webb agreed that might be a good idea.

They walked back through the business section along empty streets. Except for the gambling houses and their patrons the town seemed sunk in sleep. Inside the Legal Tender and the Silver Dollar they could hear the rattle of chips and the voices of the players. Fraser tilted his head toward the former.

"Many's the time I've bucked the wheel in there with yore dad. He was sure a wild colt when he was young."

"I've watched the little ball spin there myself some," Webb admitted.

Out of the Legal Tender poured a jet of men.

"Told you I'd take the bank to a cleaning," one of them boasted.

The huge graceless figure beside him let out a yelp of triumph. His gaze had fallen on the escaped convict. He opened his mouth to shout recognition. Instead, he gave a groan and sagged against the wall. The long barrel of Stan Fraser's pistol had crashed down on his cranium. Uhlmann for the moment had lost interest.

"Burn the wind, boy," Fraser cried, and he dived into the stairway leading to the private poker rooms in the second story.

Webb took the treads after his friend, racing up them two at a time. The roar of a forty-five from the entrance below filled the well with a noise like the blasting of dynamite. Stan flung open a door of a room where five men in their shirt-sleeves sat around a table with chips in front of them and cards in their hands.

The players stared at the two men charging through the room to the small stairway in the far corner.

"What in hell——?" one of them began to protest.

Bob Webb's arm swept the chimney from the bracket lamp attached to the wall and plunged the room in darkness. He followed his friend up the dark closed way to the trap-door above. Through it they went to the roof.

"Where now?" he asked.

Fraser did not know. He hoped there was another opening to permit descent into an adjoining building. If not, they were out of luck. As they moved forward to look for a road of escape they heard the noisy clamor of many voices below. Men were milling around in the poker room confused by the lack of light.

"Found one," Fraser called to his companion.

Fortunately the trap-door was not bolted inside. Bob went down into the dark pit after Stan, stopping only to close and latch the heavy framework of the vent. The ladder led them to a store room from which they stepped into a passage with rooms on both sides.

"Must be the Tucson Hotel we're in," whispered Fraser.

They had no time to waste. Already they could hear the stamping feet on the roof and the shouts of the searchers.

"We've walked into a rat trap, looks like," Bob mentioned. "Nothing to do but go on down and fight our way out."

A gleam of wintry humor lit the little man's eyes. "We might take a room for the night."

Bob did not answer in words. But Fraser had given him an idea. There would be small chance now of breaking through below to safety. The gambling houses had emptied into the street to join the chase. Why not invite themselves to share the room of one of the hotel guests? Under compulsion he might be induced to hide them. It would at least give them a breathing space during which they could decide what was best to do.

Very few of the rooms were locked. The habit of the country was to forget keys. Bob opened a door, looked in, and discovered through the darkness two children asleep in a bed. He withdrew and closed the door gently.

"Kids in there," he told his companion.

They softfooted down the hall and tried again. From the doorway Bob's glance swept the room. The bed had been slept in but was at the moment unoccupied.

"Filled with absentees," Webb murmured.

There was a rustle at the window. A shadow bulked close to it from which stood out a white face.

"What do you want?" a woman's voice asked sharply.

"Sorry, ma'am," Bob apologized. "Mistake. Wrong room."

Before he could leave she flung out a protest, her voice fined down almost to a whisper. "Wait. You're Cape Sloan. They are attacking you."

Bob would have known that voice among a thousand. Its low throaty cadence set the excitement strumming in his blood. He guessed that Sandra had been wakened and drawn to the window by the sound of the firing.

The shuffling of many feet on the roof above came plainly to them. Somebody was hammering on the trap-door. In another minute searching men would fill the corridor.

"We're lookin' for a port in storm," Fraser said.

"But not this one," Webb added quickly. "We'll be on our way, Miss Sandra."

"No," the girl objected. "You're safer here. They won't come in without knocking, and when they knock I'll meet them at the door."

"That will be fine," Fraser replied. "We'll stand back out of sight."

But Webb was not so sure. If it was ever discovered that she had hidden them gossip about her would fill the countryside.

"We'll find another room," he insisted.

She was at the door before him, her arms stretched wide across it. "Don't be foolish. They are on their way down now. It's all right. Father is in the next room."

Already boots were clattering down the ladder. It was almost too late to go. If they left the chance of escape was not one in ten.

"Much obliged, Miss Sandra," Fraser spoke softly, to make sure of not being heard. "We're in a tight spot sure enough."

"Get back of the bed and crouch down," she ordered. "Hurry, please. They'll be here in no time."

A man was knocking on a door farther down the hall demanding admittance. Reluctantly Bob joined his friend back of the bed.

Urgent shouts beat through the wall to them. "They didn't go downstairs . . . Must be somewhere here if they came down through the trap-door . . . Search the rooms, boys." And then the angry snarl of Uhlmann: "It was that little cuss Fraser busted me on the head."

A fist beat on the door panel of the room. "Hey! Open up here. We're searching the hotel."

Sandra flung a glance behind her to make sure her guests were concealed. The thumping of her heart was so loud that she was afraid it would be heard. As she opened the door her fingers drew the nightgown closer around her throat.

"W-what do you want?" she quavered.

She was manifestly frightened, and her fear was no disservice. The men in the corridor were rough customers, some of them scoundrels. But they had the frontier respect for good women, at least the outward semblance of it. Sandra recognized one, a man who dealt in cattle, by name Rip Morris.

He lifted his hat. "Sorry, miss. Don't be scared. We're lookin' for an escaped convict. We think he's in the hotel here somewhere."

The door was open six or eight inches. She clung to the knob. "You don't mean—in my room?"

"No need to be afraid, miss," he assured her. "If he is, we won't let him hurt you. Point is, he might have slipped in here while you were asleep."

"But he couldn't have" she cried panic in her voice. "I haven't been asleep. At the first shots I got up. Nobody could have come in without me seeing him."

John Ranger came into the room through a connecting door. "What's all this?" he demanded sternly.

"We're huntin' for that escaped murderer Webb," Morris explained apologetically. "He's around somewhere—probably in the hotel."

"Not in my daughter's room, Rip," retorted Ranger's warning voice. "You don't mean that."

"He might of slipped in to hide without her noticin' him," Uhlmann growled.

"But I told them I was awake and got up when the shooting started," Sandra explained to her father.

"That's settled then," Ranger snapped. "Get going, boys."

"Sure, Mr. Ranger," a man in the background said. "Sorry we disturbed the young lady. Might have been an empty room far as we knew. Let's go, Rip."

Ranger closed the door without ceremony. He stood there a long minute listening to the hunters troop down the hall and try the next room. When he turned at last, it was to say in a low voice, "Come out from behind that bed."

The crouching men stood up.

"We butted in, not knowing this was Miss Sandra's room," Fraser mentioned. "They were crowdin' us, and we had to go somewhere."

"I made them stay and hide," Sandra added.

Without glancing at her, Ranger said sharply, "Get back of that bed and put some clothes on."

Sandra drew back in shocked embarrassment. She had been so entirely concerned with the safety of Bob Webb that she had forgotten she was barefoot and wore only a nightgown over her slender body. From the back of a chair she snatched a garment and held it in front of her.

The intruding fugitives walked to the window and looked out. They heard the rustle of clothes and the stir of swift feet. Presently a small distressed voice said, "All right."

Fraser said gently. "We're sure obliged to Miss Sandra for helping us out of a mighty hot spot, John."

"I'll never forget it," Webb added. The thought of her young loveliness, startled fear for him stamped so vividly on her face, still quickened the blood in his veins.

"It came so sudden," the girl explained shyly. "I didn't think about—clothes."

Ranger did not discuss that point. The situation explained itself. "You're a hard man to help, Webb," he told the convict bluntly. "In your circumstances nobody but a fool would be in Tucson—or in Arizona at all."

"How often I've told him that," Fraser agreed.

All of them were speaking in voices so low that they were almost whispers.

"We were just leaving when we ran across Uhlmann coming out of the Legal Tender." Webb attempted no justification. "I know I'm a nuisance. Sorry it has to be that way. Better give up trying to help me. I don't want to get you into trouble—or Stan either for that matter."

"It's you we're worried about," Sandra reminded him.

"Better let us carry on, Webb," the cattleman urged. "We are taking the Newmans to the Circle J R to protect the husband. He will testify that Packard falsified the smelter returns. The superintendent of the smelter must have been in on the deal. I understand he now lives at Phoenix. I am going to check on the thing from that end too. It looks as if we have got something on Jug that might bust him wide open, providing we can drive our wedge in and prove a conspiracy. Frankly, you can't be of any help in this. The thing for you to do is to get out and hole up until we send for you."

"I'll keep out of yore way," Webb promised. "And I'll be very grateful for anything you can do to clear me."

He spoke to John Ranger, but the daughter of the cattleman knew that he was sending her an indirect message of thanks.

Ranger took the hunted men back with him to his room. They had to get out of town before morning. After a time Uhlmann and his companions would get tired of looking for their victims and would either return to their gambling or go to bed. The best chance for a getaway would be just before daybreak. Webb's enemies of course would check up all the wagon yards and corrals in town to find the horses of Fraser and Webb. But probably they would not succeed in finding them, since Henry Mitchell had moved them to a pasture owned by his brother on the river bottom just out of town.

18 *Enter Jug Packard*

Night still filled the sky when John Ranger walked out of the hotel to make arrangements for the escape of his friends. He stood for a moment on the sidewalk looking up and down the street. Pete McNulty moved forward from the entrance to the Legal Tender and joined the Circle J R owner.

"Ain't you up early, John?" he asked.

Ranger looked at him with disfavor. "No earlier than you are, Pete," he answered coldly.

"I'm kinda on duty," McNulty explained. "The boys think that fellow Webb is still around. We aim to cook his goose if we find him."

"Meaning just what?"

"Why, he's a murderer, escaped from the pen. You know what a desperate character he is. If he's killed resisting arrest we can't help it."

"You a deputy sheriff?"

"Not exactly. You don't have to be to collect a fellow like this with a reward on his head."

"Is there a reward offered for the arrest of Cape Sloan?"

"He's Bob Webb, that's who he is. Rhino recognized him."

"I was with Uhlmann several times in the presence of Sloan," Ranger observed. "He didn't say anything about Sloan being young Webb. If you make a mistake and kill the wrong man you might find yourself in prison, Pete. Better go slow."

"We'd ought to of hanged this bird when we first saw him in the cañon," McNulty retorted bitterly. "I said so, but you and Russ Hart wouldn't have it that way."

Ranger did not think it worth while to answer that complaint. He walked up Congress Street and disappeared in the darkness. The sentry watched him go and then reported to his associates, who were playing poker in a corner of the hall.

In the east a pale promise of light was sifting into the sky when McNulty notified his companions that Ranger had returned and vanished into the hotel.

Uhlmann slammed a hamlike fist on the table and set the chips rattling. "You can't tell me he doesn't know where that wolf is holed up. Had him down to his ranch for a while, didn't he? They don't just happen to be in town at the same time."

"Don't forget there's a pot on the table that's practically mine," Cole Hawkins reminded him, and shoved in a stack of blues. "Kick 'er up five." He slid a malicious grin at the huge ungainly cattleman. "Might be they are boilin' up bad medicine for the gent whose testimony sent Webb to the pen."

"They can't do a thing to me," Uhlmann blustered. "Webb is the one headed for trouble." He ripped out an angry oath. "If I ever get my gun on him they won't have to bother taking him back to Yuma."

"If you happened to be the lucky gent and not the one to be measured for a wooden box," Hawkins retorted. The San Simon valley man was a rustler and bad character generally, but he had, like most hardy ruffians, a sneaking fondness for cool and daring scamps. He had joined the hunt for Webb because of the excitement, yet had hoped they would not find the convict. Whatever of evil Webb might have done, he felt that the young fellow's faults were venial compared to those of Hans Uhlmann or Jug Packard.

"No if about it," the big man boasted. "I'll take that bird on any day of the week."

"Okay with me," Hawkins agreed. "Question before the house is, do you call, raise, or fold?"

Uhlmann looked at his cards again and threw them into the discard. "I'm laying down a flush. Any chump could tell you've got a full."

The San Simon rustler flipped his cards over and reached for the pot. He had two small pairs.

A man pushed through the swing doors and came back to the poker table. He was dressed in cheap and soiled clothes a sheepherder would have disdained. His unprepossessing face was seamed with wrinkles. Close-set eyes, small and shifty, slid from one to another of those at the table. The thin-lipped twisted mouth hinted at cruelty.

" 'Lo, Jug," Uhlmann grunted. "I sent for you because I

thought you'd like to know an old friend of yours is in town tonight."

"If Webb is here what are you all doing on yore fat behinds instead of hunting him down?" Packard demanded angrily.

The laugh of Hawkins was a taunt. "Dunno about the other boys, Jug, but I haven't lost this young fellow. Me, I kinda like his nerve. It will suit me fine if he makes a clean getaway."

Packard turned an ugly look on him. "An escaped murderer, isn't he—with a price on his head?"

Hawkins looked around the table coolly, his gaze on each of those present in turn. It came to rest at last on the mine owner. "Murder is a nasty word, Jug. I like killer better." The outlaw's voice was suave and pleasant. "Just a prejudice I have. Maybe some of these boys share it. If we took a private census of gents now here, I reckon the casualties they have caused would be found to fill quite a few graves. No blame intended, of course. The unfortunates likely asked for it. But I never heard that Giles Lemmon was any plaster saint."

"Webb had a fair trial and was convicted," Packard retorted harshly.

"The kid had bad luck. Far as I recollect none of us got as far as a court room."

Packard brushed aside any discussion of moral values. "I'll add another two hundred dollars reward for this fellow's scalp, dead or alive."

"I'd like that four hundred dollars," Uhlmann said. "I'll hold you to that offer, Jug."

"Where was this fellow seen last?" Packard demanded. "Tell me about it."

They gave him both facts and surmises.

"You had him cornered, and you let him slip away," Jug accused.

"That's right," Hawkins agreed cheerfully. "He said 'hocus pocus open sesame' and melted into thin air."

"He's right around here somewheres," McNulty chipped in. "He couldn't of got away. We've got watchers posted in front and back."

"Ranger knows where he's at," Uhlmann supplied venomously. "I'd bet fifty plunks against a dollar Mex."

"But none of you had the guts to tell him so," Packard snarled. "You let him bluff you off."

"Nobody is holding you here, Jug," Morris said. "You go tell him."

Packard was sly and mean by nature. He preferred to use others as tools for his villainy. But there was a substratum of cold nerve in him that lay in reserve back of his caution.

"Don't think I won't," he flung back harshly. "Where's his room at?"

They told him. He turned and walked heavily out of the place.

"The little cuss is going to put it up to Ranger," Hawkins commented. He was surprised. Packard had the reputation of getting his results less directly.

The mine owner stumped up the stairs of the Tucson Hotel, walked down the corridor, and knocked at the door indicated. A voice said, "Who is it?"

Packard did not answer. He opened the door and walked into the room. The lamp was not lit, but he could see that Ranger was not alone. Two other figures bulked in the darkness. One was standing by the window, another sitting on the bed.

A bracket lamp in the corridor lit the face of the self-invited guest. "What brought you here, Packard?" asked the cattleman.

The intruder's small eyes peered at the man on the bed, then shifted to the one by the window. Coming day was beginning to lift the darkness. Packard took two or three steps toward the man by the casement.

"Hold it, Jug," warned the sitting man lightly. He was nursing a forty-five in his lap.

Packard paid no attention. He had not expected to find Bob Webb in the stockman's room. But he had recognized Fraser and had to certify his conviction that the third man present was Webb. A little near-sighted, he had almost in that dim light to push his wrinkled face against that of the suspect.

"You're Webb," he said after a moment. The beard, the harsh lines etched in the lean cheeks, the steely hardness of the eyes, had to be brushed aside. They had been no part of the boy he had wronged. Bitter years in prison had brought them. But the bony contour of the head could belong only to the son of the Bob Webb who had been his partner.

"Sloan is the name to you," Bob corrected.

"You'd better give up and come with me without any fuss," Packard flung out shrilly. "All I got to do is shout and——"

"No," Ranger cut in sternly. "Temporarily Mr. Sloan is my guest. You'll accept that fact."

"Or go out in smoke before yore friends arrive, Jug," Fraser added genially. "And don't think I'm loading you about that."

Packard whirled on Ranger. "You know what you're doing, don't you? Aiding and abetting the escape of a criminal wanted by the law. Do that, and you'll go join Webb at Yuma, John."

"You haven't proved that Sloan is Webb," the cattleman differed.

"You know he is. You know it doggoned well. I can bring witnesses up to swear to him. Uhlmann for one."

"But you are not going to," Fraser said gently. "You're

going to sit down in a chair nice and friendly until we say 'Depart in peace,' like the Good Book has it."

"No, sir. You can't keep me. I'm going down right now to tell the boys you've got this murderer here."

Ranger confronted him as he made for the door. "Don't make a mistake," he warned. "I didn't invite you here, but since you came without being asked you'll stay. If you open your mouth to cry out I'll throttle you."

"You'll go to the pen for this," Packard gulped out.

Fraser brought a chair to the mine owner. "Sit," he ordered.

Jug glared at him. He had been top dog for so long that it came hard on him to obey. "Do you no good to hold me," he snapped sourly. "If I don't go back the boys will come looking for me."

"So they will," Fraser chuckled. "And find you tied up here nice and comfortable."

"You'll never get away," Packard prophesied spitefully. "We've got men back and front to check on you."

Fraser pushed him back into the chair. "Have to use the sheets to tie him," he said.

"We won't tie him." Webb had been watching the little plaza back of the hotel through the window. "Time to go. A friend is leaving two horses at the hitch rack for us. We'll take Packard with us and see how he likes being shot at."

Stan Fraser stared at Bob. "Take him with us?" he repeated, puzzled.

"Far as the horses. For his friends to make a target of, if they feel that way."

"Sure," cried Fraser joyfully. "Jug has a kind heart. He will protect us like we were brothers."

"I won't go a step of the way," the mine owner announced shrilly.

Sandra opened the door connecting with the next room. "Is everything all right?" she asked anxiously.

"Everything is fine," Bob answered. "We're just leaving. Sorry we barged in on you and yore father this way and forced you to hide us."

The girl knew he was trying to safeguard them against any charge Packard might make that they had aided his escape.

"Good-bye, Mr. Sloan," she said, and shook hands with him. "I hope this silly mistake about you being that man Webb will be cleared up."

Bob smiled. "We'll clear up the whole business," he said.

19 *Guns on the Plaza*

With Fraser's revolver prodding his back, Packard announced again doggedly that he was not going downstairs.

"Suit yoreself," the little man drawled. "You can go or stay. If you stay, it will be with a head busted by the barrel of my gun. Not such an easy tap as I gave Uhlmann. But don't let me influence you."

Packard shuffled down the corridor. "I'll fix you some day for this," he promised, his voice thick with fury.

Ranger watched them go from the door of the room. On his face was a frown of anxiety. It was his opinion that presently they would hear the roar of bullets from below. His daughter stood beside him, white to the lips. She felt a panic fear choking her throat.

Webb led the way down the stairs. He opened the back door a few inches and peered out. Several men were just emerging from the Legal Tender. One was Uhlmann. He had a revolver in his hand and was giving the others instructions where to take their posts. The two saddled horses were hitched to a rack a short distance from the hotel. A lank fellow in leather chaps and a blue shirt stood beneath a cottonwood carrying a rifle, evidently the guard posted to cover the back door. He called to Uhlmann that the black horse with white stockings belonged to Fraser.

To make the run from the back door to the horses, with half a dozen guns trained on them, would be suicidal. Webb saw that at once. A plan jumped to his mind, one made possible by the unwilling co-operation of Packard. There was a dark closet near the entrance where buckets, brooms, and mops were kept. Given luck, it might serve the hunted men nicely.

Bob sketched in three sentences what he had in mind, explaining curtly to Packard his part in it. "You'd better make it good," he added grimly. "If you let them suspect it's a ruse you won't live long enough to enjoy tricking me. Just one suspicious move, and I'll drop you."

"You figuring on killing me?" Packard asked, gimlet orbs drilling into those of his enemy.

"If we're discovered. You'll kick off before we do."

The prisoner started to protest, looked into Webb's bleak

eyes, and decided it was not worth while. "I'll play yore game, because I can't do anything else," he said, sullen anger in his voice.

Packard was to call his men and tell them he had discovered the hiding place of Webb. He was to head them up the stairs, bringing up the rear himself. Every foot of the way he would be covered by the guns of the two men in the closet.

"Don't get crazy and start anything," Fraser advised. "All we'd have to do is crook our fingers."

"I'm not a fool," snarled Packard. "You've got the drop on me right now, but inside of forty-eight hours you'll both be laid out cold."

Webb spoke, in his voice the law harsh grating of steel: "You murdered my father, Packard. I'm not forgetting that. You robbed my mother and lied me into prison. Pay day is coming for you soon. I'm telling you this now so that you'll know if you lift a hand or let out a word to betray us I'd as lief shoot you in the back as I would a wolf. Better not forget that for a moment. Speak yore piece now—and make these men believe it if you want to go on living."

Bob's revolver pressed against Packard's ribs as the man put his head through the door opening and called to Uhlmann. He spoke urgently but not loud.

"Hi, Rhino, I've found Webb. He's upstairs. Bring the boys and keep 'em quiet."

"Right away, Jug." Uhlmann spoke to those with him, turned, and lumbered across from where he stood to the back door of the hotel. Three men trailed at his heels. Hawkins remained where he was, at the door of the Legal Tender. The man in chaps under the cottonwood held his ground.

"Did Ranger tell you where he was?" Uhlmann asked in a sibilant whisper.

Webb drew back to join Fraser in the darkness of the closet.

"Heard him talking with Fraser—in a room upstairs," Packard answered. "Walk soft, boys. We want to surprise them."

The old treads creaked beneath the weight of their heavy bodies. They went in single file, Uhlmann leading. Jug flung a look of bitter hate toward the closet and moved along the passage to the stairs. He knew that the revolver of his enemy covered him every foot of the way and did not feel sure that a bullet would not crash into his back. There was a bend in the staircase half-way up. If he could get past that he could shout out an alarm and send his men charging down on those below. The steps of the flight seemed interminable. Four more—three

—two. He took the last at a leap and from the landing screamed at the others to come back.

"Holy Mike, what's eatin' you?" Uhlmann demanded.

Already the men hidden in the closet were bolting for the door. As they raced for the horses they heard the pounding of feet down the stairs. The cowboy beneath the cottonwood woke up and yelled, "What's going on here?" Neither Webb nor Fraser paid any heed to him. He started to run to the hitch rack, stopped, and raised his rifle.

A bullet from the door of the hotel whistled past the running men, and before the crash of the explosion had died away a second and a third shot sounded. One of them came from the gun of Hawkins. Webb pulled the slip-knot of a bridle rein and swung to the saddle of his mount. Fraser was already in motion, a few yards ahead of him. He jumped his horse to a gallop and jerked it to a sudden stop. The black had given a scream of pain and collapsed, sending its rider flying to the ground.

Bob swung round and rode back. His one idea was to pick Stan up and get away from the heavy fire centering on them. But in the second during which he faced the blazing guns his eyes took in a dozen details of the panorama in the plaza. Three or four men were strung along the wall of the hotel firing at him. Pete McNulty was drawing a bead on him from back of a drinking trough. Packard shrieked shrill orders to get him—get him. A dozen yards from the hitch rack the cowboy in chaps lay face down, his outflung hands still clinging to the rifle he would never use again.

Fraser scrambled to his feet and ran limping to his friend. He flung himself on the horse back of Bob, who whirled the cow pony in its tracks and touched it with a spur. The animal shot across the plaza like a streak of light and raced down a dusty street past the old convent. Behind them sounded the fire of the drumming weapons.

"You didn't get hit?" Bob asked.

"No. I kinda sprained my ankle when I lit after my horse went down." Fraser grinned exultantly. "We sure fooled them that time. I reckon Jug would sell himself right now for two bits."

"We'll have to pick up another horse somewhere."

"Yes, sir. On the q.t. I can see how this will make you or me out a horse thief." The little man chuckled. "I've been most everything else in my time. We're lucky to have got away whole."

"One man didn't—the man in chaps with the rifle. He was drawing a bead on me just before I reached the hitch rack. I didn't see him again till I stopped to pick you up. He was lying on the ground spraddled out, face down. Someone must have shot him by mistake for us."

Fraser could not understand that. The cowboy had not been in the line of fire. "Looks like one of Jug's warriors must of got buck fever," he hazarded. "But I'll bet my boots they lay the blame on us."

Bob thought that was very likely.

20   Who Killed Chuck Holloway?

Packard tore a sunstained and shapeless hat from his head, slammed it on the ground, and stamped on it furiously. "They got away. Goddlemighty, you lunkheads had twenty cracks at them—and missed. That devil Webb rode back again, and still you couldn't hit him."

"Must be one among us who can hit the side of a barn," Hawkins jeered. "Someone killed a horse."

"Yeah, and then let Fraser climb onto Webb's horse and ride away. After you had him on the ground practically surrounded. I never saw such crazy shooting in my life."

"We'd have got them all right if you hadn't dragged us upstairs," Uhlmann grumbled. "You fixed it nice for them to reach their horses, Jug. Don't cuss us. You're the one most to blame."

Rip Morris was kneeling beside the prostrate cowboy in chaps. He looked up and called to the others. "Quit yapping, boys, and come here. They got Chuck Holloway. He's dead."

"Dead!" McNulty looked down at the man lying on the ground. "When did they kill him? Far as I could see neither of them fired a shot."

"That's right," Uhlmann agreed. "Unless it was before I got outa the hotel."

"It couldn't of been before that," Packard objected. "I saw Chuck with his rifle raised to fire. But Pete is right. Neither of these fellows fooled away any time shooting back at us. They went straight for their horses and lit out. If that's so, one of us . . ."

The mine owner did not finish the sentence. He looked round on a group of startled faces. The gaze of each shifted from one to another, and none of them liked what they saw in the eyes staring at them. Chuck must have been killed by one of their own group.

Rip Morris put into words the thought that was in the minds of all of them. "He was standing off to the right. I don't see how any of us could have done it—unless someone got jumpy and took him for a friend of Webb's."

"Must have been that," Hawkins agreed. His glance went

coolly round the circle. " 'Fess up, fellow, whoever it was. We'll have to stand by you."

Each denied his guilt, some profanely and some with corroborative explanation, but all explicitly and with vigor.

"Just up and shot himself, seems like," the San Simon man murmured ironically.

Morris raised another question. "Did Chuck have any enemies?"

Uhlmann stared at Rip a long time, while the meaning of the inquiry seeped into his dull mind. "Holy Mike, you don't think one of us—on purpose——"

"Maybe it wasn't one of us," Morris suggested. "Someone could of slipped out from a house on the other side of the plaza and plugged him."

"Or Ranger from the window of his room," Packard said with acrid spite. "He was hiding Webb. Why wouldn't he help him make a getaway?"

"Might of," McNulty agreed. "But that won't go down so good with the public. John is a solid fellow, popular with all the cattlemen and well liked in town. I don't reckon we better hang it on him."

"That's right." Packard came to swift decision. "Webb did it. He had me covered with his gun when I called you fellows into the house. It was in his hand when he ran out to the plaza. When he saw Chuck in his way he cut down and let him have it. That's how it was, boys. I saw it. Who else did?"

"I did," Uhlmann assented promptly. "Just before he got on his horse. You saw him too, Pete."

McNulty showed his teeth in an ugly grin. "Sure I saw him. I remember now."

"Then that's settled," Packard concluded. "Webb has killed another man."

"Not quite settled." The words came crisp and clear from a speaker standing back of the mine owner. "If Bob Webb was carrying a gun he did not have it out when he ran to the hitch rack. I was watching from the window."

Packard slewed his head round and glared at John Ranger, who had stepped out from the hotel quietly and joined them. "So it's you? Butting in again. If you're so sure Webb didn't kill this boy maybe you know who did. Maybe you had a gun out if the convict didn't."

"My daughter was standing beside me at the window," Ranger said. "She can testify I didn't fire a gun, and both of us can swear that Webb didn't."

"That goes with me, Mr. Ranger," Hawkins answered. "If you were standing at the window, perhaps you can tell us who did shoot this boy."

86

"No, I can't, though I saw him fall. Several guns were fired about that time within a second or two."

"It may go with you, Hawkins, but not with me," Packard cried vindictively. "Ranger was in cahoots with these scoundrels. He threatened to strangle me if I called out to you that Webb was hiding in his room. He has played in with him ever since he met the killer in the cañon. Why wouldn't he lie for him now?"

McNulty nodded vigorously in assent. "Right, Jug. I dunno what his game is, but he has taken a great shine to the jailbird."

"I like his nerve myself," Hawkins replied. "Jug hates him for some reason. That's his privilege. And I can understand why Pete doesn't like him. But why should the rest of us get all het up to bump off the fellow or send him back to Yuma? Me, I've busted a lot of laws in my time. I've lived in the brush enough myself to favor anyone on the dodge rather than the ones hunting him."

"Is that why you were pumping lead at Webb a couple of minutes ago?" snapped McNulty.

The smile on the face of Hawkins was a little sly and mysterious. It suggested a secret source of ironic mirth.

"You got me there, Pete," he admitted. "I reckon I was some carried away by the Fourth of July you boys were pulling off."

"We'd better get poor Chuck into the Legal Tender and notify the sheriff," Morris said. "Looks to me like he's going to have a nice time finding out who did kill him."

"Carry him in, and somebody go for the sheriff," Packard ordered. He turned bitterly to Ranger. "Don't think you're going to get away with this. You aided and abetted a criminal. First you hid him, then you prevented me from getting him arrested. That's a penitentiary offense, you'll find out."

"If you can prove it." Ranger smiled blandly at the mine owner. "Your story and mine might differ. Have you any other witnesses to back the charge?"

John turned on his heel and walked back into the hotel. His daughter was waiting for him in his room. She had lit a lamp and stool tall and slender beside the table. The color had not yet washed back into her cheeks.

"Well?" she asked.

"I don't think either of them was hurt," he replied. "One poor boy who rode for Uhlmann was killed. Nobody seems to know who shot him. Probably somebody mistook him for Webb. Jug Packard was fixing to tie it to Bob when I showed up and rather spoiled his plan. Later he said very likely I did it."

"He would like to get even with you."

"Yes, but I don't see how he can prove anything against me. He has no witnesses except himself to show that we hid Webb."

"Or that we knew Cape Sloan is Bob Webb."

"No."

"The papers will be full of this," Sandra said. "You'd better see Mr. Davis again and make sure the *Star* gets the story right. Jug Packard will try to make it seem that Bob killed this boy."

"You're right," her father agreed. "Bob is the dog with a bad name. We don't want to correct a story putting the blame on him. Most of the people who read it would never see the correction."

Sandra beat a small fist despairingly into the palm of her other hand. "It's no use," she declared. "If he gets out of this he'll just get into another mix-up, and by this time everybody in the territory is on the lookout for him."

Ranger knew this was true. Yet he sympathized with the cause driving Webb to what looked like reckless folly. "You can't blame him for trying to clear his name. If he had just lit out after the jail break the stigma on his name never would have been cleared up."

"You think now it will?" the girl asked eagerly.

"Yes. We've got an investigation moving now." He added, regretfully: "But I can't promise he'll be alive when we spring our evidence on Packard, and I don't know that what we dig up will be enough to convict Jug—except in public opinion."

"If Bob Webb isn't alive, it will do him a lot of good to show he has been the victim of a conspiracy," Sandra said bitterly. "And as for the villain who sent him to prison—a lot he'll care what people think, if he escapes the law."

John put a hand gently on her shoulder. "Keep a stiff upper lip, honey," he said cheerfully. "This will work out right yet."

He wished that he believed his own prediction.

21 *Retrodden Trails*

When the fugitives left Tucson they did not have time to make a choice of roads. They took the one that led them most quickly out of range. It brought them to a cactus-covered mesa that extended eastward for miles. Bob turned out of the road into the thick growth of cholla, prickly pear, and greasewood. The scrub was tall, and inside of a few minutes they were in a wilderness of brush so dense that it made an ideal temporary hiding place.

To the north at the horizon's edge were the bare stark Santa

Catalina mountains, to the south the Rincons. They had to decide the direction in which they had better travel, after which they must find another horse.

"They'll expect us to strike for Mexico *muy pronto*," Fraser said. "Even so, I reckon it would be the smart thing to do."

"With the border closed to us, as it will be inside of an hour? Jug isn't anybody's fool. He'll wire to Douglas, Bisbee, Nogales, and all points along the line. Soon as we show our noses officers will pounce on us. I'd say for us to get into the mountains and hole up till the chase is over. We could pass through Oracle, off to the left a bit so that we won't be seen, cross the Divide, and drop down into the San Pedro valley. Once there, we can head for the White Mountains or for the Dragoons, whichever seems the safest bet to you, Stan."

Fraser nodded agreement. "I reckon you're right. But first off, I've got to get me a horse."

"Buy one or steal one?" Bob asked.

"There are objections to both," the little man grinned, scratching his head. "If I buy one the seller is going to start talking soon as he hears about the rumpus in the plaza; if I steal a bronc I'll have officers in my hair wherever I show myself."

"Not so good," Bob admitted. "We might buy you a horse and get away with it, but soon as we talk about buying a saddle a rancher is going to get suspicious. He'll want to know where yore own saddle is. Maybe we could rope a stray mount on the range, but you can't rope a saddle too."

The eyes of Fraser lit. "You've done said it, son. We'll borrow a horse to take me as far as Oracle. I'll buy one there. McMurdo is a good friend of mine. He'll fix me up all right."

They wound in and out through the brush toward the Catalinas, one walking and the other riding. In the sunlight the mountains looked as if they were made of papier-mâché, an atmospheric effect helped by the gulches and cañons that seamed the sides of the range. From the mesa they dropped down into the valley of the Rillito and crossed its bed, a dry wash that after a cloudburst was sometimes filled with a roaring torrent of water.

Bob pointed to the sahuaro slope rising to the foothills. "A bunch of horses," he said. "You had better do the roping, Stan. I'm out of practice."

The horses were not wild, though they showed a little nervousness at the approach of Fraser. He was careful not to alarm them by any hurried movement. They were cropping alfilaria in a small draw from which it was not easy to escape without passing him. He picked a sorrel gelding, and at the first cast the loop of the rope dropped over the head of the animal. The old-timer fashioned from the rope a headstall and reins and swung to the bare back of the bronco. After a crowhop or two the horse accepted the domination of its new master.

They kept away from the road as much as possible, following the foothills until late in the afternoon. It was getting near sunset when Fraser pointed out a road winding around the side of a bluff.

"That's where yore pappy made the big mistake of his life. He and two-three of his boys came on a bunch of Pachies who had trapped a freight outfit. They drove off the Injuns. One of the mule skinners was wounded. It was Packard. If they had left him right there to die everything would have been slick. But yore pappy put him in a wagon, took the sidewinder back to Tucson, and had Mrs. Webb nurse him till he was well."

Young Webb reflected with sardonic irony that this simple act of kindness had resulted in the ruin not only of his father's life but also those of his mother and his own.

Darkness had fallen before the riders reached the live oak groves of Oracle. From a hill-top they looked down on the lights of the stage station.

"I reckon I'd better drift down and have a powwow with Jim McMurdo," Fraser said. "If it looks all right we'll wave a lantern in front of the house for you to come on in."

Bob tied the horses and sat down on a flat rock to wait. Stars flooded the sky and a big red moon was just rising over the horizon. The night was peaceful as one could imagine, but there was no serenity in the heart of this hunted man. For years he had lived like a caged beast and since his escape the life of a hunted one. The trouble was that he was at war with himself. He had built a steely wall of protective hardness around his kindly human emotions, and of late he had found them seeping through and overflowing the barrier.

A light moved to and fro in front of the house below. Bob mounted and let his horse pick a way down among the boulders, the led horse by his side.

McMurdo was a stoutly built Scot of middle age. His shrewd blue eyes, rather stern, looked steadily into those of the escaped convict.

"I knew your father," he said quietly. "A fine man. Mr. Fraser tells me you have been wronged. I don't know about that, but I don't trust Packard. Never have. I've agreed to let Stan have a horse and saddle. My wife is making supper for you. While you eat, my son will feed your mount."

Before they went into the house Fraser released the sorrel gelding and gave it a cut with a quirt on the rump. The animal started on a trot down the road. Within twenty-four hours it would be back on its own range.

As they ate, Fraser told the story of their escape at Tucson,

90

omitting all reference to the Rangers. Bob noticed that the manager of the stage station watched him closely. The man had something on his mind and was hesitating as to whether he had better mention it.

It was while Fraser was saddling his horse at the stable that McMurdo came out with what was troubling him.

"Know a man named String Crews?" he asked Webb.

Bob shook his head. "Don't think I do—not to remember him anyhow."

"Drove stage for me last year."

Fraser spoke up. "I knew him. Long hungry-lookin' fellow lean as a range cow after a tough winter."

"That's the man. Quit me a couple of months ago to settle on a ranch in the San Pedro valley. Long time ago he drove an ore wagon for the Johnny B."

Webb fastened his eyes on McMurdo. "In my father's time?" he asked.

"Then, and for a while afterward." The station manager turned to his son. "Bill, run up to the house and see if your mother has that package of grub packed for Mr. Fraser." After the boy had gone McMurdo said, his direct gaze on Bob: "String told me something that maybe you ought to know."

"If it is about my father's death I think I ought," Bob answered. "I've stuck around Arizona because I want to get to the bottom of this business. I think Packard murdered my father and robbed my mother. I know he lied me into prison."

"I'll give you what String told me for what it is worth, though I don't know whether he is willing to stand by it in court. He went on a spree with a man called Uhlmann about a week after your father's death. Uhlmann got very drunk and was throwing his money away. He boasted that it came easy. At first that was all he would say, but later in the night he claimed that Packard had given him five hundred dollars for a special job, a bit of dynamiting that was worth a lot to Jug."

"Did he say just what the job was?" Bob asked, his voice rough and tense.

"It was to blow up your father, but I don't know that Uhlmann admitted this in so many words. Anyhow, String understood what he meant. That wasn't the end of the story. After Uhlmann sobered up he remembered that he had talked too much, though he wasn't quite sure how far he had gone. In a roundabout way he tried to find out from String. He said he was an awful liar when he was soused and you couldn't believe a word he said. But String could see Uhlmann was worried and he began to get scared of the fellow. A few weeks later somebody shot into the cabin where String was sleeping. The bullet passed over his body so close that it ripped the bedding. String could not prove that Uhlmann had fired the shot, but

91

he felt sure of it. That day he left his job at the Johnny B and never went back."

"Whereabouts is this ranch of his?"

"On the river. Five or six miles above Mammoth."

"I'm obliged to you, Mr. McMurdo."

"If you are innocent, I hope this will help you. Tell Crews you heard it from me."

The fugitives rode into the night up the trace which led them past the big rocks from which they could look down into the valley below, a dim gulf of space in the darkness. They made a dry camp, using their hair ropes to draw a protective circle around them against rattlesnakes. Though neither of them knew whether the rough hairs were so irritating to the belly of a rattler that the reptile would not crawl over such a rope, like a good many outdoor men of the Southwest they gave the tradition the benefit of the doubt.

By day the valley stood out in sharp detail. The silvery river wound along its floor, and here and there cottonwood groves dotted the banks. The blades of ranch windmills sparkled in the sunlight. The last time Bob had seen the San Pedro he was with his father. He remembered that it was spring, and the slope of the Galiuro Mountains which rose to hem in the opposite side of the valley had been one immense golden splash from millions of blooming poppies.

Before they reached Mammoth they left the road, cutting across the baked desert to a bend in the stream a few miles above the town. A barbed wire fence barred the way. They deflected, to follow the fence. It brought them, after two right-angle turns, to a neat whitewashed adobe house. The woman who came to the door pointed upstream.

"String lives about a mile farther up the river," she said. "On the right side."

Fraser found String as gaunt and as hungry-looking as he had been a dozen years earlier. He was directing the course of water in an alfalfa field, but he stopped to lean on his hoe while he talked. He was glad to meet Fraser and hash over old times and acquaintances. To Stan's younger friend Cape Sloan he did not pay much attention.

At Crews' insistence they stayed to eat a bachelor dinner in the unplastered adobe house of two rooms which went with the ranch. Not until they were nearly finished eating did Fraser lead the talk back to their host's freighting days at the Johnny B.

String agreed that Bob Webb had been a fine man, a good boss, always fair and reasonable. "Different from that damn fox Packard as day is from night." He pulled up and looked hard at Fraser. "I could tell you something, Stan, that would give you a jolt."

"I don't reckon you could tell me anything about that old snake in the grass that would surprise me," Fraser replied carelessly.

Crews was piqued at this cavalier indifference. "That's what *you* think, old-timer. I know better. But I reckon I'll keep my mouth shut. You're just as well off not knowing it."

That the ranchman wanted to shock his friend but did not think it would be wise to talk was clear. Bob guessed that his presence had something to do with String's reticence. When dinner was finished he strolled away to take a look at some horses in the corral.

Fraser nodded toward the retiring back of Webb. "He's all right, Sloan is, but it was smart of you to wait till he had gone to tell me about Jug." There was flattery in the wise drop of the voice, all set for the reception of confidential gossip.

It turned the scale. Crews had been telling himself he had better not tell what he knew, but now he changed his mind. He leaned forward and put his forearms on the table.

"What would you say if I told you Bob Webb wasn't killed by an accident but on purpose?" he asked.

Fraser showed the proper amazement. "Good Lord!" he gasped.

"Sure as you're a foot high."

"But—he was blown up in an explosion down in the mine."

"That's right. He was asked into the drift by a man who had set the charge and made an excuse to beat it in time."

Stan showed frank incredulity. He shook his head. "No, String. Someone must of pulled a whizzer on you. Did the fellow claim he was there and saw all this?"

The rancher hesitated. He could still stop without giving any details that might later turn out to be dynamite. But Fraser was a close-mouthed fellow, and String had an answer so pat and startling that it was not in him to suppress it.

"More than that. He told me he was the one who did it."

The old-timer felt it due his host not to discount any of the shock by reason of having heard this before. "My God!" he exclaimed. "Somebody told you he murdered Bob Webb?"

"Practically." Crews nodded his head in affirmation. "And who gave him five hundred dollars to do it."

"How came he to do it—to tell you, I mean?"

"He let it out soon after when he was dead drunk and blowing the money."

It was time, Fraser felt, to put the direction question. "Who?" he asked.

"Hans Uhlmann. Packard wanted Webb out of the way and paid him."

"To get hold of the mine."

"Yes, sir, and he got it." Crews finished the story. "Some-

93

body shot at me one night while I was in bed. Just barely missed me. I knew it was Uhlmann. You see, he kinda remembered telling me. I lit out *prontito*. That fellow is a killer, and I knew I wouldn't last long there."

Bob watched for a sign from Fraser to rejoin the others. He did not want a premature return to interfere with what Crews had to tell.

Not till after they had left did Fraser repeat to his friend what he had just learned. They discussed whether they had better try to get Crews' sworn story down on paper or wait until they needed it. Stan favored the latter plan.

"If he has to sit around and wait after going on record he might get scared and skip. Leave him lay. He'll stay put. When we need him he'll come through."

Bob too was of the opinion that there was no need to rush him.

22 On the Dodge

Bob picketed his horse and lay in the brush in the shade of a clump of ocatillos while Stan rode into Mammoth and bought supplies at the little store there. It was certain that the stage had brought up news of the fight on the plaza, but unless by mischance somebody recognized Fraser he was not likely to be taken for one of the fugitives. Cowboys riding the chuck line were common as fleas in this cattle country. Work was slack, and a good many of them were drifting from one range to another.

A couple of loafers in chairs tilted back against the wall of the store watched Fraser tie at the rack and bowleg to the store. He stopped to pass the time of day with them. They gathered that he had come down from the Tonto Basin where he had been helping on a drive of stock for the Hashknife outfit. Leisurely he rolled and smoked a cigarette before going into the store to make his purchases. Thought he would cross the line into New Mexico, he said. Never had worked over there and would like to take a whirl at it.

The proprietor of the store was a scrawny little man wearing glasses. Fraser ordered flour, bacon, a package of Arbuckle's and other supplies. He bought also a coffee pot and a fry pan. While he was packing the goods in a gunny sack for easier carrying the storekeeper mentioned that the stage had been robbed yesterday five miles from Oracle.

"The hold-ups get much?" Fraser asked.

"About two hundred dollars, mostly from the passengers."

"They don't know who did it, I reckon?"

"Not for sure. Folks think it was that fellow Webb who escaped from the pen two-three months ago—him and a pal of his. They were in Tucson day before yesterday and killed a man there."

Fraser bit off the answer that was on his tongue. This was not the time to defend Bob. "Seems like Arizona has more than its share of scalawags," he said virtuously. "We'd ought to have rangers like Texas has to clear them out."

"That's right," agreed the merchant. "We got no protection. Webb and his pardner might drop in any minute, and what could I do?"

The customer looked out of the door in startled alarm. "Don't talk thataway, mister," he remonstrated. "No foolin', I don't want any truck with bad men. But shucks! we don't need to worry. Those fellows are skedaddlin' for the White Mountains or some other outlaw hole-up. They ain't stickin' around here none."

That was likely, the storekeeper agreed. He strolled outside after Fraser and watched him tie the sack behind the saddle seat.

"If you meet up with those stage hold-ups, tell 'em from me that they don't need to do any shooting any time they want what I've got," Fraser said. "I'll hand everything over cheerful."

He left the road a half a mile from Mammoth and cut into the brush. Before he reached Bob he began to sing a stanza of one of his favorite songs. He did not want his companion to make any mistake about who was approaching. Except that his voice was cracked and that he could not carry a tune, he did very well.

> "There's hard times on old Bitter Creek
> That never can be beat.
> It was root, hog, or die
> Under every wagon sheet.
> We cleared up all the Injuns,
> Drank all the alkali,
> And it's whack the cattle on, boys,
> Root, hog, or die."

"Glad you're back," Webb told him. "I got to worrying for fear you had run into trouble, and when I heard yore foghorn sounding I was afraid you had lost a rich uncle or something."

Stan dismounted and turned a severe eye on his friend. "So you been at it again soon as I let you out of my sight," he charged.

"What have I been at?" Bob inquired. He guessed that this opening was a precursor to news.

95

"Robbing the stage near Oracle, and right after you killed a man at Tucson."

"Was the Oracle stage held up?"

"Yes, sir. Last night. They claim you did it."

"Alone?"

"Why, no, I reckon I helped you." Fraser grinned gaily at his fellow fugitive. "That's what comes of me keeping bad company."

"I expected they would say I killed that gunman on the plaza, but it's a surprise to find I'm a road agent too."

"You might call it right coincidental that some galoots have to pick the very day we're traveling that district to rob a stage," Fraser complained cheerfully. "We have the beatingest luck— killers, horse thieves, stage robbers, all in the same day. And me in my sunset years, with my bones creakin' and aches in all my joints." It was quite evident that the old-timer was well pleased with himself.

Yet he agreed with Bob that it might be well for them to put a few more miles between them and the scenes of their crimes. They rode down the valley and camped at dusk on the river. Their intention was to hide out in the Dragoon Mountains for a few days until the first heat of the hunt for them was past.

The sun beating down on their faces woke them. For breakfast they had flapjacks, bacon, and coffee. While the shadows from the east were still long they were on their way. In the early afternoon they stopped at a water hole and rested.

"Dragoon isn't more than two-three miles from here," Fraser mentioned. "It's no great shakes of a place. But we can get tobacco at the store."

"What's that up on the hill?" Bob asked. "Looks like a mine."

"Yep. Abandoned long ago. Fellow called Frenchy worked it for a year or two."

"Let's go up and take a look at it," Bob said.

"If you like," his companion consented.

The shack was falling to pieces and the windlass had already collapsed into the shaft, but on the other side of the hill was an arroyo down which a little stream trickled and watered a small grove of live oaks.

"Why not stay right here a day or two?" Bob wanted to know. "There are water, shade, and no inhabitants. We might do worse."

"Suits me," Fraser replied.

They rode down the slope, unloaded, and unsaddled. There was a good growth of alfilaria by the stream. They picketed their mounts and relaxed.

After supper they decided to ride in to Dragoon and renew their tobacco supply. Fraser did not think it quite wise for Bob to go, but after all the chances were ten to one they would not see anybody in the drowsy village who would be any danger to them. Probably no news of the trouble on the plaza at Tucson or of the stage hold-up had reached the place.

23 Wanted—Dead or Alive

The sun was back of the western hills when Webb and Fraser rode down the dusty business street of Dragoon and pulled up at the post office, but darkness had not yet blanketed the country. The storekeeper, Mose Hersey, sat in front of the establishment and drank in the cool breeze that relieved the heat of the day. He was a soft fat man, and he felt a momentary resentment at having to get up and wait on customers so soon after supper. Unfortunately the two brown travel-stained riders tying at the rack were strangers, and he could not very well tell them to wait on themselves and pay when they came out.

Mose heaved himself out of the chair and waddled into the store after them. Apparently all they wanted was tobacco. Since he was a friendly garrulous soul, his annoyance evaporated almost at once. The shiny leather chaps, the worn boots, and the big weathered hats told him they were cowboys. He asked them for what outfit they rode.

"We're on the loose right now," Fraser told him. "Know any ranch around here that could use two top riders?"

Just at the present moment Mose did not. The Bar Double X was the biggest spread in the neighborhood, but he had heard they were laying off men.

It was darker in the store than outside but still light enough to read. Webb had stopped in front of a poster tacked to the wall close to the post office cage. It offered a reward of fifteen hundred dollars for his capture dead or alive. Two hundred of this would be paid by the state and the rest by J. Packard. The man wanted was a desperate character, a murderer escaped from the penitentiary who had just killed another man at Tucson, by name Chuck Holloway, and a few hours later had robbed the Oracle stage. There was no photograph shown of the outlaw, but a very accurate description was given of him.

Fraser stowed the tobacco in his pocket and joined Bob.

"This guy is valuable," he said. "Fifteen hundred is a lot of mazuma. More than I could make in several years chasing cows. This J. Packard, whoever he is, must be real interested."

"Probably he's just a good citizen who wants to promote law and justice," Webb suggested ironically.

"Me, I could pay off the mortgage with fifteen hundred,

97

son," Fraser mentioned sadly. "But finding this bird would be like lookin' for a needle in a haystack, and when you find him yore troubles would be just beginning."

Mose Hersey laughed wisely. "You boys can have him. I don't want any part of him if he is as tough as they say."

"I'll bet he's a sure enough bad man from the Brazos who would start smokin' quick," Fraser said. "The time to get him would be when he is asleep, don't you reckon?"

"Not interested, asleep or awake." Mose shook his head. "I like money well as most men, but I'd walk a mile around any desperado when he is on the prod even if the reward was ten times that big."

"Well, you ain't liable to meet him . . . You wouldn't have any mail here for Joseph K. Ward, would you?"

The postmaster knew he had not, but out of politeness he riffled through the five or six letters in the office before answering that he had not.

"I didn't hardly expect one," admitted Joseph K. Ward, alias Stanley Fraser. "My wife ran off with a traveling salesman, but I figured maybe they would be outa money by this time and she might of writ home asking me to send her some and the letter could of been forwarded."

Bob slanted a look at his companion. It said, "You blamed little son-of-a-gun. You'd rather pull a fairy tale any day than tell the truth."

Mose murmured that he was sorry Mr. Ward's home had been busted up.

"So is the city slicker sorry by this time," the alleged bereaved husband commented philosophically. "Mary Jane has the evenest bad temper of anybody in Trinidad, though of course she ain't there since she lit out with the guy selling the rheumatism cure."

"Trinidad Colorado?"

"That's right. Do you think my son here favors me?"

"Quite a bit," the storekeeper fabricated, trying to say the right thing. "Course he's a whole lot bigger than you, and not so dark complected, and his eyes are different color, and his head ain't shaped the same, but outside of that he's the spittin' image of you."

"I got four more boys and two girls," Fraser went on mendaciously. "The other boys ain't so puny as this one. Bill here is the runt of the family."

"He don't look so puny to me," Mose said.

"Appearances is deceptive. Cough for the gentleman, Bill."

Bob said heartily, "You go to blazes."

"You hadn't ought to talk thataway to yore pappy," Stan reproached him mildly. To his audience of one, he explained: "Bill hates folks to know he's a mite on the sick side."

Through the door they could see that a rider had stirred up the yellow dust in the street and was heavily dismounting in front of the store. He stopped to exchange greeting with a man lounging outside, after he had glanced at the two horses already tied to the rack.

Fraser took one look at him and dropped his foolery instantly. "I reckon we better be moseyin' along, son," he drawled.

The new arrival came into the store. It was darker inside the building than out in the street, and he stood accustoming himself to the change, his bleached blue eyes squinting into the gloom.

" 'Lo, sheriff," Mose said.

" 'Lo, Hersey. My throat's dry as a lime kiln. Bust me open a can of tomatoes."

Bob had seen the man before, at the Circle J R ranch. He recognized at once the sunwrinkled face of Sheriff Norlin. The officer was wearing the same old scuffed boots, floppy Stetson hat, and corduroy trousers. If the checked shirt from which many washes had faded the color was not the same it must have been a twin.

Norlin had not identified Webb, who had wandered to the back of the store and was standing in the shadows. Fraser moved forward and stood directly between the sheriff and the convict. He bleated an enthusiastic greeting.

"Well—well, if it ain't Chad Norlin. You doggoned old vinegaroon, I ain't seen you for a month of Sundays. The last time was on the round-up at Three Cedars. Or have we met since? Sure is good to meet up with you again." Fraser caught the officer's hand and wrung it vigorously. His face beamed delight.

The sheriff was surprised at this burst of affection. It had not occurred to him before that there was any real tie of friendship binding him. He did not know that while Fraser was firmly but unobtrusively crowding him toward the front of the store the little man was desperately hoping there was a back exit from the building by means of which Webb could escape.

"Want to show you something, Chad, though maybe you've seen it," Fraser continued eagerly. "Here's a fifteen hundred dollars reward offered for a guy escaped from the pen. Yesterday it was two hundred. Now it has jumped into big money." He put his finger on the poster just below the name of Packard. "Jug is a tight-fisted galoot. Why for is he digging up thirteen hundred bucks to get this fellow?"

Mose had been cutting open a tomato can with the heel of a hatchet. Now he brought it forward to the sheriff.

Norlin brushed the dust from the top of the can before lifting it to his mouth. "I saw that poster at Mammoth, Stan," he said. "I can tell you something you probably don't know. 'Most all of one hot day less than two weeks ago I spent in the saddle going to have a look at this fellow. I didn't know he was Webb, since he was passing as Cape Sloan. The fellow had been accused of being a rustler, and I wanted to check up on him. He was staying at the Circle J R ranch with the Rangers. I satisfied myself he couldn't be one of the waddies who ran off stock when Spillman was killed, but I had a queer feeling I was missing something. So I was. There was Webb right in my hands, and I let him go."

"That was certainly hard luck," Fraser said. "But you can't blame yoreself. You didn't know who he was."

The sheriff tilted the can and began to drink the tomato juice. Out of the corner of an eye Fraser saw that Bob was not only in the store but was coming forward quietly, evidently with the intention of passing unnoticed in the rear of Norlin while he was drinking. As Bob was brushing past, the officer glanced at him carelessly.

Norlin's eyes froze. But his right hand was holding a tomato can two feet from the butt of his revolver and the barrel of a forty-five was pressing against a rib just over his heart. His shooting iron might just as well have been in New York.

"Go right on and finish yore tomatoes," Webb advised coldly.

Chad Norlin almost strangled as the liquid went down the wrong way. When he had stopped coughing, the weapon at his side had been removed from the holster.

"Take it easy, sheriff," Bob warned. "This isn't your day."

"I won't forget this, Stan," Norlin promised. "You worked me for a sucker."

"Don't feel too bad," Fraser consoled him, with a grin. "You were took by surprise, and if I do say it I put on a good show."

"Why are you throwing in with this criminal, Fraser?" the sheriff demanded. "It means the penitentiary for you too."

"You done said it, Chad," answered Fraser chirpily. "I'm in this up to my neck. If and when Bob killed Chuck Holloway and robbed the stage I was right by his side aiding and abetting. What makes me mad is that they're offering fifteen hundred for him and not a thin dime for me. Dad-burn it, I want you to spread the word that I'm a bad man from the Guadalupe just as much as he is, and I got a right to a reasonable amount of publicity."

"This won't be so funny when you're breaking rocks with a guard over you," Norlin told him irritably.

"Change that when to if, Chad," suggested Stan. "We ain't either of us going to prison. First off, Bob never killed a man in his life, and that perjured murderer Jug Packard knows it. The same goes for his killer Uhlmann. We've declared war on those villains, and we aim to show who belongs in the pen and who doesn't."

"Shooting off yore mouth that way won't get you off," the sheriff replied angrily. "What stands out like a wooden leg is that this fellow here is an escaped convict and it's my job to arrest him. He had a fair trial, and a jury said he was guilty. That's enough for me, and it ought to be enough for you."

"Well, it ain't," the little man snapped. "Not by a jug full. There's gonna be justice done in this case."

Bob interrupted. "No use arguing, Stan. Sheriff Norlin is right. It's his job to arrest me, but this time he doesn't cut the mustard. The three of us are going to leave here together. He'll stay with us until we think it's safe to let him go."

Norlin did not attempt any protest that he knew would be futile. He walked out of the store with them and mounted as directed. When they rode into the gathering darkness his horse was between those of the others. No attempts to escape would be successful. If he tried it, they would shoot his mount. He knew they were not going to hurt him. At the first safe opportunity they would release him.

24 Governor Andrews Advises Sandra

After telling his story Chandler Newman walked out of the governor's office to wait in the outer room. Governor Andrews ran a hand through a shock of fine white hair. He was troubled, and showed it. He shook his head slowly.

"Your evidence misses the point, John," he said. "I'll admit that Jug Packard is a crook and probably stole the Johnny B from Mrs. Webb. It looks as if he might have contrived the murder of her husband judging by what Fraser told you he learned from this man String Crews. I hope you get the goods on him. The scoundrel has a record as odorous as a hydrophobia skunk. He's sly as a weasel and poisonous as a sidewinder. Young Webb had plenty of provocation, but I can't go outside of the record. The prosecution made out a strong case. Witnesses swore that when he came to Packard's office he had the manner of one looking for trouble. He pushed his way in without knocking. Through the window two workingmen heard him angrily denouncing Jug and threatening to get him. Uhlmann backed Packard's story that the boy killed Giles Lemmon. I have read the testimony carefully. Webb made out a very weak case for himself."

"Uhlmann had to support Packard, since he had killed

101

Lemmon himself while shooting at Bob Webb," Ranger pointed out.

The governor thumped a fist down on the desk. He was an honest man, doing his duty as he saw it, and unhappy at the direction in which it drove him. "Bring me some evidence to prove that," he cried. "Something more than Webb's unsupported word."

The low-pitched husky voice of Sandra took up the attack. "Bob says there was a woman in the outer office when he went in to see Packard. When he ran out of the building after the shooting he saw her in the street looking white and scared. She was Mary Gilcrest, a daughter of one of Packard's miners. What became of her? She was not a witness at the trial, though the defense tried hard to find her. She had disappeared."

The eyes of Governor Andrews softened as he looked at Sandra. He had been a cattleman himself, from the same neighborhood as the Rangers, and, even before she was born, a friend of the family. He remembered dandling her on his knee when she was less than six months old. The gallant golden youth of the girl warmed his heart. She had a provocative disturbing face, amazingly alive, and courage in her blue eyes carried like a banner.

"Never heard of her," he answered. "If this woman knew anything of importance she would have come forward at the trial, I reckon."

"Packard saw to it that she could not be reached," Sandra retorted quickly. "He sent her away until after the trial. Mr. Lansing, Bob Webb's attorney, tried to look her up. Her father pretended he did not know where she was and her mother acted as if she was afraid to talk. It was a conspiracy. I'm sure of it."

"Where is she now?" the governor asked.

"We don't know. She was married and went away, and soon afterward her father died. The mother moved. We are advertising for Mary now."

"I hope you find her. We can learn what she has to say, if anything. But I'm afraid you are depending on a frail reed. Probably she won't have anything of value to tell. And frankly, I must make it plain that I can't indorse the pardon of any man who has broken prison and is still at large."

"Not even if he is innocent?" she cried.

"If he is innocent, let him surrender. I'm willing to reopen the case."

"He won't surrender, after spending seven years in that terrible prison. He would rather be killed than be taken."

"I don't ask whether you know where he is hiding—and I don't want to know. But if you get in touch with him, try to persuade him to give himself up—or at least to get out of the country until you've worked up the case against Packard and Uhlmann."

"He won't leave," John Ranger said. "He is filled with the one thought of proving the case against Packard. I wish you knew him, Ben. Webb is not just a wild daredevil. He is fine and strong as steel—a thoroughbred."

"I have a sheepish admiration for him, even though I haven't made his acquaintance," the governor confessed, and there was a smile on his face. "Half the people in Arizona are cheering for him and laughing at the authorities. They are making a romantic Robin Hood of him. My own wife and children say they hope he won't be captured."

"Because they think he is innocent," Sandra tossed in.

"Not at all. They don't care whether he is innocent. Because of his confounded impudence."

"Was it impudence that made him ride alone against four of Pablo Lopez' killers to save me and my brother?" Sandra asked, her eyes starry with indignation.

Ben Andrews had a moment of regret for his own vanished youth. He was happily married, but the days of romance for him were gone forever. That fine rapt look in Sandra's face belonged only to lovers. It occurred to him that Bob Webb, hunted convict though he was, might have something in his life most men would never know.

"He has plenty of sand in his craw," the governor admitted. "Maybe too much. I don't suppose you can tame your wild buckaroo, Miss Sandra. He's a little too exciting for Arizona now that it claims to have passed the days of its riotous youth. Ever since he broke loose he has been in one difficulty or another. Just check up on them. To begin with, practically caught rustling."

"And proved innocent," Sandra interrupted quickly.

The governor ignored the interruption. "Kills a Mexican scoundrel the same day and wounds another." He held up a hand to ward off the protest of Ranger. "I'm merely running through a list of his activities, John. Beat up a citizen with a quirt."

"A fine citizen," Sandra flung out scornfully.

"Is accused of another murder and stage robbery. On top of that kidnaps a sheriff starting to arrest him. The fellow is making more news in the territory than Geronimo did. I'm afraid to look at my paper in the morning for fear he has committed some other outrage."

His smile robbed the indictment of much of its force. Sandra smiled back at him. "Sheriff Norlin was probably trying to win that fifteen hundred dollar reward you say ought never to have been offered."

"Well, it oughtn't," the governor admitted resentfully. "Jug had no right to print and circulate that reward poster. He did not consult me. I would never have authorized the public to bring Webb in dead or alive, and as soon as I learned what Packard had done I called in the posters and notified the newspapers to that effect."

John Ranger nodded approval. "We know you did. That poster explains itself, Ben. You know Jug Packard is tight as the bark on a live oak. Why did he offer so much money, in an open invitation for hunters to kill rather than capture Webb? There can be only one reason. He is afraid to have Bob at large for fear he will get proof of his skulduggery."

Andrews thought that might be true. "It looks bad, John. Maybe you are right. Webb may have been framed. There is nothing I would like better than to get enough evidence to free the young fellow and to put Jug in his place at Yuma. But move carefully. And make Sandra keep out of this. If Packard thought you were working against him I wouldn't put it past him to have you drygulched."

"Nor I," agreed Ranger thoughtfully. "He has everything at stake that counts with him—property, power, even his life perhaps. Murder wouldn't stop him."

"But this time he must know somebody is raking up the past to get something on him." The governor put a hand on Sandra's shoulder. "Stay at home and tend to your knitting, my dear. This is war, and you must not be mixed up in it. Your young man has several good friends working for him now. Let them take care of this."

The color deepened in the girl's cheeks, but her eyes held fast to his. "He isn't my young man, but I want to see justice done," she said quietly.

Yet there was a touch of proud defiance in the poised grace of her fine lifted head. He might think what he pleased. She had enlisted in Bob Webb's cause regardless of what anybody might say. The governor read worry in John Ranger's troubled face. He too believed that Sandra was in love with this vagabond who had the brand of the criminal on him, and from such an attachment no happiness could come.

25 Two of a Kind

"Be reasonable, Rhino," protested Packard. "Don't get hell in your neck. All I want is for this to work out right for us both."

"All you want is for someone else to be yore catspaw," Uhlmann differed, an ugly snarl in his voice. "I'm to run the risk while you sit back not doing a frazzlin' thing that could get you into trouble, the way it has always been. By Judas priest, it won't be like that this time. If you want this fellow, you get him yoreself."

"It won't be hard," Packard continued. "He's hanging around in the brush back of the Circle J R somewheres. Locate his camp, watch your chance, and plug him in the back."

"Glad you think it's so easy, because you're going to have to nail his hide on a fence if it's done. I ain't ridin' on that kind of a job any more. My saddle is done hung up on a peg for keeps."

"Just pick your time right and there is no danger."

"Not interested," Uhlmann grunted. "You can't catch this mule with that ear of corn, Jug."

"I wouldn't wonder but what you could use a couple of hundred dollars now."

"Why, you blamed Shylock, you made a public offer of thirteen hundred," the big ruffian cried angrily.

The mine owner thought fast for an out. "That was different. If a posse had got him they would of had to divide the dough half a dozen ways."

"Webb would be just as dead if I gunned him, wouldn't he?" The German looked at Packard with a contempt he did not take the trouble to conceal. "I never met up with a human as poisonous as you. If a skunk bit you it would die awful quick."

"No use flying off the handle and making talk like that, Rhino," Packard remonstrated with no apparent resentment. "We been friends a long time, and I don't aim to get mad because you've got a mean temper."

"Friends!" repeated Uhlmann harshly. "There never was a day you wouldn't of sold me down the river if it had paid you."

Packard did not waste breath defending himself. "We're in this together, Rhino, and up to our necks. No use loading ourselves with the idea that the past is dead and buried. This fellow Webb is dangerous as a tiger that has got loose, and he has important friends helping him. Like I told you, Ranger and his daughter called on the governor Thursday, and they took with them that fellow Newman."

"Chan Newman hasn't got a thing on me," the ranchman boasted, the small eyes in his pachydermous face gloating over his accomplice. "I didn't rob the Webbs of the Johnny B. This is your chicken coming home to roost."

"That's where you're wrong. This whole thing ties up into one ball of yarn with some loose threads sticking out. Soon as Webb begins to pull on any of those threads anything is liable to come loose." The shifty eyes of Packard's evil wrinkled face fixed fast on those of his companion. "For instance, you talked too much after this fellow's father had the accident in the

105

mine. If this wolf got hold of that thread and raveled it out he would come right smack to you."

"And to you," Uhlmann added. "Don't forget that for a minute." Sullenly he followed this up with a question. "How is he gonna prove the accident to his old man was kinda intentional? The only talking I ever did was to String Crews, and we haven't heard of him for years. Last I knew he was figuring on drifting back to Nebraska to live."

"I don't say he can prove it," Packard replied. "I'm just pointing out that we're in the same boat and have got to pull together or sink."

"Yeah," sneered the other. "Only remember you're not a passenger in the boat and have got to do some pulling too."

"This fellow Webb is the rock on which we might founder," Packard went on, his voice oily with persuasion. "If he was out of the way we would be all right. Nobody else is going to bust a tug trying to get us in trouble. You could fix that with a crook of your finger, Rhino."

"No rheumatism in yore finger, is there?"

"You know I can't do that sort of thing, Rhino—haven't the cold nerve for it. You never saw man or devil you were afraid of. I always said you can outgame any fellow I ever met. Of course I'd be prepared to pay a reasonable sum."

Uhlmann was flattered at the praise, but not to an extent that it diverted him from an intent to get all the traffic would bear. He knew why he was being softsoaped.

"I'll not hold you up," he said. "This guy's grandstanding doesn't faze me any. I had rubbed out my first man before he was born—when I was a kid of nineteen. Any time he wants to come a-smokin' I'll be waiting at the gate."

"I know that," purred Packard. "You've got what it takes to stand up to any of them. Still, no use you running any risk."

"I won't," bragged the killer. "He won't know what's happening until it will be too late. Now about the price."

"You said it wouldn't be much, seeing as you have to get him on your own account too."

"It will be just fifteen hundred plunks, the thirteen hundred you promised and an extra two hundred as a bonus for having a crackajack gunman on the job who will do it right."

Packard let out a yelp of distress.

"Jumping creepers, Rhino, I'm no millionaire. Fact is, if I had to raise a thousand dollars right now I wouldn't know where to turn."

Uhlmann fished twenty-five cents from his pocket. "Go get yoreself a square meal, if you can find a restaurant that will let a bum dressed like you are sit down at a table," he jeered.

"I might go as high as four-five hundred," the mine owner said.

"You'll go to fifteen hundred, one third payable now."

"Have a heart, Rhino. Times are awful tight."

"You paid more than a hundred thousand spot cash for that Sinclair ranch last month."

"Somebody has misinformed you about that. It was one of those three-party deals with a lot of swapping in it and mighty little money. Tell you what I'll do—six hundred spot cash soon as the job is done."

"You're so poor I can't take yore money, Jug. To keep yore family from starving I'll pay *you* six hundred to do it." Uhlmann rose from the chair in which he had been sitting, stretched his huge arms in a deep yawn, and heavy-footed to the door. "Going to hit the hay. If you decide to take that six hundred let me know. But you're so slippery I can't let you have a nickel till I've seen Webb in his coffin."

"Wait a minute," Packard said. "Let's settle this now. You know you're going to do this, to protect yoreself if for no other reason. What's the sense in trying to jack up the price to more than I can pay?"

"You got mighty poor all of a sudden." The ranchman's voice was heavy with sarcasm. "Must have had some losses since you got that poster out."

"When I had that printed I expect I had got jumpy. The governor called that in, so it's off." Packard moved closer to Uhlmann and dropped his voice almost to a whisper. "If anything was to happen to Webb now, the law would take it for granted he had robbed the Oracle stage *and wouldn't go looking for anybody else.* But if he lives, like as not he could prove an alibi. I wonder if you could, Rhino, if some busybody officer started to push you around."

Uhlmann glared at him angrily. "Don't threaten me, you damned Judas. I won't take it from you. For fifteen years I've known yore slimy tricks. All I have to do is open my mouth to blow you sky high."

"Now—now, don't get off on the wrong foot. I was just showing you another reason why you had better rub out this Webb. Dad-gum it, a blind man could see he's bound to have it in for us both. It's neck meat or nothing. If we don't get him, he'll get us. No two ways about that."

"Buy him off," suggested Uhlmann.

"Not the kind you can buy. He told me we had murdered his father and he meant to get us. You have seen that ad in the *Star* for Mary Gilcrest. What would she do if she saw it?"

"She would keep her mouth clamped if she knew what was good for her," Uhlmann answered brutally. "Why do you suppose I married her, except to fix it so she could not testify against me?" He showed his teeth in a savage grin.

Packard met that smile with another as evil. "I take some

credit to myself for that happy marriage. Even when I bought off her pappy to send her to California until after the trial I knew she was still a danger to you. Webb's lawyer might get at her later. Seeing she was a nice plump pretty girl, I figured it would be a kindness to find her a husband who had just got him a good spread and a bunch of cows likely to have a remarkable increase on account of being close to a couple of big ranches. So I said, 'God bless you, my boy,' and sent you courting to Los Angeles. You being such a handsome buck, she couldn't resist you."

"Don't get funny at me," Uhlmann growled. "I don't like it."

"You know I wouldn't, Rhino," Packard replied, instantly dropping the sarcasm. "But about Mary. She's barred from testifying against you. But now they have started hunting for Mary Gilcrest they are sure to find out she is your wife. They'll contact her if possible, and if they get her to talking that will do a lot of harm."

"I'll have a little powwow with her," the ranchman promised, his voice harsh and grim. "After I have given her orders she wouldn't say 'Good Morning' to the Shah of Persia."

"I hope you're right," the owner of the Johnny B said doubtfully. "Sometimes she looks at you like she hates you, Rhino."

"I know I'm right. What do I care how much she hates me? A woman is like a horse. She has got to know who is master, and every so often you have to give her the whip so she won't forget it."

Packard did not comment on that. He knew how this ruffian beat his horses and he had suspected that he gave his wife the same treatment. There was a sadistic streak in the fellow that might some day get him into trouble. Horses had been known to kill cruel masters and this might be true of women driven to despair. If she was too cowed for this, she could run away and start talking. But there was nothing Jug could do about that. The German would have to keep his own household in order.

"What say we fix up the price after you've done the job?" Packard proposed. "I'll be liberal."

"The price is fixed," Uhlmann replied obstinately. "It's fifteen hundred."

"The standard price for bushwhacking a man has never been above five hundred."

"The cost of living is going up," gloated the giant. "But I'll make you an offer. We'll draw straws, and the one who loses does it for nothing."

Packard considered for a moment whether there would be any chance of gypping his co-conspirator and decided that it could not be done. Uhlmann would be too suspicious to let him get away with any sleight of hand trick. Jug might get the wrong straw.

Reluctantly he turned over to the killer five hundred dollars as a deposit for value to be received.

26 *Sandra Rides to Visit a Neighbor*

Jim Budd brought into the parlor to meet Sandra a shuffle-footed Negro named Sam Washington. He was the cook at the Johnny B mine, and he and Jim had become close friends. Sam was as embarrassed as he would have been at a Buckingham Palace presentation, and he stood twirling his hat in two restless hands.

Sandra rose from the piano where she had been playing a Viennese waltz. She had made Jim promise to bring Sam in to see her next time he stopped at the ranch.

"I'm glad you and Jim get along so well," she said. "Make him give you a piece of that apple pie he has in the kitchen. It's delicious. But since you are a cook yourself good food may not be a treat to you. I hear you have been at the Johnny B a long time."

"Ten years come next Christmas, ma'am."

"That's a long time. I wonder if you remember a girl whose father used to work for Mr. Packard. Her name was Mary Gilcrest."

The cook twisted his face into a grimace to help his memory. "Folks they come an' go. Seem like I got a recommembrance, but I can't jest put my mind on it."

"Her father was a miner," Sandra prompted.

Sam slapped a hand on his thigh. "Pete Gilcrest. He moved away. Comes to me I done heard he was dead."

"He died in Nevada. Do you know what became of Mary?"

The Johnny B cook nodded. He had the woman placed now all right. "She up and got married."

Sandra felt a tingle of excitement run through her. The answer to the next question she asked would bring her to an impasse or would open a road for her to follow. "Did you ever hear the name of her husband?"

Sam's eyes went blank. It was as if she had drawn a curtain over them and yet left them still open. "She married a ranchman in this valley, a man who used to work for Mr. Packard. Name of Uhlmann."

"A big heavy ugly man—the one they call Rhino."

"That's him." Sam's voice had grown sullen and vindictive.

"You don't like him," the girl said quickly. "Neither do I."

"I don' want to have no truck with that man a-tall," the Negro said with finality.

"He did you a wrong some time, maybe?"

Sam hesitated. He wanted to play safe, and on the other hand he felt a desire to express to this young woman who did not like Uhlmann his own bitter pent-up hatred. His fingers touched a long deep scar on his forehead.

"Once when he was drunk he did this—with a stirrup. Out of plumb meanness. Because when he came an hour late for dinner, after everybody else had eaten, I had things cleared off the table. For a month I was awful sick."

"He's a heartless brute," Sandra said, eyes flashing.

"Yes'm," Sam agreed. "Folks say he treats Mrs. Uhlmann terrible. I ain't ever seen her since she was married. Story is she don't hardly ever leave home."

Rumors about the Uhlmann family life had reached Sandra. Fortunately there were no children. There was a lot of gossip, some of which might not be true. It was said the man beat his wife with a whip.

Sandra had never met the woman, though the Uhlmanns lived only about ten miles up the valley from the Circle J. R. No welcome sign for visitors was hung out at the X Bar. The girl made up her mind to ignore this, for she meant to see Mary Uhlmann and have a talk with her. Of course she must make her call at a time when the husband was not at home. Since he was notoriously absent most of the time, the chance of missing him ought to be good. She might have to try more than once before she succeeded.

That her father would not approve of such a visit Sandra knew. He felt strongly that anything further done on behalf of Bob Webb must be undertaken by him and not by his daughter. Knowing her father, she was aware that he would think it unfair to work against a man through his wife. On both points she held a different opinion. Anything that could be done for Bob she meant to do, and she had no scruples about using Mary Uhlmann to get justice for him.

Her father left early next morning to look at a bunch of cows in the Sulphur Springs Valley that were for sale. He did not expect to get back until the evening of the second day. As soon as he was out of sight Sandra gave orders to have her horse saddled. She asked Jim Budd to put up a picnic lunch for her, since she probably would not return till sunset.

About a mile west of the ranch house she left the road, to follow a trail that ran up through the low hills to a rocky ridge hemming in one side of the valley for a distance of twenty miles. A gulch sown with cactus led her to the flat tops above. A fringe of bushes edged the bluff and screened her from the observation of anybody on the floor below when the path ran close to the precipice.

Now that she was in action again the girl felt happier than

110

she had been for several days. To sit still and do nothing while Bob might be in peril had been a strain on the nerves. With the sun shining and a light cool breeze ruffling her hair as she rode, the fear of impending disaster lifted from her. In a world like this, so clean and free, the alarms knocking at her heart seemed fanciful.

Swifts ran across the path and disappeared. A road runner raced in front of her for fifty yards and then veered into the brush. Beside the trail a Gila monster lay inert and sluggish. The call of a dove sounded from an arroyo. All the familiar aspects of this desert land were reassuring.

So few traveled the rough terrain of the ridge that she was surprised to catch sight of a man on horseback. He rode toward her, and she recognized Stan Fraser. The old-timer lifted his hat and waved it, a smile of pleasure on his face.

"I'm right pleased to meet you, Miss Sandra," he said. "But aren't you off yore home range some?"

"I've heard that travel broadens one," she answered.

"And a doctor once told me that the outside of a horse is good for the inside of a man. It joggles up his liver—or something."

He shifted his seat in the saddle, resting his weight on one stirrup. "You look blooming as a pink rose. If a doc did that for you, I'd like his address."

"You've kissed the Blarney Stone, Mr. Fraser," she accused. "But I'm like all women and eat up flattery."

Stan shook his head. "I dassent say half of what I think."

Her eyes sparkled. "Go on. I won't breach-of-promise you."

"That's certainly bad news," he mourned. "You'd ought to have seen me when I first began to tail cows. But that was so long ago the Rincons were still a hole in the ground. I notice the girls' eyes pass over me and light on that young high-stepper I travel with. Outside of his being thirty years younger and full of pepper and not having a face that turns milk sour, what has that hell-a-miler got that I haven't?"

"I like mature men with sense," Sandra said demurely.

"That's me. I'll be camping on yore doorsteps soon as I am no longer on the dodge."

"How nice for me!" She put the question in her mind with obvious carelessness. "And where is the—hell-a-miler? Isn't that what you called him? I hope he hasn't gone back to Yuma yet."

Fraser waved a hand widely, to include all the territory in the hills. "Back in one of these pockets. He'll holler his head off when he learns what he missed."

"Oh," she inquired innocently. "Has he missed something?"

"Bob will think so. I'll bet he won't ever stay and clean camp again." He frowned a question at her, though his words were

111

a statement. "Funny you came away up to this rough prong to take a ride."

"Maybe I thought I would like to visit a neighbor."

"Meaning a crazy bandit holed up here who is wanted for horse stealing, abduction, stage robbery, and murder?"

The color deepened in her cheeks. "No!" she answered sharply. "Not meaning him at all."

Fraser was puzzled. The cow trail she was taking led to no settlement, unless it might be the back boundary of Uhlmann's X Bar spread, and of course she could not be going there. In spite of her swift vigorous denial he was inclined to believe that she was riding the ridge in the hope of meeting Bob Webb.

"If you are going back now maybe I'd better ride along until you're off the steep trail," he offered. "A horse could easily break a leg in all those rocks."

"I'm not going back yet. And Beauty is very sure-footed. I won't need to trouble you."

"No trouble at all. A pleasure."

"For me too, some other day," she replied, with a smile that took away the sting of the dismissal.

But Sandra was still afraid she might have hurt the feelings of the old-timer, and she wouldn't do that for a good deal. She liked him, and he was a loyal friend of the man she loved. So she stayed to talk for a little longer in order to make sure he was not offended.

"I heard some news that will interest you and Mr. Webb," she told him. "That is, if it is news to you. This girl we are trying to find, Mary Gilcrest, is the wife of that villain Uhlmann."

It was a complete surprise to Fraser, but he picked up at once the adverse effect this was likely to have on Bob's chance of getting a pardon.

"Even if she wanted to she couldn't testify against Rhino now," he said. "Bob has the darndest luck. Of all men in the world she has to marry the one fellow she should not have."

"That would be a strange coincidence, if it is one," she replied thoughtfully. "It must have been some more of Packard's scheming. Well, I'll say *'Adios,'* Mr. Fraser."

"Don't forget to look for me on yore doorstep soon as this hunt quits getting hot," he said with a warm grin. "You saved my life the other day, and I certainly ain't going to let you throw me over now."

"Oh, I'm thinking of being an old maid," she laughed, turning away.

A little disturbed in mind, Fraser rode on. He was not sure that he ought not to stay with her until she was safely back in the valley. But she evidently wanted to be left alone.

A pass cut through the ridge. Sandra moved down into it and up a steep slope to the continuation of the ridge on the other side of the cut. In the distance, miles farther up the valley, she could see flashes of light from the sun striking the whirling blades of a windmill at the Uhlmann ranch. The X Bar was a small outfit, and as she drew nearer she saw by her field glasses that the buildings were ramshackle and the fences poorly kept up. The owner of the place paid very little attention to improving it.

As Sandra topped a small rise she came face to face with another rider. He carried a rifle, and a moment later she saw that the horseman was Uhlmann.

The rancher pulled up, surprised and disconcerted. His object in traveling along the ridge had been to escape observation. In front of her he jerked his horse roughly to a stop.

"What you doing here?" he demanded, suspicion in the look he slanted at her.

Sandra thought quickly. "I came to have a talk with you," she replied.

"Then why didn't you ride by the road?" he wanted to know.

She had an answer for that. "I thought perhaps you would rather I weren't seen going to your place, on account of the trouble at Tucson."

He digested that, before flinging a harsh question at her. "What do you want with me?"

"I want to ask you please to let Bob Webb alone. He has never harmed you, Mr. Uhlmann. Don't you think you have hurt him enough already?"

"How have I ever hurt him?" he growled.

"You testified at his trial that he killed Giles Lemmon, and you know that wasn't true," she said, looking straight into his small beady eyes.

"That so?" he jeered. "Who did?"

"Never mind that now. Why do you hate Bob so? Let the officers get him if they can. It's not your business."

"I want that reward."

"I shouldn't think you would want blood money," she said contemptuously.

"It will buy just as much." He added, with sudden anger: "And I won't be satisfied till that fellow is rubbed out or sent back."

"For seven or eight years he has been in that terrible place to serve a sentence for something he did not do. If he is a hard and bitter man now, his enemies made him that. Mr. Uhlmann, I'm only a girl, but I know you can't do a deliberate wrong to anybody without destroying yourself."

"Don't try to feed me pap," he broke out violently. "I know what I'm about, and I aim to keep right on doing it. My ideas don't change just because some fool girl has gone mushy about a killer."

She threw up a hand wearily. "If you won't listen, I can't help it."

He pushed his horse closer, so that his seamed leathery face was close to hers. "You do some listening, Miss High-and-Mighty. I'm dirt under your feet, by your way of it. The only reason you speak to me is because you are crazy about this Webb and are scared of what I'll do to him. Tell him for me I'll get him. It's gonna be him or me. If it's the last thing I do in this world I'll be standing up pouring lead into him after he is down." He finished with a string of scabrous epithets. The savage bitterness of his pent up venom appalled her.

She turned her horse aside to pass. He caught the bridle rein.

"You've seen me now," he jeered. "And fixed up everything nice. There's nothing to keep you from headin' for home now."

"Let go that rein," Sandra ordered.

Uhlmann's eyes narrowed. "You didn't come to see me at all," he charged, "but to meet yore fancy Dan."

"Turn loose my horse," she warned, her eyes bright with anger.

"You know where he's roostin' up in these hills, and by cripes! you're gonna take me to him."

She swung her quirt, and the lash cut across the fellow's cheek. Startled by the unexpected pain, his hand dropped from the rein. Sandra was away like a frightened rabbit, her body low over the neck of her mount. Stung to fury, the man fired at her and missed. Some saving sense in him stopped the second shot. He lowered the rifle and put his horse to a gallop in pursuit. Before he had gone thirty yards he knew his lumbering sorrel could not catch her fleet-footed mount. He ground his horse viciously to a halt and poured curses at the girl disappearing into a dip.

27 Bob Saddles

Fraser found Bob lying on his back gazing up at the thin cloud-skeins drifting across the sky.

"I'll bet you are thinking about my girl," Fraser challenged with a chuckle.

"Didn't know you had one," Bob responded cautiously, aware that there might be a catch in this. There was an air of suppressed excitement about his partner that presaged news.

"You didn't know I had a girl!" Fraser exclaimed with a show of indignation. "Shows how much you don't use yore eyes. Why, I just been out on the bluff having a nice talk with her."

Webb slanted incredulous but inquiring eyes at him. "You

114

old roué, and I've been siding you all this time without suspecting how depraved you are."

"Nothing of the kind. I've got the most honorable intentions. I told her soon as these sheriffs quit wanting me I would be right there at the Circle J R looking for her."

The prostrate man had not moved a muscle, but his gaze still rested on Stan. "So you met Miss Ranger," he said.

"You bet I did. On one of the cow trails that run along the prong."

"Not alone?"

"Why, no, there were two of us there—Miss Sandra and me."

"She had come alone?"

"That's right."

"What for?"

Fraser abandoned his bandinage. "I don't rightly know why, boy. When I hinted it might be to find you, she put me in my place quick. There was something else in her mind."

"What could it be? Nobody lives up here."

The older man scratched his head. "She said something about going to see a neighbor."

"That doesn't make sense."

"I couldn't get it. Say, she told me something I didn't know. She has found out who married Mary Gilcrest and where she lives."

"It must have been that ad Ranger put in the papers. I suppose the woman answered it."

"I dunno about that. Give you three guesses as to who the woman married."

To get it over with and find out sooner, Bob guessed, "President Cleveland, the Czar of Russia, or John L. Sullivan."

"No, sir. A dear friend of yours. She is Mrs. Hans Uhlmann."

Bob stared at him. "You sure?"

"That's what Miss Sandra told me."

"Makes it fine for me, doesn't it? Even if she wanted to testify what she heard the law wouldn't let her. You can't make a wife give evidence against her husband. I reckon they won't allow her to go on the stand."

"Old Jug sure ties up a package nice and neat," Stan said.

His friend agreed. "The girl must have heard plenty or Packard wouldn't have thought it necessary for her to be hog-tied by marrying Uhlmann."

"By now she is good and tired of that hulking rhinoceros probably. If she knows anything and will talk there must be some way of using her. You better get you a good lawyer."

"I don't know any that lives on this street," Bob answered. "When I was in town you were hell-bent on getting me out

115

where the neighborhood was more filled with absentees. Now you think——"

"Ranger will see one for you. I still think country air is more suitable for yore puny corporosity."

Bob did not answer that. His half-shuttered eyes were fixed on a stretch of mackerel sky. The consideration of another problem was occupying his mind. What was Sandra doing on this bare ridge ten miles from home? Had she come on the slight chance of meeting Fraser or him to tell them the news about Mary Gilcrest? It did not seem reasonable. She had no way of knowing that they were within fifty miles of the Circle J R, and if she had been aware of it the likelihood of running across the hunted men in these huddled hills slashed by gulches and ravines was not worth counting. Moreover, the information was not important, since there was nothing he could do about it.

He sat up abruptly. The answer to his question had flashed across his mind. She was going to the Uhlmann ranch. That was what she had meant when she told Fraser she was going to see a neighbor. And she meant to slip in to the X Bar by the back way. But why, instead of taking the easy road along the valley? If she wanted to see Uhlmann why make a secret of it? Above all, what could have induced her to go to see this ruffian without being accompanied by her father?

The only reason he could find was that she hoped to see not Uhlmann but his wife. Perhaps she had seen him passing the Circle J R on his way to town and knew that Mary Uhlmann would be alone. Bob did not like the idea at all. This fellow was too dangerous for Sandra to try to trick.

"I'm saddling," he said, and walked to his picketed horse.

"Going where?" Fraser asked.

"To the X Bar."

"Making a friendly call on good old Hans?"

"I'll tell you how friendly later—when I know myself."

"Think I'll mosey along to see the fireworks," Stan said.

"Hope there won't be any. Chances are that Uhlmann isn't home."

"But his wife will be—that the idea?"

"Not exactly. I think we'll find Sandra Ranger there."

Fraser slapped a hand on his chaps. "Right. That's where she was headed for when I met her. Never thought of that. That girl is bound and determined to help you whether you want her to or not."

Bob was worried for fear she might have involved herself in a perilous situation. Uhlmann would show no mercy toward a girl on account of her age and sex if she was making trouble for him.

"I wish she would mind her own affairs and keep out of

116

mine," he blurted gruffly. "She'll get hurt if she doesn't look out."

"Funny you didn't think to tell her that the other night when she took us in and saved our lives," Fraser retorted dryly.

He understood that his friend's irritation was born of a deep concern for Sandra's safety. To some extent he shared too in Bob's apprehension.

"She's impulsive," Webb explained. "Once I helped her when she was in a jam, and she feels she has to keep on helping me."

"That must be it," Stan agreed with a grin. "All right, fellow. Let's ride."

They jogged out of the little park where they were camped and down a stiffly sloping ledge to the plateau below. It was still rough going, but Bob put his horse to a canter till they struck a cañon that led to the ridge which made a boundary for the valley. It was impossible to travel fast through the twisting boulder-strewn gulch, yet the urge driving the younger man sent him clattering and sliding along the dry bed of the stream more rapidly than was safe.

"We won't get there any sooner if we break a leg of one of our broncs," Fraser complained. "Take it easy, boy. After all, Uhlmann isn't a fool. He daren't touch a hair of that girl's head. If he did, the men in this valley would string him up so quick he wouldn't have time to get that quid of tobacco outa his cheek."

"He might figure nobody had seen her coming to his place and he could get away with rubbing her out."

"No. If it came to a showdown Sandra would tell him she had met me and told me where she was going. I was a mite scared myself at first, but there's no sense in being afraid. Sandra will be all okay. You got to remember his wife is on the ranch—and maybe a rider or two. Rhino couldn't put over a thing."

This was probably true. None the less when they emerged from the cañon Bob put his horse at a gallop.

28 "I've Made My Bed"

When Sandra pulled up her horse, sure that Uhlmann had given up the chase, she found herself in a huddle of low cow-backed hills all of which looked alike. If she had been a tenderfoot she would have been lost, but with the sun for a guide she knew that if she swung to the left she must strike again the barrier ridge.

Her heart was beating fast from excitement. A man had shot at her. In the race to escape she had not had time to be afraid. Now that the immediate danger was past she noticed that her knees felt weak. Fear of this big shapeless brute flooded her. John Ranger was right. She ought not to become involved in a business of this kind. Not far away, in some fold of the hills, the ruffian was probably still looking for her. They might any minute come face to face.

She had no assurance as to what direction she had better choose. He was between her and the Circle J R. There was no longer in her an urgent desire to see Mary Uhlmann at once. The thought of her own safety was uppermost. If she could reach the ridge and cut down into the valley she might hit the road that led home. This would take her through the X Bar ranch, but she was pretty sure its owner would not be there. He was a stubborn man and would likely be lying in wait for her return.

Her judgment told her to keep traveling for another mile before cutting back to the ridge and to slip down into the valley at the lower end of the ranch.

This she did and came to the ridge by a ravine that cut through the barrier wall to the floor below. Though she kept a constant alert, she saw nothing of Uhlmann. Through a poor man's gate, three strands of wire fastened to poles by staples, she passed into the pasture back of the house.

She had given up her intention of seeing Mary Uhlmann, but now she changed her mind. Her alarm was subsiding. Uhlmann could not have reached the ranchhouse yet, and there was no sign of him anywhere along the ridge. He had been riding away from the place when she met him, and she could think of no reason why meeting her might bring him back.

She skirted the yard in approaching. A saddled horse was tied to the corral fence, but it was not the one Uhlmann had been riding. As she drew nearer the house, she heard voices. By a slip-knot she tied her bridle to a rickety hitching post. Before knocking she swept the ridge again with her eyes to check on the man she was avoiding. Not a trace of life showed on its barren slope.

At her knock the voices stopped. A woman came to the door. She was tall, angular, lean as a rail. Astonishment leaped to the jet-black eyes as they took in the girl's young vital beauty.

"Who are you?" she demanded sharply.

"I'm Sandra Ranger. I want to talk with you if I may."

"You'd better get away from here." There was whipped fear on the face that turned to search the terrain. "He might come home and find you."

"I don't think he'll be here just yet. It won't take a minute for you to tell me what I want to know."

"No. Get on your horse and leave."

"Wait a minute," a drawling voice interrupted. "That's no way to treat a visitor, Mary." The owner of the voice sauntered to the door. He was a light-stepping dark man, with a face both wary and reckless. Across the left cheek, from ear to chin, a livid scar stretched. Perhaps this was what gave him the sinister and dangerous look, Sandra thought. "If Miss Ranger wants to have a little talk—why, this is a free country."

"She had better go—now. I have nothing to tell her. If she stays to talk it will only make trouble."

"Let's hear what she has to say," the man demurred. "Rhino ain't the great mogul. You shouldn't let him get you whipped, Mary."

Sandra guessed that this man was one of the lawless night riders who lived around Charleston or up in the San Simon, but she was of the opinion that there was more chance of Mary Uhlmann talking with him present than if he were away.

"It's about Bob Webb," she said. "He didn't kill that man Lemmon. You were there when he was shot. You know he didn't."

"I wasn't there," the woman cried. "I didn't see a thing."

"You were in the next room and heard everything. Hans Uhlmann shot Lemmon, by accident, while he was shooting at Bob."

"No," the woman denied violently. "You can't get me to say so. Send this girl away, Scarface."

"Don't push on the reins, Mary. I've heard it said before that this boy was railroaded to the pen. Over at Charleston the other day I met him. And I like the fellow. He got a rotten deal. Why don't you spill what you know? You don't owe Rhino a thing, the way he treats you."

"I don't know anything." The sullen lips closed tightly.

"Seven years of Bob Webb's life are buried in that prison," Sandra said. "They are hunting him to send him back. Doesn't it hurt you to know that you sent him there and that every day you keep silent is another robbed out of a life you have ruined?"

"Go away. Leave me alone. It's easy for you to talk that way, but——"

She broke off the sentence and Scarface finished it for her. "——but you don't live with that devil Rhino Uhlmann." The man put a hand on the woman's bony shoulder. "You don't have to live with him either. He treats you as no decent man would use a dog. Light out of here, Mary. You can hide where he won't find you. Long as you stay on this ranch you'll be his slave."

"I've made my bed," she answered bitterly.

"You don't have to stay in it," Sandra told her eagerly. "As long as we live we can start again. You are young and can go away and make a new life for yourself."

"I'm not young," the woman differed hopelessly. "I feel a hundred years old. I've been wrung dry, all the life squeezed out of me. It doesn't matter what becomes of me now."

"It does. It matters a lot. To feel as you do is all wrong. You can make new friends and be happy."

Mary Uhlmann's thin smile was cynical. "Happy! You don't know what you are talking about. Because you are a young girl and have not made any mistakes you think all anyone has to do to make the future rosy is to just will it so. But life isn't like that. If you take the wrong turning you can't go back."

"Oh, but I'm sure you're mistaken," Sandra cried. "Come and stay with us. Forget all this. You'd be surprised."

The girl's enthusiasm beat in vain against the woman's despair. It was too late now to turn back from this marriage she had chosen.

"Why did you marry him?" the outlaw asked.

"Because I was a fool. No use arguing. I'm here. I stay. And I'll do no talking."

"And let an innocent man suffer for what he didn't do." Sandra's voice rang out scornfully. "I don't believe it. No good woman who has to go on living with herself could be so cowardly."

A touch of red burned underneath the thin tanned cheeks of the older woman. The contempt of this spirited young thing stung her. For years she had held hidden in her heart this shameful secret, and now it had been dragged out into the open.

Round the corner of the house a man came, leading a horse. Across his cheek there was a purple weal where the lash of a quirt had fallen. He glared at Sandra, openly and evilly triumphant.

"So you lied to me," Uhlmann snarled. "You came to see her, not me. I figured it might be that way, and I slipped down by the arroyo. You don't get away from me this time, you meddler."

Sandra was afraid, but she stood stiff and straight, her gaze steadily on his fat vicious face. "Maybe if you shoot at me again you might hit me this time," she said.

"Did you shoot at Miss Ranger?" Scarface asked softly.

Uhlmann glared at him. He did not want to stop for explanations, but Scarface was a tough hardy scamp he could not ignore.

"I shot past her, just to stop the little fool," he admitted grudgingly.

120

The outlaw did not raise his voice. "My friend," he replied, almost in a drawl, "that don't go in this country."

The big man started to answer, but the rustler beat down his words, a sudden sharp challenge in his tone. "I always knew you were a wolf, Rhino, but I didn't know there was a broad yellow streak of coyote in you too. We don't fight women here, and we don't let low-down coyotes do it either."

Scarface waited, still leaning against the door jamb at apparent ease. His indolence was deceptive. Every muscle was set for instant action if the call came. Uhlmann's face grew purple with ugly anger. His impulse was to draw and kill, even though he too would likely be shot down. But he dared not take the risk. For if he destroyed Scarface and lived himself the girl would be a witness against him, unless he rubbed her out too. To do that would condemn him beyond a hope of escape. All this part of Arizona would turn on him and hunt him down.

"Tell you I didn't shoot at her!" he cried.

"His bullet did not miss me six inches," Sandra said. "It cut a leaf from a shrub beside the horse."

"You was too scared to tell what it hit," the ranchman charged.

"If you were just shooting into the air why was she so scared?" demanded the other man.

"You know I wouldn't shoot at a girl, Scarface." There were tiny beads of sweat on Uhlmann's forehead. If it should be believed he had even shot at this girl his life would not be safe, regardless of the intent to hit or miss. "I was just funnin'. You know me." He ground his teeth, giving his own words the lie. "And the little devil had lashed my face with her quirt."

Scarface did not lift his steely eyes from the big leathery face. "Yes, I know you. When you come busting in here calling Miss Ranger a liar and telling her she wouldn't get away from you this time, it sounded like you were funnin'. We 'most split our sides laughing. And of course you weren't annoying her when she quirted yore ugly phiz."

"You ain't so damn lily-white yoreself, Scarface," flung out Uhlmann, searching for a defense. "Don't forget the law wants you for killing Spillman on that raid two-three weeks ago."

"All right, I'm a bad man too, even though I didn't kill Spillman. But, by God, I'm not yore kind of bad man. I don't shoot at women, and I don't rub out men for pay when they haven't a chance for their white alleys. If I was you I'd light out tonight and keep traveling till I was way deep in old Mex."

"Are you deaf, Scarface? Haven't I told you over and over you got me wrong? I'd cut my hand off before I'd do this

121

young lady a mite of harm. All I did was give Miss Ranger a little scare. Why, Goddlemighty, man, she's my neighbor. I've watched her grow up since she was knee-high to a duck."

Scarface laughed, not pleasantly. "If you can talk yoreself outa this you'll be good, Rhino. My guess is different. I'd say if you are here when the boys come you'll be kicking yore heels in the air under one of those cottonwoods." To Sandra he said, without lifting his eyes from the other man, "Get on yore horse, Miss, and I'll see you home safe."

He waited till she had mounted, then turned to the sullen worried ranchman. "I don't reckon you are crazy enough to pull any more gunplays. If you've got any such notion, discard it. You would only be driving more nails in yore coffin. And anyhow, I'll be on the alert long as you're in sight."

"What's the sense in talking thataway?" Uhlmann protested. "I don't aim to hurt you any." He pushed the rifle into the hands of his wife. "Here, take this gun since he's so scared."

The rustler turned to the wife of the harried man. "This fellow's ball of yarn is wound up, Mary," he said. "Rhino has reached the end of his trail here. Better fork his horse and ride with us."

"You can't talk that way to my wife," Uhlmann cried. "I won't stand for it."

"I *am* talking that way," Scarface retorted quietly. "That's the way it is. You light out, or——" He let a shrug of the shoulders finish the sentence.

The ranchman's bravado broke down. He was not afraid of this or any other man. What daunted him was the thought of the determined anger of the community moving solidly against him. He had committed the unpardonable offense of attacking a good and popular girl.

"I don't get it why you've turned against me, Scarface," he pleaded. "We been pals all these years. When you were in a tight spot I helped you out. You wouldn't throw down on me now, would you?"

"You threw down on yoreself," the outlaw told him coldly. He turned to the wife. "Are you riding with us, Mary?"

The eyes of the woman were bleak and wretched. After a moment she said in a low voice, "No, I'll stay."

Scarface walked beside Sandra's horse to the corral and swung to the saddle of his own mount. He started her down the road. Not until she was fifty yards on her way did he make a move to follow, and when he did it was with his body slewed round in the saddle to keep an eye on the killer.

The look on Uhlmann's face as he watched them go was one of baffled hatred. The venom of fury and hate had poisoned the man for years. But a new element had been added to these, the fear of a dreadful day of judgment riding hard on his heels.

He turned with a violent malediction on his wife. "You were ready to sell me out," he cried, moving toward her.

She fell back slowly, her eyes reading hot murder in his. "No," she answered. "I didn't tell her anything. But you've hated me a long time. Maybe you had better kill me before you are hanged."

He gave a wild beast snarl, flung her furiously against the wall, and shuffled into the house. Scarface was right. He had to get away from this part of the country. What a fool he had been to let his temper trap him into this. Two hours ago he had been sitting pretty. All he had to do then was to shoot down an enemy from ambush when he found him and from that killing get safety and a big reward. Now he had brought down on him the vengeance of the whole district. But as he flung into a sack food and the few clothes he meant to carry, one resolve hardened in his tortured mind—he would get Bob Webb before he lit out for Mexico.

29   Mary Uhlmann Breaks
a Long Silence

Bob cut the wires of the X Bar boundary fence and rode into the ranch of his enemy. Because he was worried about Sandra he had no time to steal up to the house Indian fashion. But he did take advantage of the contour of the land to follow the dips that would conceal them as much as possible. A draw about two hundred yards from the house offered the last chance of cover.

"Here we come, Rhino," grumbled Fraser. "A couple of easy marks. Pick us off real carefully. Take yore time."

He thought that Uhlmann probably had not got home yet, but some not too serious complaint was in order. During the past few days he had become very much attached to his companion and watched over him like a father. When let alone Bob was inclined to take too many chances. So the old-timer grumbled and followed him.

Young Webb emerged from the draw first. As he pulled up for a second to look over the cluster of buildings and the terrain around them his horse staggered and fell. The crack of a rifle had sounded. Bob flung himself out of the saddle and crouched back of the horse. The smoke puff came from the cottonwoods back of the house. A man was standing beside a saddled horse.

"Look out, Stan," Bob shouted. "Uhlmann is taking your advice." He rested his rifle barrel on the saddle and took aim.

"Missed," Fraser said, and dropped behind a clump of yucca. "Lemme have a crack at the wolf."

"Not if he can help it," Bob answered. "He's getting out of there fast."

Uhlmann had swung himself heavily astride of his mount and was riding through the grove. He had no mind to face both of them. Fraser fired twice, but they were random shots. The trees gave Uhlmann protection. He disappeared into an arroyo.

Bob examined the wound in the neck of his horse. The bullet had struck a major artery and the blood was pumping out fast.

"He's done for," Fraser told his friend.

The echo of Bob's revolver died away. He put the weapon back in its holster and looked down with a set face at the dead horse.

"I'll get the saddle later," he said, and started for the house.

Fraser offered no consolation. He knew that Bob felt he had lost a friend and that he would not want to talk about it yet.

A woman came out of the house and stood by the door. As Bob drew closer he saw fresh bruises and abrasions on her thin face. The eyes that looked at him were bitter and hopeless. She was still young in years, but the slavery of an unhappy marriage had robbed her of the joy that was her heritage.

"Is Sandra Ranger here?" Bob asked bluntly.

"No, She's gone."

"Gone where?"

"Home. Scarface Brown took her."

"Scarface—the rustler?" Bob asked.

"Yes. Don't worry. She's as safe with him as with her own pappy."

Fraser nodded. "That's right, Bob. Did yore husband tell you where he was going, ma'am?"

Her dreary laugh held no mirth. "To hell, I hope."

"We know that," Fraser replied. "I meant, where is he going right away?"

"He's on the dodge. Seems he shot at Miss Ranger up on the ridge this morning. Scarface told him he would sick the dogs on him and he lit out."

Bob felt his hackles rise. "Shot at Miss Ranger?" he repeated.

"She slashed his face with a quirt. Too bad I didn't do it long ago."

"He's headed for Mexico probably," Fraser guessed.

"Not yet." The woman's gaze rested on Bob. "Says he has a job to do first. He wants to kill another man. Is your name Webb?"

"Yes."

"I thought so. You're lucky he missed you this time."

"Miss Ranger is all right?" Bob asked. "He didn't hurt her?"

"No." She touched her face. "He took it out on me. It's nice having a wife when you have to beat somebody and nobody else is handy."

"I reckon Hans Uhlmann did you two more dirt than he ever did anybody else in the world," Fraser said. "Unless you think killing a man is worse than ruining his life."

The woman looked at Webb. "I had a share in what he did to you," she told him. "Marrying him was the craziest thing I ever did. He had me then. If I had ever told what I knew he would have killed me."

"What did you know?" Bob asked.

"I was in the outer office when Giles Lemmon was killed. It came so fast I hadn't time to get away before the shots were fired. I heard Hans cry, 'Goddlemighty, I've killed the wrong man,' and Jug Packard answered: 'Quit shooting, Rhino. I'll fix that nice.' Then I ran out of the building. Next day my father sent me to California. I didn't know anything about your trial till two months after you were in the penitentiary, and by that time I was married to Hans."

"If you'll tell that to Governor Andrews it ought to save Bob from going back to Yuma," Fraser said.

"I'll tell him. I would have told him long ago if I hadn't been a coward." She added, as though something inside of her was forcing her to talk at last: "Hans wasn't so—so awful—in those days. He was a big bully, but he didn't look so like a hippopotamus. I was kind of pretty then, and he fooled me into thinking he was so fond of me that I could change him. His story was that you had come in to kill Packard and that when you started shooting he had to draw a gun to save the life of his boss. Afterward I knew that wasn't true, just as I knew I couldn't change him. He was bad—not bad the way Scarface or Cole Hawkins is. They are wild and reckless, and I reckon both of them have killed men in fights, but they are kind-hearted and they are always gentle to me. Hans is evil. There is something about him that makes my flesh creep." Her voice broke. She was thinking, as she had done many times before, that she had been a vile creature to have lived with him so long, knowing what he was.

"You're through with him for good and all," Fraser reminded her cheerfully. "We'll take you where you will be safe—where he can't reach you."

"There's no place I can go," she said. "I don't know anybody now but riff-raff and outlaws."

"My sister would be glad to have you stay with her at Tucson," Bob said. "But if Uhlmann found you she couldn't give protection from him."

"Miss Ranger asked me to come to their place, but I expect her father would feel differently about it," the woman said. "Anyhow, I wouldn't ask him."

"The very place for you," Fraser cried. "John Ranger is a man among a thousand. Of course he'll want you there, just as Miss Sandra does. I happen to know they were trying to get a housekeeper a week or two ago when they were in Tucson. You'd be fine for the job."

"I think I could look after a house," Mary admitted doubtfully.

"Of course you can." Fraser assumed this settled. "Rhino shot Bob's horse. We'll have to run up a couple, one for you and one for him."

"I didn't say I'd go," the woman protested.

"We'll kidnap you," Fraser laughed. "Bob and I are old hands at it. We've just turned loose a sheriff we kidnapped."

Bob brought his saddle in from the knoll where his dead horse lay. Fraser roped two other mounts in the pasture and led them to the stable. Shortly the two men and Mary Uhlmann were on their way down the valley.

Mary's life had filled her with a sense of unworthiness. The man she had married had not only abused her physically but had trampled down her spirit by his jeers and the humiliations to which he subjected her. Now she was full of fears about the reception she would meet at the Circle J R. She was the wife of a man good people despised. Her clothes were old and patched. Long ago she had lost the knack of meeting new acquaintances pleasantly, largely because of the defensive barricade she flung up, a manner dry and short even to rudeness. What would the Rangers think of her?

30 *Uhlmann Borrows from a Friend*

In the darkness Uhlmann's horse picked its way through the brush up Double Fork. Until nightfall he had lain hidden in a hill pocket. He did not know whether any posse of cattlemen was out after him, but he had to keep from being seen for fear his presence in that locality would be reported. There was an open season on him now. His overbearing ways had made plenty of enemies, and any one of them could shoot him down with no risk of a penalty.

The narrow valley of the Double Fork widened into a small park. At the foot of a rocky bluff, sheltered by a few scrubby live oaks, were a corral, a stable, and a small cabin. There was a light in the house, and as Uhlmann rode forward a dog began to bark. At once the light winked out.

"You alone, Pete?" the fugitive called warily.

There was a long silence before an answer came. "I can't do a thing for you, Rhino. The boys are aimin' to tack yore hide on a fence. You better light out for the border damn fast now."

"Open that door," Uhlmann ordered.

"You hadn't ought to of come here," the man in the cabin reproached. "This is the first place they'll look for you. If you had any sense you would know that. Like as not somebody is lying back there in the brush with a rifle trained on you this very minute. When I light the lamp he would get you as you come in. Smart thing for you to do is to slip back into the live oaks and beat it hell-for-leather in the darkness."

"Yeah, you're mighty anxious for me not to get hurt," sneered Uhlmann. "If I was shot you wouldn't go down to the store and tell everybody how fine it was I had got my come-uppance at last, seeing I always had been a killer and a bad man. Not you, Pete." The voice grew suddenly harsh and imperative. "Fling open that door, damn you. And don't light the lamp. We won't need it."

McNulty's wheedling voice protested. "Now looky here, Rhino. Down at the store a couple hours ago I was warned to keep outa this if I knew what was good for me. I don't mean to let myself get drug in. Course you got my best wishes. My advice is——"

"I'll blast my way in and come a-smokin' if you don't open," the hunted man threatened savagely.

"That's no way to talk to a friend," Pete grumbled. "I'll let you in, but there's nothing I can do to help you. It's not my fault you got yore tail in a crack. You'll have to ramrod yore own way out." He drew back the bolt and opened the door.

"Have they started a posse out after me?" Uhlmann asked.

"I dunno. They were still talking when I left. But the boys are crazy mad. They'll get you sure, if you don't pull yore freight. What in tarnation made you shoot at the girl?"

Uhlmann had not come to make explanations or to defend his case. "I'm caught short," he said bluntly. "I want money."

"I was down to the store buying supplies," McNulty answered quickly. "I ain't got but three dollars left. I'll divvy with you fifty-fifty."

"I'll take three hundred dollars. Get it outa the hiding place where you keep yore dough." In the big man's harsh voice there was an ultimatum.

"Three hundred dollars," wailed McNulty. "Why, I haven't got that much in the world. You're crazy with the heat, Rhino."

"Dig it up. I'll give you a bill of sale for enough of my stock to cover it."

"How could I use that bill of sale? The boys would know

I had contacted you and they would string me up for helping you to make a getaway. They would claim I always had been in cahoots with you."

"I don't care whether you use it or not," Uhlmann growled. "It's the money I want."

"But I tell you I haven't got it." Pete pulled from his pocket a small handful of silver. "You can have all I got. Here it is."

Uhlmann's small eyes glittered like those of a cat in the darkness. "The boys are gonna hang me, you claim. Or maybe shoot me as they would a wolf. They can't do any more to me for rubbing you out too. *I want that money.*"

"If I had it, Rhino——"

"Don't talk," interrupted Uhlmann. "Get busy, or I'll let you have it in the belly and do the hunting myself."

In the pit of McNulty's stomach there was a dreadful sinking sensation. He loved the ill-gotten treasure he had piled up a little at a time. By nature he was a miser, and when he was alone he often got it out and fingered the gold pieces fondly. To give them up was far worse than letting somebody pull out his teeth. The loss of three hundred dollars would be bad enough, but he knew this ruffian well enough to be sure that he would take the whole hoard. Pete felt despairingly that he could not give up his savings, not at least without trying to talk Uhlmann out of the hold-up.

"I dunno where you got the notion that I've got money hidden away, Rhino. There's nothing to it. I hope a bolt of lightning will strike me dead if I'm lying."

"A bolt of lightning is gonna do that in about five seconds if you don't get busy," jeered Uhlmann, the barrel of his forty-five jammed into the stomach of his host. "I'll count ten. One—two—three——"

"I'll get it—the three hundred," McNulty moaned. "If you'll just step outside a minute while I find it——"

"I'm staying right here. Think I want a slug in my back?"

"Maybe I got a little more than three hundred, Rhino. You'll let me keep the rest, won't you?"

"Sure—sure. I wouldn't rob you, Pete."

McNulty's dragging feet took him to the far corner of the room. He knelt down and lifted from the puncheon floor a length of timber the face of which had been squared by a broad-ax. His fumbling fingers found a tin box and lifted it from the hole beneath. This he carried to the kitchen table. He searched for a key in the hip pocket of his jeans and brought it out reluctantly.

"I'll take that bill of sale, Rhino, though I don't reckon I can ever use it," he said.

On Uhlmann's pachydermous face was a dreadful smile.

"Like you say, maybe you can't ever use it. That's yore lookout. Open the box."

The key in the trembling hand found the hole with difficulty, even after Uhlmann struck a match with his left hand. The revolver was in the right, held against Pete's backbone just below the shoulder-blades. The flame flickered out. A second lighted match showed to the robber's gleaming eyes a pile of gold coins that half filled the box.

"Good old Pete, you've been saving money for me all these years and didn't know it," he said.

McNulty slewed his head around, in time to catch that gloating look before the match went out. "You promised me you'd only take the three hundred, Rhino," he pleaded. "God knows how many years I've scraped and slaved to get this little backlog. You wouldn't take it all from me, after we've been friends so long."

With cruel pleasure Uhlmann tasted this minute of victory after so many hours of bitter impotent anger. There was no feeling of mercy in him toward his helpless victim.

"Money is no good to you, Pete," he answered, derisive triumph in his heavy voice. "You only put it in a hole. Thinking of what a good time it is giving me will give you a kick."

McNulty made a fatal mistake. He tried to bargain. "It wouldn't be so good for you if I was to tell the boys you are holed up in this neck of the woods."

"Not so good," the hulking villain agreed.

Pete realized at once his error. He wished to heaven he had left the lamp alight. In the darkness this big devil was appalling. The only detail of the big leathery face that stood out was the dreadful shining eyes. The threat in them filled Pete with terror. A sickness ran through him. Weakness plucked all the manhood out of him.

"I wouldn't do that, Rhino—not to you," he murmured, his teeth chattering. "And us such good friends."

"Sure you wouldn't," the gunman taunted. "You'd stay right here and not make a move—till I was out of sight."

The roar of the forty-five filled the room. Into the prone body the killer flung bullet after bullet. He snatched up the money box and ran out of the cabin. Dragging himself to the saddle, he galloped wildly into the night. He had not meant to kill Pete when he rode up Double Fork. It had been the farthest thing from his thoughts. But he saw now that it was the only way out for him. McNulty would have set the hunters on his track and they would have run him to earth. With every added mile between him and that dark cabin of death he felt easier in mind.

31   Sandra Talks with a Bad Man
and Likes Him

As Sandra rode down the valley with Scarface Brown she felt
an odd jubilance of spirit. The sense of danger that had been
heavy on her was gone. She was safe, riding in the warm
sunshine beside a man who would fight to protect her as
quickly as Bob Webb had done against the raiders of Pablo
Lopez. Her companion was the most notorious rustler in
Arizona. Probably he had killed oftener than Uhlmann. But
she knew she had no need to be afraid of him.

She slanted a smile at the long dark man riding knee to knee
with her. "I've heard of you, Mr. Brown," she said demurely.

Scarface caught her mood instantly and responded to it.
"Nothing but good, I hope," he replied, and flashed his fine
white teeth in a grin that for the moment wiped from the
brown face its sinister wariness.

"I think maybe those who told me were a little prejudiced
against you," she answered.

"Some are," he admitted. "But I dare say they would allow
that I have taking ways."

Sandra laughed. "Yes. They would agree to that. I'm awfully
glad I met you. I don't know any bad man except by sight.
Now I have one all to myself for an hour or more." Her mis-
chievous eyes mocked him. "You *are* a bad man, aren't you?
I thought I heard you tell Hans Uhlmann so."

"I don't teach in a Sunday school."

"But you stood up for me against that ruffian and made him
let me go."

"That was a pleasure," he explained. "I never did like the
big bully, and it seemed like a good time for a showdown."

"I was dreadfully afraid of him, but not after you spoke
up." She guided her horse around a chuck hole in the road. "If
you are a bad man, there must be something wrong with me.
I like you."

Though he laughed, he was much pleased. His way of life
did not bring him into contact with girls like this one, but
he understood exactly the quality of her liking and did not
intend to presume upon it. It was probable that he would
never again be alone with her, since he moved outside the
laws that sheltered her. Yet the memory of this meeting would
always be one to remember.

"It's right funny how words are thrown at you and they stick," the scamp philosophized. "They call me a bad man, and I can't kick. I'm a pretty rough hombre, and I've ridden a lot of wild trails. Uhlmann is a bad man from where they laid the chunk. Not excusing myself or anything, he's bad in a different way from me."

"You don't need to prove that to me," Sandra agreed.

"All right. I won't start whitewashing myself. We'll take another case, this Bob Webb. He gets hot under the collar account of what Rhino and Jug Packard did to his parents, and it lands him in the pen. He breaks loose, and right away he is a bad man, a rustler, killer, stage robber, and general trouble-maker. A good citizen is beaten up by him, and a sheriff who starts to arrest him is kidnapped. I happen to know half of those things are not true, and the other half can be explained. But there he is, the dog with a bad name."

"It's very unfair," the girl protested. "People are so stupid. He isn't a bad man at all, if they would only let him alone."

"In one way he is," the rustler differed. "Sometimes when you speak of a bad man you mean one who is dangerous, a fellow not to monkey with but to ride around real careful if you want to stay healthy. Now there was old John Slaughter.* He was little, but 'Gentlemen, hush!' When those cold eyes of his blazed at you there was a funny feeling in the pit of yore stomach. He chased me all over the White Mountains once. That was what he was paid for, and I hadn't any complaints. But to my thinking he was a bad man—dangerous back of a gun when he was after you. Don't get me wrong, Miss Ranger. He was a first-class citizen, and one of these days Arizona will likely put up a statue to him. This young fellow Webb is bad the same way. If he was an enemy of mine I'd hate to crowd him."

"He won't be your enemy," Sandra said.

"Not if I can help it," the outlaw answered dryly.

"What do you mean when you say that half of these things Bob Webb is accused of he didn't do? How do you know that? What half is false?"

Scarface took his time to reply. It was in his mind to tell her certain facts, but he did not intend to say too much. A man on the dodge as he was, a leader of the riff-raff who preyed on the property of other men, learned by the underground route the true story back of all the lawless deeds committed in his district. The obligation was on him not to divulge any of these to anybody who might carry information to the

---

*Sheriff of Cochise County, Arizona, in its wild days. While he was cleaning up his territory he served notice to the rustlers, "Get out or get killed." During his term of office there was a considerable migration of night-riding gentry.

authorities. But he had his own code of right and wrong. It did not include the protection of a smug two-facer like Jug Packard or a hired assassin such as Uhlmann, who were trying to shift their crimes to the shoulders of another man.

"First off, Webb did not kill Giles Lemmon. Uhlmann did it, while he was shooting at the boy. Packard fixed it up to frame the kid. Uhlmann brags too much when he is drunk. I could tell you too who shot Chuck Holloway, but I am not going to do it. I will say it was neither Fraser nor Webb."

"Father and I can testify to that. We were looking through the window watching them as they ran for their horses. Neither of them fired a shot."

"Some of the gang with Uhlmann that night give yore father credit for the shot."

"It's not true," Sandra denied indignantly.

"I know," Scarface nodded. "Holloway was a very bad character. He had been fixing to ruin the fifteen-year-old daughter of a man who was present that night. This father would not have shot him down without giving warning. I'm sure of that. Not if an emergency hadn't jumped up and kinda forced his hand. He liked Webb, and he was against this ganging-up to kill him. The man followed Uhlmann's pack of wolves out the back door of the Legal Tender. About the first thing he saw was Chuck Holloway standing not a dozen yards from Webb raising his rifle to fire at him. He couldn't miss. This man I am telling you about is a crack shot with a forty-five, one of the best I ever saw. He fired once. That was enough. Later he told me about it. Now I'm telling you. His life may be in yore hands, Miss Ranger. Some of these birds might ambush him if they knew."

"I'll be very careful," the girl promised. "The testimony of Father and me will clear Bob. We don't need to know this man's name."

"I hope you're close-mouthed. If you are not, just remember before you talk that my friend's life may hang on it." Scarface passed to another charge against Webb. "Also by the under-ground whisper I know that Webb and Fraser did not hold up the Oracle stage. Uhlmann and another man did it. I won't say any more about that."

When they rode into the yard of the Circle J R, Sandra was surprised to see her father dismounting from a horse.

"I thought you intended to be away two days," she said.

Ranger's eyes could not conceal their astonishment at the companion she had brought with her to the ranch. He said, "There was a letter in the mail-box that made it unnecessary for me to go."

"Father, I have done something foolish," his daughter said.

"I'm getting used to that," John Ranger replied coldly, his gaze still on the desperado. "What was it?"

"I found out that Mary Gilcrest is Uhlmann's wife, so I rode to the X Bar ranch to talk with her."

The face of the cattleman flushed angrily. "I didn't think that even you were foolish enough to do that," he told her.

Sandra had made up her mind to tell the whole story and face the consequences. "I went up along the ridge, so as not to be seen. I saw Mr. Fraser there, and after I left him I met Uhlmann." She related what had occurred there.

"He shot at you?" Ranger repeated, his face dark with anger.

"Yes." She went on to tell the rest of the story.

Once Scarface interrupted, embarrassed at the credit she gave him. "Come, Miss Ranger, all I did was to tell Rhino where to head in."

"You stood up to him and told him what he was," she cried. "You made him let me go with you and told him you would set the ranchers of the valley on him to hang him. I thought once he would shoot you."

"I knew he wouldn't," the rustler answered lightly. "I was watching him. Fact is, Mr. Ranger, I only did what any white man would do." On his face was a sarcastic smile. "If you and yore friends ever catch me with the goods there is nothing to prevent you from hanging me to a cottonwood. No obligation on yore part. I been waiting for a chance to step on that bully Uhlmann's corns."

Ranger was embarrassed. It had not been a month since he had almost caught this man driving away his stock, and if he had been captured he would certainly have been hanged on the spot. Now the man had intervened to save his daughter from the results of her folly.

He managed a smile. "Mr. Brown, you have me in a cleft stick. No matter what you say I am under a very great obligation to you. And I don't see how I can repay it. You have chosen a crooked trail to travel, and you know where it is likely to end. Unless you leave it, there is nothing I can do for you."

"Just what I've been telling you." There was a flash of teeth in the brown face as the outlaw smiled hardily. "We understand each other perfectly. I'll be saying *adios*."

"Father!" the girl murmured unhappily. She could not let the man leave on that note.

Scarface came to the rescue. "It's all right, Miss. Nothing else Mr. Ranger can say or do. He's not throwing me down. It has to be this way."

After he had mounted, Sandra impulsively walked up to

him and offered her hand. "I'm not a cattleman," she said. "Whatever you are, I can't help it. I know you stood up to that villain Uhlmann and brought me back home safe. No matter what happens, I won't ever forget it."

He held her small hand in his large brown one for a moment, a smile on his face that relaxed its habitual vigilant wariness.

"That goes double, Miss. I won't forget either."

He turned his horse and rode, a lithe and graceful figure, to whatever fate destiny had in store for him.

Ranger turned to his daughter, a worried frown on his face. "I'm glad you told him that. Though he is a scoundrel and a thief, he is a generous fellow with a clean streak in him. You put me in a nice spot, girl. He goes out of his way to help you when you are in trouble, and all I can say to him is that I hope I won't have to help hang him. Can't you stay at home and behave yourself, Sandra? Do I have to lock you in your room?"

She told him she had learned her lesson and promised to do nothing more without consulting him.

32   *Sandra Forgets Her Bringing Up*

Mary Uhlmann need not have worried about her welcome at the Circle J R ranch. John Ranger lifted her from the saddle and gave her a smiling greeting in Spanish—*"Esta es su casa de usted."* His daughter put strong young arms around the guest's thin shoulders and gave her a quick hug. It touched Mary deeply to be told that this was her home, to feel the warmth of the Rangers' friendliness pouring into her starved heart.

Though she did not know it, her young hostess was more emotionally disturbed than she. Sandra had given Bob Webb a very casual greeting, but her cheeks were flying signals of excitement. The man she loved was back again, unhurt, and the clouds that had hung heavy over him were breaking. She was afraid to look at him, for fear her face would tell too much.

Fraser came forward, spurs jingling. "Didn't I tell you I would be camping on yore doorstep, *compadre*, soon as the heat was off?" he asked, a twinkle in his sun-faded blue eyes.

The girl was grateful for his badinage. She knew he was giving her a chance to ease back to the normal. "Good to know there is one faithful man alive," she laughed.

"I'm him." Stan lowered his voice to a stage whisper and jerked his head toward Bob. "Course he had to drag along. Some folks never know when they are not wanted. We'll fix it to get rid of him."

Ranger was pointing out to Mrs. Uhlmann the pass over

134

which the Apaches had crossed the Huachucas to sweep down on the valley less than twenty years before. Bob was watching Sandra and his friend, a sardonic smile on his strong-boned face.

"We mustn't hurt his feelings by hurrying him off—now he is here," Sandra pointed out.

"Oh, we'll let him stick around a little while—say about sixty years." Fraser slapped his hat against the shiny chaps and gave a small whoop of triumph at his hit.

The girl looked at him reproachfully. "You know so much! Just for that I'm going to leave you." She moved to join her father and their guest. As she passed Bob she murmured, "Want to see you alone before you go."

Webb nodded without speaking. He had something to say to her, and he preferred to say it when nobody else was present.

Sandra showed Mary to the room she was to occupy. It was the sort of bedroom the older woman had dreamed about, bright and cheerful, with chintz window curtains, a big easy-chair and soft bed, a good rag carpet. Shy embarrassment made her almost speechless. As Sandra fussed over little details that made for comfort, Mary had a feeling she ought to fight against the gratitude that was melting the protective ice so long stored in her. She was afraid to let herself be glad, for fear of the pain that would follow when she found her joy illusory.

The girl left her to wash off the dust of travel. She found Bob Webb alone on the porch. Fraser had drawn John Ranger to the barn on pretense of wanting to look at the new Hereford bull the stockman had recently bought.

"Let's go into the orchard," Sandra said. "It will be cool there."

As soon as they were among the peach trees Bob opened his attack. "Don't you know better than to go fooling around with Uhlmann?" he demanded sharply. "I've told you it isn't safe for you to try to find out anything he and Packard want kept secret. If you would only let me manage my own affairs!"

She looked at him in surprise, astonished and hurt at his brusque vehemence. "I thought that—"

"Can't you get it through yore noodle that if you learn too much about these blackhearted villains they will rub you out?" he interrupted. "They won't stop because you are a woman. That devil might have killed you today. This isn't a game they are playing with me. They mean to destroy me, just as I mean to destroy them."

Sandra knew his irritation had its genesis in his anxiety for her safety, but her anger rose at his dictatorial manner. He might make some allowance for the urge that had driven her and for the fact that her interest had uncovered the evidence that might save him.

"That's my lookout," she snapped, hot temper in her eyes. "I don't have to ask you what I can or can't do. I'll go on doing as I please."

He took her by the shoulders and shook her till her teeth chattered. When he freed her she stood staring at him in astonishment, too breathless to talk. Sandra was no more amazed than he. Until the moment that his hands were on her he had not had the remotest idea of what he was going to do. How could he explain to her that it was his dark fear for her that had boiled up in heady anger?

"Just another Uhlmann," she said. "But you haven't blacked either of my eyes yet."

He might have retorted that she had not lashed him with a quirt, but he had no spirit for contention. He had burnt out his exasperation in action. All she had done for him flooded up in his mind, not only her brave fight to save him from approaching catastrophe but of even more importance the rebirth of hope and faith in him her trust had inspired. With a little gesture of defeat he turned to go.

"Wait a minute," she ordered.

They looked steadily into each other's eyes. Mirth began to bubble in hers. "It's not fatal to shake up a girl—when she needs it," Sandra mentioned. "Maybe it will improve her, as it does medicine in a bottle."

He was still shocked at what he had done. "I don't know how I came to lay hands on you. I must have gone crazy."

Her face had crinkled to laughter. "You're very vigorous in your punishments, sir," she said, with mock demureness, and she lifted some stray golden locks to prove it. "My hair has tumbled every which way."

All he could say was, "I don't want these villains to hurt you."

"If it has to be done, you'll do it yourself," she added with neat friendly malice.

"You wouldn't listen to me, and I thought it might make the difference between life and death for you."

"I'll listen now." A queer song of joy was singing in her breast. He would not have been so violent if it had not been for his interest in her. "And I'll promise from now on to stay at home and not lift a finger. Does that suit you?"

"It suits me fine. I'll shake hands on it."

Their hands met and clung fast. Out of that contact some magnetic force flowed that drew one irresistibly to the other. His arms went round her and their lips met in a long kiss that set the blood pounding.

He pushed her from him. "What am I doing?" he asked in a low rough voice. "There can't ever be anything between you and me. We both know that."

136

"But there is," she denied exultantly. "There always has been since the first moment we met."

A savage joy beat up in him, but he set himself grimly to fight it down. "No," he answered harshly. "There is the curse of the prison on me. All through your life it would rise up to destroy your happiness."

"If it is proved you are not guilty?"

"People would forget that. They would remember that I spent years in a penitentiary."

"But you are wrong," she cried. "And it wouldn't matter what they thought so long as we knew the truth."

"Not today or tomorrow maybe, but in the years to come. It would be a blot on our children's future. I've been having an impossible dream, but I've got to face facts now."

"We'll wait until you're cleared and talk of this again," she said.

"No," he flung back unhappily. "Never again. There's a wall between us we can't break down."

The girl looked at him with high spirit, her lovely young head held high. "You are wrong, Bob Webb. There's no wall except one your silly pride has built up. You can't kiss me like that and throw me over. I won't have it, for I know you love me. My future has its rights as much as yours. You can't decide this alone without consulting me."

"It's you I'm thinking of, a lovely young girl, sheltered and—"

"Fiddlesticks!" she interrupted. "I thought you had more sense. A woman doesn't sit on a pedestal, making sure her hands are lily-white and that there is no common dust on her skirts. Unless she is a fool she goes out and—and meets life. She loves and marries and has children, if she is lucky. Her hands roughen and her face wrinkles. Griefs and trouble wear her away, as they do a man. And in spite of that she is happy, given the right mate by her side."

Slender and erect, she faced him. A warm glow beat through the clear skin. Her starry eyes challenged him. She was as spirited, he thought, as a young Joan of Arc. The gospel she flung out so hotly was heresy against the traditions in which she had been brought up, that a good girl must wait demurely, eyes downcast and innocent, until the man came to seek her. She would have none of that mincing philosophy. If her happiness was at stake, she meant to fight for it.

"When I am wearing my striped uniform I am Number 4582," he reminded her gently.

"The only thing that matters about a man is what he is, not what people say about him," she retorted.

He was puzzled at her sureness. She was so young, and had

137

gone such a little way in life, yet somehow had cut through conventions to essential truth.

"Where did you learn so much?" he asked her, a smile in his eyes.

She knew she had won. "I thought it out nights in bed when I couldn't sleep for worrying about you. I found out what was important and what wasn't." An impudent little smile wrinkled her face. "If I'm a forward hussy, I don't care."

He took her in his arms again. "I've just found out how much I like forward hussies," he told her.

33 *Uhlmann Makes a Refund*

Jug Packard sat behind an old scarred desk figuring a payroll. He was seated in a cheap kitchen chair. In one corner of the office were piles of old accounts tied together with strings. Dirt and disorder were everywhere.

An observer who knew Jug well would have noticed that he was expecting a visitor and had made preparations not to be surprised by him. The soiled curtains of the windows were drawn closely to prevent anybody outside from seeing into the room. A box half filled with papers had been set against the closed door so that it could not be opened without warning. The drawer of the desk was out about six inches, and in it lay a forty-five, the butt of it within six inches of Jug's fingers.

The expected caller had given Packard no advance notice of a visit. His expectation of one was due to his knowledge of a certain man's psychology. Probably the fellow had not sent word to Pete McNulty that he was coming, but Pete ought to have been ready anyhow. Jug did not intend to be taken unaware.

He had not made up his mind yet whether to kill his uninvited guest or not. It would be a popular thing to do, and just now with the cards running against him he could use some public good will. It might be the safest course, since dead men tell no tales. On the other hand it might be that he could still use Uhlmann to get rid of Webb.

The door handle turned slowly. Packard's right hand dropped into the desk. He watched the box being pushed farther into the room. His fingers came out of the drawer and rested on the desk. They were holding the revolver.

"Come in, Rhino," he invited, his voice suave and mocking. "I've been looking for you."

The box slid across the floor as the door whipped open.

Uhlmann stood on the threshold. The two men stared at

each other. Packard was smiling, derisive mockery on his hatchet face.

"Nice of you to drop in on me," he jeered. "You visiting all yore old friends before you leave the country?"

"Put that gun down, Jug," growled Uhlmann. "You don't need it."

"Any more than Pete McNulty needed one," Packard reminded the other. His thin lips tightened. The foxy slyness in his face was gone, in its place a cruel implacable wariness. "Sit down in that chair, and put yore hands on its arms. Move slow. Don't forget that I can fling three-four slugs into yore belly before you drag out that gun you're thinking about."

Uhlmann glowered at him sullenly. "You gone crazy with the heat, Jug? We've always been side-kicks, you and me."

"Like you and Pete were," the man behind the forty-five said, his voice low and ice-cold.

"Any man who says I killed Pete is a liar," the big man blurted out. "I ain't seen him for a week."

"I say you killed him. This whole country says it. You were seen headed up Double Fork."

"I went to get some money he owed me, but he wasn't to home."

"If he hadn't been he would have been alive today." Packard did not let his voice lift out of its low even register, but his words dripped with an imperative menace. *"Get into that chair now, or go out in smoke."*

The leaden feet of the huge killer dragged forward. He slumped down into the chair, more like a rhinoceros than ever. The small sullen eyes, the wrinkled skin of the face hanging in heavy folds, the gross body huddled into a shapeless mass, all suggested that brutal and insensitive pachyderm.

Scarcely six inches from Uhlmann's hairy hand the butt of a revolver pushed out from its holster. He knew that Packard had not forgotten this. The man was taunting him, gloating over his helplessness. There was mockery in the cruel eyes. They invited him to take a chance, to reach for his weapon and make a fighting finish. But the catch was that there was no chance. Jug was lightning-fast, and at that distance he could not miss. Before the big killer could fire a shot his great body would be crashing to the floor.

"Don't be that way, Jug," Uhlmann growled. "I came up here to figure out how I was going to get Webb. Fellow told me he and Fraser were roosting in the hills back of the Circle J R. My idea was to do the job tonight."

"Yore idea was to slip in on me and play the same trick you did on Pete," corrected Packard. "First rob me, then shoot me into a rag doll. You knew I was always here alone at night, so you figured it would be easy. That's the kind of a lunkhead you

139

are. From the moment I heard that you were on the dodge there hasn't been a second when you could have pulled yore heavyfooted trickery on me."

"You got me wrong, Jug." Uhlmann brushed his coat sleeve across a perspiring forehead. "I wouldn't do you thataway. We've been pals a long time, you 'n' me. When you've needed help you've come to me, and I've been with you every time. Ain't that so?"

"Water over the dam. Anything you ever did for me I paid you for. And while we're talking about that, shell out the five hundred I gave you as advance on a job you didn't do."

"I aim to do it tonight, like I told you."

"Fine," answered Packard, with a titter. "I'll pay you when you've done it. Until then I'll keep the five hundred for you. Dig it up."

Uhlmann made no motion to get the money. "You can't do that to me. I'm going through with this. I don't aim to leave until I've settled Webb's hash."

"When you do, you'll have fifteen hundred coming to you. But I reckon I'll make sure, Rhino." The man's mouth tightened. He leaned across the desk and let the end of the barrel tap gently on the wood by way of reminder. "Shell out my money, fellow."

"If I have to light out I've gotta have dough," Uhlmann pleaded. "Don't be a hog, Jug. Five hundred is nothing to you, and I aim to earn it inside of two hours."

The eyes of the mining man glittered. "When I pull this trigger there won't be any questions asked by anybody. Everybody will give me the glad hand for rubbing out a mad wolf. Don't make a mistake about this. It's the last call."

From a dry throat Uhlmann grunted surrender. It was in his mind that when he reached to open the money belt his fingers would tilt up the revolver and fling a bullet through the holster.

"Just stay where you're at," Packard ordered brusquely. "Leave yore hands on the chair arms." He rose, walked around the desk, passed back of his prisoner's chair, and drew the revolver from its case. "I wouldn't want an old pal like you to commit suicide."

The short blunt fingers of Uhlmann counted out five hundred dollars in bills and left them on the desk in front of the other man.

Packard slid the money into the open drawer and closed it. "If you really must go I won't keep you any longer," he said.

"Do I get my gun back? To fix Webb."

"You have yore rifle beside the saddle."

"I want my six-gun too," Uhlmann insisted doggedly.

The miner gave this consideration. "All right. You get it— after you are in the saddle. Let's go."

Uhlmann lumbered out of the room first, in obedience to a wave of his captor's hand. He did not feel comfortable, for he knew that though sly and cautious Jug was a man who had no regard for human life. His intention might be to destroy the trapped man before he had taken a dozen steps. The big ruffian talked, his voice not under very good control. He had to fix it in Jug's mind that he was setting out to find and kill Bob Webb.

"They're in that old Baxter cabin—the one in the foothills back of the Circle J R. I can sneak up and get Webb sure as you're a foot high, Jug. That will be fine for both of us."

"If you do, I'll send you the money, Rhino. That's a promise."

Hans Uhlmann did not believe he would keep it. Just now he was not interested in whether he would or not. The killer knew he had been a fool to come here. If he got away with his life he would be doing all right. As he flatfooted forward he half expected a bullet tearing through the muscles of his back.

"Climb up," Packard ordered, after they had reached the post to which the horse was hitched.

Uhlmann pulled himself heavily to the saddle. He still was not sure whether Jug was going to kill him. "Everything will be all right," he said hoarsely. "I'll get that fellow Webb sure."

"I'll believe it when I see him dead."

Packard broke the gun and emptied the shells into his hand. He tossed them on the ground and flung the empty revolver away.

"You can pick them up after I have gone," he said, and ran swiftly back to the office.

From a window he watched Uhlmann dismount and search the ground for the shells and the weapon. After he had apparently found them the big killer pulled himself to the back of the horse again and disappeared down the road.

Hurriedly Packard put the five hundred dollars safely away, blew out the light, and slipped out of the office. A saddled horse was waiting back of the building. A minute later he was following Uhlmann down the steep mountain trail over which ore from the mine was hauled to the plains.

34   "Till A' the Seas Gang Dry, My Dear"

After Sam Washington had washed the Packard supper dishes he carried a pail of refuse to the gulch back of the kitchen and emptied it over the precipice that fell away for a hundred feet to the floor below. It was as he was walking back to his quarters

141

that he caught sight of a shadowy bulk which resolved itself into a man on horseback. The rider dismounted in the darkness and moved forward to the office cautiously.

Sam recognized the lumbering gait. The furtive visitor was Hans Uhlmann, who in the past forty-eight hours had become a fugitive from the vengeance of his neighbors. The cook had a large bump of curiosity tempered by caution. From an old leather trunk in his bedroom next to the kitchen he took a revolver and checked to make sure it was loaded. He did not know what Uhlmann was doing here but he meant to find out if he could. That his employer and this evil man had been accomplices in wickedness at times Sam was pretty sure. Hans might have come to plot with Packard, or he might want to destroy him as he had McNulty.

The door of the office was closed and all the curtains were drawn tight. Sam could neither see into the room nor hear anything that was said. It was impossible for him to tell whether this was a get-together meeting. He found out later, when Uhlmann slouched out of the room with a forty-five pointed at the small of his back.

By that time Sam was crouched in the brush at the edge of the gulch, a few yards from the spot where the horse of the ranchman was hitched. As Uhlmann moved through the darkness he talked, and there was something very like panic in his whinning voice. He was telling Packard that Webb was in the old Baxter cabin and he would sneak up and kill him. The answer of the mine owner made clear his position. He would pay the killer after he had done the job. But it was also plain that he did not trust his hired assassin, for he kept him covered until the man was astride his horse and left him weaponless while he backed away to safety.

Sam waited in the bushes and saw both Uhlmann and Packard ride down the road, though not together. The cook was puzzled at this set-up. It was plain that Jug meant to keep an eye on Rhino. Was it to make sure the gunman would kill Bob Webb? Or was it in his mind to rub out the villain who was doing his work?

The cook scratched his woolly thatch and talked aloud to himself. "Now looky here, Sam Washington, this plumb ain't any of yore business. Go to monkeyin' around with these two wolves and you'll ce'tainly buy yoreself a mess of trouble. What you wants to do is to include yoreself out."

He continued to grumble to himself as he saddled his old white mule and took the trail after the other two. But though he chided himself, he could not keep out of the business. He had to let Miss Sandra know about the plot to murder her friend. Very likely he would be too late. If Webb was at the Baxter cabin, and if Uhlmann rode straight there, it would take only a few seconds to call the convict to the door on some excuse and riddle him with bullets.

The road went along the rim of the cañon to the foothills. No short cut could be taken by Sam. Nor was there any chance of slipping past the men in front of him, since the trace ran along a ledge wide enough only for a wagon to pass. More than once he stopped to make sure he was not getting too close to Packard. But no sound of hoofs in front came back to him in warning.

He came out of the cañon into the roll of low hills that stretched like waves to the valley. A path that was little more than a cow trail deflected from the main road and ran toward the ridge back of the Circle J R. Sam guessed that both of the riders had taken this cut-off, but he by-passed it and headed straight for the ranchhouse.

He tied his mule to the corral fence and crossed the yard to the kitchen. Jim Budd was grinding coffee for breakfast. He slewed his head around and grinned at sight of his friend.

"What you doing here this time of night, fellow?"

"I gotta see Miss Sandra."

"Wha' for?"

Sam did not intend to let anyone else steal the credit of his news, not after having ridden twelve miles to tell his story.

"Nem' mind about that. This is impo'tant. Where is she at?"

"She's entertaining comp'ny. You cain't go bustin' in on her. You tell me what you want and I'll see—"

The mine cook turned his head to listen. From the parlor came to him the voice of a girl. She was singing, "O my luve's like a red, red rose."

"You go tell Miss Sandra quick—or her pappy, one, I don' care which—that I'm here to tell some info'mation—and there ain't no time to fool around."

"Now, Sam, you an' me is friends," Jim began, with the patient manner of one arguing a case to an unreasonable child.

Sam did not listen to him. Miss Ranger was not fifteen steps from him. Her young voice came to him clear and vibrant:

> "Till a' the seas gang dry, my dear,
> And the rocks melt wi' the sun,
> I will luve thee still, my dear,
> While the sands o' life shall run."

Jim was still talking. Sam ducked past him and through the door. He ran along the passage and into the parlor. A young man was standing at the piano beside the girl, but the colored man paid no heed to him.

"Miss Sandra," he cried, "that Uhlmann is ridin' right now to the old Baxter cabin to shoot Bob Webb."

The man leaning on the piano whirled round. "What's that?" he demanded abruptly.

If his errand had been less urgent Sam might have hesitated to tell it before this unknown visitor, but under the circumstances he blurted out details. "I done heard them talkin', Packard and Uhlmann. Jug is gonna pay him soon as he kills off Webb. I followed them down the cañon to tell you, Miss Sandra."

"Packard is with him?" the stranger demanded.

"No, sir. Jug came down after him. Rhino doesn't know it. Jug is checkin' up on him, looks like." Sam told about the miner coming out of the office on the heels of Uhlmann with a gun covering the killer.

"He doesn't trust his hired assassin."

"Not none. But both of them are out to get this Webb. If he is at the old Baxter shack they'll do it."

"This is Mr. Webb, Sam," explained Sandra. "We'll not forget that you took the trouble to warn us."

Bob looked at the Negro searchingly. This might be a plant arranged by his enemies. Sandra guessed what he was thinking.

"No, Bob," she intervened before he could speak. "Sam is our friend. Uhlmann gave him that scar on his forehead. Jim and I know he is all right."

The troubled eyes of Webb shifted to the girl. "Stan may be in the cabin. If he is—"

He did not finish the sentence. She knew what he meant.

"You said you didn't sleep in the cabin, but in a hill pocket somewhere back of it," she reminded him.

"Yes, but he was reading that Dickens story you lent me when I left. He may not have gone from the cabin yet." He added, his voice sharp with anxiety, "I'll have to hurry."

Jim Budd was in the doorway. Sandra turned to him. "Get the boys in the bunkhouse. Tell them to saddle fast." To Webb she said: "I wish father were at home. But anyhow there are five of the boys in the bunkhouse. They won't keep you waiting more than a few minutes."

"I can't wait for them." His eyes were quick with excitement. "Tell them to follow soon as they are saddled."

"It won't be more than five minutes," she pleaded.

"Five minutes is as long as five hours sometimes." He took her by the arms to move her out of the way. As he looked down at her the harshness died out of his face. "Don't worry about me. I'll be careful."

She did not trust his promise. He would be careful only if recklessness was not necessary to save his friend. His hard steely eyes had softened for the moment, but she knew that when he reached the battle zone the safety of Stan Fraser would be his first thought.

144

"If you all rode together," she urged, and did not get a chance to finish.

He kissed her, smiling into her troubled eyes. The assurance he gave her had nothing to do with his danger, at least not on the surface. His words came lightly, as if in jest, but she knew how much he meant them. " 'Till a' the seas gang dry, my dear,' " he said with cheerful nonchalance.

Spinning her gently out of the way, he strode from the room.

35 *Stan Writes a Note*

Fraser grew tired of reading. This fellow Dickens was all right, but he sure was a word-slinger. The folks who read *Dombey and Son* must have had more time to burn than a sheepherder. He yawned deeply, stretched and looked at his watch. A quarter to ten. Time for all honest people, except lovers, to turn in for sleep. Since Bob was one of the exceptions, he probably would not leave the Circle J R for hours yet. When a man was with the right girl sleep was something he had no use for.

Stan grinned. That young chump was getting a break at last, after a helluva lot of lean years. Uhlmann was a fugitive. With evidence piling up against Packard as it was, looked like he might go to the pen instead of Bob. On top of that young Webb had won the nicest and best-looking girl in the county. Good going for a convict with a price on his head.

The old-timer blew out the light and sauntered from the cabin. A young moon rode a sky of scudding clouds and at the edge of these stars peeked out. Sam untied the horse he had left at a post and stood at sharp attention. He had heard the hoof of another horse strike a stone. A bullet whistled past his ear.

"Holy mackerel!" he grunted, and vaulted to the saddle.

A leaden slug punged into the adobe wall back of him. He lifted the cow pony to a canter, his body low on the animal's neck, and reined his mount sharply to the left, to put the building between him and the rifleman. At the back of the house he pulled up and reached for the Winchester in the scabbard beside the saddle.

Another gun sounded. "Two gents hunting," he said aloud, and started for an arroyo fifty yards away.

The pony staggered, lost its footing, and plunged to the ground, badly wounded by the last shot. Fraser landed on his shoulder and was for a moment stunned. He heard a triumphant yelp. It was too late now to get the rifle. He ran for the

145

arroyo. Fortunately the moon had gone under a cloud. Though one of his attackers fired again, he reached the arroyo safely. Up this he raced to a boulder pile below the rim rock of the ridge.

Among the rocks was a scatter growth of cholla and prickly pear. Fraser realized that if he lay crouched here he would neutralize the advantage held by the attackers. Their rifles would be of no more use than revolvers at short range, and they would have to creep up close to dig him out from the rocks. Lucky for him it was a night battle. If it had been in the day-time one could have held the exit from the arroyo while the other rode up to the rim rock and picked him off from above.

What worried Stan was not his own situation but that of his friend. In thirty minutes, or an hour, or maybe two, Bob Webb would come along anticipating no danger and ride into an ambush. By a near miracle Fraser had escaped the first blast, but the killers would make sure of their victim next time.

Stan was trapped. He could not climb the sheer rock wall behind him, nor could he expose himself on either rim of the arroyo, for the clouds had been swept away and the moon shone bright over the desert. But he might be able to give Bob a warning, at a considerable risk to himself, by firing shots at intervals. If he could keep this up long enough, Bob would hear and be on the alert.

For a million years rocks had crashed down from the ridge into the small boulder field at the end of this pocket. The terrain was ideal for defense, but not so good if one every ten minutes kept calling the attention of the enemy to his position.

Fraser fired toward the mouth of the pocket and scuttled through the brush to the shelter of a boulder ten or fifteen yards distant. As he had expected, two explosions sounded so close to each other that the second seemed almost an echo of the first. He settled down in his new place, watching to make sure the enemy were not stalking his cover. He was a cool customer, with nerves and muscles co-ordinated perfectly. Long habit as an outdoor Westerner had trained eyes and ears to catch the slightest stir of movement or rumor of sound. Warfare against the Apaches, terminated only in the past few years, had put a premium on still and vigilant patience.

A ruse to lessen the risk occurred to him. He picked up a bit of quartz and flung it against the face of a boulder twenty yards from his shelter. The guns of the ambushers sent bullets whistling up the draw in the direction of the sound. The old-timer chuckled. He had lured them into giving the warning without having to do it himself.

Stan knew he was in a tight spot. His assailants could not wait till morning to get him. He felt sure that they were taking

146

advantage of the cover and of the darkness to move closer to him. But he was less distressed about this than about Bob's reaction to the warning of the shots. Webb would be alarmed at the danger of his friend and might come charging forward without taking any precautions.

A rustle in the bushes a stone's throw distant, so faint that only keen hearing could have detected it, told Stan that one of his enemies at least was working nearer through the brush. Fraser shifted his position back of the rock noiselessly. All he could do was wait until the rifleman was within range of his revolver. If the fellow stealing up on him got an open shot now he could hardly miss. Stan crouched low in the shadow of the boulder back of a clump of cholla.

His hunter was working very slowly and cautiously to the right. The moon was out again, and soon he would see his prey, a solid bulk back of the cactus, only partially protected by the embedded boulder. Fraser could not wait any longer. He had to take a chance. There was nothing for it but to dash across an open space to the refuge offered by a sunken hole back of a sandstone slab.

Stan came out on the run. From the darkness a startled voice ripped out an oath. The old-timer was in moonlight bright and clear. He was half-way to the slab when a shot rang out. A blow struck his shoulder but did not stop him. His body plunged down into the sand hole and slid along it. Though bruised and winded, he clambered to his feet and peered around the edge of the rock. A shifting shadow crossed the floor of the arroyo in front of dense shrubbery, the figure throwing the shadow concealed by the foliage. Fraser fired, guessing at the man's position. A bullet flung an answer, striking the sandstone at an angle and flying off on a ricochet.

Pain obtruded itself into Stan's consciousness. He put his hand to his shoulder and found his shirt soggy. Warm blood seeped down his back and arm. Fraser grinned wryly. This was a heck of a note. He hoped the wound was not too bad, since he was too busy just now to go see a doctor.

With divided attention he gave himself first aid. While he took the bandanna handkerchief from around his neck and tied it about the wound to stop the bleeding, he checked up intermittently on the position of his foes. If they rushed him, he wanted to be ready to give as good as they sent.

The old frontiersman was a realist. It was a three to one bet, he guessed, that he had come to the end of the trail. His hunters probably thought that the victim they had trapped was Bob Webb. They might not discover their mistake until he was dead, and if they did he would be rubbed out anyway, on the principle that a dead man could not bear witness against them.

147

His attackers were taking no unnecessary chances. They were huddled back of cover just as he was. The silence in the arroyo was long, broken only by the sounds of night life peculiar to the desert. In the brush were murmurs of small creeping things, almost too faint to be heard. A more strident note was the sudden clamor of a cicada. On a far-away hill a coyote lifted its mournful howl.

Still watching for the attack or for any shift in the position of his enemies, Stan put his forty-five on the ground beside him and took from a pocket an old notebook and the stub of a pencil. By the bright moonlight he wrote:

Son, they've got me trapped in the arroyo. Might be trail's end for me. There are two of the birds. Uhlmann must be one of course. Don't know who the other is. They shot Jack Pot as I was leaving the cabin and I had to skedaddle without my rifle. One of them sent a pill into my shoulder.

A bullet whistled past Stan. He put down the pencil and picked up the revolver. Very cautiously he risked a look around the edge of the sandstone slab. He could see nothing like a gunman in the dark masses of shrubbery within his vision, but he knew that one at least of his attackers lay there hugging the ground. For moral effect, to let them know he was still dangerous, he sent a shot into the chaparral.

Another stretch of silence followed. Stan wrote again.

Just swapped shots with a gent hidden in the rocks. No damage, I reckon. I'm writing you, son, to tell you—if they send me West—that I've had a good go of it since I met you that day at my corral. Unbeknownst to you, boy. I've kinda adopted the son of my old friend. I've had fun scooting over the hills and watching from a ledge now and then posses hunting us. Made me feel young again.

Got to quit. One of these Injuns is crawling around to get me on my unprotected side. So long, son. A guy can't live forever anyhow.

Stan put the note in his boot leg and picked up the forty-five.

36 Sandra Turns Nurse

Bob found the stirrups after he had flung himself into the saddle. He wheeled his mount and sent it galloping down the lane. Very likely Stan had left the cabin and was safely in the hills before the arrival of Uhlmann. But the old-timer's habits were not predictable. He might have decided to sit in the shack reading until Bob returned from the ranch.

There was a good deal of the Indian about Uhlmann. He liked to do his killing from ambush, and if Fraser was still at the Baxter hut the old man might never know what had hit him. For Bob had no doubt that the outlaw would not hesitate to shoot down Stan, even though the man he really wanted to get was Webb.

It was Bob's habit to ride with consideration for his horse, but tonight he plunged ahead as fast as he could drive the animal. When clear of the fence he left the road and cut across a rough uneven flat to the hills shaping shadowlike in the distance. Even when the moon sailed out from behind a cloud the pace was dangerous, for there were gopher holes into which the gelding might stumble and break a leg.

He was driven by fear that his old friend might fall at the hands of an assassin. Without a moment's hesitation Stan had joined fortunes with him, refusing to be rebuffed, cheerfully determined to make a gay adventure of their hardships. No man could have asked for a more loyal or faithful companion. He had put up with Bob's moods and diverted him with light chat when the black devil care rode on Bob's shoulders. Now the little man might be lying crumpled on the dirt floor of the adobe cabin with a bullet through his heart.

Faintly there came to him on the night breeze the faraway pop of a rifle. Bob did not slacken the pace, though his stomach muscles collapsed at the sound. A killer had fired the gun, had very likely shot down Stan without warning. A sickness ran through Bob's lithe body. If the worst had taken place, it was something he could never forget. In him burned a hot fierce rage. He would get the man who had done this, if he had to follow the trail for years. But that would not bring back to life his whimsical and warm-hearted friend.

There came a second explosion, and a third. Hope quickened in Bob. If the first bullet had destroyed Fraser there would have been no need for more. It might be that Stan was forted in the cabin—fighting back—standing off his enemies until help came.

Breathing heavily, Bob's horse pounded forward. The sound of firing came occasionally to Webb, louder as the distance lessened. He could tell now that Stan was not in the cabin. The hammering of the guns came from the arroyo south of the house. Rifles were making most of the noise, but more than once a forty-five blasted out its challenge. Stan must be penned up in the arroyo among the rocks and brush.

Bob swung to the left and crashed through the cactus. He tore up a rise to the hill crown from which a slope dipped into the arroyo. He flung himself from the saddle, slipped back of a clump of prickly pear, and lifted a yell to encourage the beleagured man.

149

A call, weak but undaunted, came back to him.

"Hi yi, Bob. Look out these devils don't get you."

Bob heard the rustling of somebody scuttling away through the brush. He fired a random shot then ran down the slope toward his friend, blundering among the boulders and the shinnery to find him. Stan spoke again, to localize himself.

"You all right?" Bob asked as soon as he saw Fraser.

The old man grinned up at him indomitably. "Not too all right. One of the damned wolves plugged me in the back. Up near the shoulder. Reckon a doc can fix it."

They heard a galloping horse taking off into the night, and before the sound had died away the drumming hoofs of a second.

Bob gave immediate aid as best he could and carried the light body of Fraser to the cabin. The bleeding had not stopped, and the jolting of the trip had done the wounded man no good. As soon as Bob laid him on the bed he fainted. While he was still unconscious Bob washed and dressed the torn shoulder.

Stan opened his eyes. "I must of fainted. Like a girl." His smiled derided himself. "You've sure got a pal who can take it."

"The best ever a man had." Bob escaped from emotional ground quickly. "Were there only two of them?"

"That's right—two."

"They ambushed you?"

"One of 'em took a crack at me when I came outa the house. I ducked round it, and the other fellow shot my horse. Seeing I couldn't get at my rifle, I legged it for the arroyo."

"Could you tell who either of them was?"

"I didn't see but one of the birds, and then only for a moment. That skunk Uhlmann."

"The other was Packard," Bob said.

They heard a shout and the clop-clop of horses' feet. Bob moved swiftly to the door, revolver in hand.

"Circle J R riders," a voice announced. "That you, Fraser?"

"Stan has been wounded," Bob answered. "Webb talking. Uhlmann and Packard lit out."

A slim figure slid from a saddle and came forward. "Is Stan badly hurt?" Sandra asked.

"What are you doing here?" Bob asked.

"I had to come," she replied in a low voice. "We'll talk of that later. What about Stan? If he's hurt, I can nurse him."

"Yes," Bob nodded. "I'm glad you came, though you shouldn't have. The wound is serious. I don't know how bad. Come in."

He had dressed the wound in the dark, but now he lit a lamp. With four armed Circle J R men on the scene there would be no more shots out of the darkness.

150

Sandra sat on the bed and put her fingers on the pulse of the wounded man. She looked up at Bob. "We can't move him now. Better send one of the boys for Doctor Logan."

In Fraser's tired eyes there was a flicker of laughter. "This is one time I put Bob's nose outa joint," he murmured. "I'll bet he's sore at me being the whitehaired boy."

"Hurry up and get well," Bob said. "Then we can talk about that."

"I don't aim to hurry a doggoned bit, if Miss Sandra is gonna be my nurse," Stan announced weakly.

"As long as you need me I'll stay with you," she promised.

Bob asked Jim Budd to ride for a doctor, and as soon as the colored man had gone drew Sandra to one side.

"I'm not sure whether the bullet went into Stan's lung or not," he said. "But anyhow this is going to be a long sickness. If you can stay here that will be fine. I'll leave word at the ranch to relieve the boys after a while. Two guards must stay with you all the time."

"Where are you going?" she asked in quick alarm.

"I've got a job to do," he replied grimly.

She noticed how hard and stern his eyes were. "You mean——?" The question died on her lips. Sandra knew what he was going to do.

"Don't worry about me," he advised. "I'll be as safe where I am going as you will be here."

"You're going after this villain Uhlmann," she charged.

He said: "Stan has given for me these last weeks everything he had. I'm not going to let this fellow get away with this."

The girl's heart died under her ribs. "Do you have to do this, Bob? Can't you leave it to somebody who isn't already in trouble?"

"No. Stan got this wound for me, not for somebody else."

She had known what the answer would be before she put her question. When he made up his mind it was as fixed as the Rock of Gibraltar.

"I don't see how you're going to find him," she said, and could not keep out of her voice the hope that he would not. "He'll be hiding in the hills, as you were."

In his harsh bony face was the day of judgment. "I'll find him. Right now he's riding hard to reach Mexico."

"But if he gets across the line."

"I'll go across too."

"But he'll be safe on Mexican soil. You can't touch him there."

"Can't I?"

Looking into his bleak cold eyes, Sandra shuddered. This was not the man who had promised to love her till all the seas went dry. He was as relentless as fate, and he would follow

151

the trail until his victim was destroyed. She had to find out one thing more.

"Are you going to bring him back to Arizona for punishment?"

"That's up to him. I'll give him that chance."

"You talk as if you were God," she cried. "He may lie in wait . . . and shoot you."

"It won't be that way," he promised.

With one of the Circle J R riders he looked over the horses and picked the one with most stamina. The cowboy watched Bob fix the stirrups to the right length.

"Good luck, fellow," the ranch hand said, rage at Uhlmann surging up in him. "Blast hell out of the Dutchman."

Sandra joined them, and the cowboy slipped away into the house. Bob finished tightening the belly-band. She found no comfort in his hard and stony face.

But when he turned to her his gaze softened. He took her in his arms and held her close without speaking. She thought, despairingly, "I can't let him go—I can't." But she knew it had to be that way. How full of fear her heart was she could not let him know. She said shakily, clinging to him: "The best eating place at Nogales is Dan's Café."

"Take care of Stan," he said. "Don't let him die."

He kissed her and swung to the saddle. Without looking back he rode away. She watched him until his figure had blurred into the landscape and he was no longer even a shadow in the night.

37   *When Rogues Fall Out*

On his way down from the mine Uhlmann had been in a swither of doubt. He was heading for the safety of Mexico, but he could not make up his mind whether to make a short detour and try to get Webb on the way. A man in the hills had given him a straight tip that the convict was at the Baxter cabin. He could ride across the hills below the rock rim and take a look. If he was in luck a shot in the dark would be enough.

But a new hate was simmering in his warped mind. He did not want to pull any chestnuts out of the fire for Jug Packard, who had just robbed him of five hundred dollars and sent him down the road at the point of a gun. No dependence could be put on Packard's promise to pay him for getting rid of his enemy.

The trouble was that the convict was Uhlmann's enemy too. Perhaps because he had so greatly injured young Webb he had for him a bitter malevolence, and when he came to the fork in the road that rancor tipped the scales and led him to the Baxter cabin. It would do no harm to blot out Webb if it could be done conveniently. That would be one score settled.

He drew up on the summit of a rise and looked down at a light gleaming in the darkness. The information given him had been correct. Webb and Fraser were staying there. If he had a break he could get them both.

The sound of a moving horse behind him sent a stab of fear through the man. He had been drinking a lot and his nerves were jumpy. A man had seen him on the rim rock the day before and shot at him. To be alone against the world, without friends, filled him with a dreadful loneliness.

Drawing off from the trail, he stood back of his horse with the rifle across the saddle seat. The traveler back of him did not appear. Perhaps he had imagined the sound. More than once in the long nights he had conjured up danger that did not exist.

He waited, while dragging minutes passed.

A mocking voice, from the brush behind him, put a jeering question. "On the lookout for a friend, Rhino?"

The big man swung round, incredibly fast for his size. "Where did you come from?" he demanded.

Packard gave the tittering tee-hee that passed with him for a laugh. "Thought you might need a little help."

The hunted man did not like being dogged in the darkness by the plotter whose tool he had been. Suspicions flitted through his mind, and with them ugly thoughts. He pushed them into the background, to be dragged out later.

"There's a light in the cabin," he said sulkily.

"I saw it."

"Maybe we could let him have it through the window."

"And if Fraser is there too?"

"He'll have to go with the friend he's so crazy about."

"There's a back door to the cabin," Packard said. "I'll swing round and cover it from the brush. Give me ten minutes before you start the fireworks."

Neither of them trusted the other, but each knew that their desires ran together in this matter. And each villain hoped to destroy his confederate later.

The light in the cabin was blown out before Uhlmann was ready to fire, but the crack of his rifle sounded when a man came out of the cabin. Half a minute later Packard dropped their victim's horse and Fraser bolted for the arroyo. They had the fellow now, since he had lost his Winchester. It would be only a matter of time before they got him. They moved into

153

the arroyo cautiously, wary as Indians, taking advantage of all the cover there was. But before they could finish the job that fighting fool Webb had broken their ambush and driven them away.

Packard flung himself on his horse and galloped out of the battle zone. In spite of the sly mean streak in him, the safety-first instinct in him that prompted the use of others to do his evil deeds, he was a hardy scoundrel afraid of neither God nor man. His flight was not a question of lack of courage. He had his reputation to consider, the fiction that he was a respectable and law-abiding citizen. It would be a great mistake to be recognized here as an ally of Uhlmann.

One of his worries was that Rhino knew too much about him. If the fellow was captured and not killed, he would implicate the mine owner in his crimes. Packard blamed himself for not having killed the man when he had the chance. He had been too greedy. It had been asking too much to hope that his accomplice would get rid of Webb and then let himself be trapped by Jug.

A man always cautious, he pulled up to listen. He was not expecting immediate pursuit, but it was better to make sure. On the light night breeze there came to him the beat of hoofs. A horse was traveling fast toward him. He guessed the rider of that driven animal was Uhlmann.

Under the shadow of a mesquite beside the trail he waited, revolver in hand. The huge body of Uhlmann was on the horse that came pounding down the road. Packard fired a thin split second too soon. The bullet shattered the saddle horn of the laboring animal. Uhlmann flung himself to the ground on the far side of his mount, hanging on to the bridle with his left hand.

Startled at the explosion, Packard's horse bucked violently. The rider was flung from the saddle and hit the sand hard, his weapon tossed a dozen feet from him. While one could have counted ten he lay there, jarred and breathless. It took him a long moment to scramble to his feet and another to get his fingers on the forty-five. A slug ripped into his belly. Two spat spurts of dirt from the road. A fourth struck his foot.

Packard sank down. He was through with living and knew it. But the urge to kill was still strong in him. By a tremendous effort he pushed himself up from the ground and raised the revolver weakly. The bullet went whistling into the brush.

Uhlmann did not wait to learn how desperately wounded was his foe. The man was still alive and fighting. Clumsily he pulled himself astride his horse and spurred into the chaparral. He rode up a low ridge and looked down into a swale along which men were moving at a gallop. They were headed for the Baxter cabin. Though he could not identify them in the moonlight, he had no doubt they were Circle J R men.

He knew that if he was going to get out of the country alive he had to hurry. His horse's head he pointed south. Not until he was deep in Mexico would he feel safe.

38 *A Body in the Dust*

Uhlmann opened cautiously the back door of the Silver Dollar saloon and looked the place over before entering. It was the slack morning hour, and there was nobody in the room except two Mexicans, a cowboy, and the bartender. He moved forward ponderously and ordered a drink. The man in the white apron put a glass and a bottle in front of him. The customer showed evidence of having traveled far. He was dusty and sweat-stained, and his little eyes were red and sunken.

"Resting yore saddle after a long ride?" the bartender asked, to make talk.

The big man glared at him sullenly. He was in a very bad humor. His horse had gone lame and added several hours to the journey. As a result he was both weary and exasperated. The bartender was bald, fat, and forty. He looked like a safe man to bully.

"That any of yore business?" Uhlmann demanded truculently.

The cowboy playing solitaire laughed. "One for you, Mike," he said. "Now will you be good?"

Mike's slaty eyes rested appraisingly on the surly giant. "No offense meant, stranger," he mentioned. "I wasn't asking where you came from or why."

A dull anger beat into Uhlmann's face, but for once he let discretion rule him. This was no time to make another enemy. *He knows who I am,* the killer thought. *I'd better drift.*

A man came through the wing doors and stopped abruptly before he reached the bar. He was Cole Hawkins from the San Simon country. His eyes fastened on the fugitive.

"So you're here," he said.

Uhlmann's ugly face broke into what was meant for a friendly smile. "Have a drink on me, Cole," he invited.

"I'll buy my own drink, you damned sidewinder," Hawkins replied harshly.

The huge ruffian glared at him. "You can't talk thataway to me, Cole. I won't take it."

"You'll take it, you dirty murderer. I heard what you did last night."

Uhlmann spread his huge hands in placatory explanation. "Now looky here, Cole. I had to do it. Jug lay in wait for me. He had first shot. It was him or me, one."

155

"Jug?" exclaimed Hawkins in surprise. "Jug too? That's a new one on me. I was talking about Fraser."

"I didn't kill Fraser. That was Jug."

"You were there with him. You were recognized."

"Some mistake, Cole. I see now why you were sore at me. No, sir. You might know I wouldn't hurt good old Stan."

"You don't have to lie to me, Rhino. Save that talk for the man outside lookin' for you."

"What man?" Uhlmann cried.

"The man whose father you killed years ago—whose friend you shot down last night."

"You talkin' about Webb? Is he here—at Nogales?"

"He's here. To put a rope round yore neck and drag you back to be hanged."

The eyes in the leathery face of the killer betrayed him. Hawkins knew that cold despair was clutching at the man's heart. Uhlmann had not expected his enemy to be here so soon.

"Where's he at now, Cole?" the hunted man asked, his voice fallen to a hoarse whisper. "You wouldn't be joshin' me, would you? You gotta have yore little joke."

"No joke. And I'll say this. If Bob Webb didn't have first claim on you I'd drag yore big carcass back myself."

"Gimmie five minutes, Cole," Uhlmann pleaded. "I'll light a shuck across the line and never come back. You 'n' me have had good times together, old man. You wouldn't throw me down now."

The man's wheedling tone stirred contempt in the other. "You've thrown yourself down, you fool," Hawkins told him bluntly. "I never did like you even when I did business with you. Had a feeling you were rotten bad. Now I know it."

Uhlmann flared to weak passion. "I'm no more a killer than you. Think I don't know you shot Chuck Holloway that night at Tucson?"

The eyes of Hawkins narrowed and grew chill. "If I did, he had it coming—as you have." He was silent a moment, watching the harried man who had come close to the end of his croked trail. When he spoke, his voice was low and the words spaced. "It's a show-down. Pull yore freight, wolf, right damn now, or I'll do the job the hangman is waitin' to do."

The dry lips of Uhlmann opened, but no words came from them. He wanted to fling out a defiance, to drag out his forty-five and start shooting, but he could not drive his flaccid will to obey the urge. Out of his throat came a strange animal sound of distress. His dragging feet took him through the screen doors to the narrow adobe street. Up and down the street his gaze swept. A few men were in sight, a group of three not

156

twenty feet from him, but none of them showed any interest at his appearance.

He had made a mistake in stopping on the United States side of the line, but it might not be too late yet to get across to the Mexican side of Nogales. He would keep going, deep into Sonora, where a fugitive was safe. First, he would have to buy another horse. But not until he was in the old town.

His gross body, his flatfooted slouching gait, made him an uncouth sight. He knew this, and usually he resented the looks that followed him. But just now all his thoughts were concerned with reaching the horse he had tied in front of a dry-goods store. As he moved down the sidewalk his eyes darted from right to left and back again. He could not believe that the avenger was so close on his heels. Probably Hawkins had been lying to frighten him. None the less when he was twenty yards from his horse he broke into a shuffling run.

Abruptly he pulled up. A slim man, coffee-brown, walked out of the dry-goods store lithely as a panther. The killer's stomach muscles tightened. An icy wave drenched him. But it was now or never. Webb was looking leisurely down the street. In a moment he would turn his head and see him.

Uhlmann fired in panic haste. Before Bob had his gun out a second bullet tore through a hanging sign above his head. He was so sure of himself that he shouted an order at the frenzied man.

"Drop that gun!"

The revolver of the killer roared again.

Bob took deliberate aim at the huge body and sent a slug crashing into it. A second one struck the desperado just below the heart, not four inches from the first. The revolver dropped from Uhlmann's fingers. He spread his two hands over his great stomach, dragging it in to ease the pain, and stumbled forward half a dozen paces. One foot caught on the other, and the giant figure pitched heavily to the sidewalk and rolled from it to the dust of the street.

Bob's harsh face, the hardness of battle still stamped on it, looked down at the inert mass of flesh and bones that had a moment earlier been quick with life. A thin trickle of smoke rose from the barrel of his forty-five. He felt no emotion, no shock. This had been a possibility he had looked forward to for years, and now that it was fulfilled he had no sense of elation. It was just something unpleasant he had been forced to do. This was no longer his enemy. It was the body of a stranger who had brought about his own destruction by his folly.

A voice said heartily. "No regrets—he's better dead."

Bob looked up, and saw Cole Hawkins. "Yes," he agreed dully.

"You're in the clear. He took three shots at you before

157

you fired. I never saw the beat of how cool you were."

"That's right," another man spoke up. "Three-four of us saw it all. Self-defense."

"I meant to take him back to be hanged," Bob explained, his tone still lifeless. "He shot my best friend last night."

"And your worst enemy," Hawkins added.

The surprised eyes of Webb questioned him without words.

"He told me back there in the Silver Dollar," the San Simon rancher continued, "that he rubbed out Jug Packard last night."

Bob stared at him in astonishment. "Are you sure that is what he meant to tell you?"

"Dead sure. He trapped himself. I called him a murderer for what he did last night. He thought I meant Packard and said Jug tried to ambush him and was killed."

The convict made no comment. This was not the way he had planned his vengeance, but he could see that it might be better for Packard to fall at other hands than his.

He drew a long breath. "I reckon if there are no objections I'll ride back to the Circle J R and see how Stan is making it."

"Nobody will stop you, Mr. Sloan," Hawkins said, stressing the name. "We'd better see the sheriff and explain how this happened."

Webb took the advice of the ranchman and gave the sheriff the name of Cape Sloan, which meant nothing to the officer. He told Bob that since the killing had been clearly self-defense no arrest would be made.

Hawkins said, "I'm going north, and if you have no objections I'll ride part way with you."

When they came to the parting of the ways, a few miles south of the Circle J R, Bob made a remark that surprised the other.

"I've been told you saved my life once."

The cattleman glanced at him quickly. "News to me," he answered.

"On the plaza back of the Tucson Hotel not long ago."

"Funny how news gets around," Hawkins commented dryly. "One man saw me fire that shot. He wasn't going to tell anybody. Now two people inside of an hour accuse me of it—you and Uhlmann."

"I'm not accusing you," Bob replied. "I'm thanking you."

"No need of that. I had an axe of my own to grind. When I saw his rifle aimed at you I let him have it. Understand, I'll deny this if anybody else puts it up to me."

Bob assured him that nobody would ever hear of this through anything he would say.

Hawkins nodded. "That's all right. I'll be saying *adios*, Mr. Webb. Good luck."

They took different trails. The one Bob followed led him to the Circle J R.

39 *"While the Sands o' Life Shall Run"*

Sandra walked out of the cabin with the doctor and looked an anxious question at him.

"Fraser is a tough old *hombre*," he said. "Barring unexpected bad luck he's going to make it. What he needs is good nursing more than a doctor—and I can see he's going to get it."

"I'm glad," the girl said, deeply pleased. "When his friend, Bob Webb, comes back he will be so happy."

The doctor slanted a smile at her. "I should think he might be." He had heard stories of Sandra's eager interest in Webb.

She replied, with a sigh, "I wish he hadn't felt he had to go and bring that villain back. You don't think——?"

Doctor Logan finished her uncompleted query. "I think your young man will come back sound as a dollar. He's too hard a nut for Uhlmann to crack."

Sandra's attention had strayed. A rider was coming over the hill. She watched him, in her eyes a queer look a suspended hope. The man on horseback waved a hand at her. He put his horse to a canter, and she broke into a run. Doctor Logan smiled again. Her young man had flung himself from the saddle and taken her into his arms.

"By golly, I was right," the doctor said aloud, and walked into the house.

Bob's first word was, "Stan?"

"Doctor Logan says he's going to be all right."

"Glory hallelujah!" he cried. "I've been worrying all day about him."

"You didn't find Uhlmann." she said.

His voice and manner changed. "Yes, I found him."

"Did—did you leave him at the ranch?"

"No." He added, gravely: "I left him at Nogales."

Back of the words she read futility. An anxious excitement set the blood pounding through her heart. "You killed him." It was a statement, not a question.

"Yes."

"Tell me."

"I came out of a store and he fired. He had the first three shots and missed. Several men saw it. The sheriff said I was free to go."

She held him close in her strong young arms. "I've been so frightened. I kept seeing you—trapped. And now he's gone. And Jug Packard too. Did you know that Uhlmann killed him near here after the fight in the arroyo?"

"I heard so."

"All your enemies are gone. We can forget the long nightmare of the dreadful years that have passed. We'll be together—always."

He laughed, happily. " 'While the sands o' life shall run.' "

It was surprising what a change the laughter made in his harsh bony face. The years and all they had done to him were lifted from it. She thought. *I'm going to make him laugh often. I'm going to make him forget all he has been through.*

She said: "Governor Andrews will pardon you now. He's been waiting for a chance. We have plenty of evidence now. And you'll be a hero for ridding Arizona of that bad man."

He did not like that. The thought of public acclaim for what he had done disgusted him.

Yet the papers were full of the story. Editorials demanded that he be pardoned. Almost unanimously the people of the territory agreed that a great injustice had been done him. No act of the administration of Governor Andrews was more generally approved than the pardoning of Robert Webb.

One unexpected result was the attitude of the Packard heirs. The family of the mine owner had been alienated from him for years. He was the skeleton in the closet of their lives. They had lived in Tucson and had seen him only at rare intervals. Even before the pardon his son had come to Bob with an offer of restitution. He suggested turning over to Webb a majority of the Johnny B stock.

Bob wanted no part of the mine. He hoped never to see it again. But since he wished to get hold of a cattle ranch he made it clear he would accept a fair monetary compensation. Young Packard suggested he take the Sinclair ranch with all the cattle and equipment on it. This was a fine spread, recently bought by Jug for close to a hundred thousand dollars. Bob looked the place over and accepted the offer.

The young couple moved to it. On it a large family of Webbs were born and brought up. Among her noisy and turbulent brood Sandra moved happily, ruling lightly and wisely. With the passing years she retained the loveliness that had distinguished her youth. When her husband looks at her today, gray-haired, the toll the decades have taken stamped on her face, he still thinks her the paragon of women.